PAYING TUITION

LECY ELLIOTTE

1

THE RAMSKELLER

Fordham Rose Hill Campus, September 1991

I
f there's one thing more depressing than sitting in a bar
drinking alone, it's sitting in a bar alone, too broke to drink. The
Ramskeller is the Fordham campus pub. The school mascot is a
ram, so the name is supposed to be funny if you speak German, I
guess, which I don't. I don't usually come here on weeknights, or any
night for that matter, but I've had a really shitty day.

There are two types of sophomore girls at our little Jesuit enclave
in the Bronx. Type I's study all the time and never go out. Type II's
never study and go out every night. The Type I's, e.g. my roommate
Laura, and me before this afternoon, are squirreled away in Duane
Library or the computer center, writing a theology essay or doing
chemistry homework and thinking about hitting the sack for a good
night's sleep before their 8:30 a.m. classes. The Type II's, e.g. my other
roommates, Deirdre and Melissa, are comparing outfits, putting on
makeup, and pre-gaming before heading out to Clark's or the Lantern
around 10:00.

Neither type would be caught dead in the campus pub at 8:00 p.m. on a Tuesday night, which is why it's a perfect place for me to sit at the bar, get drunk, and feel sorry for myself. Or rather it would be if beer cost no more than a Diet Coke which, I have now discovered to my embarrassment, it doesn't. (Remember? Type I. I never had reason to come to the pub before now. So many things left to learn. So few I actually will, unless I figure out how to come up with $20,000 by the end of the month. But I'm getting ahead of myself.)

Until this afternoon I was right on track from Jenni to Dr. Jennifer McGrath, DVM. Third highest GPA in my high school class. 98th percentile on the SAT. Early admission to a not-quite-Ivy League but still respectable college. Financial aid package big enough that my parents didn't have to take out a second mortgage. Straight A's in everything except chemistry lab. (I'm pretty good on exams and essays, but I broke too many test tubes before I figured out I should let my lab partner do all the measuring and titrating.)

Vet school was in the bag. Then kaboom. One letter from the bursar popped my dream like the soap bubbles Jorge Leister likes to blow in lab when the T.A. isn't looking.

———

STUDENT MAIL IS DELIVERED to the campus post office in the basement of McGinley Center. The office is only open between one and three in the afternoon. You can rent one of the old-fashioned art deco P.O. boxes that line the wall and pick up mail at your convenience. However, this is one of the optional fees I economized on, so this afternoon I stood in line with the other cheapskates.

Today I was hoping for the latest issue of Discover or a letter from my big sister. Janine writes me every week, even if nothing ever happens back home in Easton. She's married and almost twice my age. Yes, I was a "surprise." Her oldest boy, Brian, has been in a running battle of wills with his third grade teacher. Last week he refused to draw the school-approved bunnies and ponies during art class. Instead, he drew a picture of the teacher dressed in a witch costume being burned at the stake. Janine enclosed a copy of the drawing with her last letter. I was impressed at his command of symbolism and color at an age where most boys are drawing dog poop; but somehow neither the teacher nor the principal saw it that way, and he was put on a three-day timeout. I was curious to see how it all turned out.

However, instead of one of Janine's hand-addressed envelopes, the bored work-study student behind the counter handed one of those crinkly, computer-printed envelopes that does double duty as the letter, like the school uses for paychecks and report cards. Only I didn't get a paycheck, and the semester's barely started so it can't be a report card.

I tore the tabs off the edges, slid my finger through the top to open it, and unfolded the paper. It was a bill from the bursar's office. The red letters at the bottom caught my eyes:

Your payment of $19,832 for the Fall 1991 semester is now past due. Please remit the balance by October 1, or your registration will be cancelled.

———

"CAN I GET YOU SOMETHING?" the bartender asks. He's about twenty-five with soft blue eyes peeking out beneath his curly blond hair.

"Some more water, please?" I ask, timidly.

"Sure thing, I'll be right back." He's probably a grad student in one of the softer subjects, psychology or theology. Maybe I should pick up a few pointers from him since working a bar is the most I'm going to be qualified for with one year of college and no degree.

The bartender returns. He puts down a paper coaster and places the glass on it.

"Thanks," I say.

"No problem. Anything else?" He smiles at me in a big brothery sort of way.

I bite my lip. Maybe I could tell him what happened? He looks nice enough. Bartenders are supposed to listen, right? Only, what if he thinks I'm trying to scam a free drink? Before I get up the nerve to speak, he's off to pour beers for actual paying customers and I'm left alone again with my ice water and my thoughts.

———

AFTER I GOT over the initial shock of the letter, I reverted to practical mode. The bill was simply wrong. There was no way I could owe that much money. Fordham's expensive, but they offered me a really nice financial aid package. I had almost a full ride. It was the only way I could afford to come here.

I scanned the details on the rest of the page. There was the usual list of charges—$16,890 tuition, $6500 dorm, $2300 meal plan, and a bunch of mandatory fees—followed by a thin column of credits.

I scanned the bill one more time and breathed a sigh of relief. They had left off my financial aid grant. I chose Fordham instead of Georgetown or Scranton because they agreed to cover my financial aid with grants while the others only offered loans and a little work study. At Fordham, I could graduate without a lot of debt and be in better financial shape for vet school. Just another bureaucratic snafu at a university whose computer systems were out of date in the 1960s. Two weeks ago I had to explain to the registrar that no, Physical Education was not the same as Physics, and could she please put me in the right class? Still, I thought I should take care of this right away before they decided to charge me interest or late fees or something.

———

THE LINE TO see someone at the bursar's office stretched around the corner. It was 3:15 by the time I finally reached the front, and a plump, middle-aged woman waved me over to her counter. She looked exhausted.

I smiled as I handed the letter across the counter. "I'm afraid there's been some sort of mistake. My grant-in-aid got left off the bill."

She didn't even look up. "Name and social security number?"

I reeled off the information, and she typed it into her computer. She frowned and typed some more. "I don't see any grant-in-aid listed for you."

"That can't be right. I get almost $30,000 a year."

She scowled, and tapped at her keyboard again. "I see a grant for last year, but nothing for this year. Are you sure your grant was renewed?"

"Of course, it was a four year grant." A hint of nervousness was creeping into my voice.

She typed some more. "I'm sorry, I don't see anything here. You'll have to go see the sophomore dean." She wrote down his name and office number on a piece of paper and handed it across the counter.

———

SOMEHOW I AVOIDED BREAKING down in front of Dean Maresca when he insisted that the bill was correct.

"I'm sorry Miss McGrath. We try to keep tuition in line with academic standards. I'm sorry the financial aid is not what you expected. It seems many students had some misapprehension about the period of their grant this year. At least the tuition didn't rise as much as we originally thought it was going to. That's something, right?"

Then he smiled, like I was supposed to be grateful. He was still leaving me with a $20,000 hole to fill. And another next year. And the year after that. The bill might as well have been twenty million dollars for all the chance I had of paying it.

One thing in my favor. I didn't necessarily have to get all the money right away. The dean told me about a short term loan that let me pay in installments over the school year (with 8% interest) but that still worked out to more than $2000 a month. I might have enough savings bonds from nineteen years of grandparents and relatives to cover one payment.

When I got back to my dorm room (thankfully empty; I didn't think I was ready to tell my roommates they were going to have to start looking for another fourth or accept whomever housing assigned them) I flopped down on my bottom bunk and ran through my options.

Option 1: Find a job, work nights and weekends, and go to class during the day. I took a notebook and pen off the desk and did the math. Minimum wage was $4.25 an hour. Putting in forty hours a week that was about $170 a week. Four weeks a month times nine months made $6120, less than a third of what I needed, and that was assuming nothing got taken out for taxes. Plus, when would I study? Maybe if I dropped the meal plan and ate ramen noodles, I could save a few dollars? Yeah, that would be real healthy. A diet of nothing but ramen noodles and any wine and cheese I could scrounge from faculty party leftovers.

Option 2: Summer job. But that was more than eight months away, and what kind of summer job paid $20,000? I heard about one student who worked a fishing boat in Alaska, but even if that wasn't a campus legend, I felt pretty sure that wasn't for me.

Option 3: Call my parents.

Our dorm room didn't have a phone, but there was one in the hall I could use with a phone card. I gritted my teeth and dialed the number. Just as I was sure the answering machine was going to pick up and grant me another hour's reprieve before I delivered the bad news, my mom picked up. "McGrath residence." Her voice sounded a little off.

"Hi Mom, it's me."

"Oh, Jenni. Hi. How's school?"

"OK. Is Dad around?"

My mother didn't say anything for several seconds. When she finally spoke, her voice sounded a little tight. "Now's not the best time, honey. Can he call you back tomorrow?"

A bad feeling started to rise from my stomach, like school-cut-all-your-financial aid bad. "Is something wrong? Is Dad OK?"

"He's fine, dear, it's just that..." Her voice trailed off.

"Mom, you have to tell me. What's wrong?"

"We don't want to worry you. You focus on your schoolwork. It'll be OK."

"Mom, you're scaring me now. What happened?"

She sighed. "Your father was laid off yesterday."

For the second time in two hours my stomach crashed below my feet. This could not be happening. Not now. "What happened?" I finally asked.

"IBM closed the whole office. Said they didn't need it anymore. They offered to relocate some of the managers, but not him."

Dad had worked for IBM for as long as I could remember. He loved that company. "How's he doing?" I asked, biting my lip.

"He's in a bit of a funk. It's natural. He just got the news yesterday. I'm sure he'll be better tomorrow."

My Dad's "funks" usually involved a lot of alcohol and sitting in front of the TV watching the weather channel. This was not good.

"Are you going to be OK?"

"Don't worry about us, honey. We'll tighten our belts for a little while until he finds something else. I may look for a job at the library or down at the mall until he does."

Maybe I was projecting my own problems, but she didn't sound very confident.

"Mom, do you think I should come home?"

"Of course not, sweetie. This is just a bump in the road. We'll see you at Thanksgiving."

"Are you sure? I know you'll need money. I could get a job."

"Honey, your job is going to school. You'll have the rest of your life to worry about money. Hang out with your friends. Go to a party. Don't worry about us old fogies."

I didn't actually have a lot of those sorts of friends here, and of course school might not be an option. I might have to move back in with them. I didn't ask the dean exactly when they'd kick me out of the dorms if I didn't pay. But since I didn't want to add to her troubles, I didn't tell her that. Instead, I said, "OK, if you're sure."

There was a sound like glass breaking over the line. "Oh hell, the cat knocked something off the table. I have to go now, Jenni. Thanks for calling. It's really good to hear from you. Keep in touch, OK?"

"OK. Bye bye." She hung up first, and I stood there like a dummy with the phone in my hand. What the hell was I going to do now?

Somehow I made it as far as the hall bathroom, thankfully empty, and locked myself in a stall before the tears started to come. It was over. All of it. My thoughts raced around in circles, one bleeding into the next before I could complete it. I wasn't going to finish college. I wasn't going to be a vet. I'm would have to move back home.

Six minutes into my crying jag, I was startled by the sound of the bathroom door opening. I tried to choke back the tears and be quiet. Just as quickly, the door shut again. Girls crying in the bathroom are a disturbingly common occurrence here. I hoped whoever it was didn't recognize me. If they did, by dinner everyone would be whispering about how my boyfriend broke up with me. My lack of anything approximating a boyfriend wouldn't stop them. There may be ten thousand students on campus, but sometimes Fordham feels smaller than my AP Latin class in high school.

I tore a piece of toilet paper off the roll and daubed it at my face. If only my problems were as simple as a bad date or my boyfriend dumping me. I wished I had a boyfriend to dump me. Until now my limited experience had consisted of an awkward make-out session with my debate partner, and six minutes in heaven at an eighth grade party with Jimmy "The Rottweiler" Neilson. Maybe it's better that I didn't. If I did, it would be one more thing to lose when I leave.

I wasn't ready to go back to my room. Laura, Deirdre, and especially Melissa would have too many questions I didn't want to answer. One look at me, and Melissa would know I'd been crying, that it was about money, that the money was for school, and probably get within a hundred dollars of the amount. She can read people like no one I've ever met.

I'd have to tell them the story eventually, but not yet. I could have gone to the cafeteria, but I didn't have an appetite. The library seemed pointless with nothing to study for. And that's how I found myself in the Ramskeller for the first and possibly last time of my college career.

———

TECHNICALLY NINETEEN IS TOO young to be hanging out in the campus pub, but no one cards on Tuesday nights, and it's mostly hypothetical anyway since I can't afford to drink. Maybe a guy will offer to buy me a drink? I've heard of that happening. Well, seen it on TV at least. However, on TV the girl the male lead buys a drink for is a sexy cheerleader with C-cups or a sophisticated blond woman from the Upper East Side in the perfect little black dress who can walk in six-inch heels without wobbling. Melissa can pull off that look, but I can't.

I scan the room, looking for my white knight with a wallet. The prospects are not promising. A gaggle of sorority types—Fordham doesn't have sororities, but they sure have the type—are giggling and pretending they're drunker than they are. Two grad students in thin glasses and elbow-patched jackets are arguing about some dead German. A single gray-haired professor I half-recognize from the chemistry building is drinking alone, drowning his nightly disap-pointment at being stuck in this backwater school. A couple wearing clothes too formal for campus are chatting quietly at a table in the corner. The man has his back to me, half-blocking my view of his companion, but I can tell they're too old to be students and too young to be parents. Maybe alumni visiting the campus? Finally, several theater geeks dressed in head-to-toe black are laughing it up. I'm pretty sure the chubby one with the curly red hair is gay. He's gazing intently at the leading man, a blond J. Crew type who has two female theater geeks hanging off his every word. All things considered, the gay actor is my best bet.

Even if boys do buy girls drinks in real life, a point I am none too sure of, they don't buy drinks for plain brunettes from Pennsylvania in jeans and tennis shoes, even ones who are watching their dreams of college and vet school drain away like the last water in my glass. That's me, the girl standing in the corner (or sitting at the bar) being ignored by both the cool kids and the geeks. Your classic plain Jane. Not pretty enough or distinctive enough to be noticed.

Somehow I thought college would be different. College guys would be smarter. They'd look past how much makeup a girl wore or how blonde her hair was. Instead it's like high school all over again: everyone chasing the same pretty ditzes. The only difference here is that a few of the pretty girls actually have a brain in their head.

Melissa's one. Not only is she skinny and gorgeous, she got a near perfect score on her SATs. Deirdre's another. Super cute and not bad on a test if she remembers to study. Laura's even smarter, and the only one of us who's managed to land a serious boyfriend, even if Joshua is something of a hippo.

I'm going to have to tell them I'm leaving. Maybe they'll get lucky and have a spare bed for the rest of the semester. It's stressful enough being cramped up with three other girls in a room marginally larger than a prison cell, even more when one of them is randomly selected from the list of involuntary roommate reassignments.

I swallow the last of my water as my gaze wanders to the couple across the room. The man pushes his chair back and stands up, giving me an unobstructed view of the woman he's with. As he steps aside, the light from the ceiling falls on her like a spotlight and I gasp involuntarily. The woman is stunning.

She looks like she stepped out of the pages of one of those fashion magazines Deirdre reads. She's wearing a green dress that is slit down her leg and shows off every curve of her body. Curly red hair cascades down past her shoulders, and when she tilts her head I'm pretty sure the things sparkling in her ears are diamonds. She's a little younger than I initially thought, about the right age for an assistant professor but better dressed and far too attractive. And her face is perfect, like one of those Botticelli paintings my art history teacher is always going off about.

But it's not so much her features that pull me in as the way she holds herself. This woman is confident in her own skin, self-aware, self-possessed. She has no doubts, about anything. She is exactly the opposite of me, a messy bag of doubt and insecurity. Even if I had her looks, I could never manage the casual elegance she exhibits. This is a woman with grace, and I am a girl from Pennsylvania who is going back there soon if I don't figure out where to get $20,000, fast.

I swivel the stool back around and hold up my glass to the bartender. "Can I please have some more water?" I whisper. He smiles and takes the glass from me. Since I'm not even tipping, I don't feel entitled to pour my troubles out on him, but at least he doesn't make me feel guilty for drinking water.

"Perhaps I could offer you something stronger?" says a man's voice from behind me.

I swivel around to see who said that and almost fall off my stool. Redheaded woman's friend is standing there, smiling at me. I don't know where she's disappeared to, but in the moment I don't think about that because if she was Botticelli's Venus, he is St. Sebastian.

2

DAN CORTLAND

I feel myself slipping off the stool and by reflex grab onto St. Sebastian's shoulders. He catches me around the waist, and somehow I avoid going splat on the floor. Way to make a first impression.

"Careful there, a chara," he says as he slides me back onto my stool. "It would be unlucky to break a leg before you've even met me." I feel his arms flex as he lifts me without visible effort.

He's smiling at me like I've forgotten something, but I can't take my eyes off his face. It really is like looking at a piece of art. Shit, my hands are still on his shoulders. Self-consciously I drop them and clutch the side of the stool to keep from falling off again. I still feel a little dizzy, even though I haven't had anything stronger than water tonight. I reposition myself on the stool and try to recover what little is left of my dignity. "Thanks for the catch."

"No problem." His blue eyes sparkle with amusement, not threatening, just friendly. He is tall, much taller than me, clean shaven, and wears a suit that probably cost more than my entire wardrobe. It is the suit more than anything that marks him as out of place in the Ramskeller. Men safely past college age are not uncommon here, mostly professors too tenured to care who sees them drinking, but none of them dress like they work on Wall Street.

It's my turn to speak, but I honestly cannot think of a single word. What do you say to a man who's stepped out of a Renaissance painting and magically appeared in the Bronx? Somehow, "Would you like to come to my friend's kegger?" doesn't seem right.

Fortunately, the bartender is a little more familiar with the protocol than I am and interrupts us. "What can I get for you, sir?"

"Bourbon, rocks. And a gin and tonic, with a twist, for the lady." He hasn't asked me what I want, but gin and tonic sounds good. If he's paying, maybe he gets to choose? I'm not accustomed to men buying me drinks. To be honest, I'm not accustomed to boys, much less men, paying any attention to me at all. He can't really be interested in me, can he?

He holds out his hand. "Dan Cortland."

"Jenni McGrath," I reply, taking his hand. He holds it a second longer than normal, then lets it drop.

"Um, thanks, I think," I mumble.

"You're welcome. You looked like you could use a real drink."

The grad student behind the bar returns with our drinks before I can fashion a reply.

"Can you run a tab for us?" He hands the bartender a black credit card, and the grad student's eyes go wide. He fumbles a bit, and almost drops it on the floor. "Yes sir. Right away, sir."

I take a sip of my drink, and the fizzy heat of the alcohol pops in my mouth. "That was strange. Is your credit card radioactive or something?"

"Something like that." His lips curl upward like I said something funny.

I take another sip. Yes, I could definitely get used to drinking gin and tonics.

"Look, don't take this the wrong way. I appreciate the drink and all, but are you sure you haven't confused me with someone else?"

Dan laughs. "Trust me. I know exactly what I want."

"It's just that boys don't usually notice me. Those girls seem more like your type." I point at the sorority types who have started playing quarters in the corner.

Dan's gaze doesn't follow my hand. Instead, his eyes stay focused on me, not at all like the college boys who alternate between looking at their feet and my chest, not that my chest has a lot to look at.

"I suppose boys might not notice you. Men know how to look a little deeper. At least I do."

I mentally kick myself. I still think of myself as a girl, and by extension that makes the other sex boys. But he's right. I'm not sure how old he is—a couple of streaks of silver edge his curly black hair—but he is clearly well past being called a boy, in both maturity and age.

Before the silence gets awkward, Dan asks me a direct question. "You look like the studious type. What brings you out on a school night?"

"I felt like I needed one of these." I lift my glass. "Only the pub doesn't take flex points from the meal plan."

Dan laughs once, a short, sharp bark. "No, I don't suppose they do." Then he smiles at me again.

I look away and take another sip. The pleasant warm fizziness must be liquid courage because instead of making my usual awkward excuse and racing for the exit, I say, "And how about you? What brings you to the Bronx on a rainy night? Are you a professor?"

Dan laughs again. "No, not a professor. I'm afraid I never got past my B.A., though I do keep my finger in on campus. Tell me about yourself. Who's Jenni McGrath? Why is she sitting alone in the Ramskeller on a Tuesday night?"

I bite my lip. "It was a really bad day, you know?"

"Boyfriend trouble?"

"I wish."

"Roommates then? I seem to recall that when I was in college, my female friends had more drama with each other than with us."

He's not wrong about that. Last week the R.A.s in Hughes had to split up a room because one of the girls was staying up all night screaming at the other two. Fortunately that wasn't me. "No, my roommates are great. Melissa's my best friend, I guess. She's really pretty. Laura's smart, very stable, almost like an adult. And Deirdre's the sweetest girl I know. We get along."

"Four? Do you have a suite in Walsh?"

"No, we share a quad in Hughes."

"I'm glad you get along, but even so, Hughes rooms aren't that big. Four is a lot of girls to share one room."

I don't think to ask how he knows so much about the layout of the Fordham dorms. "Most sophomores share a triple at most. But a quad's cheaper and we got along great last year, so it made sense to room together again."

"Is that an issue for you, then? Saving money?"

My face betrays me.

"Ah, so it is money."

"No," I say, though I'm lying. Then, looking down. "Yes." I don't know why I'm so embarrassed by this, but I am.

"I'm sorry."

"It's not your fault."

"Tell me about it."

"I don't know. I think..." My voice catches in my throat. I'm afraid I'm about to start crying, but I choke it back.

"Take your time. You don't have to talk about it if you don't want to."

"You know, actually I kind of do, want to talk about it. Only..." I take a deep breath and gulp half the glass down. It burns, but it's a good burn. I'm beginning to see why people like drinking.

Dan picks up my glass and motions at the bartender for a refill. Maybe it's the alcohol, or maybe it's just that this man doesn't know me from Eve so there's no way he can think less of me. Whatever it is, the whole story pours out of me, how my parents saved up to send me to college, how the school promised me a lot of financial aid and then cut it once I was committed, my father being laid off, how I'm going to have to drop out and move back to Pennsylvania. By the time I finish, the bartender has refilled my drink twice. Telling your troubles to someone is supposed to make you feel better, but it just makes me feel pathetic.

Dan's taken the stool next to me. He motions to the bartender for another bourbon and wraps his arm around my shoulders so I have to lean into him. I'm a little woozy from the gin so I'm grateful for the support. "You've got money problems. That's all."

"That's all?" I am incredulous. "It's a pretty big deal to me."

"Money's not hard to find, if you know where to look."

"You think I'm going to find a big bag of tuition in the middle of Edwards Parade?"

"No, that's the mistake so many people make. They play the lottery, or wait for a wealthy uncle to die. It's a sucker's game. You need to go where the money is."

"So where do I go to find this magic pile of money that's going to solve all my problems?"

"I've got money," says Dan. He reaches his hand out and brushes a wave of hair out of my face, while looking directly into my eyes. Suddenly I am very conscious that this man I have been pouring out my troubles to is a *man*, and however nice he's being, he wants things. Things he's willing to pay for.

My whole body tenses up as I realize I've been blind to what's happening here. Melissa probably would have read the subtext immediately, but I'm too far outside my comfort zone.

I can't help myself. I freeze like a fawn in the headlights of an oncoming truck, but to his credit Dan doesn't run right over me. He pulls the truck over and steps out, and oh God this metaphor has gotten completely out of control and can I please start over? "You're looking at me like I'm the one ugly puppy in a pet store window," I finally manage.

"More like you're a piece of art that's been overlooked by the plebeians and fashionistas." He takes a miniature leather wallet out of his coat pocket and extracts a business card which he hands to me. I don't know what to do except read it:

Daniel Cortland

Investments

212-555-7474

Then Dan reaches over and puts his hand behind my neck. He leaves it there just long enough for me to start feeling its heat. Without quite lifting me off the stool, he pulls me toward him and leans in, and then we're kissing. Not the tentative play acting of a couple of teenagers who don't know what to do and aren't actually all that into each other but want to see what all the fuss is about. Dan kisses me hard, like someone who knows exactly what he wants and what he's doing. As my tongue reaches up to touch his, almost without conscious thought, my body starts to respond. For the first time since I got the letter, I'm not thinking about tuition, or how I'm going to pay for school. I'm sure the alcohol is part of it, but for one brief ecstatic moment I'm lost in the sensation, all volition and worries about the future vanished from my head.

Then, too soon, Dan breaks the embrace, and I'm sitting on the stool staring at him wide-eyed.

Dan stands up from his stool and smiles at me one more time. "Call me if you decide you're ready for a fairy godfather." Then he turns and walks away.

If my body were functioning, I'd follow him out, no matter what he wanted; but between the gin and tonics and the kissing, I'm barely able to think, much less walk. By the time I regain enough control to move my legs and climb down from the stool, Dan is gone. But I have his card.

3

DO I OR DON'T I?

When I wake up Wednesday morning, my head feels like it's been rolled down an inclined plane in physics lab, my stomach feels like I was drinking the leftovers from the Erlenmeyer flasks in chem lab, and to complete the set, my tongue feels furrier than any three mammals in zoology. What the hell did I drink last night? Oh yeah, gin and tonic. How many did I have? Add that to my list of things never to do again.

My vision is still a little blurry and it's hard to focus, but I assume the amorphous shape at the desk is Melissa, doing her makeup like she does every morning. I don't see Laura in the bunk across from me so she and Deirdre have probably left for breakfast. Melissa skips breakfast, whether because she eats approximately nothing or because she needs the extra time to work on her makeup, I don't know. Laura, Deirdre, and I are probably the only people on campus who know what she looks like without foundation; and that's only if we catch her when she isn't looking, since she won't look at anyone before she has her face on. I don't know why she works so hard at it. She's prettier than the rest of us put together, but I guess that's why she's her, and we're us.

I force myself to sit up in the bed. Bad idea. My stomach does not approve and punishes me for the effort with a wave of nausea.

"Ah, you're finally awake." Melissa says. She touches her eyelashes with a brush and checks herself in the mirror. Satisfied, she leans back and looks at me. "Laura thought maybe we should call the campus ambulance for you. I told them I'd stay here until you woke up and make sure you didn't choke on your own vomit or anything."

"Thanks," I mumble, clutching my head in my hands. At least the room isn't moving from side to side anymore, and my eyes are beginning to focus. "I didn't throw up, did I?" That would really suck. Deirdre spent a long night puking in her sleep last year after drinking some punch the chemistry majors had spiked with pure ethanol, and our room smelled like vomit for the rest of the semester.

"No, though given how green you looked, I'm a little surprised you didn't. You hold your alcohol better than I thought. Where were you last night?"

"I went to the Ramskeller." I grimace as the god of hangovers drives another iron spike through my head.

"Really?" Melissa sounds surprised. "Trust you to pick the nerdiest place possible to do your drinking. Pre-med party or something?"

"No, I just thought I needed a drink." My stomach chooses that moment to start climbing up out of my throat. I leap out of bed and race for the bathroom. By some miracle, I make it to a stall in time to spew in the toilet instead of on the floor.

Melissa follows me and stands in the bathroom door behind me to shoo off anyone from the floor who might choose this moment for a shower. I kneel on the tile floor clutching the bowl while I wait for the rest of it to come up. I notice I'm still wearing my pants from last night. God, how drunk was I? My stomach heaves again to answer my question.

When I'm convinced no more is coming, I push myself to my feet, grab the edge of the stall to steady myself, and kick the handle with my foot, trying not to look at the evidence of my debauchery. The stall is still disgusting, though nothing out of the ordinary for any dorm bathroom on Sunday morning. Of course, it's Wednesday.

I stumble over to a sink, turn the water on, and start splashing it in my face.

"You're not usually the party type. What inspired this mid-week bender?"

I should probably tell her now, only it wouldn't be fair to Laura and Deirdre. Plus, I don't really know what I'm going to do yet. I know I'm not going to take Dan up on his offer. Of course not. That would be...weird. Only that means I have to leave school, and—

My thoughts have run away with me again. Melissa interrupts. "Jenni, are you OK?"

I say the first thing that comes to mind. "I met somebody, and he bought me drinks."

Melissa's voice jumps an octave. "Jenni, did he do something? Did something happen?"

I look up in shock. "What? No, nothing happened. He didn't even leave the pub with me."

"OK, good." Melissa looks relieved. Me too. I promised myself I was not going to be one of those girls crying in the bathroom after a bad date. Of course, I also I promised myself I wasn't going to be one of those girls who got so drunk she couldn't stand, so that's one promise broken.

"Who was he?"

"A man from off campus. He bought me drinks, and I drank them. Too many. It's nothing. I'll probably never see him again."

"How many?"

"Just one. He was alone." Was he alone? My memory is a little hazy, but wasn't there somebody with him?

"Not how many guys, silly. How many drinks?"

"I don't know. I didn't count. A few. Four? Five?"

Melissa laughs. "No wonder you're plastered. I don't think I've seen you drink more than a beer since freshman orientation. Come on, let's go back to the room."

I'm still a little wobbly so I lean on Melissa as we walk back to our room. Once I'm safely back in my bed, Melissa pulls up a chair and begins to pump me for information. "Tell me about this guy who was buying you drinks. What's he like? Is he cute?"

How much can I tell her? How much do I really know? Not much. I settle for, "Yes, he's cute."

Melissa proceeds with the full third degree. I try to answer as monosyllabically as possible, half because saying more than a couple of words at a time makes my head pound and half because if she digs too deep, I'll have to tell her why I was in the campus pub scrounging drinks in the first place. Still, she manages to get out of me that his name is Dan, he's not a student, and he's older than us. Finally I beg off with the excuse that I need to shower before class.

By the time I get out of the shower, it's too late for breakfast, not that I could keep anything down if I did eat. I throw on a sweatshirt, grab my backpack, and race out the door to chemistry class.

Usually I enjoy chemistry, but today I'm too distracted by the other kind of chemistry (well, biology to be precise) to concentrate. My mind keeps wandering back to last night when it should be focusing on covalent bonds. Instead, it focuses on Dan's eyes. He had this way of looking at me as if he could see everything, like I had no secrets from him, which is silly. I just met the man. He doesn't know anything I didn't tell him.

I take his card out of my pocket and flip it between my fingers. The name and the phone taunt me. Should I call him? Do I want to? What will he do if I don't call him? Would he come looking for me? Did I tell him where I live? I try to remember. I know I told him more about me than I probably should have. We just met and I don't know him from Adam, but damn it, it felt so good just to have someone listen.

In the morning light, and with weak nausea replacing the vodka-induced haze, Dan seems a bit dangerous. Not Henry Portrait of a Serial Killer dangerous, more like James Bond dangerous, but still someone who could get me in way more trouble than I'm ready for. I doodle in my notebook as I think about it.

Of course, if I don't call him I still have the rather large problem of how to pay for school, which is probably what I should be focused on. How did my adult problem of paying for my education turn into some schoolgirl drama about whether I should call a boy?

Well, not a boy, exactly. Dan is a man. There's no mistaking it. Even those brawny guys Deirdre and I were checking out at the rugby party last week now seem weak and incomplete by comparison. It's hard to even imagine Dan as a boy.

Which brings up another issue. How old is he? He's not a teenager, that's for sure. I'm reasonably certain he's on the far side of thirty, and not yet collecting social security. Between those two mile-posts, though, my judgment of men's ages is a little fuzzy.

I picture his face. It wasn't a baby face, but it wasn't wrinkled either. Those light blue eyes sparkled like he knew a secret about me I didn't know myself. I could lose myself in those eyes. Maybe I did. I can't say they looked old, or young. More playful than anything.

He's not going bald yet, that's for sure. I imagine running my fingers through his hair, and the thought starts to warm me up. Focus, Jenni, focus. There was definite gray, or more like silver, around the temples, though on him it works. That might only mean he has a good colorist, though somehow Dan doesn't seem like the sort of man who would see a colorist. Tom's in my class and he's already grayer than Dan is. So maybe Dan's forty? Forty-five? Fifty? Can I be with someone who's fifty? That's older than my father.

And speaking of my father, what would he say about this? Or my mother? Or Janine? I imagine bringing him home for Christmas. "Hi Mom. Hi Dad. I'd like you to meet the man I'm sleeping with to pay for school since you couldn't afford it." Awkward doesn't begin to describe it.

Then again, I don't think Dan's looking for the sort of relationship that involves meeting my parents. He made that pretty clear last night, even if he never said the words.

And that's the final question. Is he serious? Will he really pay for school if I sleep with him? If he'd asked me last night, I think I would have gone with him, tuition or no tuition. In the morning though, with a little distance between us and the alcohol wearing off, it seems sort of, well, not cheap—if there's one thing Fordham isn't, it's cheap —but seedy, definitely seedy. There's no denying I'm attracted to him, but it's hardly romantic that he wants to pay for it. At the same time, a small part of me is excited that he thinks I'm worth paying for. All those blond girls in the bar last night, and he picked me. I'm the plain girl, the best friend. The idea that he thinks I'm the hot one is validating. I like it.

Maybe I'm overthinking this. Maybe he doesn't want to sleep with me at all. Maybe he hangs out in college bars offering to pay young girls' bills out of the goodness of his heart, like on that old TV show that plays on basic cable? But then there was the kiss. That was not a friendly kiss. That was a full-throated kiss from someone who wants to merge bodies and not come up for air for about a week. God knows my body responded to him. Even now the memory makes me start to flush.

Why didn't I follow him out last night? I was drunk and I was ready. I was more ready than I knew I could be. Why did he have to make it so damn complicated by dangling tuition in front of me? Like I didn't already have enough to worry about.

Too many questions. Too few answers. Before I know it, the rest of the class is standing up and packing their books and notebooks away. Crap. That's one lecture missed. Frantically, I try to copy the assignment off the board before the next class comes in. School hardly seems worth paying for if I don't even pay attention in class.

———

DINNER in the cafeteria is marginally less disgusting than usual. Wednesday is the weekly special night. Tonight they're serving prime rib. At least they call it prime rib. My mother called it pot roast. But what the hell, I'm almost certain it's actual beef for a change.

Deirdre and I have splurged on the meat. Laura is having the chicken. Melissa sticks to her usual salad. I'm sure she eats protein sometime, but I've never seen her do it. I'd think she was a vegetarian if she hadn't spent two weeks talking Deirdre out of it last year: "Men don't like girls who don't eat red meat, Deirdre. If you won't eat a burger, the only boyfriend you'll get will be some tie-dyed hippie who doesn't shave, spends all his time playing hacky sack, and expects you to pay for dates."

Thanks to the prime rib, the cafeteria is more crowded and noisier than normal. As long as we face each other around the table, it's actually possible to have a relatively private conversation.

I'm half-expecting Melissa to start up again with questions about Dan, but it's actually Laura who goes there first. "So Jenni, what happened to you last night?"

"Yeah, Jenni," says Deirdre. "Are you OK? You looked pretty green this morning."

"I'm fine. I had too much to drink. That's all." I'm tempted to add "and you should know," but I restrain myself. Of the four of us, Deirdre is by far the heaviest drinker.

Deirdre leans forward across the table. "Was there a party? You should have told me. I would have gone with you."

"No, no party. I just went to the Ramskeller and had a couple of drinks."

Laura pipes in. "More than a couple, I'd say. When you got back to the room last night, you were so hammered I thought I was going to get drunk on the fumes."

Laura, of course, hardly drinks at all.

"Jenni had some man buying her drinks," Melissa volunteers.

Damn it, I wasn't going to tell anyone that. I wouldn't have told Melissa this morning if I wasn't too hung over to think straight.

"Jenni," Deirdre squeals. "Did you sleep with him?"

"No, I didn't sleep with him," I retort. "He was a perfect gentleman. Better than the three of you are being, I might add." Well, not perfect. That kiss was definitely over the gentleman line. Not to mention his suggestion. But I am *not* going to tell Deirdre, or any of them, about that.

"A perfect gentleman who got you drunk," Laura, always the practical one, says.

"I think we should let Jenni tell us what she wants to tell us and

not press her. I'm sure if there's anything serious she'll let us know,"
says Melissa. "Isn't that right, Jenni?"

"Thank you. And no, it isn't serious. He bought me some drinks. I
drank them. I came home. That's it. I'm probably never going to see
him again. Now can we please eat dinner?"

"Sure Jenni, if that's what you want," says Deirdre, looking a little
disappointed there isn't more gossip. Before long she's chattering
away about an illegal barbecue some girls in her sociology class are
throwing in Martyrs this Friday while I pick at my meat. I wish I was
as confident about not seeing Dan again as I told them, because I've
been trying to talk myself out of it all day, and failing.

―――――

I DO NOT SLEEP WELL. I lie on my back looking up at the bottom of
Melissa's bunk, obsessing over what I'm going to do.

By 1:00 a.m. I've decided the whole situation is ridiculous. It's not
going to happen. First thing in the morning, I'll tell Melissa and
Laura and Deidre I'm dropping out. I'll call my parents, go to the
registrar to give the official notice as soon as they open, and by the
time my father drives up from Pennsylvania, I'll be packed and ready
to go. There. Done. Decided.

At 1:30, I realize I'm insane. Am I going to throw away all the work
I've already done? All the parties I didn't go to in high school so I
could study? Not like I was invited exactly, but maybe if I wasn't such
a grind I would have been. And my parents already spent a lot of
money for my freshman year. How can I tell them they wasted it,
especially now that my father's been laid off? No, I'm not going to
throw it all away. If there's any chance, any chance at all, I have to take
it. I'm going to do it. I'm going to call Mr. Cortland. If he really can
pay for me, if he really is that rich, I'll do it.

2:00 a.m. What the hell was I thinking? I'm not that sort of girl.
I'm still a virgin, for Christ's sake. What kind of girl does he think I
am? Not the kind of girl I am, that's for damn sure. What would

everyone say? What would everyone think? This is not what I studied for.

2:30 a.m. Jesus, I know I don't really believe in you anymore but if I'm wrong, would you mind helping me out a little here? Tell me what to do? Or give me a third option? Oh crap, this isn't like that joke about the flood and the boats and the helicopter Father Boudreaux told us at senior retreat, is it? Is Dan my helicopter? You wouldn't do that to me, would you?

2:45 a.m. Why can't I get Dan's face out of my head? Those blue eyes that look right at you like they understand everything and make you believe it's all going to be OK? Would it really be so bad to take him up on his offer? If I wasn't in trouble, if I didn't need the money, I'd still want to be with him. And he can make it all better. I want to believe.

3:00 a.m. Stupid girl. How could a man like him want a girl like me anyway? This is all some cruel frat boy prank, a pig party for rich Wall Street jerks who compete to see who can seduce the most pathetic loser. I'll agree to it, and then he's going to videotape it to show to his buddies while they all laugh. I should throw his card away and forget this ever happened. I wish I'd never met him. I wish, I wish, I wish.

3:30 a.m. I'm crying into my pillow, and trying to not sob so loud I wake Melissa. Why can't life be easy? And why, in the face of losing my education, my friends, and my future, is the thing I'm crying about that I'm not going to get a chance to be with Dan?

I don't remember falling asleep, but I must have because the next thing I know, it's 7:00 a.m. and my alarm is going off. I still don't know what I'm going to do.

I gather up my bath supplies and head for the shower. Is there anyone I can talk to about this? Certainly not my parents or my priest. Not my teachers. Deirdre's too flighty and she could never keep it a secret. Laura would totally forbid me the moment she heard.

Melissa's the one person who might listen and not immediately judge me for considering taking Dan up on his offer. She's smart and knows how much an education means, even if she tries not to show it.

She's got a Presidential scholarship, for Christ's sake. Full ride guaranteed. No FAPSFA forms for her. And she's not rich. None of us are, but she's more not rich than the rest of us, I think. She's a little cagey about the details, and I'm too polite to pry, but her mother does medical billing and I've never heard her mention her father. She'll understand my dilemma if anyone does.

When I get back to the room, Laura and Deirdre are leaving. Perfect. Melissa is putting the finishing touches on her makeup. I sit down on my bed. "Melissa, can I ask you something?"

"Sure Jenni," she says without looking away from the mirror. "What's up?"

I open my mouth and freeze. "Can I borrow some lipstick?" I finally blurt out.

"OK," Melissa says with a querulous tone. She opens a drawer, takes out a lipstick, and hands it to me.

I know. I'm a coward, but I can't tell her.

I SIGNED up for microeconomics to fulfill the core requirement in social science because it was mathy enough to be an easy A. I'd break the curve while all the business majors tried to remember cross-multiplication from Algebra I. Only I didn't count on Professor Gibbons having a monotone that makes the teacher in Ferris Bueller sound like Sam Kinison. Most days I doodle in my notebook while Gibbons drones on, but today something he says jolts me awake.

I stick my hand up excitedly. "Excuse me, could you repeat that?"

Professor Gibbons looks at me and raises one eyebrow. For him, that's major emotion. Maybe it indicates surprise. It's the first time anyone has asked him to repeat anything this semester, maybe this career.

"Yes, Miss McGrath. I was saying that proper risk management requires keeping the maximum possible number of options open. Options have value. Putting off decisions can be a highly rational strategy when additional information might become available before you exercise them. In short, don't make a decision today you can put off until tomorrow."

Gibbons never uses three words where he can use three hundred, but he's right. I don't need to make up my mind today. I just need to keep all my options open. Maybe there's some point to the core curriculum after all.

After class I go straight back to the dorm so I can use the hall phone before I lose my nerve. I've already memorized the number from Dan's card. My stomach is doing flip flops. This isn't a commitment, I tell myself. I'm not making a decision, not yet. I'm keeping my options open. That's all. It's not like I can't drop out if I call him.

I pick up the phone and start to dial. I punch in the last digit, then slam the phone back on the hook. I repeat this three times. Each time I hang up before it can start ringing on the other end. This is silly. Breathe, Jenni. You can do this. He asked you to call him. Finally, the fourth time, I let it ring through.

After the first ring, someone picks up and a woman's clear voice says, "Cortland Investments, Mr. Cortland's office. How may I help you?"

Shit! A secretary. I assumed I'd get Dan. I guess men like him have secretaries. "Um, it's Jenni Mcgrath," I say in a voice barely above a whisper. "Dan, um, Mr. Cortland, gave me this number." I pause while I try to think of what to say to this woman on the other end of the line. "It's personal."

"I'll put you right through," she says with an air of cold efficiency, and I breathe a sigh of relief. I don't know what I would have told her if she wanted to know what my business was with Dan.

Dan comes on the line almost immediately. "Jenni, I was hoping you'd call." I hear his voice and my heart does a little dance. This is bad. Why am I so happy to hear him? His voice is strong and confident, exactly what I'm not feeling.

"So, I was thinking about what you said, and I was wondering…"

I pause, not sure how to ask the question that's occupying my mind. How exactly does one go about negotiating something like this?

"Go on," Dan says.

I take a deep breath. "So, you're able to cover my tuition?"

"Tuition, room and board. Maybe a small allowance. Money's not the concern here."

The hell it isn't. Money's my major concern. Well, that and the next question. "And in exchange for this, you'd want?" I leave the question hanging.

"Nothing too kinky. Just some underwater acrobatics in scuba gear with my church choir."

I gasp audibly over the line.

Dan laughs. "Just kidding. Why don't we meet for dinner and talk about it? My treat, of course. I know a nice restaurant in the Village. No pressure. No obligations."

I consider it for a moment. Dinner isn't too bad. I have to eat, and it would be nice to eat something a few levels better than the "fit for human consumption" food Marriott feeds us. OK, that's probably another campus legend, but it's not like the food in the cafeteria is actually good. I'd love to have some salad that wasn't half brown for a change.

Then a thought crosses my mind. "Somewhere public?" The scuba comment still has me a little rattled.

Dan laughs again, but a friendly laugh. "Of course. I'll have my secretary set it up. I can send a car for you tomorrow, say at 7:00?"

I nod, then realize he can't hear me. Why can't I think when I'm talking to him? "That sounds good," I murmur.

"Great. Wear something nice. I'll see you tomorrow. Bye now."

"Bye bye," I say, as he hangs up. Shit, now I have to find something to wear.

4

FIRST DATE

Melissa helps me plan my outfit while Deirdre kibitzes. Deirdre really, really wants to know who I'm going out with, but I beg off. "It's a first date, and I don't want to jinx it. I'll tell you if it looks serious." That's not exactly a lie, just not the whole truth, right? OK, maybe it's 10% of the truth, but I simply cannot tell her what I'm thinking about doing. I can barely admit it to myself. Melissa knows it's the man I met at the Ramskeller Tuesday, but not a lot more than that.

Melissa wanted to go shopping, but there is no way I can afford new clothes right now. My bank balance is at zero. My parents gave me a credit card for emergencies, but since my father was laid off I don't want to surprise them with an extra bill. And I absolutely do not want to have to explain the nature of an emergency that requires a trip to Macy's.

Instead, we pick a frilly, dark blue blouse that's a little too low cut for comfort from Melissa's side of the closet and a black skirt from Deirdre's that she hasn't worn yet this semester. It's the closest we can manage to a little black dress.

I've never been any good at walking in heels, but when I show Melissa the shiny black canvas slippers I bought two years ago for senior prom, she looks at me like I've announced I'm going to wear a grass skirt and a coconut bra. So it's the sensible black heels I only brought to school because my mother insisted I could not wear tennis shoes all the time. I hope I don't break an ankle.

Finally, Melissa insists on doing my makeup, and for once I let her. "I've been wanting to do this for a year," she says. I usually don't go fancier than washing my face and maybe adding some light lipstick and bit of mascara if we're going out to a party or a bar, and it drives her nuts.

Laura returns halfway through the process and scowls. If there's one fault line between the four of us, it's the significance we attach to fashion or lack thereof: Deirdre and Melissa on one side, Laura and me on the other. Seeing me dolled up like this, she must think I've switched sides. "Where are you going?" she asks.

"Jenni's got a date!" Deirdre squeals in her little girl voice before I can answer. "Isn't it exciting? Some man is taking her out to a fancy restaurant in the city, only she won't tell us who. It's mysterious."

Laura looks like she's about to say something, but instead she goes to the dresser she shares with Deirdre and takes something out of a drawer to hand to me.

"What's this?" I ask, looking at the shiny silver object she's dropped in my hand.

"It's a rape whistle. If he gets out of line, you blow it."

Deirdre makes a face. "She's not going to need that."

Will I? I look to Melissa. She shrugs. "Better safe than sorry, I guess."

"OK. I'll keep it in my purse."

It takes Melissa another thirty minutes to finish my makeup. Deirdre keeps hopping up to inspect and make suggestions. Finally, Melissa tells her to sit on her bed and be quiet or she'll kick her out of the room. Deirdre is so happy she's practically bouncing up and down on her bed. "Jenni, you look so cute. You should dress this way all the time!"

Yeah, right. Like I have three hours a day to spend on makeup and clothes. But for one night I can manage it. If I'm going to do this, I might as well do it right.

When we do the final check in the mirror, I'm stunned. It's like a different person is looking out at me. "Wow," is all I can say.

"Told you you should wear more makeup," says Melissa.

———

DAN SAID the car would pick me up at 7:00, but the four of us are standing outside Hughes Hall at 6:30. Melissa and Deirdre fuss over my clothes, while Laura gives me advice I'm too nervous to pay attention to. The main thrust of it is that if he tries to rape me I should knee him in the balls and run.

It's a surprisingly chilly evening for September, so I ask Deirdre to run upstairs and grab a sweater for me. At 6:45 she returns with a leather jacket studded with enough rhinestones to embarrass Dolly Parton. "I know you wanted a sweater, but this is cuter," she says, beaming.

"Um, thanks." I hold the jacket in front of me and try to figure out how to politely decline.

At that moment, Kenny and Tom, two sophomores from the second floor, pop out the front door and bound down the steps before coming to a screeching halt right in front of us. Oh great, just what I need. An audience.

"Holy shit, Jenni, what got you so dressed up?" says Kenny, his eyes laser focused on my chest.

"I don't think I've ever seen you wear a dress before, Jenni," Tom adds. At least he's able to talk to my face. It's like a steel rod is connecting Kenny's eyes to my cleavage.

"I'm meeting someone for dinner," I mumble.

"At the Ramskeller?" Tom asks.

"Who dresses like that for the Ramskeller, doofus?" Kenny looks away from my chest long enough to punch Tom in the arm, then returns his attention to my breasts.

"She's meeting her parents in the city for dinner," Melissa says.

I'll have to remember to thank her for the lie later. The last thing I want is news of this spread around campus. I'm not sure what would be worse, the truth—whatever it is—or the stories the rumor mill would concoct in lieu of it.

Before they can ask any more awkward questions I don't want to answer, a black car pulls up. It's not a limo, thank God. This is going to be hard enough to explain as is. Why didn't I tell Dan to send the car to the parking lot instead? At least it's nicer than the beat up Bronx cabs from AD-11111 and TU-22222 that usually make forays onto campus.

"Wow," Tom says, momentarily taken aback. "Your parents must have some money."

If they did, I wouldn't be out here. A Spanish man in a dark suit gets out of the driver's side, and walks around to the curb. At least he isn't wearing a little hat, or I'd never hear the end of this. "Miss McGrath?" he asks.

I nod, and he opens the rear door. Before I get in, Melissa takes me by the shoulders. "If anything happens, you call," she says softly enough so the boys can't hear. "We'll come get you if you need us, OK?"

I nod. I don't know what they could actually do, but that gives me an idea. As discretely as I can, I slip Dan's business card out of my purse and press it into her hand. "Just in case," I say, and Melissa nods. I know I'm being paranoid. I really don't expect the police to fish my body out of the East River tomorrow, but it's good to know someone has my back.

"OK guys, bye," I say and scramble into the backseat. The windows are tinted so they can't see in, but I can still see out. Kenny and Tom start chatting up Deirdre and Laura as soon as the door closes, while Melissa stares at the car until we pass out of sight.

The driver is mercifully silent on the ride into the city. I sit in the back seat and try not to bite my nails. This is only a date, right? I'm meeting Dan in the city, not miles out in the suburbs. If I don't like it, I can leave any time and take the D train home. I don't have to do anything I don't want to do. If I tell myself that enough times, maybe I'll even believe it.

The ride takes about forty-five minutes. I'm not sure, but I think we're somewhere in the Village when the car finally stops. I grab my purse and fumble with the door, but before I figure out the lock, the driver has opened it for me from the outside. I step out, and almost twist an ankle as my heel catches the curb. The driver catches me, and I steady myself on his shoulder and pull myself back to a fully upright position. That's when I see Dan standing next to the doorway, smiling in amusement. Shit, he saw the whole thing.

Dan steps over to the curb and takes my arm, as he casually slips a bill into the driver's hand. "Thank you, Hector, I'll take her from here."

"Thank you, Mr. Cortland."

Dan smiles. "Hello, Jennifer, nice jacket."

I look down and blush. I'm going to kill Deirdre! "Thanks, I guess."

Dan puts his right arm on the small on my back and escorts me across the sidewalk to the door. It feels a little controlling, like he's pushing me where he wants me to go, but on the other hand I'm a little wobbly in the heels so it's not exactly unwelcome.

Inside, Dan helps me off with the jacket and hands it to the coat-check girl. I twinge when I realize she's dressed better than me. Dan taps me on the shoulder. "Let's get our table." He walks up to the maître d', a blonde woman of about twenty-five standing behind a podium, wearing a ponytail and a pant suit. She could have stepped out of Vogue. Even the servers here are gorgeous.

"Cortland, table for two."

"Yes sir, Mr. Cortland. Good to see you again. Right this way." She gives him a big smile and wide eyes, like they're best friends with a lot of benefits. She doesn't even glance at me.

As she escorts us toward the back, I sneak sideways looks at the other diners. The men range from Dan's age to early senior citizen. The women average a few years younger, though not young enough to keep me from feeling like the child at the grownups' table. I am so underdressed.

At the table, the maître d' hands us over to our waiter for the evening, a man who introduces himself as Justin. He pulls out one chair, and I stand there for a long fifteen seconds before I realize he's pulled it out so I can sit down. I blush with embarrassment and scoot in. Only then does Dan sit down. I do not know how to behave in a place like this. I hope they don't have seven different kinds of forks, or finger bowls, or something.

I try to scan the room discreetly while Dan talks to the waiter. Aside from the school cafeteria—about which the less said the better —the restaurants I'm accustomed to run the gamut from dingy to grimy, the sort of places that mood-light to hide the food. This restaurant is attired more like a museum, airy and bright. Parallel lines of lamps draped in white cloth march along the ceiling, illuminating softly. The bottles behind the bar and the glasses hanging above it glisten like they're made out of crystal. If Versailles and the Met had a baby together, and that baby grew up to become a restaurant, this is what it would be.

Dan is chatting with our waiter about the wine list. They might as well be speaking Greek for all I understand. He could have any single woman in the room, and probably a few of the married ones. The maître d' was practically saying "Fuck me" with her eyes. What the hell does he want with me?

Dan orders a bottle of wine I've never heard of, which only means it's a brand not advertised on TV during Cheers reruns. Justin scrambles off to fetch it.

Dan picks up his menu and opens it so I do the same. The menu seems to be a mix of English, French, and Italian. I only recognize half the words. What exactly is polenta? Or Muscovy Duck? They don't even have pasta. Is tortellini pasta? I think so. Then I notice something weird. "That's funny, there aren't any prices in my menu."

"Don't worry about it. What's your favorite dish?"

My favorite dish is my mom's spaghetti and meatballs, but somehow I don't think this place serves that. Instead, I say the fanciest thing that comes to mind. "Shrimp scampi." I always order that at the Olive Garden back home.

Dan scans the menu. "Hmm, doesn't look like they have shrimp on the menu tonight, but the poached lobster with sevruga and a yuzu emulsion is exceptional if you like shellfish. You should have that. Do you like oysters?"

"I don't know," I reply honestly. Easton isn't exactly a big seafood town.

"Well, let's not be too adventurous then. I suspect you'll enjoy the caviar pie for an appetizer, everyone does. Perhaps the celeriac velouté to round it out?"

"OK." I have no idea what I have just agreed to eat. I hope it's not something hideous like sheep testicles.

Justin returns with the wine. "The 73 Montelena, sir."

Dan waves his hand, and Justin makes a show of uncorking the bottle. He pours a splash of wine into Dan's glass. Dan swirls it around and sniffs it. He seems to think for a minute, and Justin starts to look nervous. Finally, Dan nods, and Justin exhales.

Justin pours two glasses, first mine, then Dan's. I taste the wine. It's a white, all right. That's as far as my knowledge of wine goes.

Dan gives Justin our order. After he retreats to the kitchen, I ask the first question that pops into my head. "Can you really do that? Tell if the wine's good or not?"

Dan lets out a laugh. "Honestly? No. And I'll let you in on a secret. Neither can anyone else, but everyone expects it. It's part of the show. They'd be disappointed if I didn't at least pretend I might send the bottle back."

For the first time tonight, I crack a smile. It's a relief to realize Dan doesn't take all of this too seriously. It is a little over the top.

"You look very nice tonight," Dan says.

I can't help myself. I beam a little. "Thanks."

"I hope I didn't take you away from your classes to get ready."

"No, on Friday my last class is art history, and it's over by 2:00."

"Oh, are you interested in art?"

"Some of it. I like Botticelli."

This proves to be a mistake. I only took art history to fulfill the core requirement, but Dan, it turns out, actually knows something about art. As far as I can tell art is divided into modern art (finger painting) and classical (dead white guys who liked to paint naked fat women). Fortunately, Dan seems fully capable of holding forth on the subject with no help from me.

I sip my wine and nod occasionally without really paying attention. I study Dan's face, and his arms, and his hands. I couldn't care less about the museum Dan is talking about now. But Dan himself. Now that's art I can appreciate, a lot more interesting to look at than some old painting hanging in the Met. The way his hair dangles over his forehead. The way his eyes sparkle. The animation in his face. If he taught art history instead of Professor Neff, attendance might be a lot higher, at least among the girls. Hell, probably a few of the boys too.

By the time Justin brings our soup, Dan's moved on from the old masters to modern photographers.

"How's your soup?" Dan asks.

"Good," I answer truthfully, and raise another spoonful to my mouth. Quite good, creamy and salty, with a flavor I don't think I've tasted before. Apparently celeriac velouté is some kind of cream soup, with celery I guess. Who knew?

Dan leans forward. "I seem to be monopolizing the conversation. Tell me about yourself."

I look down at my soup. "There's not a lot to say. I'm just another girl from the suburbs. Nothing special."

Dan picks up his wine glass and takes a sip. "Really? Nothing that makes you uniquely you? Maybe something you've never told anyone, you keep it to yourself."

I blush. It's that way he looks at me again, as if he sees inside me, not naked exactly but like I can't hide anything from him.

Justin returns with the next course before I have to figure out something to say to that. The soup was good, but the caviar pie is amazing. I've never had caviar before and I'm not sure what to expect, but the salty, black fish eggs (which look nothing like eggs, more like coffee grounds) on top of the world's creamiest egg salad is heart-stopping. Being rich must be nice if it means you get to eat like this all the time.

I was worried the lobster was going to be a big red thing, looking at me, but it's served already shelled, and stacked into a tower with vegetables and pureed potatoes. It's so elegant I'm almost afraid to take my fork to it. Of course when I do, it's wonderful.

Dan has ordered the filet mignon, rare. It, too, looks more like a museum piece than actual food. The meat is cut into a perfect circle, placed on top of a circle of whipped potatoes, and topped with a small tower of mushrooms, carrots, and onions, as well as some green leaves I don't recognize.

"I've never seen food that looks like this."

"Like what?" Dan asks.

"So fancy. It's like they're cutting it into pieces of art."

"That's pretty much what they are doing. The chef is known for that. I can introduce you if you like."

"Thanks, but for tonight I think I'll just eat if that's OK."

"That's fine." He cuts off a piece of steak with his knife and knocks the food tower to the plate. "Tell me about school."

"School?"

"Yes, school. Let's start with why you're in school."

I chew my lobster and think about what to say. "I went to a Catholic high school, and my guidance counselor thought Fordham was a good school, not too close, not too far away."

"Not why you're at Fordham. Why are you in college at all? Is there something you want only college can give you, or did you go because it was the expected thing?"

Surprisingly few people have asked me that, but I do have an answer. "I want to be a vet. You can't get into vet school without college first."

"Definitely a vet, not a doctor?"

That question I have been asked before, by every pre-med advisor, guidance counselor, and relative since I was in 8th grade. "I want to work at a zoo, or maybe wildlife rehab. Being a vet is the best way to do that."

Dan stops chewing and looks thoughtful. "Not the answer I was expecting. Most girls would say they love animals."

"I do love animals. My parents tell me that when I was a little girl I used to follow our cat around the house and listen to her heart with my toy stethoscope. But wild animals are more exciting. It's another reason I picked Fordham. It's next to the Bronx Zoo."

"My building is across the street from the Central Park Zoo."

"Is that a nice neighborhood?"

Dan laughs again. "Why yes, I think most people would say it is. I can tell you haven't spent a lot of time in Manhattan."

I cut another piece of lobster. "I've been to Manhattan. More than once. Only it's a long way from the Bronx on the D train, and everything costs so much money. Sometimes it's easier to stay on campus for the weekend. And I didn't come here to party in the city. Everyone back home thinks I did, but I didn't. I picked Fordham because they have a good zoology program, and they offered me a bunch of financial aid. Only then they took it away." I feel myself starting to get angry just thinking about it. I finish off my glass, and almost as soon as I put it down Justin is there to refill it. Has he been doing this all dinner?

Dan has finished his steak. He wipes his lip with his napkin and looks thoughtful. "Sounds like you have it all planned out then. Of course, vet school costs money, even more than college. It could be hard to do if you're carrying a lot of debt from your student loans already."

I nod. I've been too occupied with the immediate crisis to think further ahead, but he's right. Even if I could find a bank willing to loan me the money to keep going before I get kicked out, I'd be six figures in debt by the time I graduate. Add vet school to that, subtract what I'm likely to make in my career discounted to net present value, attach compound interest; I could starve in a box on Fordham Road and still not break even. Sometimes being good at math really sucks.

"Only none of that's going to happen if I can't pay for it," I finally say.

Dan smiles. "And that's why you're here tonight."

I take a deep breath and try not to let my nervousness show. Despite the wine, my entire body feels clenched tight. "Yes."

Dan takes a pen and a small notebook out of his jacket pocket and starts writing. I can feel his gaze on me, sizing me up, calculating whether I'm worth the price. I look down at my plate. There's some lobster left, but I don't think I can eat it. Not because I'm full. My stomach is doing flip flops and food is the farthest thing from my mind.

"$17,000, plus room and board. Add books and clothes and we're probably talking more like $30,000 a year, for three years. Make it a nice, round hundred thousand dollars. That's a lot of money."

My face falls. "I know. It's too much. I'll go. Thanks for dinner." I want to get out of there before I start crying. What was I thinking? It was a pipe dream. There's no way a man like him is going to pay for a girl like me, not when he can have any woman he wants for free.

I push my chair back, but Dan puts up a hand. "Wait. I didn't say no. I just want to be clear about what's on the table."

"But it's so much," I object without thinking.

"I can afford it," he says. He reaches across the table and takes my hand in his. Then with his other hand he puts a finger beneath my chin and lifts my head up so I'm looking straight into those big blue eyes of his. I'm holding my breath and I can hear my heart beating.

"I want to make sure I'm getting what I'm paying for."

"You will," I promise softly. When he's touching me like this, I don't think I could say no to him even if he wasn't offering to pay. I can feel the blood pumping in my neck. It's like there's no one else here, just me and him, and I can't look away.

"This is not a one-time thing. I expect you to make yourself available as long as I'm paying your tuition."

I nod. I understood that.

"And if I do this for you, pay your tuition, what are you prepared to do for me?"

I should probably look into his eyes and be flirty and coquettish, but instead I look at the tablecloth. "Whatever you want," I say. I think about adding a "Sir" since we are on decidedly unequal footing here, but that might be a step too far. For my sake, I need to keep the illusion that this is still a date and not a, well, exactly what it is.

"Whatever I want. I don't know. I can want quite a lot. I'm sorry, Jenni, but if I'm going to do this for you, I need to know that you understand what you're signing up for. I need you to be explicit."

I clench my fists around my utensils. Oh God, he's going to make me say it, out loud. "I'll have sex with you," I murmur as quietly as I think I can get away with.

"Good girl. Now that we're clear on what we're agreeing to, we can discuss the terms. I'll pay your tuition, room, and board; whatever isn't already covered by financial aid. Are you on birth control?"

"Yes, the pill." My girlfriends and I went to Planned Parenthood to get prescriptions for the pill junior year in high school, several years earlier than I needed it, as it turns out. Still, better safe than sorry. I'm not going to end up like Alicia Kiliccote, our class valedictorian who somehow wasn't smart enough to avoid getting knocked up when her boyfriend came home from Harvard last Christmas.

"Good," says Dan. "You should be healthy. If you need to see a doctor for that or anything else, I can send you to someone in town. I know the campus health service doesn't handle birth control."

I hadn't thought of that, but he's right. I can't imagine going to Dr. Boetha back home if I catch something. He's been my pediatrician since I was born. Just one of the many people I absolutely cannot tell what I'm doing. In any case, he's back in Pennsylvania, so I'm probably safe on that front.

Dan continues. "When we're together in public, you'll maintain yourself in a stylish and attractive fashion. I'll help you purchase clothes that are appropriate for any events we may attend. But you need to fit into my world. No inside out sweatshirts. No ripped jeans. No concert T-shirts. No grunge."

That describes 90% of my wardrobe. I'm not exactly an evening gown and party heels sort of girl, but if he's paying for it, I can swallow my pride and wear skirts. "OK, what about in private?"

"When we're at home, you can be more casual if you like. Clothing optional."

"Does that mean naked?" I ask, shocked.

"Is that a problem?"

I grit my teeth. I've already agreed to have sex with him. A little naked won't kill me. "No. Do you want me to cook and clean for you?"

"No, you're my companion, not my maid, and I rather enjoy cooking myself. We'll eat in more often than we'll eat out. This is one of the few restaurants in Manhattan that meets my standards."

He must have some pretty high standards. I've never seen food like this before.

"You'll spend four nights and three days with me each week."

The wine is really hitting me hard now, but I need to concentrate. This is important. "That won't work. I have class every day. I can see you on weekends, Saturday and Sunday."

Dan cocks an eyebrow. "You can study at my place. I'll call a car to take you back to school for class."

"No, I need to concentrate on studying during the week, no distractions. I need to keep my grades up or I won't get into vet school." I don't say what I'm really afraid of. What we do, what we're going to do, I can't get it mixed up with school. I can tell my roommates I'm going home for the weekend. But if I start disappearing during the middle of the week, they'll know something's up.

Dan takes a sip of wine and thinks. "OK, weekends. Friday night, Saturday, Sunday. I'll send you back to campus first thing Monday morning. Add four floating nights a month at a mutually agreeable time so they don't get in the way of your classes. If you miss a weekend because you're sick or need to study or any other reason, you'll make the time up later."

"Three floating nights," I counter.

"Deal," says Dan. "so long as you remember, you're not my girl-friend. When I'm not with you, I'm free to do what I want, see who I want. So are you. No strings attached. No drama. Can you promise that?"

I nod. It hurts a little when he puts it that way, but I suppose that possibility went out the window when I agreed to take his money.

Dan continues. "Now if this arrangement isn't working out for you, if you decide to leave—"

"I won't. I keep my promises."

"Good. Nonetheless, two things. One, you don't simply disappear on me. You don't have to explain why you're leaving, but you do need to let me know you're quitting. If you do, we'll pro-rate your time."

"OK." Honestly I'm more worried he'll break it off with me first. I'm still not sure what he sees in me.

"Final thing. This one's not negotiable. Everything else is, but not this." He pauses long enough to take a thick envelope out of his jacket and slide it across the table.

I pick it up. It's not sealed. I slip out the papers and look at the first page. It's dark with intimidatingly small type. "Is this a contract?" I'm surprised he'd want to put this in writing. I'm not sure what we're talking about here is exactly legal.

"Not exactly. It's a non-disclosure agreement."

"A non-dis what?"

"Jenni, I value my privacy. I go to great lengths to keep my name out of the press and to keep my private affairs private. The world I work in, the world I live in, it's not like school. There are people who would use you against me if they could. I need to know I can count on you to be discreet, no matter what happens."

"Of course." That's easy to promise. It's not like I want everyone in New York knowing what I'm agreeing to here either.

Dan shakes his head. "Don't be so hasty. You need to think about this. You need to understand, even after you leave, no matter what happens, this stays between us, forever. No talking about me to room-mates, family, therapists, anybody. If in fifty years you're writing your memoir, I won't be in it."

I gulp. His voice has gotten almost stony. He sounds really serious about this.

Dan continues. "An NDA is a binding legal document that compels you not talk about anything that happens between us, or about anything you learn about me or my business."

"What happens if I break the agreement?"

"Don't," he says forcefully. "You wouldn't like the outcome," and for the first time since I met him he looks hard and not a little scary. A shiver ripples across my back, and not a fun shiver. This is not a man I want to upset.

He senses my hesitancy. "Take your time. Read it over. You don't have to sign. You can walk away now if you're not comfortable with it, or take the weekend to think about it. Even bring it to a lawyer if you like. But if we're going to be together, I need you to agree to this much."

His face is rigid, his mouth closed. I pick up the papers and scan them. It's four pages of single spaced type, and full of phrases like "Receiving party's obligations under this agreement shall survive termination of the relationship," and "Disclosing party shall have the right to injunctive and monetary relief in event of a breach."

This is way too scary. The only thing I understand about this contract is that I don't understand it. I'm about to say no, but then I glance up from the pages and catch Dan looking at me.

He looks away, almost like he's embarrassed that I caught him staring, but before he does I see something in his eyes, a hint of pleading, like he desperately wants me to sign and he's afraid I won't. It is the first hint of vulnerability I've seen in him.

What the hell. What's he going to do, sue me? I'm already broke.

I pick up the pen, flip to the last page, and scribble my name below his.

"When do we start?"

5

THE APARTMENT

Dan has a black car waiting for us outside the restaurant. It looks the same as the one that picked me up before but the driver is different so it must not be. The car is spacious enough, but somehow when we get into the back seat I find myself pressed up against him. He is incredibly warm, almost feverish. He puts his arm around my shoulders and gives the driver the address, somewhere on 5th Avenue. I'm too distracted to catch more than that. My heart is starting to pound with the realization of what's about to happen. That is, if I can keep myself from chickening out at the last minute.

I'm spinning around in so many directions I don't know which way is up. I'm scared and excited and nervous and elated and ashamed all at the same time, and, oh yes, not a little buzzed, which probably contributes to the confusion. That's a good thing, though. If I wasn't, I don't think I could go through with this.

My sense of time is one of several things I'm lacking at the moment, along with propriety and good sense, so I'm not sure how long it takes for the car to arrive at Dan's building. A few minutes? An hour? It's not around the corner and it's not back in the Bronx. That's about all I can say.

The building we finally arrive at is one of those ornate gray stone apartments like you see on Park Avenue, not brick and not brownstone. It's after dark and I can't properly see the building, but I get the impression it's fancy. Oh, who am I kidding. It's fancy like a Tiffany necklace is pretty. I have no idea how much money it takes to live here, but I'm beginning to realize that $100,000 may be pocket change to Dan.

Dan gets out first, then holds the door for me as I slide out. He offers his hand to steady me, for which I'm grateful. The wine is hitting me hard now and I'm more than a little wobbly. I don't want him to stop touching me, like I'm afraid that if we lose contact, the spell will be broken. Once I'm steady, more or less, he walks me to the door.

A sixtyish gentleman with a silver mustache in a blue uniform opens the door for us. "Good evening, Mr. Cortland," he says.

"Good evening, Carl," Dan replies. I'm ready to go in but he stops to chat, and I almost scream. "How's Mia? Still playing Lacrosse?"

"She's doing well. They're 3 and 0 so far. She may make All-State this year."

"Good to hear. Keep me up to date."

"Will do, Mr Cortland, will do." He steps to the side so we can enter.

Inside, the building lobby feels like a museum. The floor is, well probably not marble, but some sort of slick stone, definitely not the institutional plastic I'm used to. Freshly cut flowers in vases lightly scent the room. I don't really know anything about art, but the paintings on the wall look like original canvases, not prints encased in glass. Dan whisks me back to the elevator before I have time to drink it all in.

The inside of the elevator is different than the ones I'm used to. The buttons are numbered one to eight, along with two at the bottom labeled L and B and one at the top marked R. There's a five-pointed black star to the right of the L and keyholes next to the others. Dan takes a key out of his pocket and turns it in the keyhole next to the R button. L must be Lobby, and B is probably basement. What's R?

As we ascend, the little orange numbers above the door light up. We started in L, then passed 1, 2, and on up through 8. Finally the R lights up. Christ, it couldn't mean roof, could it?

When the door opens, Dan waits for me to exit first, so I step out into the hallway, only it isn't a hallway. The door has opened into a room that looks more like an art gallery than an apartment. This one room is probably six—no make that ten—times as large as the dorm room I share with three other girls, and I don't think this is a studio. It is as minimally and tastefully decorated as our room is crowded and cluttered.

"Welcome to my humble abode," says Dan.

I don't know what to say. Finally, I mumble, "It's nice."

For the first time since I met him, Dan really laughs, not a polite little chuckle to acknowledge a joke, but a big, full-throated guffaw. "Nice she says!" He laughs again, a bit more restrained this time. "Most women take one look at this apartment and start planning the wedding. You think it's 'nice.' Come on. I'll give you the grand tour."

He escorts me across the room while I try to absorb it all. My shoes click loudly on the hardwood floor as I hang onto Dan's arm to avoid slipping. Several oddly curvy, translucent chairs—I think they're chairs, they might be art—are positioned strategically throughout the room. Two vases are filled with a dry autumn mix of sticks and herbs, though no actual flowers. A large, black leather couch is pushed against one wall, a glass coffee table positioned in front of it. Two glossy magazines, not four, not three, but two, lay on top of the table, carefully positioned in opposing thirty degree angles to the couch. A large canvas, black paint on cream, hangs on the one wall. At first I think it's abstract art, but as we pass it the picture shifts in my head like the optical illusion of the old woman and the young girl, and I realize it's a semi-realistic portrait of a nude woman, half-laying on the floor, looking away from the artist with her hair flowing over her shoulder.

Dan positions me in front of the large window on the far side of the room. He puts his left arm across my stomach, while he stands behind, pressing against me. My body is starting to heat up from the nearness of him. Cars and their lights are passing on the street below us, followed by an expanse of dark. "What am I looking at?" I ask.

"That's Central Park," Dan whispers in my ear from behind. "Admittedly, the view is more impressive in the daytime."

I feel Dan's hand grasp lightly at the zipper of my blouse and begin to pull, and I flinch involuntarily. He lets go. "Would you like a drink?" he says. He doesn't wait for an answer.

While I wait for him to return, I stand there looking out over the park, holding my arms across my chest. What have I gotten myself into? Can I possibly go through with this? I've barely even petted. And here I am, about to sell my virginity to this man I barely know (this very rich man I barely know, my inner mother corrects me) and for what?

Well, that is the kicker. For an education. It's not like I'm going to blow the money on clothes or jewelry or drugs. If anything's worth this, isn't my education? Everyone keeps telling me that, anyway. I can still hear Mrs. Breaux all the way back in seventh grade: "Candy and video games are over in day, but an education is going to be with you for a lifetime."

Or Sister Noreen at St. Agnes. "Life isn't a fairy tale. There are no Prince Charmings to swoop down in horse-drawn carriages and sweep you off your feet to their castle. You have to rescue yourself." The nuns drilled into us that we had to be smart and educated, that we had to go to college and take care of ourselves. We couldn't count on a man to do it for us.

So am I doing that? Am I taking care of myself here? Or is this just another way of waiting for Prince Charming to come rushing through the forest on his white horse to rescue me? Is it different now that he's really here?

Tough questions. Before I come up with any answers, Dan is back with a gin and tonic over ice. He hands the glass to me, and I take a sip. "Let's go to bed," he says.

There are so many reasons to walk away: I don't love him. He doesn't love me. He's paying me. The first time is supposed to be with someone special. He leans in to kiss me, and I feel myself weaken. His tongue probes into my mouth, finding my tongue waiting for him, the heady passion mixing with the sweet tingling of the gin and tonic.

That's when I know I'm going to do it. Good idea or not, feminist or not, empowering or weak-kneed, I'm going to do it. It's not the money. Even if Dan took the money off the table, even if he'd never put it on the table, I want this. I want this in a way I have never wanted anything before, not intellectually or emotionally but physically. I want his body wrapped around mine, pressed up against me, inside me. There are probably a million reasons I shouldn't do this, but as he slides his tongue against mine and my body responds, I don't think of any of them. I don't even think of trying to think of any of them. This is going to happen, and I'm going to let it.

6

FIRST NIGHT

Dan pulls me down a hallway that seems to go on for an impossibly long time, or maybe that's my nervousness. Black and white photos hang on the walls, tastefully illuminated by track lighting. They're all artistic nudes, both men and women, but they barely register. I'm too focused on what I'm about to do.

He stops in front of one to kiss me, and as his lips meet mine I let myself go completely for the first time, no inhibitions left. His tongue touches mine as his arms wrap around my back, bringing me in so we're pressed against each other, front-to-front. Then we move a little further down the hall, and he kisses me again. A little further, and another kiss. I have never felt anything like this. All rational thought is gone. I am completely in the moment.

Finally, we reach the end of the hallway, and Dan ushers me through another door into his bedroom. Like the rest of the apartment, it is large and impeccably decorated. In the center of the room there's a king bed, covered in blue silk sheets. It's what he brought me here for.

Dan leans down and kisses me again, slowly but forcefully. I'm on edge, every part of my body tingling in anticipation.

He reaches behind me and unzips my blouse. This time he doesn't stop. He leans in and kisses my neck while he hooks his thumb under the sleeves and slips it off my shoulders. The blouse falls to the floor. Gingerly, trying not to trip, I step out of it.

He kisses me on the mouth again, hard. Language has left me. Even if I wanted to say no, I don't think I could form the words.

With one hand, he reaches around and unhooks my bra. He lifts the straps off my shoulders, then drops the bra to the floor. He looks unapologetically at my naked chest and smiles. For a second, the first blush of shame starts to wash over me, but before it can take hold, he's embraced me again and we're kissing, my arms around his neck. This time, he places one hand on my right breast which tingles deliciously at his touch. My nipples are embarrassingly, almost painfully erect.

Then, with his other hand, and without breaking the embrace, he reaches down and unclasps my skirt. Before I fully know what's happened, it's on the floor with my blouse. He slides his left hand up and down my side, and my body quivers in reaction to his touch, all of it, making me feel like I have never felt before.

His hand stops on my thigh, and I take in a breath.

"All the way," he says, and I nod. Then I hook my thumbs into my panties and pull them down. They drop to the floor, and I step out of them. He looks me up and down and smiles. Suddenly conscious of my nakedness, I cross my arms over my breasts. I haven't been naked in front of anyone since I was a child.

He shakes his head and takes hold of my hands, which he pulls away from my chest, back down to my sides. "I want to see you," he says. He puts his lips on mine, kissing me hard and wet. As his tongue meets mine and slips along it, I begin to shiver. It is the most erotic thing I have ever felt.

When he breaks away I'm trembling, not with cold but with an excitement I can't name. At the same time I'm acutely aware that I'm standing naked in front of this man in his apartment. There is nowhere for me to run, nowhere to hide.

Dan must sense my nervousness because he asks, "Would you like me to turn down the lights?"

Unable to speak, I nod.

He walks over to the door and turns a knob while I stand in the middle of the room, unsure what to do. The lights dim, though they don't extinguish completely. When he returns, he smiles and takes my hand to lead me to the bed, motioning for me to sit, which I do.

Dan slips off his shoes and kneels down in front of me. He unbuckles my right shoe and slips it off. He runs a finger down the center of my sole, sending a shock wave of excitement from my foot all the way up through my head. Then he takes off the left shoe and does the same. It feels like every nerve in my body is tingling.

He puts his hands on my knees and pushes them a little further apart. I've never been this exposed to anyone before, not even my doctor. With a wicked smile he reaches out his hand and brushes the tip of his finger against my sex, and I explode. My back arches, my toes curl, and I emit a cry of sheer non-comprehension. Without conscious control, I throw my arms back and my legs clamp around him.

When I come to my senses, he doesn't say anything, but he's smiling at me like he knows something I don't. A small voice from somewhere in my Catholic school past whispers that I'm supposed to be ashamed about this, but I'm too spent to pay any attention to it.

He pushes my legs off him, then stands and removes his jacket, tossing it over a nearby chair. He unties his tie and throws it over the chair too, not taking his eyes off me as he does so. I am suddenly very aware of my nipples. Maybe I should cover up, or hide under the sheets but it's like his gaze has me locked in place. I can't move, can't hide.

He unbuttons his shirt and tosses it on the floor. He's wearing an undershirt, and as he pulls it over his head, his muscles ripple. The sight almost makes me explode again.

I think he's going to take off his pants, but instead he sits on the bed next to me and looks into my eyes. He kisses me once, lightly, then lays me down on my back. I close my eyes as he kisses me again, harder this time. Then he takes my right hand in his and places it between his legs where I can feel him. Gently, he moves my hand along the thin fabric of his pants. God forgive me, I want that inside me so badly.

He shifts position and backs away an inch, but doesn't stop kissing me. With every probe of his tongue, I get more and more desperate. He moves his hands away for a second and I hear him unbuckling his belt. The bed shakes and his pants hit the floor. I don't know if I can stand it any more.

Then he's back on top of me. He grasps the back of my neck in one hand and holds it there so I have nowhere to look but at him. With the other he holds my left hand, fingers intertwined. Without breaking eye contact, he slips a knee between my legs, then the other one, parting them. He positions himself against my sex and thrusts.

I know the first time is supposed to hurt, but it doesn't. My body feels as loose as a cat draped over a friendly lap. This is where I should be, what I'm meant to do. All worries, all fears, vanish in the feeling of the moment. He begins to move up and down inside me, maintaining an even rhythm. As he continues to move, I close my eyes and squeeze his hand so hard I think I might draw blood. It is the most exquisite thing I have ever felt.

Then, just as I'm beginning to get the rhythm and develop a feeling for this new sensation, he pushes himself up on his arms and changes the angle so that on every stroke he's sliding right across the top. I think I scream as the feeling rolls over me again and keeps coming. I don't know how long this lasts as I have lost all self-consciousness. All I can feel is the now of my body, his body pressed up against and inside of me, touching parts I didn't know I had.

Finally, I find myself returning to awareness. I am lying in the bed under him. I'm breathing hard and fast, mostly through my mouth, but I can still smell the rough scent of him.

From a couple of inches away, Dan smiles at me like we now share a secret, just the two of us. Then he rolls off and pulls me up against him, my back to his front. I let him hold me like that and luxuriate in the warmth of his arm wrapped around my chest, the way we fit together like two carbon atoms in a double bond. I have never been happier and more content than I am at this moment.

7

THE MORNING AFTER

Sometime in the middle of the night, Dan wakes me to go again. I'm still half asleep. My thoughts are disconnected, almost dreamlike. He penetrates me and I gasp. Although my body feels him, my mind is elsewhere, sailing in a sea of dreams and hallucinatory images of puppy dogs and clouds and chemistry class. I'm halfway between conscious and unconscious, unsure if this is really happening. When Dan finishes and rolls off of me with a grunt, I do not know if we've been making love for seconds or days.

Without a word he puts an arm under me and rolls me over so I'm lying on my side facing him. He slips a finger down between my legs and begins rubbing softly. In my half-conscious state the friction sends me over the edge.

When I'm done, the sheets around us are wet, hot, and sticky, but I'm too sleepy to care. I just wrap my arms around him and hold tight. I fall back asleep almost instantly, the boundary between consciousness and dream still hazy in the night.

WHEN I WAKE up for real (nude, I neglected to bring any form of nightclothes with me), Dan's not in bed, but I hear the shower. I lie in bed waiting for him, listening to the water run, thinking about what I can do to him. Without fully realizing it, I reach my hand down between my legs. Nothing serious, just a little soft rubbing. Then the shower stops and the door to the bathroom opens. I jerk my hand back out over the covers, just in time. Crap, what if he caught me?

Dan strides out of the bathroom without even a towel. This is the first really good look I've had at his body, and oh my God, is he gorgeous. Dan naked is, if anything, more stunning than Dan clothed. He's no gym bunny, too much hair for one thing, but he's got muscles in all the right places. When I first saw him he reminded me of Botticelli's Sebastian, but no Renaissance painting ever did for me what Dan's body is doing for me now.

And his penis is, wow. I had that inside me? I catch myself blushing and look away.

"Good, you're awake," Dan says, as he pulls on a pair of blue silk boxers.

"Have you been up long?" I ask. I bring myself to a seated position, gathering a sheet around me. It's funny after everything we did last night—it's not like there's anything new for him to see now—but it still feels weird to be naked in front of him.

Dan laughs as he pulls on his T-shirt. As he slips it over his head, I sneak a glance at his abs. Not quite a six-pack, but God are they tight.

"You were asleep when I got up, so I went for a run around the park. There's coffee and juice in the kitchen. I can crack some eggs if you like."

The thought of breakfast actually makes my mouth water. Surprisingly, despite everything I ate (and drank) last night, I'm quite hungry. Apparently sex works up an appetite. Who knew?

I wait for him to leave the room before I hop out of bed and hunt for my clothes. Sometime in the night a good fairy picked them up off the floor and folded them neatly. Realistically, Dan must have done it, though I wouldn't completely rule out the possibility that he has a maid hiding somewhere in this apartment that's larger than my parents' house.

Oh God, what if he does? If so, she saw me with him. For a minute my mind races, weaving utterly implausible stories in which a maid chases me out of Dan's apartment with a broomstick, before I calm down. I suppose if she lives with Dan, she must be used to his dalliances by now. There's no way I'm his first. And of course, my real problem is back in the Bronx.

I glance at the digital alarm clock next to the bed. Quarter past seven. Laura undoubtedly spent the night in Joshua's room, and she'll probably go to brunch with him, so she won't be back till maybe 10:00, 11:00 if I'm lucky. Deirdre was going home to New Jersey for the weekend, which leaves Melissa.

If Melissa went out, she might have come back too late and too drunk to realize I wasn't in my bed. Better yet, if she stayed out herself, I might be able to get back before her. That's a lot of ifs. I don't like my odds, but if I'm going to have any chance of not getting the fifth degree about where I spent the night, I need to get rolling now.

When I find the kitchen—further away than I would have guessed; this apartment is huge!—Dan is cracking eggs over a skillet.

"Over easy OK?" Dan asks. "Or there's yogurt and granola if you prefer."

"Eggs are fine as long as they're quick. I have to get back to the Bronx before my roommates wake up."

"I thought you'd spend the weekend."

"I can come back." Oh God, do I want to come back. "Only I didn't plan for this. If I'm staying over all weekend, I need some books so I can do my homework. And clothes."

"We could go shopping." Dan hands me a glass of orange juice and a plate with five pills on it. "My treat."

"What's this?".

"Juice, and some vitamins. It will help with the hangover. You need to get something in you."

Now that he mentions it, I am feeling a little headachy. I pop the vitamins in my mouth and wash them down with the juice. It's extremely good, sweet and thick and full of pulp, nothing like the watered down concentrate we get at school.

"It's not just the clothes. If I go now, I can sneak in before my roommates get up. If they wake up and I'm not there, well, you know how girls talk."

"Why? Haven't you ever stayed out the night before?"

I look down.

Dan's brow furrows. "You haven't stayed out before, have you?"

"No," I say softly.

"Jenni, was this your first time?" He sounds surprised. I don't know why. It's not like I told him I was Little Miss Experienced.

"Don't be angry."

"Jenni, you should have told me. I would have... I would have..." He stops. For the first time, since I've met him Dan Cortland is at a loss for words.

"I wanted to make you happy."

"Oh Jenni, you did. Only if you told me I could have gone slower, been more gentle."

"It's OK. I liked it too."

Dan puts his hands on my shoulders. They're warm from the cooking, but that's not why I start to heat up.

"You're sure?" he asks.

I nod. Then I put my arms around his back and lay my head against his chest. "I'm sure."

"OK, but I may have to teach you a few things. Now if you'll release me for a minute, I need to flip the eggs before they burn."

Reluctantly I let go. I pour myself a cup of coffee while I sit at the counter and watch him cook. Dan hums absent-mindedly as he waits for the eggs to be done.

Finally satisfied, he turns off the stove and slides the eggs out onto a plate. He brings two plates over, lays them on the counter, and sits down opposite me.

"So, you did enjoy yourself last night?" he says with a grin. It's not really a question.

I blush, hard.

"I'm going to take that as a yes," he says.

"Yes," I confess in a soft voice.

"Good," he says. "A deal always works better when both parties get something they want out of it."

———

DAN WANTS to call a cab for me, but that feels too extravagant. Ridiculous, I know. It's not like he can't afford it, but I'm a subway kind of girl. He offers to walk me to the 4 train, but I demur. If I can handle the walk home down Fordham Road, I can certainly manage a couple of blocks by myself in Manhattan. Besides, I need a little alone time to think, and walking helps clear my head.

When the elevator comes, he stands in the door and keeps kissing me. "Just one more," he says and then does it again. I giggle, but it's actually a little annoying. I have to get moving if I'm going to be back on campus in time. Finally, he lets me go when I promise I'll see him again for dinner. Right before the door closes he slips a white envelope into my purse. "For later," he says. I shake my head. Fun's fun, but I have got to get back to the Bronx and quick if I'm going to have any hope of keeping my dignity intact.

The train gods are with me. The 4 train rolls into the station just as I squeeze through the turnstile; and amazingly there aren't any smelly homeless guys sleeping in my car, only a few random New Yorkers, up early or up late.

Usually I'd read a book on the train, but there wasn't room for one in this teeny purse. That's when I remember the envelope. He said "for later." Well, now's later, isn't it? I take it out. It's a plain white envelope without even my name on it. It isn't sealed so I open the flap.

Crap, it's cash. Hundreds. I don't think I've ever even had a hundred dollar bill before. Suddenly, I'm a little scared. I try to look at my fellow straphangers without being too obvious. Are any of them muggers? I think I can rule out the church lady with the purple hat and the Jehovah's Witness magazines. The unshaven dude in the UPS uniform looks a little sketchy, but he's probably on his way to work.

I hold the purse in my lap and try to make it look like I'm hunting for a lipstick as I flip through the bills. One, two, three, four, five, ...holy shit. There's a thousand dollars in here! What the hell did I just do?

8

ROOMMATES

I turn the heavy dorm key, stamped with "Do NOT Duplicate under penalty of expulsion," as softly as I can. The deadlock thunks open and I wince. I needn't have bothered trying to sneak in. Melissa is already sitting at her desk doing her makeup.

"I see somebody had a good time last night," she says without looking up. Her back is turned to me, but I can see her smirk in the mirror on her desk.

I suppose I could lie, but let's face it. I'd have as much credibility as a parish priest sermonizing about chastity after being caught in flagrante with an altar boy.

"OK, I spent the night," I admit, as I stuff the envelope into the back of my underwear drawer. "Please don't tell anyone."

"Fine, but you have to give me details. How was it? Did you blow him?"

"Melissa!"

"Well did you?"

"No, I didn't. He was a perfect gentleman."

She spins around in her chair to face me. She's grinning like a grad student who just passed their qualifiers. "Oh, I very much doubt that. Even you couldn't be that boring. You had sex with him, didn't you?"

I don't say anything, but my red face is answer enough.

"So spill. What was it like? Did you enjoy it? Did it hurt?"

"No, it didn't. It didn't hurt at all. It was...nice."

"Nice? That's it?"

I kick off my shoes and lay on my bed. "OK, it was wonderful."

Melissa squeals. "Jenni, that's great."

"But you can't tell anyone, OK? I mean it, not even Laura and Deirdre. Deirdre would tell everyone. You know she would, and Laura—" I stop. I was about to say Laura wouldn't approve, but then I'd have to explain why Laura wouldn't approve. "I'm just not ready to tell them yet."

Melissa leans back in her chair and looks at the ceiling. "You know they're going to figure it out. If you're running out to your boyfriend's every night—he is your boyfriend right? Not just some hookup?"

My stomach clenches involuntarily. I'm glad Melissa can't see my face from where she's sitting. No, he's not my boyfriend. He's my—I don't even know what to call him. Is there a word for what he is to me? There are a lot of words for what I am to him, none of them pretty.

"We haven't really talked about it, but he does want to see me again, tonight, in fact. And tomorrow. I need to get some books and some clothes, but he wants me to spend the rest of the weekend at his place."

Melissa rolls her chair around the desk so she can look at me. "Wow, sounds pretty serious. Already spending the weekend. He must really like you."

Does he? Or does he just want to get value for his money? Anyway, I'm certainly not going to tell Melissa that.

Melissa continues. "Is his place nice? Does he have roommates?"

"No, no roommates." If Melissa assumes he's twenty-two and lives in a studio in the Village, well, I didn't exactly lie about it, now did I? This is one of my few good qualities. I know how to say very little.

"Look, Jenni, if you're not sleeping here, Laura and Deirdre are going to wonder. You have to tell them something."

"I'll still be here during the week. I thought I could tell them that my father's sick and I have to go back to Pennsylvania. If I do that, can you cover for me? Not let on where I really am?"

Melissa plops herself down on the bed next to me and grabs me in a big hug. "Of course, that's what best friends are for. I'm so happy for you Jenni."

I'm glad she is. That makes one of us.

———

I TOLD Dan I'd be back before dinner, which still gives me a few hours to decompress and figure out what exactly is going on. Since it's Saturday, I spend them in the laundry room. That way at least I'll have clean clothes to bring to his place tonight. Usually I go back to my room until the clothes are done, but I'm not ready to face anyone else just yet. Instead, I sit in the laundry room and do my organic chemistry homework while I wait.

Halfway through the spin cycle, Laura bangs through the door. "Jenni, Melissa told me you were down here. She said something's wrong with your father?"

For a second I panic and almost ask her if someone called. Then I remember, this is the story I asked Melissa to tell. "Yeah, I have to go back to Pennsylvania. I'll be back Monday."

"Is it serious? Did he have a heart attack?"

Crap. I really didn't think this through. Maybe if I was premed instead of pre-vet I'd know what to say, but the first thing that comes to mind is hoof-and-mouth disease. "Yes, it's a heart attack."

"Do you need someone to come with you? Or if you need to stay at home longer, I can get your assignments for you."

OK, now I really do feel like shit for lying to her. Maybe I should tell her the truth, but I can't. Instead, I lie again. "My mother says it's not that bad. It's just a little attack. It'll be OK. I'll be back Monday."

"OK, if you're sure."

Laura sits there with me, holding my hand in silence as we wait for the laundry to be done. Then she helps me fold. I don't usually fold, just sort of toss everything in a basket; but I can't refuse her. She's so concerned. Why didn't I think up a better excuse?

———

LAST NIGHT it was too dark and I was too drunk to see properly to pay attention to my surroundings. This morning I was in too big a hurry to beat Melissa and Laura back to our room. But now, on the walk from the 4 train back to Dan's building, I take the time to stop and really notice the neighborhood. Wow. This is about as far from the Bronx as the Bronx is from Pennsylvania. The buildings are like something out of an Edith Wharton novel. Heck, this is Manhattan. For all I know, these *are* the buildings from an Edith Wharton novel. I cannot imagine having enough money to live some place like this, but clearly Dan doesn't have to imagine it.

I expect to see Carl at the door, but instead a pudgy, bald man about Dan's age stops me before I can go in. "May I help you?" he says. His tone makes it clear that I don't belong.

"Um, I'm here to see Dan Cortland."

"Wait here." He goes inside the door and picks up a phone hanging on the wall. He's on the phone for what feels like an eternity while I shuffle my feet outside in the early autumn chill, wishing I had dressed warmer.

Finally, he returns. "The elevator will take you to the eleventh floor." He doesn't look happy about it.

"Do I need a key?" I ask, remembering the elevator from last night.

"Guests are not allowed to have keys," he replies brusquely, like that should be obvious.

Sor-ree. It's just a question, OK? As I walk to the elevator, I feel him staring daggers at my back. I hope I'm not going to have to deal with him every time I come over.

However, the rude doorman is right. I get into the elevator, press

R, and it lights up without the key and starts moving. Sixty seconds later, the door opens and I step out into Dan's apartment. He's walking around the living room in his stocking feet, talking on a cordless phone in a raised voice.

"I don't care what it costs. I told you to buy the damned trailers. We'll figure out the financing later. Are you telling me I hired the wrong man?"

While he listens to whatever the person on the other end is saying, he glances at me out of the side of his eye and waves to acknowledge my presence. I'm not sure if I should stay or go.

"Listen, get Paxson up from Georgetown. She comes from there. She knows how those folks think."

He puts his hand over the mouthpiece and lowers his voice. "Sorry, Jenni, business. I have to take care of this. Wait for me in the bedroom."

I nod and head for the hall, glad to get away. It's like he's a whole different person than the one I met in the Ramskeller. Frankly, it's a little scary. Behind me Dan continues. "No, nothing, just a friend. Ignore that. Tell her to get on the next shuttle to New York. I'll see her at my office to sign the papers at 9:00, no make that 8:00 a.m. Monday. We need to get this taken care of before the bank opens. Now, what are we going to do about Morgan?"

His voice fades out as I pad down the hallway, past the nude photographs. I stop to look at the last one before the hall turns. The girl in the photo is looking down, long dark hair covering most of her face. She looks about my age, give or take a year. Maybe it's my imagination, but she looks a little scared. Silly. She's much prettier than I am, probably a professional model who does this all the time and can switch from happy to scared to flirty at the click of a shutter. I wonder who she is? Or was? There's nothing in the photo to suggest a time or place, just the girl against a plain background. For all I know, the picture was taken thirty years ago, and now she's my mother's age with kids of her own.

Dan told me to wait for him in the bedroom. One problem, I can't find it. How big is this place anyway? I'm not sure what I should do.

Open random doors until I happen across it? Go back to the living room, assuming I can find that, and ask him? Or just park myself somewhere and wait for him to find me? I decide the last is the least scary option, and wait in the third room I think is the bedroom but isn't. This one is decked out like a 1920s speakeasy, complete with bar, mirrors, and plush red couches and chairs.

I'm not sure how long he's going to be. I figure I might as well get some homework done while I wait so I get Chaucer out of my backpack and open to the Wife of Bath's Tale. I already read it in high school, but now we're supposed to read it in actual Middle English instead of translation, which only makes it more boring. Sometimes I wish I'd picked a school with a less comprehensive core curriculum.

Next thing I know I'm waking up to a hand brushing against my cheek. I open my eyes and Dan is sitting next to me. "I see you decided to do some exploring."

I smile up at him sheepishly. "Sorry. I got lost. I couldn't find the bedroom and I didn't want to disturb you. What time is it?"

"A little after seven. I got hung up. I really did plan on spending the afternoon with you."

"Is everything OK? You sounded sort of upset when I came in."

"Just business. Nothing for you to concern yourself with."

"Are you hungry? I can make you something. I do a really nice spaghetti and meatballs." Actually, it's about the only thing I can cook, but he doesn't know that yet.

"Maybe later. In any case I didn't hire you for your cooking." He smiles at me again, this time not so softly. Then we get to the thing he did hire me for.

———

AFTER WE'RE FINISHED, I'm half-lying, half-sitting on the couch next to Dan. He touches a finger to my nipple and it stiffens under his touch. Then he runs his finger along the other one. "I like your breasts," he says.

My face heats red. It's not even the naked so much as the compliment that makes me uncomfortable. I still don't know how to respond to deliberate attention to my body. I flip over so my back is toward him. "I wish they were bigger."

"Why?" He sounds genuinely puzzled.

"Sometimes I look like a twelve-year old boy. I should be more curvy."

Dan laughs and grabs me around the tummy. He flips me back over and holds my shoulders down so I can't hide. "Trust me, Jenni, like this no one is going to mistake you for a boy."

He reaches his index finger down and strokes once between my legs, well, between something a lot more intimate than that to be honest, and I shiver.

"I don't want everyone doing that just to check that I'm a girl."

"You just need some more feminine clothes, something that shows off your figure, some heels to push up your calves, and a skirt instead of jeans. Maybe tomorrow we can do something about that."

"I have to study tomorrow. I've got an English essay due next week, and a lot of chemistry homework."

"OK, next weekend then. You don't have to study right now, do you?"

"No, not right now."

He gives me that wicked grin again. "Good," he says; and with that we're off for round two.

9

THE ENVELOPE

The weekend zips by. Dan keeps his promise to let me have time to study on Sunday. The rest of the time I spend studying him. One thing I learn. He is an insanely early riser. I know girls who don't get back from the bars as early as he's out the door for his morning run around the park.

Monday I piddle around in the kitchen for a little while after he's left, drinking coffee and listening to the radio, but it's boring without him. Consequently, earlier than I would normally force myself out of bed for an 8:30 AM class, I'm on the 4 train back to the Bronx.

Having the money in my underwear drawer makes me a little nervous. There's no real crime on campus, but I don't know how I would explain a thousand dollars in cash if one of my roommates found it because they were borrowing a clean pair of socks. It would have been easier if Dan wrote a check, but maybe he doesn't want a paper trail. The legality of our arrangement is something I haven't really considered, but if he feels the need to pay in cash, maybe I should.

By 9:00 a.m., I'm first in line at the bursar's office in Faculty Memorial. The little window comes up with a rattling sound. "Good morning, may I help you?" says a bored looking, middle-aged woman behind the counter.

"Hi, I'm here to make a payment on my tuition plan."

"ID please."

I pass my school ID across the counter, and the woman starts typing into her terminal.

Her face scrunches up. "Hmm, that doesn't look right."

I do not like the sound of that. What can possibly have gone wrong now? The dean told me I had two weeks to make the first payment. They can't have thrown me out already. The woman types some more as my stomach drops.

"It says here your bill is being sent to your home. Only the address doesn't match up." She types some more. "Looks like it was just changed to 35 Wall Street, Suite 2800. Is that your father's office or something?"

"I don't know."

"In any case, you're all paid up for the semester. Wire transfer. It came in over the weekend."

"Wait, what? I don't owe anything? Are you sure?"

"Nope. Not till Spring. You're all set, honey."

"Um, thanks," I mumble. I walk away in a daze. I know what happened. It had to be Dan. This is what I signed up for, and he could probably make the bill go away with the spare change in his leather couch. But then what the hell am I doing walking around with a thousand dollars in my backpack?

In the end, I stuff the envelope as far back in my underwear drawer as it will go and try to forget about it until the weekend.

––––––––

THE SCHOOL WEEK passes with the usual classes and labs: physics, organic chem (my bête noire), microeconomics, art history, and English. It's a heavy load, even for a pre-vet. Most schools let the bio majors load up on science and slide by with an English course or two in their freshman year for liberal arts. Unfortunately, Fordham has this Jesuit idea that all students should be well-rounded, or at least that's how they spin it. If they really believed in a well-rounded education, they'd make the English majors take some real science instead of Physics for Poets or Bio for Babies.

I shouldn't complain. I knew bio was not a jock major when I signed up for it. At least this week, unlike last, I'm able to concentrate in class and focus on the work, now that I don't have to worry about tuition. I even do most of my homework the day it's assigned and the rest the following day. This is a total first for me. I usually start it on time, but agonize and rework until the last possible minute. However, since the weekend is committed to Dan, I don't have time to do it over.

Not a lot of time for socializing either, aside from meals with my roomies, but that's OK. I got more socializing done last weekend than in my entire freshman year. If I'm honest, more than in my entire life before now, even if we didn't go out after Friday night. Dan is *very* sociable. I still get warm thinking about it.

———

DAN TOLD me to meet him at home at 7:00. My last class on Friday ends at 2:00 which leaves me way too much time to fill. I'm packed and out the door by 3:30. By 4:45 I'm climbing out of the 59th street subway station that comes out next to Bloomingdale's. I have the envelope with me. I could do some shopping, but I promised myself I'd give the money back to Dan. Paying my tuition is one thing, but I cannot take cash from him. I simply can't.

I settle for a little window shopping, then wander without a fixed direction, eventually landing at Central Park. I've heard stories about crime in the park, but I think that's the other end. This side is filled with tourist couples and nannies with baby strollers.

I meander up the path and to my surprise run straight into the Central Park Zoo. I've been to the Bronx Zoo, but not yet Central Park's. Unfortunately, it's closed for the evening. I wonder if Dan would take me? No, that's probably too childish for him. He's so serious. It's hard to imagine him enjoying things like zoos.

By 6:40 I figure I've killed enough time. Dan won't mind if I'm a few minutes early. I'm relieved to see Carl is out front instead of the bald doorman.

Carl smiles at me and opens the door. "Good evening, Miss McGrath. Mr. Cortland said I should send you straight up."

As I ride the elevator up, my breath starts coming faster and I can feel my heart pounding. I've been waiting all week for this. My head still has doubts but my body has none. I'm embarrassingly eager to see Dan again.

Dan is waiting at the elevator to greet me. He's dressed casual tonight, jeans and a white T-shirt that's way too tight. He's holding a glass of something brown, maybe bourbon?

"Hello," he says with a wicked smile. There's a low vibrato in his voice that makes me shiver. He puts down his drink on the side table and takes me in his arms to kiss me hello. As our lips and then our tongues meet I can taste the alcohol on his breath. It's not nearly as intoxicating as the sheer scent of him is.

"Shall we take this to the bedroom?" he asks, and I almost forget what I promised myself I was going to do first thing.

"Yes, but first there's something I need to give you."

"Oh?" He raises an eyebrow in puzzlement.

I open my purse and pull out the envelope. "Here. Thanks, but I can't accept it. I want you to take it back."

"Really?"

"I'm not ungrateful. I appreciate the gift, but it's too much. I can't take it."

"Why not?" His voice has shifted from seductive to serious, and maybe a little stern. "I thought that was our deal."

"The deal was that you'd pay for school."

He interrupts before I can finish my thought. "And that was paid?"

"Yes, it was, thank you."

"As I recall I also agreed to pay for your books and expenses."

"I already bought my books for the semester, and I have a meal plan."

"Have you taken economics yet?"

"I'm taking it this semester."

"Ask your professor what *fungible* means. And what about clothes?"

"I have clothes."

"You need better ones. You can't wear jeans and sweatshirts all the time."

"I thought you liked my jeans and sweats."

"I do, but I don't plan on spending all my time with you camped out in my apartment. You need some things you can wear to the Met or the Belmont without sticking out like a shelter dog at Westminster."

Crap. How can I explain this to him? "I know it's not rational, but cash feels different. It's not the same thing. It feels, I don't know, dirty, somehow."

"Maybe I want you to feel dirty." He smiles. It's the smile that tells me he's playing with me. Thank God.

"Here." I shove the envelope into his hand and this time he accepts it. "If you want me to be dirty, you're going to have to take your money back first."

"Yes ma'am." he says in a tone that leaves no doubt about who's really in charge here. "But I am going to buy you some new clothes, and I'm not going to take no for an answer. Now let's be dirty."

And then he brushes a finger behind my ear, applying just the right amount of pressure I start to tremble, and we don't make it to the bedroom before we get very, very dirty.

10

SHOPPING

Dan is an insanely early riser. Did I say that already? It still surprises me. I'm not sure exactly when he wakes up, but it must be well before dawn. It's certainly before I'm even remotely conscious since he's already back from his morning workout by the time I'm trying to force my eyes open. It must have been intense. He's soaked in sweat and his T-shirt looks painted on his body. His black hair, always a tad on the unruly side, is a complete mess.

"Where have you been?" I ask, still half-asleep.

"Running. You should come with me some time."

I purse my lips at him. "I don't think so. Once I got out of high school, I promised myself I'd never see the inside of a gym again."

"Not a gym. The park. But if you're not going to run with me, you can still help me wash up."

"Excuse me?"

"Let's shower together."

"I don't know, in there? Isn't it sort of weird?"

Dan laughs, a soft, masculine laugh, and sits down on the bed. I try to cover myself with a sheet, but he takes my hand and I let the sheet drop. Ha, fooled him. I'm wearing a big T-shirt I put on after he fell asleep last night.

"Jenni, on the list of top ten weirdest things I want to do with you, showering together probably comes in around one thousand two hundred and eighty-three. Come on. Let's go."

He stands up and takes my hand. Nervously I let him lead me into the bathroom.

He positions me standing on a bathmat facing him and reaches down to grasp the bottom of my shirt. "Put your arms up," he says, and I do. In one quick motion he pulls it over my head. When it's off, I look at him, but he's not looking back at me. He's looking down at my naked body and smiling lightly. There's no hiding it. Dan is looking.

I feel my face prickle and I know it must be getting red. I cross my arms across my chest. Standing here, in front of him in the hard light of the bathroom as his eyes linger over me. I can't help it. My eyes start to water, and I emit a quick breath of anxiety.

It takes Dan a second to catch on, but he finally tears his eyes away from my body and looks up far enough to notice my red eyes. "Jenni, what's wrong?"

"It's OK. Let's do it."

"Jenni, tell me. What's going on?"

"It's just, I'm...embarrassed." I look at my toes. It's not so much being naked as seeing him see me naked, the raw intensity of his gaze.

Dan puts his hand under my chin and lifts it up so I'm looking at him as he looks straight into my face. "Jenni, listen to me. You have a beautiful body. I like to look at you. You have nothing to be ashamed of."

I nod once, but my eyes are still watering.

"Maybe it would help if I get naked too?" He reaches down and rips his T-shirt up over his head. Then, with a quick motion, he doffs his shorts too. Surprisingly, that does make it a little better. I can't help it. I glance down. Dan is three-quarters already. I feel my face start to heat again, though only half from embarrassment.

Suddenly, Dan is pushing up against me, front to front. His tongue finds my mouth and probes inside. His arms wrap around me. I have one arm around his side, and one arm pushed up against his hard, hairy chest. The kiss is hot and wet, like that first kiss in the Ramskeller, only this time there are no clothes standing in the way, nothing to prevent our bodies from doing what they want to do.

Slowly, without breaking the kiss, he edges me over to the shower. I'm too lost in the moment to see him do it, but he must have turned the shower on because when we step inside the water is already pulsating.

Dan turns me around and leans me up against the wall. He slips his hands between my thighs and pushes them apart. Then he takes my hands and places them on the wall above my head so I'm leaning against the tile, supported on my feet and forearms.

"Close your eyes," he says, and I do.

I think I know what's coming next, so I gasp when instead he runs an unexpected fingernail down the center of my back. He follows it with slippery pressure that must be a bar of soap sliding down. Next he repeats the motion down my sides, first fingernails, then soap.

I'm breathing hard now, my nakedness forgotten. My body is ready for this, but Dan makes me wait. He slips his firm but soapy hands under my hair and begins to massage my neck. Then down to my shoulders. I'm almost panting, trying hard to breathe through the hot steam that surrounds us.

Still standing behind me, he moves his hands to my front and begins slowly moving his hands down across my shoulders, then down. When his fingers touch my nipples and begin circling, pinching and touching, I moan involuntarily.

He slides his hands down my stomach, massaging as he goes, and right as he's about to reach the spot and release the building tension, he moves his hands to the sides and slides them down my thighs instead. I let out a grunt of frustration.

Dan ignores it. Instead, he kneels behind me and continues his path down my body. Massaging first my thighs, then behind my knees. His hands are strong, and reach almost all the way around my calves. In isolation it feels amazing, but right now this is not what I need, not where I want him.

When I think I can take it no more, he stands again and leans into me. He wraps one arm around my stomach, cradling me, supporting me; and slips the other through my legs and begins to slowly stroke. The tingling starts to rise inside me, and I think I scream as the convulsions wash over me. I almost lose my balance, but he's there, holding me up until I'm done.

I'm exhausted, spent from the long buildup. I want to lay down under the warm water and let it wash over me, but he leans me back up against the wall. "Another minute, a chara," he says.

I'm so relaxed and wet with soap and water that I hardly feel it as he slides into me from behind. I'm barely capable of conscious thought at this point, but somehow I grab the bar of the soap dish with my left hand and try to stay standing while he pushes in and out of my body.

Finally Dan lets out a groan of his own, and his arms clench around me. Then he's done, and I can finally slide down to the floor. He sits behind me holding me in his arms on the bottom of the shower as we let the warm water cascade over us.

He whispers softly in my ear, "If you're going to stay with me, you're going to have to get more comfortable with nudity. It's one of the things I want from you. I want to be able to see you, all of you. This apartment is my refuge. I have money and I like to use it to make my home beautiful and elegant. I hire a decorator to design it. I buy the best furniture to equip it, beautiful art to hang on the walls, and the most beautiful girls to adorn it."

"Girls? More than one?"

"Does that bother you?"

"No." I can't be here all the time for him. And it's too much to expect that he'd wait for me. Dan is a not a man who waits. In the post-coital glow, it doesn't seem so bad.

———

FOR BREAKFAST, Dan makes scrambled eggs with onions and peppers and bacon on the side. He is definitely not a fat-free yogurt and granola sort of man. I'm really glad he doesn't want me to cook for him. No way I could measure up to his standards. I don't know what he does to the eggs, but they are delicious, salty and spicy and way tastier than the cafeteria's Saturday morning brunch. The cook is a lot more interesting to look at too.

"We should get you some clothes," he says.

"Clothes?" I ask, through a mouthful of egg. A bit of yellow dribbles down my cheek.

He waves at my T-shirt with his fork. "Some things for home, some things for wearing out. You should have some clothes here."

"OK. I'll bring a bag over the next time I come." What I can spare? I don't have a large wardrobe. Most weeks it's a challenge to make it from one laundry to the next without repeating outfits. Usually I throw on a sweatshirt and jeans since no one expects those to change.

"We'll go shopping today," he says.

"I don't know. I don't usually shop in Manhattan." Walmart is more my style, or Sears if I'm feeling upscale.

"I do. I'll introduce you to my personal shopper. Something for you. Something for me."

"OK." He's paying for my time. If that's how he wants to spend it, I guess I can go shopping with him. It can't be any more painful than shopping with my mother.

———

IT IS nothing like shopping with my mother. I figure maybe we're going to Macy's, you know, with the parade? Or Bloomingdale's, which is where I have heard the rich people go, but instead he tells me he likes to buy clothes at Barneys. Like Uncle Barney's Discount Warehouse?

Apparently not. We are met at the door by Genova, a model-thin, dark-eyed brunette in a knee-length red dress and heels that bring her almost to Dan's height. She seems to know Dan better than I'm comfortable with. I bite my tongue as she kisses her hellos with him. I strain to hear what she's saying as she whispers in his ear, but only catch the hint of some accent I can't place. She reminds me of the mysterious femme in an old French movie, only in color and three-dimensional. Very three-dimensional in certain places.

After greeting Dan for sixty seconds longer than necessary, Genova finally deigns to notice me. "And who's this lovely young thing, hmm?"

Dan nods at me. "Genova, I'd like you to meet Jennifer. She's why we're here today."

She puts a finger to her lip and considers me. "Jennifer, well I can't fault your taste in names, can I, Daniel? I'm sure we can do something with her. Now, where to begin?"

Genova starts us off in the shoe department "so the rest of the outfits can be fitted right." I object that I already have enough shoes, and she looks at me like I've announced that I grew up on Mars. She ropes in two more salespeople to bring us shoes, and keeps them running back and forth to the stockroom. Black shoes, gold shoes, open toe, closed toe, sandal, strapless, all with heels at least two inches higher than I can walk in. By the time we're done, she has selected and Dan has approved more shoes than I currently own, and that's including the old sneakers taking up space in my parents' garage.

Then we're off to the women's department. I make the mistake of looking at a price tag on a pair of jeans I think are cute and almost collapse in shock. They are $250! For jeans! I slide them back onto the shelf like they're made out of gold foil which, at that price, they should be.

A bright sundress with yellow flowers catches my eye. "That looks pretty," I say.

"No, absolutely not," Genova barks. "We are not shopping for the church picnic." She turns to Dan and her voice gets softer. "A black dress, for starters, I think. And she'll need a cocktail dress, I assume?"

Dan nods. "The usual. We're starting from scratch."

Again, Genova summons two salespeople to help her, a redhead named Brigitte and an Asian woman named Mina. Neither of them is quite as striking as Genova—they're both closer to my height, for starters—but they still make me look like the poor homeless girl Dan took pity on and brought in from the street. It never occurred to me I should get dressed up to go shopping for dress-up clothes. Why didn't he warn me? Brigitte and Mina bring one dress after another for Genova and Dan's approval.

After Genova has picked out some outfits she deems acceptable, she takes me by the hand and sweeps me off to the dressing room while Brigitte and Mina follow behind, carrying the clothes Genova has designated.

Once again I'm reminded that this is not Sears. Instead of an oversized closet guarded by a matron who counts your garments as you go in and out, Genova ushers me into a carpeted room bigger than my parents' den. Mirrors line two and a half sides. There's a silver coffee urn and an equally ornate water pitcher, but Genova doesn't offer me any. Instead, she motions with her hand. "Undress now, please."

"Um, is there like somewhere a little more private I can change?"

"Ah, you are shy. How cute. Tell me, are you this shy with Mr. Cortland, hmm? Brigitte," she snaps.

Brigitte reacts like she's been slapped. "Yes, Genova?"

"Set up the screen for the Little Miss Jennifer." She points to a folded screen lying against the wall.

Brigitte picks up the screen. As she unfolds it in front of a padded red bench, I see it's decorated in a vaguely oriental scene with birds and trees. Brigitte hasn't said more than two words at a time—mostly, "Yes, Genova"—since I met her; but as she's setting the screen down she turns her head away from Genova so that only I can see her face. She cocks her lip and raises an exaggerated eyebrow. Somehow it is a spot-on impression of Genova's authoritarian demeanor. I have to stifle a laugh. I have at least one ally in this room.

Even before the screen is up, Genova is handing me the first dress. "Quickly now, young girl. You mustn't keep Mr. Cortland waiting too long. You never know who might come along and snatch him away while you're dallying about, hmm?" She smiles like she's made a joke.

The first outfit is way too sexy and absolutely not me. Maybe Melissa could pull it off. The skirt is too short, the waist is too tight, and the neckline drops almost far enough to expose my breasts. No, absolutely not, I decide. Only the next one is three inches worse. And the third, well, maybe if I were six inches taller, two cup sizes bigger, and completely without any sense of shame. We'll have to start over with something less slutty.

Genova, however, does not agree. She keeps up a running patter of, "Yes, excellent," and "Mr. Cortland will appreciate that look." She only hesitates over a two-button pinstripe pantsuit. It is by far the most conservative of the outfits they selected, though I have no idea where I might wear such a thing. She asks me to turn around in front of the mirror, then again.

Finally she nods. "I think this one we will leave on the rack, yes? It is not the look Mr. Cortland has brought you here for, now is it?"

I should ask her what she means by that—she is the first person I've met who actually seems to know Dan—even if she's not exactly friendly. I'm a little dizzy and worn out though, so I nod my head and let her take the suit back.

I've lost track of where Dan is while Genova is shuffling me in and out of these outfits. Maybe he's off looking at ties or running clothes or something. When we finally leave the dressing room, Dan is standing outside, looking as enigmatic as always.

"Did you find something you like?" Dan asks.

Can I tell him I don't really feel comfortable in any of this? They're all gorgeous but they're not me. If anyone back at school saw me wearing these clothes, they'd think I was showing off. I'd stick out more than if I were walking out naked. But the goal was to find clothes that would fit into his world, not mine, so I nod and say, "Yes, they're very nice. Thank you."

Dan smiles. As long as he's happy, I can wear them with him. It's not like I have to wear them to chem lab.

I'm not sure how many of the outfits I tried on we've actually bought. I do know it's more than I have ever purchased at one time in my life. When I see the total ring up on the register, I gasp audibly. It's more money than I have spent on clothes in my entire life. Dan seems nonplussed by an expense that would bankrupt a medium-sized Caribbean island, or pay a goodly part of a Fordham tuition bill. I have to figure out how to get him to stop spending money on me like this.

"Perhaps now we should visit the makeup counter," Genova chimes in.

"No, I don't think so. That's enough for today," Dan replies.

Genova cocks her head as if to look at me from another angle. "Are you sure? You do not find her rather...plain?"

"I prefer Jenni as she is," he says, gruffly enough that Genova actually takes a step back. I'm glad he doesn't use that tone with me.

"Very well, then. Shall I have your items delivered?"

"Yes, except these." He picks up a pair of gold sandal pumps with four-inch heels from the table where the booty has been accumulating. "We'll take these with us. We'll need them at our next stop."

11

EDEN

Outside the store, the doorman is waiting for us with a cab. Since when do department stores have doormen? Sears has a guard to catch shoplifters. Does that count?

The cab drops us off in front of an empty storefront between a Moroccan restaurant and a real estate office. Someone has written "For Lease Good Space" in white soap in the window. Is Dan planning on selling his apartment or is he ready for lunch?

Neither, it turns out. Dan shows me to a door between the storefront and the real estate office. There's a street number over the door, but no other signage. He presses a button, and a few seconds later the door buzzes to let us in. Dan holds the door for me, as I look down the dingy hallway and hesitate.

"It's OK," he says. "They're expecting us."

Who exactly is expecting us—his favorite drug dealer? I hold my breath and step carefully over the threshold.

Once my eyes get used to the light, it isn't that bad. Just another old building in New York. A small elevator waits at the end of the hall. The car is already there, so we step inside. Dan pushes the button for the fifth floor.

The elevator rattles on the way up. "I know it looks a little funky," he says, "but they really do have the best product in New York."

Which product is that? Crack or heroin?

The elevator arrives without dropping us to our deaths, and we step out into another institutionally lit hallway. The first door down the hall is an accountant's office, the second some sort of travel agency. Dan stops at the third. The address plate on the door reads "Eden Private Intimates."

Before we can knock, the door swings open. "Daniel," squeals a curvy brunette in a form fitting purple gown about two sizes too small and five years too young for her. Six inch platform heels do not make her any shorter. If Genova looked like a fashion model, this woman looks like a centerfold in one of my uncle's magazines, perhaps a little older but still stunning in her own way. She has curves on top of curves, and the purple dress clings to every one of them. Does Dan know any woman who isn't a perfect ten? Maybe his grandmother? Oh, who am I kidding. If she gave Dan his genes, she probably looks better at ninety than I do at nineteen.

She plants a kiss on Dan's cheek, leaving behind a noticeable lipstick stain. "You naughty boy," she says with breathy fake annoyance. "We haven't seen you for months and months. You must come visit us more often. And who's your friend?" She turns to look at me.

"Amanda, this is Jennifer. Jennifer, Amanda. I brought her to you to get her properly outfitted."

Amanda looks me up and down like she's inspecting a used car, no, a used bicycle. "Yes, I think we can do something with her." She takes Dan by his left arm and me by my right, and sweeps us inside.

I'm not sure what I'm expecting to find behind the door, but it certainly isn't a set from Cabaret. A stage is centered on the far side of the room. At least, I think it's a stage. Four high-backed, upholstered chairs are positioned in front of it, as if for a small audience. Track lighting is positioned to illuminate the platform. Not quite a spotlight, but it draws your attention. The back of the stage is mirrored on three sides, almost like a dressing room. A wet bar on the right runs the length of the room.

"Megan, can you come out here?" Amanda shouts. A girl only a little older than me emerges from somewhere behind the stage. Megan, to my relief, looks like a normal human being instead of a model. She's chewing gum and wearing jeans, sneakers, and a T-shirt.

"Megan," Amanda says, "can you take Jennifer to the back room and get her ready? Maybe something from the Athens line?"

Megan snaps her gum. "No problem." She has the brassy voice of one of the commuter girls, though her hair is dyed platinum and chopped short, instead of black and piled up in a tower of hairspray. "Jennifer, huh? You want a drink before we get started?"

A drink sounds like a very good idea right about now. "Do you have gin and tonic?"

"Of course we do. What kind of place do you think this is?"

I know better than to answer that. Megan puts some ice in a glass and takes a bottle from the bar. Megan hands me the glass and I take a swallow, then another. Fortified by the alcohol, I let her lead me behind the stage where a door leads to another room, the same size as the front. However where the front is outfitted like a nightclub, this room is more Filene's Basement. Racks of clothes extend from one end to the other, squeezed in so close together you can't walk without brushing up against them. It is the complete opposite of Barneys. It looks like what you'd end up with if you stuffed the entire Sears women's department into a Fordham dorm room. OK, it's bigger than a dorm room—anything larger than a token booth would be—but it's even more packed.

Megan puts her hands on her hips and sizes me up. "Let's see, you're about a size 4, petite, A cup?"

I nod.

She lifts a hanger off one of the racks and hands it to me. It's a white lace, baby doll nightie. Not exactly my style—my sleep attire runs more toward T-shirts and sweatpants—but if Dan wants me to wear it, I guess it won't hurt.

"OK, let's try it on. See how it looks," says Megan.

"Where's the changing room?"

Megan giggles, with one of those "isn't she special?" looks you'd give to a young child who mispronounces a word she doesn't understand. "Where does he find you girls? It's OK. I'll turn around."

Seriously, does nowhere in Manhattan believe in modesty? I kick off my tennis shoes, then unbutton my jeans and slip out of them. I pull my T-shirt over my head so I'm down to my underwear. I hold the nightie in front of me. I don't think I'm supposed to wear this with a bra.

Megan is pointedly facing the other way. She looks back over her shoulder toward me and snaps her gum. "You need a hand there?"

"No." I take a deep breath and take off the bra. Then I put the teddy on as quickly as I can before she gets too impatient with me.

"You done?" Megan says.

"I guess so." I pick up my street clothes and hold them awkwardly to my chest.

Megan turns around. "Oh sorry, let me take those for you," and she grabs my clothes away before I can object. She looks me up and down, and I blush.

"Cute," she says. "Now put on your shoes and let's see you in the mirror."

I strap on the gold pumps we bought at Barneys. Megan takes my hand and positions me in front of a mirror nailed to the wall.

I look in the mirror and gasp, half in shock, half in embarrassment. The nightie is see-through, and it's cold in here. "Is there maybe something a little less revealing?"

"Trust me, he's going to love this. And if he doesn't, he's gay. And I know he's not gay," Megan says with a wink.

She walks over to a table on the side of the room, and fiddles with a CD player. Some thumping club music I don't recognize starts playing. "Come on. Let's go show him how sexy you look."

She grabs my hand, but I finally find the strength to resist. "You want me to go out there? In this?" Suddenly the nightie feels even more see-through, if that's possible.

"Sure, silly. We've got the lights set up so you'll look your best. The men love seeing their girlfriends model for them."

My heart rises to my throat. "I...I don't think I can." The only thing that would be worse is if he wanted to take pictures of me in these clothes. Strange that this is where I find my limit after everything I've already done with barely a moment's thought. But there's something about showing off. I can't do it.

Megan coos and puts a hand on my shoulder. "Don't worry. You've got nothing to be ashamed of. You look great, really sexy. You're going to drive him nuts. He won't be able to take his eyes off you."

Megan's trying to be friendly and reassuring, but it doesn't help. It's bad enough when Dan looks at me, the wanton desire in his eyes, but to deliberately show myself like that. To ask him to look at me that way. To present myself. I'm Jenni McGrath from Easton, Pennsylvania, not some Manhattan model for Victoria's Secret. I want to run all the way back to my childhood bedroom and hide under the blankets like I'm ten years old.

Instead, I nod.

I let Megan lead me by my hand to the back of the little stage while some female singer warbles lyrics I'm way too nervous to pay any attention to. I don't know what's louder, the thumping of the music or the thumping of my heart in my throat.

Then I freeze. It's irrational but I have a sudden realization that this is all a huge practical joke. Everything that's happened since I got the letter from the bursar has been a big setup. I'm going to step out and my roommates and my parents and all the boys from school are going to be waiting like some horrible, evil surprise party and laugh at me for daring to think that I can be sexy.

It's going to be the second grade play all over again. I forgot my lines. I stood there on the stage, opening and closing my mouth like a goldfish trying to breathe in air. Everyone was looking at me, my teacher Mrs. Duncan, my parents, my grandparents, my big sister Janine, all the other kids' parents. The longer it went on the worse it got, everyone looking at me. And then, the pièce de résistance, my bladder opened and I peed on the floor, right there in front of the entire second grade and their families. It was the single most humiliating experience of my life.

That's right. It was. This can't possibly be that bad. Megan pulls a scarlet curtain aside, and I step through.

Dan and Amanda are sitting in two of the chairs chatting like old friends. Dan has a whiskey in his hands. I stand there awkwardly, unsure whether I should interrupt them. But then Amanda says something, Dan turns to look at me, and his mouth makes a silent O.

"I think we have a winner," says Amanda smiling.

Dan recovers long enough to say, "Let's not be too hasty. Let's see the back."

"Turn around dear. Hold your hands over your head and stretch" says Amanda.

I do as instructed and spin around as best I can in the heels so I'm facing the mirror. Wow, is that me? The woman in the mirror looks about five years older and way hotter.

"Arch your heels, dear," says Amanda, and I push up as much as I can manage on my toes.

"That's good," she says. With a sigh of relief I relax back down. This is three kinds of weird. I know some girls dream of this, but being a model has never been one of my fantasies.

"Megan," Amanda says.

Megan sticks her head through the curtain. "Yeah?"

"I think Mr. Cortland will be taking that one. Help Jennifer find a few more. Maybe the celeste teddy from Naples, and we'll need a white lace-up corset set, with stockings. And let's try some of the new bikinis Pierre sent us."

Dan whispers something to her I can't make out.

"Oh, and some demi bras, something with lift."

"No problem, boss." Megan snaps her gum again, and helps me back through the curtain.

We repeat the procedure several more times as the outfits get progressively more revealing. Amanda is a booster. She compliments me on each outfit, and finds something nice to say about each one. I get the impression she's actually happy for me, whereas with Genova I couldn't shake the feeling that she was doing me a favor by deigning to waste her time on me. Against all odds, between her compliments and Dan's obvious interest, I actually start to feel a little sexy.

I finally draw the line when Megan brings out a set that consists of white stockings and garter belt, a half cup lace bra that doesn't cover my nipples, and *no panties*!

"No, just no," I tell Megan. She looks disappointed as she hangs the ensemble back on the rack, but there are limits. Maybe I could wear that for Dan in his bedroom, but there is no way I'm modeling that in front of Megan and Amanda. I can keep that much of my dignity at least.

Finally we've picked out enough outfits for Dan's satisfaction, and I'm allowed to change back into my good old jeans, T-shirt, and sneakers. Dan pays Amanda, and she kisses him goodbye on the cheek. A few minutes later, we're in a taxi on the way back to his apartment.

"So do you like your new outfits?" Dan asks.

"They're more...daring than I'm used to."

"I want you to look sexy."

I'm not sure if the clothes make me look sexy or just slutty. For Dan, I'm not sure there is a difference. Still, for the first time, I think I may be able to see what Dan sees in me. I mean, I'm still me; but now it only seems a little implausible that Dan chose me, not aliens from the moon landed on my front lawn to bring me a cheesecake implausible.

12

HOME

The packages from Barneys beat us back to Dan's apartment and are waiting for us when we step off the elevator. The doorman must have brought them. I hope he knows when not to come up. If anyone walked in on us while we were, well, you know, I think I'd die. I still can't believe what I'm letting Dan do. OK, that's not fair. What I'm doing in this place.

Dan slips off his shoes and pours himself a drink from the bar. "Why don't you put the clothes away? You can use the bedroom next to mine as a dressing room. When you're done, put on one of the new pieces and come back here."

"Which one?" There are so many to choose from. Does he want to go out or stay in?

"You pick. Something sexy."

OK, that answers that question. In it is.

There are so many outfits it takes me almost half an hour to hang them all. I'm glad he has space for me. I wasn't looking forward to trying to make room for them in my dorm closet. Not to mention what Melissa, Deirdre, or, God help me, Laura would say if they saw even one of these.

As I put the clothes away, I try to decide which one to wear. The pink bikini? The scary black bustier? The sheer white negligee he seemed to like so much back at Eden? I've never worn anything like these before today, and now I have enough to wear till Valentine's Day without doing laundry. I wish Dan had given me a little more direction.

I decide to start with a frilly white bra and panty set. I add white stockings and the gold stiletto sandals he held out from our purchases at Barneys. They're about two inches too high for comfort. I figure I probably won't be wearing them for that long.

I do a quick spin in the mirror to check myself out. I crane my head back over my shoulder to check my back. Turns out with heels I actually do have a butt. Who knew? Cute, but not exactly living room attire. What else?

There's a blue jacket that looks really good on me, but is more office material than boyfriend bait. The red cashmere sweater is really comfortable, but perhaps needs more cleavage than I can muster to qualify as "sexy." Finally I top it off with a sleeveless white blouse and a black miniskirt. Let him imagine what's underneath.

By the time I get back to the living room, Dan has made himself comfortable with a bourbon on the couch. His shoes and jacket are off and his shirt's undone far enough for me to see his chest hair. He has the hungry look that makes my insides go all weak.

"Turn around," he says and makes a circle with his index finger.

I'm still not used to the heels, but I do the best pirouette I can manage. I don't think I did too badly, because when I finish the 360, Dan's lips are curled up in that wicked smile I'm learning to recognize.

I move to join him on the couch, but he puts up a hand to stop me. "No, stand in the middle of the room, where I can see you."

"OK," I say, though I'm not sure where this is going. I stand about six feet in front of him. He's leaning back on the couch with his legs wide, his right arm resting on the back. He looks at me like a cat, no make that a tiger, considering a mouse.

"Undress, slowly."

It's not the first time I've undressed in front of him, but doing it like this, in the living room instead of the bedroom, feels different, more powerless. I reach around behind my back to unbutton my blouse. The awkward position makes my breasts jut out. Somehow I don't think it's an accident that he bought this top for me. When it's unbuttoned, I slip it off my shoulders and let it fall to the floor behind me.

"Now the skirt," he says.

That's simpler. I unhook it and release the zipper. I wiggle so it slides down my legs and kick it away. I'm not naked yet, but I'm close enough to feel it.

Dan smiles, but it's not a nice smile; more like he's won a game I didn't even know we were playing. "Underwear," he says.

I pull my bra straps down and twist it around to the front so I can unhook it. My panties follow. I stand as straight as I can, my hands at my sides so Dan can see, well, everything. My breasts are standing at attention. No hiding that from him now.

"Shoes too," he says.

I pick up my left foot to remove the pump, then the right. At least I can relax now that I don't have to wear stilettos for whatever comes next.

"I know you aren't very experienced," Dan says, "but it's time for you to learn to do some things for me."

I don't answer, but my heart begins to beat a little faster. My nervousness about what he's going to ask does nothing to stem the growing dampness between my legs.

"First, get down on your hands and knees,. Keep your eyes on me."

I kneel down as instructed and sit back on my heels. I look up and try to maintain eye contact since I'm too nervous to look straight ahead.

"Now, put your hand on my pants."

I don't have to ask him where. I reach my right hand out and lay it on his crotch. Underneath the soft fabric he is rock hard.

"Unzip me, and take it out."

OK, I can do this. Very carefully, I pull the zipper down. I spread his fly open and slip my hand in. I barely touch him, and it pops out, pointing to the ceiling. I gasp, half in surprise, half in reverence. This is not the first time I've seen it, of course. But I've never looked at it from this angle right in front of my face. It was something I caught a glance of sideways and looked away, I sit there on my knees, simply admiring it.

I flash back to Jamie Goller showing his thing in gym and all the girls making exaggerated retching noises. I know I'm supposed to be grossed out by his maleness, but I'm not. It is one of the most beautiful things I have ever seen. It feels so right that I am here, now, in front of it.

I reach up to touch it, but Dan takes my hand and shakes his head no. Then he touches his finger to my lips. "Use your tongue."

I sit back on my heels and take a deep breath. I was hoping Dan wasn't one of those men who wanted this, or that he wouldn't ask me to do it, but so much for that. At least he's got a nice one. Oh, who am I kidding? It's gorgeous. If any penis were lickable, it's this one.

Tentatively I lean in and brace my hands against his thighs to balance myself. I stick out my tongue and give one quick lick along his shaft, pulling away before I get to the top. There! I did it!

"OK, now again," Dan says.

You mean I'm supposed to keep doing this? How long? Surely not until he comes? "Don't you want to have sex?" I ask.

"No," he says. "I want you to do this," and as if to emphasize the point, he puts a hand on the back of my head and pushes me down into his crotch. I want to close my eyes, but I'm afraid I'll miss if I do.

I stick out my tongue again, touch it to the point where he emerges from his fly, and lick upwards.

"Again," he says.

Unsure what else I can do, I comply. Then without being told, I do it again. He is now holding my head to him with both hands, and starting to breathe heavily.

On the next stroke my tongue laps up a drop of what must be cum, and I almost halt in surprise. It's salty.

"Don't stop," Dan grunts, as much a plea as a command, so I keep going. He is breathing harder now.

"Flick your tongue along the top," he says through clenched teeth. I reposition my head from the base to the thick pink head. Another glistening drop of liquid is beginning to ooze out of it, and I dutifully lap it up. I risk a glance up and his face is scrunched tight, his eyes half-closed. He looks surprisingly vulnerable like this, not fully in control for perhaps the first time since I met him.

Suddenly he grabs my head and thrusts up across my tongue, though fortunately he misses my mouth. His semen shoots out, mostly splattering him, the couch, and the floor, though a drop manages to find my left eye where it stings like I went swimming and opened my eyes underwater.

Dan lets go of my head and exhales, then leans back into the couch. "Not bad for a first time," he says as he tucks himself back into his pants. "You'll get better with practice. Now go wash off, and I'll clean up out here."

I don't think he intends to be mean, but his comment hits me like a punch to the gut. All that for "not bad"? I want him to like me. I want to be good for him, not just good for the first time. I should say something, but Dan pats me on the head; and instead I stand up, grab my clothes off the floor, and run back to the shower.

In the shower, as the hot water rushes over me, I gradually return to myself. Was that actually so bad? OK, so it was new and I never did it before; but so was sex less than two weeks ago, and that didn't bother me like this.

In fact, thinking back on it, the whole thing was sort of hot. I can totally see doing it again, staring at it, stroking it, kissing it, loving it. The shower is steamy, but it doesn't feel like all the heat is coming from the water.

Without quite admitting what I'm doing, I begin washing between my legs. Two minutes later I'm leaning against the shower wall, quivering in relief. It feels like I was stuffed inside a bottle, and someone popped the cork to let me out.

So if it wasn't the blowjob that bothered me, what was it? I'm not sure, but I resolve that if blow jobs are what he wants, I'm going to learn to give Dan the best blow jobs he's ever had.

13

BACK TO SCHOOL

Monday morning comes too soon and too early. I have no idea how Dan can be so awake when it feels like we went to bed an hour ago. Went to sleep anyway. To bed was somewhat earlier. Then again, we don't get out of bed as soon as I wake up either. In fact, I might be spending more time in bed and less time sleeping since I met him. I haven't done the math.

For breakfast, he makes a huge monterey jack omelet with green onions and sausage. It's a little too exciting for my stomach, especially at this hour. Seven o'clock and he has the audacity to tell me that he's staying home late for me! At least I talked him out of mixing in fresh jalapenos. Yesterday he snuck them in without telling me. I bit into one and almost went through the ceiling.

Dan slides about a third of the omelet onto my plate, which is still about twice as much as I normally eat. I'll probably skip lunch.

"I don't know why you won't let me call you a car," he says.

"I get car sick. It's too much trouble to drive in the city. I'd rather take the train." This is a lie. I don't know how to tell him that all the money he's spending, the things he's buying, it all makes me uncomfortable. Tuition is one thing, but that's enough. He shouldn't have to pay for me. I should be able to take care of myself. Taking the subway instead of letting him call a cab is a small thing, but it's mine. I have to do it if I want to have any hope of remaining an independent person, not just another fancy accessory on his arm. Only I can't explain any of that without sounding ungrateful.

"If you took a car, you could stay longer."

"If I take the train, I can read. I need to get ready for my organic chemistry test."

In the end Dan agrees to let me take the train home, but in exchange he gets to pick me up from campus next weekend. I can live with that, provided no one sees him pick me up and starts asking questions I don't want to answer. Melissa was way too curious about the black car that first night, and the way Tom drooled over it I'm surprised the story isn't all over campus.

Anyway, that's four days away. I have more important things to worry about first, like my organic chemistry test and a Chaucer paper I've barely thought about.

———

I'VE BEEN PANICKED about the first organic chem midterm for weeks. Turns out I needn't have worried. It's a breeze. It's still not a crib course and I'm glad I studied; but I finish the exam in half the time allotted, spend another twenty minutes compulsively checking over my answers, and walk down the aisle to hand in my blue book while most of the class is still frantically scribbling.

Theresa, the grad student proctoring the exam, looks at me funny when I hand the paper in. "Are you sure?" she whispers.

Should I take it back? Check it one more time? No, I'm being paranoid. I've already checked it over twice, and it's not like the questions were super tricky or anything. No reason to spend the next forty-five minutes sitting in the lecture hall twirling my hair and listening to the rest of the class mumble, especially when outside the weather is pleasantly sunny, a really perfect October afternoon.

I figure there won't be a lot more days like this before winter hits, so when Melissa suggests we study on the grass on Edwards Parade instead of going to the library, I agree. The disadvantage of this plan is that there's no prohibition against talking on the parade, so instead of actually studying, Melissa grills me about my weekend.

"He took you to Barneys?" Melissa's eyes are the size of lab goggles. I do not think I have ever seen her so completely off balance.

"That's right."

"Barneys? On 18th Street?"

"I guess so. I wasn't really paying attention to where we were."

"Did you buy anything?"

"A few outfits." More than a few, all of them safely residing in Dan's apartment. I can still barely imagine wearing them with him. There's no way I can wear them on campus.

"More than one?"

"And shoes. He really likes shoes." In fact, he liked them even more when that was all I was wearing, but I am not going to tell Melissa that part.

"Is he going to marry you?"

"Melissa!"

"Seriously, is he?"

"We've only known each other for a couple of weeks. I think it's a little soon to be talking marriage."

"If he's buying you clothes, it sounds serious."

He's buying me more than clothes. He's buying me the right to be here, hanging out with my friend on this verdant college campus, inexplicably situated in the middle of the Bronx.

"It's not that serious."

"Are you sure? You sound pretty serious."

"I. Am. Not. Serious." I emphasize each word. "I'm nineteen. That's too young to get engaged. I have to graduate, go to vet school, and start my career. Marriage is for older people."

"Jenni, he's older."

I'm tempted to grab a handful of grass and throw it at her, but instead I scowl. "We're not getting married, OK?"

"If you say so." Melissa does not look convinced.

I can't afford to be serious. Dan likes me well enough, I think. But I'm under no illusion that he thinks I'm marriage material. Thinking otherwise is pointless.

14

THE GIFT

Another week goes by. Another weekend arrives. Dan offers to take me to the Met, but I suggest the Central Park Zoo instead. What can I say? I'm a sucker for animals. It's sort of how I got into this situation in the first place. We scandalize one tourist family by kissing a little too passionately in front of the snow monkeys. They had twin girls who were arguing in loud whispers about whether Dan was my father or my boyfriend, and I think we answered that question for them.

Otherwise, the weekend is more of the same, which sounds boring, but trust me, it's not. Quite the opposite, in fact. Weekends with Dan are the most fun I have had since, well, ever.

Before I know it, it's Monday morning again. Dan's tying his tie in front of the mirror. Last week he wanted one last quickie, and I didn't object too strenuously (OK, not at all), but he did make me late for my first class. This time I decide to try to sneak out before breakfast. I stand up on my tiptoes to give him a peck on the cheek. "See you next weekend," I say.

"Hold on a minute," he says. "I have something for you before you go."

"OK, but make it snappy. I have a nine o'clock class."

"Got it. Wait for me in the living room."

I wait on the couch in the living room as instructed, looking at my watch every thirty seconds. I can be late for class if I have to be, but I'd really rather not. After what seems like an eternity, Dan meanders in. As usual, he is impeccably attired in a dark three-piece suit that probably cost more than I knew clothes could cost until a couple of weeks ago. He has the master of the universe look down pat.

There is, of course, no sign that he woke up at 5:00 a.m. so he could have one last sweaty, groping, sex session in the dark before he sends me back to the Bronx for another week. I don't know how he does it. My hair looks like lab rats have nested in it, my panties are I don't know where, and despite my best efforts with makeup, my face suggests I've spent the last three days in a centrifuge. I need to go back to school just to rest.

Dan sits down on the couch next to me. "I have a present for you." He hands me a beautiful, cream-colored box, about the size of a shoebox. A big, red bow adorns the top. I wish he would stop giving me things, but I don't have time right now to argue.

"Open it," he says with a smile.

The box isn't wrapped, so I lift off the top. Inside, a long white plastic wand with a big bulb on the end lays in a pile of crinkly pink paper. I pick it up and stare at it quizzically. An electric cord dangles from one end. "Thank you. What is it?"

"It's a vibrator. I want you to use it while you're away and think of me."

My face goes bright red, and I shove it back in the box.

Dan laughs. "You've never used one of these before then?"

I look over my shoulder, away from the box, and shake my head no. I've heard of vibrators, but I've never seen one before. I've certainly never used one. It's not like there were a lot of sex shops back in Easton. We had enough trouble buying condoms at the drugstore without the pharmacist telling our parents.

"That's OK. I'll show you."

"There's no time. I have class. You have to get to your office."

"Shh," he says, and puts one finger on my lips, the gesture I am coming to learn means he wants me to be quiet and do what he says. "There's always time when you want it."

He takes the device out of the box and leans over the back of the couch to plug it in. Usually I'd be entranced by the view of his ass this provides me, but I'm too worried about what's coming next.

Dan has to unplug a lamp to free an outlet. He comes back up and holds me close with his left arm so I'm leaning into his side. He flicks a button on the device, and it starts to hum.

"There are three settings," he says. "Soft, nice, and Oh my God. We'll start you out on soft."

Dan lifts my skirt up a little. I suddenly wish I had made more of an effort to locate my panties this morning, instead of trying to sneak out before he had time to get ready again. He reaches up under my skirt with the device and touches it to my upper leg. It feels funny, tingly and sort of weird.

He moves it across my thigh, slipping it around to the inside, not quite there but close enough to start me building up, really fast. Involuntarily, my toes clench inside my sneakers. I close my eyes and wrap my arms around Dan's neck. Holy shit, this is intense. It's not at all like sex, more direct and genital. I can't feel anything except my vagina wanting more of this. I'm about to go over the edge.

He slips the wand up a millimeter further so it touches me in the right spot and I explode. I'm bucking and screaming and I have no idea what is coming out of my mouth. Finally, when I'm finished and limp, Dan flicks it off.

"Well, that was easy," he says.

Too stunned to speak, I nod. When I think I have my wits about me again, I say, "That was...intense."

Dan smiles and looks at me. "I want you to use this every night when you're not here. I want you to think of me when you make yourself come. I want you to imagine it's my hands touching you, my cock that's inside of you."

"Wait a minute. You want me to use this in my dorm room? I can't. I have roommates. They'll hear me."

Dan laughs as he pulls a tissue out of a box on the coffee table and wipes off the toy. "You're a clever girl. I'm sure you'll think of something. Just remember, every night, OK?" He pulls the cord out of the wall, puts the magic orgasm wand back in, and hands me the box.

On the subway back to school, I'm going in the opposite direction of all the commuter traffic, so I get a seat. The box rests demurely in my lap. I hope it's not obvious what's inside it.

I still have no idea where my school panties went to, so I keep my legs tightly pressed together. All the underwear Dan bought me is way too sexy for my dorm room. I'll buy some cheap ones on Fordham Road and bring them to his apartment next weekend for future emergencies.

———

WHEN YOU SHARE a shoebox sized dorm room with three roommates, "alone time" is a slightly more improbable fantasy than a Manhattan millionaire who picks you up in the school bar and sweeps you away to his penthouse love nest. If Melissa's at rehearsal, Laura's studying in the room. If Laura's at Joshua's, Deirdre is chattering away about the math professor she's crushing on. (I don't have the heart to tell her, but he shares a one-bedroom studio in the Village with my English professor.)

By the time a gaggle of boys have stopped by to collect Deirdre for the nightly excursion to Clarke's and I have once again demurred, though at least this time without feeling like I may be missing out on the chance to meet my future boyfriend, Melissa will be back doing her nightly beauty routine. And if by some miracle the three of them are all out of the room at the same time, I'm probably on the other side of campus with my organic chem study group.

The four of us have an agreement, hypothetical so far, to put a sock on the door if one of us has a boy over; but I don't think that extends to masturbation sessions. I figure my only opportunity to do my "homework" with some chance of privacy is during dinner, so when six o'clock rolls around I beg off and claim I'm not feeling well. I can grab a burger at the Ramskeller later. I'll have to figure something else out tomorrow. If I skip dinner every night, they'll think I have an eating disorder. Melissa will congratulate me, Laura will lecture me, and Deirdre will want to help me shop for a new wardrobe.

As soon as the three of them are out the door, I retrieve Dan's present from my dresser drawer. Second problem: the cord doesn't reach all the way from my bed to the nearest outlet. The outlet's closer to Laura's bed, but I don't think she'd appreciate me using it for this. I could ask the RA for an extension cord, but she'd want to know what it was for.

Even if she has one, I don't think I have the time. I'm not sure how long this is going to take. It was damn fast with Dan this morning, but I always am with him. Even the smell of him is enough to start me on the way. By contrast, my previous solo expeditions back home (remember, three roommates) have been somewhat long and drawn out.

Our desk chairs are flexible and reasonably comfortable, the one piece of furniture in this institution that is, so I decide to try sitting down instead. Suddenly the thought flashes through my head that I may not be the first girl to have done this in this chair. Ick! OK, I'm definitely going to buy an extension cord in Little Italy tomorrow.

I unplug a desk light and plug in the wand. I lean back into the chair and unbutton my jeans, but that's as far as I'm going. This is going to be embarrassing enough if anybody catches me without having my pants around my ankles.

I flick the wand on and it starts buzzing loudly. If anyone walks by in the hallway, they're going to think I have a lawnmower in here. I touch it lightly to the outside of my pants and immediately snatch it back. Wow. OK, it wasn't just having Dan sitting next to me. Maybe I can finish this before the girls return. I push it back down, aiming a little more carefully this time, and yelp when it makes contact. It's even more intense than this morning, so intense it hurts, like when you accidentally get a mouthful of saccharine instead of sugar. Am I doing it wrong?

Tentatively, I touch it to my belly button and immediately yank it away. It feels like I'm being bounced down a mountain road in the back of pickup that lost its last shock absorber three miles ago. I stare at the device. It's all I can do to hold on to it. It's like it's trying to jump out of my hand.

Flash of insight: the thing has three settings and is switched to high! I thumb it back to low, then touch my belly again. OK, that's tolerable. I move it down and let it rest on top. Not unpleasant. There's a nice tingling sensation. I rub it a little, press in a little harder. Umm, that's nice. Not as nice as when Dan did it, but nice. I wish he was here now. I think about him putting his big arms around me, whispering in my ear while he reaches his hand down, touching me. The way he holds me, not letting me move, while he rubs me down there, up and down, up and down, up and Oh my God. Suddenly I'm shuddering, my whole body tightening and untightening, as the feeling sweeps over me. I barely maintain enough control to keep my teeth clenched and not cry out.

Finally, I gasp one last release and flick the switch. I'm spent. Wow, I'm really glad I didn't try to do it under the covers after we all went to bed like I first thought about. It would have been really obvious what I was doing.

I stand up and lay the toy on my desk. I snap my jeans and zip them up. That's when I notice I've left a wet spot on my chair. Memo to self. Next time use a towel, like I really hope whoever had this chair before me did.

———

THE TOY IS SURPRISINGLY ADDICTIVE. If I didn't have roommates, I might wear it out. Why doesn't every girl have one of these? I was a little peeved at Dan for his presumption in giving it to me, but I may have to eat my pride and thank him for it.

Tuesday morning I sneak a baggie of Cheerios out of the cafeteria after breakfast to save for dinner while the other girls are out. Wednesday I do the same. It's not like mystery meat, wilted lettuce, and canned green beans are any great loss. I even manage an extra session Wednesday afternoon when my art history professor cancels class, and the other three are out.

I'm learning that it doesn't actually take me that long to finish, especially if I put the toy on medium and think about Keanu Reeves before I plug it in. Dan told me to think about him, but what he doesn't know won't hurt him. It's not like I'm ever going to meet Keanu, and *My Own Private Idaho* is the hottest movie ever.

By Thursday night, I figure I can scarf down dinner in the cafeteria with Melissa, Deirdre, and Laura, then race back to Hughes Hall. If I'm quick I can do my "homework" before they finish dessert, at least except for Melissa, who wouldn't touch dessert unless she thought a diamond engagement ring was hidden in the cake.

I grab the wand out of the back of my underwear drawer and plug it into the extension cord I bought. Then I pull down my jeans and panties and lay down on my bunk. No time for preliminaries tonight, I'm going straight for the good spot.

I close my eyes and picture Dan in my head. In my fantasy he's naked, not that hard to imagine. He rubs his big hands down my back, then reaches around my chest to feel my breasts. I touch one hand to my left breast, and massage it through my T-shirt, imagining his hands are rubbing me. Then I think of him turning me around and kissing me, that long, slow wet kiss that sets my entire body tingling. I turn the wand on and slip it between my legs.

He lowers me gently onto my back. He reaches down between my legs where he finds me ready for him. Slowly, he climbs up and slides himself into me, all the while looking into my eyes. I can see in his strong, blue eyes how much he wants me. He begins moving back and forth, back and forth, first slower, then faster. I'm rubbing the vibrator along in sync with his imaginary motion. I feel myself getting ready. "Faster, Dan, faster," I whisper.

Dan pushes himself up on his massive biceps so he's thrusting into me from above, where he brushes against it with every stroke. "Oh Dan, Oh Dan," I can barely control it now, and as I feel it coming over me—

"Jenni, what are you doing?"

The image of Dan vanishes as my eyes fly open. Deirdre is standing right there over my bed staring at me like I'm on some nature documentary. My pants are around my ankles, and the vibrator is still humming between my legs. I flick it off, but it's far too late. Why didn't I at least do it under the sheets? Get at least that thin layer of plausible deniability so I could pretend I was doing anything except exactly what I was doing.

Deirdre has a huge smile on her face, like she knows she shouldn't be but can't help herself. "Wow, you were really into it. You didn't even hear me come in."

"You could have knocked."

"It's my room too. You should probably put a sock on the door or something. Anyway, Laura and Melissa are right behind me. You should cover up."

I pull my pants up with as much grace as I can muster, which is to say, none. My face must be scarlet.

Deirdre picks up the wand and holds it in front of her face, still grinning like a kid who found her parents' entire stash of Halloween candy. "So, a cord, not even battery-powered. That's serious stuff. I'm impressed. I didn't think you had it in you."

I snatch the toy out of Deirdre's hand so I can stuff it in my underwear drawer before the other two arrive. I shove it as far back as I can and slam the drawer closed. Right now I don't care if I never see that thing again.

"So who's this Dan whose name you kept repeating?" Deirdre asks. She sits down on her bed, but she's practically bouncing. Isn't there anything in her life more exciting than catching her roommate masturbating?

"Come on, you can tell me. Is it Dan Soto on the first floor? He's hot. I'd do him. Or is it that senior we met at Clarke's last month? Oh wait, I know, it's Dan Marcus from the black frat!" I look away for a second, and she must take that as confirmation because she squeals loudly. "What does it look like? Is it really big?"

I finally find my voice. "No, it's not any of them. No one on campus, no one you know, OK?" Laura and Melissa arrive, chattering to each other, before Deirdre can interrogate me further about my private fantasies. I brush past them as I rush out the door, shoes in hand. I'm going to have to tell Dan I'm not doing any more of his homework assignments, not unless he wants to pay for me to have a single room first.

Friday night, Dan laughs when I tell him that Deirdre caught me with his present.

"It's not funny. I was humiliated. I couldn't go back to my room. I slept in the common room."

Dan puts down his drink. "I know, sweetie. I'm sorry. If you knew how many times boys catch each other, it wouldn't seem like such a big deal."

"It was to me." I sniffle and look at my drink. Damn it, I wanted him to be more understanding, sympathetic even. Instead, he's treating it like it's some big joke. Only I'm the butt of it and it doesn't seem very funny at all.

"OK, tell you what. You don't have to use the toy every night. If your roommates are around, you can skip it. Or just use your hands under the sheets after they go to sleep."

"Thank you."

"And if you ever can't go back to your room again, whatever the reason, you can always call my work number. If I'm not around, my secretary can get you a hotel room."

"Thank you," I say again. I briefly wonder why I can't come here instead, but I viciously push the thought down. Of course, I can't just show up at his apartment. That's what he's paying me for, right? To be there when he wants me, and not there when he doesn't.

15

HALLOWEEN PARADE

Back home, things are not looking up. Dad hasn't found a job yet, and Mom keeps muttering about finding something at the mall. In Janine's latest letter she mentioned that she and Mike had to make the last payment on my parents' mortgage; but they've got two kids and a house of their own so they can't do that every month. At least I'm not a burden on them right now, and I can't let myself become one. If it comes to it, I'll take the job at the mall.

That, however, is all back in Easton. In New York, the last few weeks have zipped by faster than an acid-base reaction. Much to my surprise, autumn is coming to a close. It feels like Dan just found me in the Ramskeller yesterday. Yet if I'm not careful, I catch myself acting as if I've always been with him, I'll always be with him, and the rest of my life was just prologue.

I squelch that feeling down hard. That is not who I am. I'm not going to school to get a Mrs. degree. I'm going so I can have a career, and I'm with Dan so I can go to school. That's it. This is a transaction, nothing more. If I have some fun along the way, so much the better; but I can't lose sight of what's at stake here, namely my entire future.

Dan's taken me to Central Park to see the turning leaves. The fall foliage is actually prettier in the Bronx Botanical Garden across the street from campus. It's almost like you're not in the city at all, but there's too much chance of running into someone I know there.

We're walking through an area of the park Dan tells me is called the Ramble. The air has a nip to it. The pink cashmere sweater he bought me is warm enough, but it's a good excuse to wrap my arm through his and press close as we walk side by side. He's so solid and warm. It's like there's a furnace burning inside him. Are all men this warm or just him?

It feels good, like there's a magic bubble around us when we're together. As long as I'm with him, I don't have to worry about school or money or roommate drama, or anything. Whatever happens, it's going to be OK.

Then, as usual, Dan opens his mouth.

"What would you like to dress up as for Halloween?"

"Aren't we a little old for trick or treating?"

"You could still get away with it, I think, but that's not what I had in mind. I thought we'd go to the Halloween Parade down in the Village, then maybe clubbing. You could wear a mask, in case any of your friends saw us."

"That doesn't seem likely." The advantage of living in a city of eight million people. The chance of running into anyone I know is small, even when we're out in public like this. I don't know why I even think about it. If any of my friends do happen to see us, not that they ever go farther from campus than Clarke's Bar, they'll just think I found myself a boyfriend a bit this side of age-inappropriate. It's not like my price is tattooed on my forehead.

———

DAN WANTS to take me shopping for a costume, but I've already experienced what Dan calls "shopping." If I let him take me, I'll end up wrapped around a stripper pole in a G-string and six-inch platform heels. I'm going to choose my own costume, thank you very much.

Instead he loans me his credit card, and I cab it down to a store advertised in the Village Voice. "Largest Selection of Adult Costumes in New York!" the ad shouts in 48-point bold type. The window display is a surprisingly artistic tableau of witches, bats, black cats, and cobwebs, half of them animatronic. They probably hired a Broadway set designer to create it.

However, the inside is rack after rack of some of the cheesiest outfits I have ever seen. The pictures on the packages are all adult porn stars wearing clothes that might have fit them at age twelve. Sexy nurse, sexy lawyer, sexy policewoman, pretty much any occupation you can imagine, only with a miniskirt and the word "sexy" prefixed. I briefly consider going as "sexy scientist"—I could substitute my actual white coat from chemistry lab so it wouldn't be nearly so revealing—but what the hell. It's Halloween. It will be dark, and I have Dan's credit card.

With the help of a salesgirl who'd be cute if not for electric green hair and an upper lip piercing, I finally settle on a suitably dark outfit. Thigh-high fishnet stockings and garter belt, a glossy black PVC pleated miniskirt, a white ruffly top that dips low enough to embarrass the St. Pauli Girl, and a short red pleather jacket I could almost wear some other day of the year. A top hat, flapper wig, and sequined midnight blue mask complete the outfit. I have no idea what I'm supposed to be, but Asphyxia, as the salesgirl asserts her name to be, assures me that my boyfriend will love it.

The Halloween store also carries a wide selection of glow-in-the-dark makeup, but instead I buy a bright red lipstick at Duane Reade that will last past Halloween and some pale foundation, mostly for my chest which is going to be more exposed than it was since I was nine. Yes, I'm one of those girls who wears a really solid onesie at the pool in the summer.

Last stop is Payless ShoeSource for a pair of glossy black you-know-what pumps that show off my toes in the fishnet stockings, since Dan has such a thing for my feet. They're two inches higher than I'm comfortable with, but as long as I can lean on Dan's arm, I'll manage.

Total expenditure including cab fare: $312.37. It's a rounding error to Dan, but it's more than I've ever spent on clothes for myself before.

———

HALLOWEEN, I leave the Bronx early to give myself time to prepare. I left the outfit at Dan's apartment and made him promise not to look. Not that I could really keep him from doing anything he wanted to do, but you know.

After getting dressed, I inspect myself in the mirror in the master bathroom. I barely recognize the girl looking back at me. The mask helps. She's sexy and flirty and thoroughly mysterious. She's certainly not a mousy little wallflower from Easton, Pennsylvania. But she isn't the sophisticated Upper East Side society girl Dan likes to decorate his arm with either. She is original, her own creation. I'm going to have fun with her.

When I enter the living room and present myself for Dan's inspection, he's lounging on the couch in a tuxedo with a blue homunculus peeking out of his jacket pocket. He isn't struck speechless, but the expression on his face tells me I've piqued his interest.

"Why Miss McGrath," he says, "I do believe I've misjudged you."

"Tonight I'm not Jenni McGrath. I'm," let's see, "Victoria, and I have a secret."

"And what might that be?" Dan asks, intrigued.

"That would be telling," I reply, cocking my lip and raising my eyebrow in imitation of Dan's iconic smirk. "You're going to have to find out."

———

DAN SUGGESTS WATCHING the parade from a bar he knows that has a balcony overlooking Sixth Avenue. The cover charge is $50. Dan hands a hundred to the doorman like it's lab tissue. Inside, I catch him slipping another bill to the hostess when he asks for a table on the edge. I don't catch whose face is on it, but I'm pretty sure it's not George Washington's. I'm still not used to how rich he is. We've barely started and he's already dropped enough cash for me and my friends to drink all night at Clarke's.

By the time the parade arrives we've covered the two-drink mini-mum. I'm not sure what I'm expecting. Something like Macy's Thanksgiving Parade on TV but with pumpkins instead of turkeys? Whatever I'm expecting, it's not this. Skeleton puppets, eyeball balloons, mothers pushing baby strollers containing infants made up to look like miscarriages, and some things I know are anatomically impossible.

There's a whole separate category for public nudity. Many of the marchers are wearing (or not wearing) outfits that would get them arrested in Easton. In high school I didn't even like showering after gym class, and here half the women are parading down the middle of the street in G-strings or less. No wonder I've never seen this parade on network TV. A TV van is set up down the block to film the action, but they're going to have to slap a black bar across three quarters of the screen.

I'm not sure how much of the parade has gone by, but I gulp down the last of my drink and grab Dan's arm. "Let's go down to the street. I want to be where the action is."

He raises an eyebrow, but follows without objection when I hop up and drag him back downstairs. Even by New York standards, Sixth Avenue is packed. I can't see most of the parade, but it doesn't matter. The real action is on the street. I'm pushed up against every possible piece of humanity. Black, white, green, purple—male, female, and indeterminate—half wearing costumes, some incredibly elaborate, some almost not there at all. Usually this would terrify me, but tonight the joyous mood of the crowd is infectious, and I find myself laughing and going with it. For once, I'm the one dragging Dan around, craning my neck to try to get a better view of every passing float and drag queen.

After the parade passes, the party spills out into the street. Traffic is blocked off, and crowds of costumed revelers roll down Sixth Avenue. The mood is gay in more ways than one. I've known gay people before. My best friend Lucy back in high school is now calling herself a bisexual, and our Spanish teacher was an open secret; but I have never before seen so many men flaunting it so openly.

Some of them are dressed in leather bondage outfits, but they don't even achieve the level of twelve year-old vampire costume scary. More like a cross between a biker and a teddy bear. Quite a few of the younger boys are walking around in nothing more than tennis shoes and sequined gold Speedos. They all have great bodies, a little like Dan but with not an ounce of fat and no body hair whatsoever. I'm tempted to ask for grooming tips. They're pretty in the way a statue in a museum is pretty: absolutely flawless but not quite real, look but don't touch. I squeeze Dan's hand tighter and snuggle up against him, relaxing into the smell of him. Dan is look and touch, and very, very real.

However the ones that really get me are the—and I hesitate to use this word because I know it can be mean, but in this case it's quite literal—fairies. Mustachioed men with hairy legs in tutus and gossamer wings with sparkly wands, like a five-year-old girl's princess costume. They're silly but completely uninhibited. More than anybody else they own their attitude.

I try to imagine myself that free, and yes, the costume helps. I'm not little Jenni from Pennsylvania. I am the dark and mysterious and powerful Victoria from, let's see, London.

I put my arm around Dan's neck and nudge it. He gets the message and leans down.

"I want to do naughty things with you," I whisper in his ear, though actually it's more of a normal tone of voice since with this much clamor around us nothing softer would be audible.

Dan smiles that wicked grin of his. "I know just the place."

16

AFTER PARTY

Dan leads me out of the crowd onto a side street that intersects at an oblique angle. After a few quick turns onto other weirdly angled streets, I'm completely lost. We're still in the Village—too many men in hoods are tethered by neck chains to bare-breasted women in leather jackets for us to be anywhere else, even on Halloween—but otherwise I have no idea where we are. Downtown geography is still a little hazy to me, and the predictable Manhattan grid is dosed with LSD below 14th street.

The industrial area he takes me to would be scary if it was deserted, but this is New York City at 11:00 p.m. on Halloween. Nowhere's deserted. More people are wandering down the middle of the street than you'd see in a week in downtown Easton. Many are drunk, high, or both—the smell of marijuana is everywhere—but they're all happy. It's a great night, and one big party. I can't believe I spent last Halloween watching Friday the 13th with Laura in the dorm lounge when we could have been in the Village watching this.

Dan stops at a large brick building where a suited bald man even taller than him and twice as wide holds a velvet rope in front of the steps leading to the door. He's wearing stuffed antlers in deference to the holiday, but somehow still manages to look like a rock of seriousness amidst the bacchanalia. A line of drunken revelers extends down the block.

Out of habit, I aim for the back of the line, but Dan drags me forward. He says something to the giant guarding the door, and the man unbuckles the rope and waves us in. It feels wrong to cut the line, but I assume Dan knows what he's doing.

As soon as we step inside, I hear the distant thumping of dance music. The bass is rumbling the floor underneath us. "Where are we?" I ask while I can still hear myself talk.

"A club I know. I don't think it has a name."

He leads me down a dark staircase, the music getting louder the closer we get.

At the bottom a punk-looking girl with dyed blonde hair and too much makeup is sitting on a stool in front of a heavy metal door. "Forty dollars," she yells, loud enough to be heard over the music vibrating through the door.

Dan pulls out his bank roll, peels off two twenties, and hands them to her. She shoves the cash into her bra, then bangs twice on the door. It opens, and we pass through into the club.

The room is dark but sporadically lit by spinning disco balls. After my eyes adjust, I take in the tableau laid out before me. People in a wide variety of costumes are dancing, twirling, or jumping manically. Some have no costume at all. Is naked a costume? It seems to be tonight. A man dressed as a satyr, complete with exposed tumescence, whirls by with two women in tow, one dressed as a Greek nymph and the other as a biker chick. The biker chick sort of spoils the Greek theme, but I doubt anyone cares.

The room is hot, but not uncomfortably so, probably a good thing given the costumes some of the crowd are not wearing. It smells raunchy and raw, full of sweat and hormones and sex. Jenni, I think, would be terrified; but screw that. Tonight I am Victoria, and Victoria is afraid of nothing.

Dan takes my hand and leads me out into the center of the room. I briefly think of objecting that I don't really know how to dance—I went to my prom stag with Lucy and we spent most of the night guarding the punch bowl and making fun of the cheerleaders—but for once I stop myself. The whole room is too high, too crowded, and too loud for anyone to pay any attention to what anyone else is doing. If I make a fool of myself dancing, who cares? Victoria certainly doesn't.

Dan smiles as I find the beat. I shake my hips from side to side. My hands wave in the air. I even forget about my shoes and dance like I'm wearing sneakers. How I stay afoot I don't know, but Victoria does and she is in control. It is exhilarating. This must be what Deirdre feels like all the time.

One song blends into the next. At various times we're joined by other people in costume: fairy princesses, devils, drag queens, and swimsuit models. Most of them are just pretending, but one woman I think I've seen on the cover of Sports Illustrated. Either that or she's the best drag queen ever. Through it all Dan pays polite attention to their artistry, but always returns his attention to me.

Of course he does! I'm Victoria, and Victoria is hot. She is the queen of the night, the ultimate sexy. She can have any man she wants. I spin around and flash him a flirty smile over my shoulder that says he is lucky to be with me. He returns an appreciative look that says he knows it.

I'm not sure how long we dance, but eventually the D.J. slows down the music and Dan takes me in his arms for a slow turn. I'm covered in sweat. I probably lost five pounds of water weight since we began. "Can I have a drink?" I ask.

Dan nods. "Of course," and leads me off the floor to the bar. I'm tempted to order a gin and tonic, but I'm still a little high from what I drank back on the balcony. I'm more thirsty than anything.

"Perrier," I say to the shirtless bartender, who has a well-trimmed beard, matching nipple rings, and no chest hair whatsoever. He's cute in a smooth sort of not-Dan way, and I smile at him as he pops the cap off a green bottle, and hands it to me.

For once, I gulp it down without worrying about the extravagance of bottled water. Victoria drinks nothing but bottled water, I decide.

Dan orders his usual bourbon on the rocks and lays a twenty on the bar.

We're both too out of breath for small talk. Who knew dancing was this much exercise? I enjoy the clean, cold water while Dan sips his bourbon and admires me/Victoria. A redhead in a sparkling black dress and wide mask covered in green feathers sweeps in from behind him. The mask does not hide the fact that she's gorgeous, movie-star gorgeous. She sidles up against Dan on his right side and slips her arm around him. "So is this the little one you were telling me about?" She says it in a voice a cat might use to comment on a baby bird it was about to eat.

"This is Victoria," Dan says. He uses her name, which I'm a little too buzzed to catch, but he obviously knows her. How well I wonder?

"Victoria?" she says, as if it's a question. She looks me up and down, as if sizing up the competition. Normally I'd be freaking out about now, or trying to shrink into my shoes, but Victoria does not shrink from competition. She welcomes it. I strike a pose of sensual nonchalance, and throw her smile back at her. Not even a threatening back off smile, but a confident "He is mine and there is nothing you can do about it, so I can be magnanimous," smile. I love Victoria. I should be her all the time.

The woman must like what she sees—maybe Victoria's confident stoicism impresses her—because after a few seconds she holds out her hand, and I take it.

"Pleased to meet you," she says. However instead of letting go of my hand as I expect, she pulls me in close to her, puts the other hand on my back, and slips her mouth up to my ear.

"Don't hurt him," she whispers, in a tone that sounds more like a command than a request. She says it so quietly I'm not sure I heard it at all. Shocked, I lean back but she's smiling like nothing out of the ordinary has happened. Dan is smiling at the both of us. I don't think he heard.

What the hell did that mean? I'm not offended or anything. It just doesn't make any sense, like telling a baby gazelle not to hurt a hungry cheetah. The idea that I could do anything that would hurt Dan, even that Victoria could, is laughable.

Feather-mask woman has turned her attention back to Dan. The two of them are chatting like old friends about some movie or TV show or something. After a few minutes, she pecks him on the cheek and sweeps away, leaving me with lots of questions and no answers.

Dan puts his empty glass on the bar. "Let's go to the back room" He takes me by the hand, and I lay my bottle on the bar and follow him.

The next room is darker and the music softer and mixed with an out of sync beat track that doesn't keep time. The room is not as crowded, though a few couples are swaying slowly in the middle of the room. It's also cooler. I'm grateful for the reprieve. Much as I enjoyed it, I don't think I have the strength for more dancing.

Dan leads me to an empty couch along the wall. We sit down, and a wave of relief flows through me. I didn't notice it while we were dancing but my feet hurt, like sharp, shooting pain in my arches hurt. Victoria may be mistress of the dance, but she lives in Jenni's body, and Jenni isn't used to wearing four-inch heels, much less dancing in them.

Dan wraps his arm around me and I relax into him. I begin to open my mouth to kiss him when out of the corner of my eye I spot the satyr and the nymph sprawled across a bed doing what satyrs and nymphs do. I draw back in shock. Are they really? I suppose they could be faking it, but I doubt it. Her legs are wrapped around him and her head is thrown back, and suddenly the general background noise of the room snaps into clear focus. It's not part of the music. People are making those noises! And those noises are...

I swivel my head to scan the room. There's more furniture in here than I realized at first, and most of it is taken. Those are bodies moving up and down, nude or in costume or halfway in between. There are couples and triples and even one quartet (or quintet, it's hard to count the body parts in the dark) in various stages of undress and copulation. And it's not all boy-girl either. A burly football player (well, he's wearing a football outfit, at least the top half) is bent over in front of a gay biker. I can't help myself. I stare at them blatantly. The football player's face, what I can see of it, is strained and grunting.

Dan takes my hand. "First time in a back room?"

I nod, without really paying attention to him. I can't take my eyes off the football player and his...friend. I know what gay men do. I'm not that naïve, but I never thought I'd see them do it, not live and in person at least.

Dan grasps my head more firmly in his hands and turns me toward him. I know what he's up to. He thinks he's going to see how far he can push me again. Only he's forgotten that tonight he's not with little Miss Scaredy Jenni. He's with Victoria, and Victoria takes what she wants.

Before Dan can kiss me, I grab his neck with my hands, and I'm kissing him, pushing my tongue into his mouth. He recoils for a second, taken aback by Victoria's aggressiveness, but then he relaxes into it and lets me guide him.

I reach my left hand down to his pants and brazenly place my palm on his crotch. As I expected, he's already hard. I rub my hand along the soft fabric, up and down. Dan moans. His breathing gets harder and deeper.

I take my hand away and Dan emits a plaintive sound I don't think I've heard from him before, but I smile and put a hand on his chest. He gets the message and lets me push him down onto his back. I unbuckle my shoes and drop them on the floor. Then I reach up under my skirt, pull my panties off, and dangle them in front of his face like I'm teasing a cat. I drop them on the floor next to the shoes. Dan looks dumbfounded. He's not used to me taking charge, but I'm not taking charge. Victoria is.

Carefully, I position myself across Dan, straddling him about waist high. I run my palm along his crotch again, and he's still hard. Good. I unzip his trousers, and try to reach in. It's surprisingly tricky, and I end up grabbing a handful of cloth. I guess there are some things even Victoria can't do.

"Let me," he whispers with some urgency. He reaches down and does something with the fly that balked me; and there he is, hard and tall and ready. I think I'm shielding it from the rest of the room, but I doubt anyone really cares if I'm not, Dan included. I take hold of him and grasp it tight in my hand. I lean down and whisper in his ear as I stroke it, "No coming, I want you for me."

Dan's usually on top, but not tonight. I let go, lift myself up a few inches and scoot forward. As I do, we touch momentarily, and a shiver runs through me. I am so ready for this. I reach behind me and take hold, then guide him into me. I slide backward down him, and it feels amazing.

Once he's all the way inside, I lean forward, placing my palms on his chest for balance. We're still clothed aside from the fun parts, and those are mostly hidden by my skirt. And if they're not, we're still not the most naked in this room by quite a lot. I grip the pleats of Dan's white tuxedo shirt in my hands as I begin to rock my hips back and forth, feeling his warmth inside me.

For once, I don't worry about him, or what I look like, or whether I'm doing it right. I move myself back and forth, finding the rhythm I like, making sure he's at the right angle for me. I close my eyes and go with it, and when the feeling starts to wash over me, I keep going.

When I'm done, I collapse on top of Dan, breathing heavy. I didn't notice him finishing, but he slips out of me, and he's a lot softer than he was a few minutes ago, so I guess he must have. I lay there on top of him, panting until I regain my strength.

Being Victoria is fun!

———

BEING VICTORIA IS ALSO MESSY. Dan and I were already sweaty from the dance floor, and after our romp on the couch we're positively drenched. Plus, the sticky residue is starting to drip down my leg. I find a tissue in my purse and try to wipe up discretely, but it's hopeless.

In retrospect, I wish I'd paid a little more attention to where I was tossing my underwear. Now that it's been on the floor, I'm not sure I want to put it back on my body. I can see what people are still doing on the floor, and God only knows what they've already done. And I am not even going to think about who might have used the couch before us. I take one last look at my panties and kick them under the couch. They probably won't be the strangest thing the janitor's had to sweep off this floor.

I'm tempted to do away with the shoes too, but the thought of putting my stocking feet on the floor is beyond gross. As I buckle my shoes back on, my legs remind me how much I've been abusing them tonight.

Dan is, if anything, even more disheveled than me. His white shirt is askew across his cummerbund; and his hair, never all that straight to start with, looks like he swam through a hurricane. But he is smiling. I like to see him smile. He can be so intense and serious sometimes, almost scary, but then he's like this and all is right with the world.

"I need to clean up," I whisper to him.

———

THE LESS SAID about the ladies room the better. The word "biohazard" may begin to describe it. I'm afraid I'll leave filthier than I entered. I clean up as best I can. At least the water in the sink isn't obviously brown, but I wouldn't want to put it under the one of the microscopes in the bio lab.

When I exit, Dan isn't waiting for me. He must have gone looking for the men's. Probably twice as gross, if that's even possible, but at least he doesn't have to sit to pee. Being male does have its advantages.

I stumble my way back down the dimly lit hall, running my hand along the wall for balance and trying not to fall down in my too high shoes. When I get home, I'm going to wear tennis shoes for a week. I open the first door I come to and get a glimpse of two people before one of them slams the door in my face. OK, next door then.

It seems louder in this direction, though truth be told there's so much thumping coming from every which where it's hard to be sure. Carefully, I push through the second door, and find myself back in the room we came from. I'm sure it's the right room because the football player and biker are still going at it. I have no idea what they're on. Even Dan doesn't last that long.

What do you do at an orgy while you wait for your date to get back to from the bathroom? Is it polite to stare or should I look at my shoes and pretend I don't notice the rampant sex? Not exactly a question I ever had reason to ask before.

When in doubt, fall back on what you know. I plant my back against a convenient wall and try to fade into the furniture. This got me through what few parties I was invited to in high school. Hell, with the lights down low enough this could be mistaken for one of Michelle Neiderbach's makeout parties. The only difference is that I'm really waiting for my date instead of imagining him in my head.

I must have dozed off for a second or two, because the next thing I know I'm jolted awake by something wet running along my cheek. I open my eyes to find a man in a red spandex devil suit and black eye shadow leering across my peripheral vision.

"Um, what?" I murmur, still half-conscious.

"Shh," he says, and slips one arm around my back. With his other hand he starts running a finger down my chest. "It's OK."

"Hey, back off," I try to shout, though it comes out more as a whimper. I bring my arms up to push him away, but I'm too close and don't have any leverage. It's like trying to push open a barred metal door.

"Come on girl, don't be like that," he slurs. "I know you're good to go. I saw you with Mr. Tuxedo a little while ago."

"I said no," I say, a little louder this time, and turn my head to the side to avoid his probing tongue, which hits my cheek again. Oh, gross!

"Don't be a tease. Let's see if you're ready for it." He slips a hand under my skirt. Panicked I clench my legs together, which only makes me more wobbly in the heels.

He takes his hand away from my legs, grabs my right wrist, and starts dragging me with him. I don't want to go. I should scream, or knee him in the groin, or something, but instead I'm frozen in fear as he half pushes/half drags me toward the couch. I'm trapped in a bad ABC Afterschool Special: What happened to the girl who only thought she was a bad girl when she went to play with the big boys. Where's Dan? It's dark, and is anyone going to realize something's wrong?

A woman's voice comes out of the dark. "Hold up there, cowboy, I think the lady's spoken for."

Shit. It's green feather mask woman. She puts a hand on his shoulder, and Devil guy turns to see who spoke. I look at her plaintively. Help, please, I say with my eyes, though my lips still aren't moving.

"Leave us alone," he snarls. "Unless you want to join us?"

Green feather woman gives him a look you might reserve for a cockroach, right before you step on it. "I don't think so," she says. "The lady's going home with me."

"Bitch," he says and lets go of me long enough to slap her, right across the face. Green feather woman hits the ground and gags like she's trying to vomit.

Devil man turns back to me. "Come on." He grabs my arm again. Only he's not looking at green feather woman, who is trying to stand. Please stay down, I think. Don't let him hit you again, but she isn't listening, and I'm not really talking.

She braces one hand on the ground and somehow manages to push herself to her feet with the other hand in her purse. Maybe it's the mask, but her face looks surprisingly calm for someone who just got beat down.

"Hey, dick breath," she says, loud enough to be heard through the music.

Devil man whirls around to face her, yanking my arm in the process. His face is contorted with anger. "I thought I told you to go away. If you don't leave us alone, I'll—"

But I never hear what he's going to do because she shoves a can right in his face and sprays.

My accoster screams and lets go of me to claw at his eyes. I don't know what she sprayed him with, but it smells awful. Most of it hit him, but just the whiff of it is making my eyes sting.

Green feather woman grabs me by my wrist. "Come on, let's go, before some idiot gives him a towel."

"OK." I seem to have found my voice again. I let her lead me out of the room. The thumping music and flickering lights are still playing havoc with my perception. I think she's taking me back to where we came in. Instead, we end up in a smaller room lined with plush couches. This room is better lit and quieter since there's no music playing here, only a distant throb from the one we left.

On the couch in the far corner, talking to a dark-haired woman in a Zorro costume is, "Dan!" I shout.

Dan looks up at me like nothing has happened. "Ah, there you are."

It's too much. I practically throw myself down onto the couch and grab him in a full-bodied hug.

"Something I should know about?" Dan asks.

"No," says green feather mask woman before I can compose myself enough to answer. "But I think you should keep a closer eye on this one in the future. Someone's liable to steal her away from you."

Dan flashes her a dark look, but she just smiles enigmatically and fades back into the crowd. I hold Dan tight, and promise myself I'm not going to let go until I'm safely home, no matter how badly I have to pee.

———

OUTSIDE THE CLUB, Halloween is winding down. Only a few packets of the drunkest revelers remain. Thankfully, it only takes Dan a couple of minutes to flag down a yellow cab. He holds the door for me, and I scramble in. He slides in next to me.

"Fordham College, Fordham Road and Southern Blvd, in the Bronx," he tells the driver.

The driver isn't happy at the prospect of going all the way up to the Bronx; but Dan slips him a twenty as a "pre-tip" and promises him a fare back to Manhattan after they drop me off.

Dan doesn't press me for details on what happened when we got separated, for which I'm grateful. I'm a little worried what he'd do if he knew, and I'm a little embarrassed by the whole thing. It does feel good to realize I, or at least Victoria, took care of myself for once. OK, with not a little help from Green Feather Mask woman my conscience reminds me. I have to remember to ask Dan who she is. I owe her a big thank you.

But that's all past now. I snuggle up to Dan as the cab turns onto the West Side Highway and picks up speed. Being Victoria was fun for a night, but I think it's time to put her away until next year. Halloween only comes once a year.

17

NOVEMBER

Halloween marks an inflection point in my relationship with Dan. Inflection point: where the curve keeps going in the same direction, but the second derivative changes sign. I scored a 5 on my AP calculus exam.

We're still not exactly equals—that would be tricky as long as he's paying my bills—but he seems to ask more and tell less. The shift is subtle, but it's there. Or maybe it's that I'm looking at me with a little more respect. Either way, I stop waiting for the other shoe to drop and begin to settle into a comfortable rhythm. Schoolwork during the week. Fun during the weekend.

There must, however, be a law of conservation of stress because all the energy I don't spend stressing over Dan, I devote to worrying about my second organic chem exam. Riding the 4 train to and from Dan's place, my chemistry text weighs heavily in my lap. PKe values, unsaturation, parent chains, Newman projections, enantiomers, and oh my God, how did I ever think I was going to be able to cram all this in? Why didn't I major in something easier like 12th Century Latin or High Energy Physics?

Fortunately, Dan is not adverse to me brushing up on carbon-carbon bonds and stereoisomerism during some of the time he's paying for. His apartment's actually pretty quiet, certainly quieter than a Hughes Hall quad with three roommates or even Duane Library. He shows me how to use his home PC to write my English paper. That's like a thousand times easier than waiting two hours for one of the machines in the computer lab to get free.

One evening over dinner I ask him why, but the only answer I get is, "Your education matters, Jenni." Well duh, my father could have told me that.

Turns out I needn't have worried about the test. It's a breeze, even easier than the first one. Why does everyone panic about this course so much? Spend some quality time reviewing class notes, memorize a couple of formulas, and do a few practice problems from the textbook, ones the professor didn't already assign. Last time, I noticed that half his questions came straight out of the even numbered problems at the back of the chapters. There's the A, easy peasy. This time when I hand Theresa my blue book with an hour left in the exam period, she sighs and accepts it without comment.

———

MAYBE I SHOULD HAVE BEEN a little more worried. At the end of lab the next day, Theresa comes over while I'm putting the glassware away. "Jenni, do you have a minute? Professor Bolotowsky wants to see you in his office."

"OK, I'll go as soon as I finish cleaning up here."

I spend the two minutes it takes for the elevator to arrive becoming progressively more panicked. Why does the professor want to see me? Did I miss a page on the exam? Does he think I cheated? Is he secretly a thousand year old vampire who maintains his youthful appearance by drinking the blood of talented young undergraduates?

That last one's ridiculous. No one would accuse Professor Bolotowsky of being youthful.

By the time I finally knock on the open door of his office, I'm half convinced the NYPD is waiting inside to arrest me for cooking meth during lab.

Professor Bolotowsky looks up from his computer. "Oh, Miss McGrath. Thank you for coming. Please come in and have a seat."

Hesitantly, I walk in and sit in the armchair in front of his desk. "Is something wrong Professor? If it's the exam, I'm sorry. I know I can do better."

Professor Bolotowsky raises an eyebrow. "No, not at all. In fact, you did very well on the exam. We haven't finished grading them all, but it looks like you may have the highest score in your class."

Woah. That can't be right. I know I'm smart, but I'm not the smartest girl in the class. Plus, all the pre-meds spend all their time studying, weekends included. I spend more time studying Dan than organic chem. Professor Bolotowsky is still talking, but I'm not hearing him. I force myself to tune back in.

"...so we were wondering if you had thought about majoring in chemistry. There are likely to be some research opportunities available junior year."

"You want me to major in chemistry?"

"That's right."

"But I'm not any good at chemistry. I'm a complete klutz in the lab. I broke about a thousand beakers and the hood last year."

"Your grades say otherwise. And everyone has a bad freshman year in lab. It's why we give you the cheap equipment. Now the hood, yes, I do seem to remember hearing something about that."

How could he forget? Mulcahy Hall had to be evacuated until the fire department gave the all clear.

"I don't think we've had an undergraduate break one of those before, at least not during normal lab hours, but your TA's all agree that you've improved dramatically this year. I'm sure we can find a place for you."

"I don't know what to say. Thanks? I'm glad you think I'm good enough, but I'm pretty set on vet school. That's why I'm a bio major."

"If that's still what you want when you graduate, I don't think you'll have any trouble getting into vet school with a chemistry major. But I also don't think you'd have any trouble getting into a top graduate program in chemistry, MIT, Cal Tech, maybe Columbia if you want to stay in the city. And chemistry's not physics. There are always jobs outside academia for a good chemist."

A chemist? It seems about as likely as playing linebacker for the Giants or singing the lead in La Boheme. Finally, I a utter a weak, "I don't know. Maybe?"

"Promise me you'll give it some thought, OK?"

"OK. Thanks. I will think about it."

"That's all I ask." He smiles. This may be the first time I've seen him smile all semester.

———

LAURA and I are in the Hughes Hall lounge working together on our English papers. We're taking opposing sides on *The Tempest*. Laura is claiming Miranda is an incidence of Shakespeare's misogyny while I'm arguing she's a proto-feminist. Neither of us actually cares about or believes what we're writing, but it cuts the research in half.

The four of us agreed to take the same core classes so we can trade ditch days and the girl who goes can tell the others what they missed. At least, that was the plan. In practice, Laura and I have missed a grand total of twenty minutes of class since the beginning of freshman year; and fifteen minutes of that was when we got lost on the way to theology our first week. Deirdre, by contrast, is lucky if she makes it to half her classes. Melissa, I sometimes think, is only pretending to attend this university. She's secretly a twenty-five-year-old undercover reporter who snuck onto campus to write an exposé on college life. Then again if that's what she wanted, she could have picked a more scandalous group of roommates.

None of the others are science majors, but Laura at least understands about grad school admissions. She's majoring in poli sci in prep for law school. When I tell her about Professor Bolotowsky's unexpected proposal, she scowls. "Seems the same to me. Does it really make a difference if you're going to vet school?"

"I don't know. I never really thought about majoring in anything except bio. But he's right. Chemistry might actually make it easier to get into vet school. Everyone applying to vet school is a biology major. If I were a chemistry major, I'd stand out. What I don't understand is why they want me to switch now, just because the class got a little easier."

"Did it?"

"Well, yeah. I didn't get 95s on the exams in General Chem last year. And I studied like, all the time. This year, I'm studying less."

"Are you studying at home on the weekends?"

I still haven't told her where I'm really going, and so far my secret hasn't slipped out. Keep that up for the next two-and-a-half years and everything's going to be A-OK.

"Some, not as much as I used to. I'm actually sort of busy on the weekends. A lot of family stuff, you know." The lies get bigger. I start spinning a story in my head about my father's illness, and how I have to take care of him on weekends so my mother can have some time off, but fortunately Laura pulls a different thread instead.

"I remember. You'd keep the light on all night to study."

"Did I? I'm sorry."

"It's OK. It didn't bother me that much, and Deirdre and Melissa were usually out half the night anyway. But you're not doing that any more. Most nights you're in bed before me. Maybe you're finding your stride now. A lot of women struggle their first year in college, even the smart ones. Remember Audrey? She was smart and she flunked out."

"Yeah, but she also ditched pretty much the entire second semester."

Laura laughs. "I think weed had something to do with that. But you can study too much. There has to be a happy medium between getting high and playing guitar all the time and cramming every waking minute. You need time to lie back and process it all."

"If I'm studying less, shouldn't I do worse?"

"Jenni, don't take this the wrong way, but last year you seemed sort of afraid."

"Afraid?"

"Maybe afraid's too strong a word, but certainly nervous. You didn't talk much, you'd sit in the back of every class. You'd slouch down and try to fade into the wall. Now, I don't know, you seem more confident somehow, calmer, more comfortable in your skin."

Wow. I had no idea Laura felt that way. But nothing's changed. Well, one thing's changed, but Laura doesn't know about that yet. I'm still me. It's not like being with Dan gives me extra IQ points or anything.

I don't know why, but suddenly I feel closer to her. Maybe I can tell her what I'm doing. Before I get up the nerve to say something, the door to the lounge bangs open and Deirdre bounces in with Tom from the second floor.

"Hey guys, we're going down to Little Italy for pizza. You want to come?"

"Sure," Laura says, "I'm not getting anywhere with this damned essay anyway. Let me grab a sweater from the room."

"How bout you, Jenni?" Tom asks. "You in?"

"Sure, why not?" Might as well enjoy college while I can.

———

BACK IN MANHATTAN, November is getting cold, so Dan shifts our excursions around the city from parks and zoos to museums. It is here I experience our first real incompatibility. Dan loves the Met and adores MoMA, both of which I find as interesting as dry paint, which, when you think about it, is literally what we're going there for.

I, on the other hand, could happily descend into the corridors of the Natural History Museum and not come out till Spring while Dan thinks the dinosaurs and dioramas are "kid stuff." To each their own, I suppose. At least we're still compatible in Dan's apartment.

The Sunday before Thanksgiving, Dan takes me to the Met again. We hold hands while we take in the Temple of Dendur, one of the few exhibits I actually appreciate. The winter light through the glass walls is soft and peaceful. Everyone around us whispers, almost as if they're in church. I guess if they were ancient Egyptians, they would be. Then I unexpectedly step into a minefield.

"When would you like me to come over next week?" I ask Dan absent-mindedly as we admire the Temple.

"You're off from school on Wednesday, right? That should be fine. I'll make reservations at Café des Artistes for dinner."

"I just wondered if you wanted to spend Thanksgiving with your family."

"No."

I look at him. "It would be OK if you did. You don't have to worry about me. The dorms are open or I can go to back to Pennsylvania for the day."

"I said no," he says loudly enough for several fellow museum-goers to turn and look at us.

Shit, he actually looks angry. This is the first time he's raised his voice to me. What did I say?

"OK, I'll come over Wednesday," I finally mumble.

"Fine," he replies while staring fixedly at the sandstone building.

Wow. I seem to have touched a sensitive spot. Was it his family? He must have parents. I mean, of course he has parents. I am a biology major. But he never mentions them. Are they alive? Dead? For all I know he could have children. He might even have a child my age. Now that would be creepy, but I'm pretty sure this isn't the right time to ask him about it.

———

MY MOTHER DOESN'T TAKE it well when I tell her I'm not coming home for Thanksgiving.

"Honey, don't you want to see your grandparents? They miss you."

"I'm sorry, Mom. I really have to study. Finals are coming up, and I have two term papers to write." Not quite a lie. I do have term papers, and finals are coming up; but of course that's not why I'm staying in New York over the break.

Fortunately, Mom is not good at detecting half-truths, maybe because until now I haven't given her a lot of practice. Instead, she asks about food.

"What will you eat? Do they keep the cafeteria open?"

"I can get pizza in Little Italy." Another half-truth. I could get it, but I won't.

"Pizza isn't turkey, honey. Can't you come home, just for Thursday? You can take the bus back Friday morning. You're smart. I'm sure you can afford the time off."

"Really, I don't need turkey, Mom. I'll be fine."

Finally, reluctantly, she agrees. Thank God. For a moment, I thought she was going to suggest coming to the city to see me. Now that would be a pickle. "Mom, Dad, I'd like you to meet the older gentleman who's paying for me to go to school." That's a conversation that can wait for another day, preferably one about ten years after I begin collecting social security.

18

RADIO CITY

Thanksgiving goes at off without a hitch. Dan even takes me to see the Macy's balloons being blown up the evening before the parade. The nighttime temperature is below freezing and I'm bundled up in three layers of wool, but even through my gloves his hand feels like a space heater. He's probably not the least bit chilly. His temperature runs about ten degrees hotter than mine at all times. I can be shivering with goose bumps in flannel pajamas (when he lets me wear pajamas, that is), curled up under three blankets, and he'll be lying on the mattress half naked without a single sheet on him.

After Garfield has inflated, we stop in at a faux-French bistro for hot chocolate. I sit there with the warm mug between my hands, smiling at him and watching the first flakes of snow drift down outside; though I swear the mug isn't quite as hot as he is.

In hindsight, New York City was clearly the better place to be for the holiday. Dinner table drama with my extended family and shopping Black Friday sales for tea towels at the Palmer Park Mall, or fooling around with my super-rich boyfriend and playing tourist in the city? It really is no contest. A niggling little voice in the back of my head reminds me that he's not really my boyfriend, but I tamp that thought down hard.

Still, when he's holding my hand as the crowds that pack Manhattan for the holidays magically part around us, it's hard not to think of him like that. Whatever this is, whatever he is to me and I am to him, when I'm with him it feels like nothing can go wrong. I never want the feeling to end.

I call my family on Thanksgiving from Dan's place. Janine is hosting this year so she picks up the phone. She's too busy wrangling her boys to talk much, but I learn the cat knocked the turkey on the floor, her youngest Alex has a newly discovered allergy to cheese mites, and Mom's jello mold went up in flames. I make a mental note to ask Professor Bolotwosky how it's possible to set a jello mold on fire. Maybe there was a little too much rum in the mix this year? Or gasoline?

When Mom gets on the line, she sounds happy. She tries to guilt me a little for staying at school. That's how I know she's doing OK. If she were down in the dumps, she'd be blaming herself instead of me. Dad hasn't found a job yet, but he isn't worried. They all sound happy. I'm happy too. I just wish we could be happy together. If this goes on, I will have to tell them eventually, but I'm not going to spoil the holiday.

Of course, all good things must come to an end, and long, lazy holiday weekends are no exception. Sunday is our last full day together until exam week. Somehow all my finals this semester ended up on the first three days of the exam period. Plus, I have two term papers due. I'm going to have to tool every waking minute for the next two weeks to keep my GPA up where it needs to be. That's what this is all about, right?

Dan agrees to let me stay on campus for the next two weekends so I can study, provided I make up the time after finals are over. He's surprisingly accommodating when it comes to schoolwork, about the only thing he is considerate of. I can study at his place if I need to, but he's a little too distracting for a young girl in—No. I am not going to go there. We are snuggled up on his couch, and that's all this is.

"Anything special you'd like to do for our final night together? Maybe something Christmasy?" Dan asks.

Hmm, Christmas in New York. What to do? The tree isn't up yet at Rockefeller Center, and I do not ice skate. The last thing I want is for Dan and the rest of Manhattan to see me falling on my ass. Then an idea hits me.

"Can we go see the Rockettes?"

"The Rockettes?"

"You know, at Radio City Music Hall. It's silly, but I've always wanted to see them live. I've only seen them on TV."

Dan furrows his brow. "You know, I've never been to see them either. OK, the Rockettes it is."

———

THE NIGHT IS COLD, well below freezing, so Dan makes sure I bundle up. He even insists I wear pants and sneakers. I'm a little disappointed that I don't get to wear the cute outfit I prepared, but Dan is adamant that I'd be uncomfortable in it.

When we get out of the cab five minutes before the doors open and we're standing in line in the sub-freezing chill, I decide he was right. I'm wearing a wool sweater, long underwear, and my heaviest puffy coat and I'm still cold. I try to press up against him to suck up as much warmth as I can while we wait on 51st street. Dan slips his hand down to pat my rear, then leaves it there. Tonight I'd let Professor Bolotowsky put his hand there if it made me two degrees warmer.

A man in an usher's uniform comes out and addresses the crowd. "Folks, there's a problem with the electrical inside the theater. We're getting it straightened it out, but it's going to be a few minutes before we can let you in."

An audible sigh of disappointment ripples through the line. A fat man with a red face, but bald and beardless so not Santa Claus, pushes past us to argue with the usher.

I hop from foot to foot, trying to warm up. "Bejeezus, it's cold."

Dan laughs. "Maybe I can think of something to keep you warm," he says with a smile in his eye. I'm already pressed up against him, so his mouth doesn't have to reach far to find mine. I'm not sure if his kisses really do warm me up, or if they merely distract me from the incipient frostbite. Either way it works. Usually with Dan it's a quick hop from deep kissing to heavy petting to our clothes flying off and rutting on the floor; but in public like this there's not any further it can go. Instead, I enjoy the feeling as my body shivers with each probe of his tongue.

A child's high voice pipes up from behind us. "Mommy, why is that Daddy kissing his daughter like that?"

For a moment we freeze, then break apart. If my face isn't blue from the cold, it must be red from embarrassment. I completely forgot we were standing in a crowded line full of children.

Dan has a different reaction. He is laughing so hard he can barely breathe. I've heard him laugh before, but never like this. It's not a polite acknowledgement of a joke, but a drunken torrent of insane mirth. He finally gets control of himself, looks at me, and collapses into laughter again. Well, I'm glad he doesn't feel any shame about putting on a show for a bunch of ten year olds and their parents.

He regains control just as the doors open. The line begins to move past us, and a woman about my mother's age with a wide-eyed girl in a ballerina outfit gives us a look that would freeze ice, if it weren't already freezing. "You should be ashamed of yourself," she chides us.

"And Merry Christmas to you too, Ma'am." Dan doffs his hat and bows politely to her. "Please don't mind us. I'm just getting my little girl warmed up before she sits in Santa's lap."

The look on the woman's face is priceless. Her daughter is staring at us like we're Santa Claus on a date with the Easter Bunny carrying a big bag of Halloween candy. It is too ridiculous to behold. I forget my humiliation and start laughing. And that sets Dan off again. I don't think either of us could stand up alone, so it's lucky we balance on each other.

Half the line has moved inside by the time we're able to talk again. Those who were too far back to see the exchange probably think we're high. Finally, he takes my hand, and joins the rest of the line as we push forward into the theater.

———

THE THEATER IS AMAZING, like something out of a black-and-white movie from the thirties, only three-dimensional and in color. Glittering glass chandeliers hang from the ceiling. Balls of electric light illuminate the red and gold walls. The clerks pushing programs and T-shirts are dressed in red and gold uniforms that make them look like they stepped out of a children's picture book.

After too little time gawking like a tourist from Pennsylvania, Dan leads me up the stairs to our seats, right as the orchestra begins to play. Dan puts his big hand on top of mine, and they both rest on my leg. The orchestra starts playing, the curtain rises, and dozens of sequined women begin to dance down the stage. I squeal in surprise and delight when the bow wrapped presents on the stage unexpectedly stand up and begin dancing with a young girl.

A woman in the row in front of us turns around and make a loud shushing noise, her finger pressed to her mouth. Her face is red and, oh my God, it's the woman from the line outside whose child thought Dan was my father! I didn't recognize her with her coat off.

"You two," she says in a tone one might use if you unexpectedly stepped in an ice cold slush puddle in open-toed shoes while crossing 42nd Street.

I can't help it. I giggle. It's too over the top, all the wonder taking place on the stage and she has a look that would scare Scrooge tattooed to her face.

"I don't know why they let perverts like you into a children's show," she says in a harsh whisper. "I should call an usher and have you thrown out. When we get home, I'm going to write a letter to the owners so they can keep people like you away from the children."

"I look forward to reading it. I'm always happy to hear from one of our patrons," says Dan.

"Shhh," says someone from down the aisle who's more intent on the spectacle onstage than the one unfolding behind them.

"No, I'm not sending it to you. I'm sending it to the owner," the woman hisses.

"Yes, and I'll be happy to read it." He sticks out his hand to the woman. "Dan Cortland, principal investor in Radio City Music Hall. Pleased to meet you."

She looks at his hand like it's a dead fish, then up at Dan, then back at his hand again. Her mouth is making motions like she's trying to talk, but all that's coming out is, "But, but..."

She grabs her daughter by the hand and yanks her out of the seat. "Come on, Emily, we're going."

"But Mommy, Santa Claus hasn't come yet," Emily objects.

"Emily, let's go."

"No, I want to see Santa Claus!" Emily shouts. Now other people are starting to look at her. Someone else directs a shush at them.

"Now, Emily," says the woman, standing and trying to extract the child from her seat. Emily is holding onto the armrest for dear life, and screaming, "No, no, no."

Everyone's looking at them, and the chorus of shushes is beginning to drown out the show. The mother gives in. "Fine. Sit. Be quiet, and don't look back."

As I'm watching the spectacle and wishing I could disappear into my chair, Dan whispers in my ear. "What do you say we really give her something to shush us about?" Before I can process the question, he picks up my hand and moves it from my leg to his lap. I can feel his erection straining underneath the wool trousers. He slips off my coat and lays it across his lap, covering my hand.

"Dan, there are children here," I say in as loud a whisper as I think safe, my attention suddenly diverted from the spectacle in front of us.

"Well, then we'll have to be quiet, now won't we?"

He begins moving my hand back and forth slowly across his pants.

Crap. What if somebody sees us? I scan the faces of my seatmates. They all seem absorbed in the show.

Dan wraps his left arm around me and whispers in my ear, "Unzip it."

It takes a bit of fumbling but I find the zipper. I pull it down and slip a finger in. That's all he needs to pop right out like the jack-in-the box onstage. As we watch the ballerina perform her pas de deux with the toys and stuffed animals, I stroke him under his coat. It's funny how it can feel so hard and silky at the same time. When the ballerina twirls and the music hits the climax, so does Dan. I'm afraid someone might hear his muffled cry, but it is lost in the clapping.

I return my hand to my lap, wiping it on his pants as I go. His hands fumble underneath his coat to push it back in. He's definitely going to have to have his suit dry cleaned. Or buy a new one. I cannot believe what I have just done. The woman in line was right about me.

Dan hugs me close to him, careful not to let his coat fall off his lap, and kisses me. The shame falls right out of my head like it was never there. I will do anything for this man. If this is what he wants me to do, this is what I am going to do. And if the suburban moms of the world don't like it, too bad for them.

Later, in the lobby, as the audience is filing out, I ask him the question that's bothering me. "Do you really own Radio City Music Hall?"

"Well, I suppose Radio City Music Hall is part of Rockefeller Center, which Mitsubishi bought a few years back, which is owned by its stockholders, who include some mutual funds I have positions in, so I guess you could say I own it. At least a small part of it."

"So you were lying to that woman?"

"Stretching the truth, and in the end no harm done. I'm sure she'll be regaling her friends with tales of wickedness in New York for years."

"What if she had called an usher?"

"Then I guess we would have had to leave," Dan replies.

19

FINALS

Final exams make the end of the semester the most stressful time of year. I can't begin to think about Christmas until my last blue book is handed in. Laura, Melissa, and even Deirdre are all wound tighter than a bobcat's tail. OK, that makes no sense, but I'm way too tired and too stressed to think of a better metaphor.

Everyone's trying to catch up on all the studying they didn't do and term papers they didn't write for the first eleven weeks of the semester, which means at least one of my roommates is in the room pretty much all the time. Consequently I can't use Dan's present, and I am missing him something fierce. This is the longest I have been without sex since, well, the beginning of the semester now that I think about it. Funny how easy it is to get used to regular sex, and how you miss it when it's suddenly taken away. Nineteen years with as close to no sex as is mathematically possible didn't seem like any great burden, but after three months of having it, then having it suddenly cut off (at my own request, damn it) I'm climbing the walls.

Maybe I shouldn't have been so hasty to take a couple of weeks off, but it's too late to change my mind now. Dan said he was going to take the opportunity to visit some friends in Boston, so even if I hopped the train down for a quickie he wouldn't be there.

It's not only the sex I miss. Sleeping alone is lonely. Even though my bottom bunk is barely big enough for one person, it feels like there's a huge Dan-sized hole next to me every night. It's worst in the early morning hours when I'm lying awake listening to Laura snore and watching the shadows cast on the wall by an occasional passing car outside.

I'm not the only one who's punchy either. Laura and Melissa almost come to blows over a hairbrush. It's not even a nice hairbrush, just a ninety-nine cent piece of pink, plastic junk from a closeout store on Fordham Road. The fight is loud enough that the RA knocks on our door to ask us if we're OK.

The simple truth is that four girls is two too many for one room. In the end, we make it through finals week without any involuntary roommate switches, and only Deirdre has to take an incomplete. Laura and Melissa make up over beer.

My finals wouldn't be that hard, except that I have two the first day, two the second, and one the third, the last one being the dreaded organic chem. The exam takes three full hours, and this time I do use them all. The final isn't harder or more complex than the midterms, but it covers the entire semester. Thank God for reading days, or I never could have crammed all the formulas into my head in time.

By Wednesday afternoon, I'm done with organic chemistry until next semester, and I am studied out. That's when the flu decides to invade my overworked body, and my temperature spikes to 101. I should be a good scientist and report that in Celsius instead but I'm too sick to do the math, and it's not as high a priority as making sure I reach the bathroom in time.

This happened to me right after finals last December too, and at the end of the Spring semester. I may be detecting a pattern here. My body can only function so long on Entenmann's cookies, Manhattan Special Coffee Soda, and Diet Coke before it rebels. I spend the next thirty-six hours in bed. Laura and Deirdre smuggle Cheerios and bananas out of the cafeteria for me, but I barely touch them.

I make one, half-conscious call to Dan's office from the hall phone to tell him I'm staying on campus a little longer than planned. Miss

Parenton, his secretary, takes the message. More time to make up later, but somehow I don't think holding my hair back while I vomit in his toilet is how Dan wants to spend his time; or, for that matter, how I want him to think of me. Despite the surprising amount of alcohol I consume when I'm with him, so far I've managed to avoid puking in his bathroom. I'd like to keep it that way.

By the time I'm recovered enough to brave the 4 train again, it's almost time to go back home to Pennsylvania. I briefly imagine skipping Christmas and spending the holiday in New York. From my mother's phone calls, I don't think things are in great shape at home. Dad still isn't working. Per her reports, he sits in his recliner in the living room watching the Weather Channel all day. Mom's taken a temporary job in the Men's department at Sears for the holidays. Finally, both my nephews have been diagnosed with some psychological condition I've never heard of, but which requires expensive medication their insurance doesn't cover. I knew there was something wrong with those two!

This is all family drama I could do without, but the dorms are closed over Christmas. If I don't come home, my parents might start to wonder where I'm living, another question I can't have them asking. So I shove enough dirty laundry for a couple of weeks into my father's old Army duffel bag, add a few plastic tchotchkes I picked up on Fordham Road to stick under the tree, and throw it over my back for the hike to the 4 train.

The duffel bag is so heavy I walk like a hunchback up Bedford Park, then drop the bag at the foot of the stairs and drag it up to the platform. I should have done my shopping back in Easton, or maybe not brought all my dirty laundry to wash at home. Either that or taken my mother up on her offer to get my father to drive out and pick me up. Honestly, I think she just wanted him out of the house. However, I do want to see Dan one more time before New Year's, so I told her I'd take the bus.

At least it isn't snowing. The temperature is just high enough to turn last week's leftover snow into black slush, the kind that looks like pavement until you step in it. By the time I hump my overstuffed duffel out of the elevator into Dan's apartment, I'm soaked in sweat that has frozen and thawed and frozen again and is now starting to thaw one final time. Whoever said New York looked beautiful in the snow never tried to drag a fifty pound sack three blocks through a slushy Manhattan. I feel like a drowned hood rat.

Dan takes one look at me. "Bath, now," he says.

"And hello to you too."

"Now," he repeats.

"Fine," I say, and drop the bag to the floor, rattling a fancy antique side table that probably cost more than everything I'm carrying put together. "I'll take a bath."

———

As my naked body relaxes in the warm water, I start to let go of some of the tension of the last few weeks. In hindsight, a bath was a pretty good idea, maybe exactly what I needed. I'll have to remember to thank Dan for thinking of it. I haven't had a bath in I'm not sure how long. The dorm only has showers, and the water there only has two settings: lobster and vichyssoise. You can't appreciate the true luxury of fully functional plumbing in a private bath until you share a communal shower with a hall full of sophomores for a semester.

Like everything else Dan owns, his bathtub is outsized. Melissa and I could share it without even getting into any weird lesbian positions and—woah, where did that come from? OK, I'm clearly a little too relaxed. Let's focus on the task at hand. Where's the soap?

There's a glass jar full of little purple rocks on the side of the tub. Maybe it's bubble bath? I scoop out a handful of pebbles, toss them in, and am rewarded with a pleasant lavender scent. Not bubble bath, bath salts.

"Salt: an ionic compound formed by the neutralization reaction of an acid and a base," my mind recites before I can stop it. I guess I haven't lost all the crap I crammed in for the exam yet.

There's a knock at the door, and it opens a crack.

"Are you indecent yet?" Dan asks through the door.

He doesn't wait for a reply, but steps in uninvited. He's still fully clothed in jeans and a black T-shirt. He moves to about a foot away from the edge of the tub, then stands there looking down at me and smiling.

Self-consciously I cross my arms over my chest. Why couldn't I find the bubble bath?

Dan sits down on the edge of the tub, a little behind me, and starts to stroke my hair. "I thought by now you'd be used to being naked with me."

"With you, yes; for you, no."

"What's the difference?"

He runs a finger down my back, and I shiver involuntarily, but I don't take my arms off my chest.

"It's different when we're together."

Dan reaches around and pulls my hands away from my chest. My nipples are painfully, embarrassingly, hard. Why does my body respond to him like this?

"Aren't we together now?" he asks, his voice deep and warm, as his fingers slowly massage my areolas.

Oh God, I've been away from him for too long. I can feel it rising up in me already. I don't think it would take more than a touch in the right spot to send me over the edge.

I clench my fists tight and grit out a response. "It's different when you're naked too."

"Is that all? That's easily remedied."

He stands up, and in less time it takes me to take off a lab coat, he's stripped down. Unlike me, he has absolutely no shame. From this angle I have a better than normal view of his penis. He's half-erect already and it's growing as I watch. I blush and turn my head away.

Dan steps into the tub, then slides down behind me so his thick legs encircle mine. He wraps one arm across my breasts and pulls me against him. I can feel him pressing in the small of my back.

"Is this better?" he whispers in my ear. It's all I can do to exhale in response. Has the water gotten warmer or is it me?

He reaches his other hand down and puts it between my legs and strokes up, and I can no longer hold on. I too forget about my nakedness and relax into the warmth.

———

I WISH we could stay in the bath until June, but nothing lasts forever, not even (especially) sex. Despite a lot of enthusiastic friction and shared body heat, the water does eventually grow tepid. If I'm to have any hope of getting to Easton before midnight, I have to be on my way. Dan offers to drive me, but why I'm showing up in a Lexus with a man twice my age is a conversation I am so not ready to have with my parents.

I tell Dan he doesn't have to see me off, but I'm secretly grateful when he insists on accompanying me to the bus station, and not only because he tosses my overstuffed bag over his shoulder like it's filled with stuffed animals and marshmallow fluff. The Port Authority has always made me nervous. It is virtually impossible to walk a hundred feet without at least one incredibly creepy dude either:

1. Asking me if I need a place to stay.
2. Expressing his appreciation for my womanly parts in graphic detail, then calling me a bitch or worse when I ignore him and keep walking.
3. Grabbing my arm and insisting on protecting me from previous creepy dude.

Today, however, hanging on Dan's arm, I am miraculously unaccosted. It's like he exudes a bubble of protection that other predators know not to test.

I'm afraid Dan will want a final quickie in the men's room, but for once he's on his best behavior. We kiss our goodbyes outside gate 309.

One silver lining to the general skeeviness of the Port Authority: unlike Radio City, no one here looks twice at a man deep kissing a girl young enough to be his daughter, though I do think the homeless guy sitting on the stairs may be touching himself.

"I'll be back at New Year's," I promise.

"New Year's Eve," Dan corrects. "I have a party to attend. I expect you to be there."

"New Year's Eve," I confirm. On impulse, I close my eyes and wrap my arms around him, laying my head against his chest. He reciprocates, and for a minute we stand like that, holding each other and saying nothing like two commuter statues.

Dan breaks the silence. "Your bus is here."

I nod. I don't want to let go, but it's time. Easton awaits. Reluctantly, I release him. He tosses my bag over his shoulder and escorts me through the door to the side of the bus where the driver is loading up luggage. He hands the driver my duffel, who slides it into the bottom of the bus. I give him one final peck on the cheek before I climb the stairs and look for an empty window seat on the left side of the bus. It takes me a couple of minutes to find one. I look out the window into the neon lit corridor for one last glimpse, but Dan has already gone.

20

HOME AGAIN

The commuters who usually pack the Easton bus must have already knocked off for the holidays because for once I get two seats to myself. It's nice to look out the window without being squeezed in next to some sweaty accountant. The ride from New York City to Easton takes about two hours, and I thought I might use the time to read something fun; that is, not Chaucer or Organic Chemistry. I borrowed a paperback romance from Deirdre, the kind we'd get sent to detention for bringing to class in eighth grade. It's the first non-school reading I've had time for in months. However, when I get to the bottom of page two and realize I have no idea what I just read, then read it again and still don't know what happened. I slip it back in my purse. I guess I'm too nervous about what's waiting for me at home to lose myself in escapist fiction. Instead, I gaze out the out the window into the night and watch the exits roll by.

This semester was the longest stretch of time I've been away from home in my life. Freshman year I went home almost every month, at least for a weekend. Of course, that was before I had Dan demanding all my free time and a few days extra. Not like I haven't enjoyed my time with him, but I do feel guilty that I haven't been home for so long. I know money's tight for my parents right now so it's probably good that I wasn't there to be an extra mouth to feed, but four months is a long time and I know they miss me.

Mom kept saying everything was OK. I shouldn't worry, but I could hear the anxiety underneath her voice. She's worried about my father. The couple of times she got him to come to the phone, he grunted his hellos before handing it back to her.

———

MOM USUALLY PICKS me up at the Greyhound station, but tonight my father is waiting for me when I step off the bus.

"Dad!" I grab him in a big hug and let him wrap his arms around me as I nestle in.

"Good to see you too." He kisses me on the cheek and pats me on the shoulder. "Come on, princess. Let's get your bags."

As we wait for the driver to open the luggage compartment, I smile. I was so worried about him, but he looks a lot better than my mother has been leading me to believe.

He launches into the usual dad questions. "So how's New York been treating you? I hope you aren't finding any worms in the Big Apple."

He seems to think that's a joke so I smile. "School's good. Exams went OK." That's an understatement. I crushed them.

"How are your roommates? Laura, Melissa. Who's the other one? I can't keep track of their names. Do you like having all those roommates? You were practically an only child growing up. Are you all getting along?"

"Her name's Deirdre. And yes, they're all fine." While we wait for the bus driver to unload the bags, I give him a summary of the semester, suitably edited for parental consumption. He doesn't need to know about Deirdre's pregnancy scare or the homeless guy who got caught living in the Hughes Hall boiler room.

Finally, the driver heaves my duffel bag out onto the concrete. I reach for it but Dad stops me and takes it. I grit my teeth while waiting to see if he'll collapse under it, but he grunts and lifts it off the ground without herniating himself.

"What do you have in here, Jenni? Half the books in the library?"

"You don't have to take that. I carried it from Fordham to the station," minus an intermediate stop I'm not going to tell him about.

"The car isn't far. Come on," he says, and he's off. I guess he still thinks of me as his little girl going to sleep-away camp for the first time. OK, I can be his little girl for a week. It might even be a relief.

It's only ten minutes from the bus station to our house, at least without traffic, and there's never any traffic in Easton. Dad tunes the radio to some sappy Christmas songs and hums along when "It's The Most Wonderful Time Of The Year" starts playing. He's always been a sucker for Andy Williams. Me, I want to shove lab stoppers in my ears when I hear Moon River.

"You seem like you're in a good mood," I say.

"Things are looking up. I meant to ask, do you need some money for Christmas shopping?"

"No, Dad, I'm fine. I got most of my shopping done already. Anyway, I don't want to be taking money from you."

"Don't worry about that. Everything's going to be fine. My old college friend Barry—you remember him?"

I nod. Bald, smells like Listerine, and drinks too much at my parents' July 4th barbecue every year, after which he invariably puts his hand in my hair and makes some inane comment about how tall I'm getting. He's been doing it since I was eight. How could I forget?

"Barry's offered me a job managing his Utica office, but we don't want to move so I'm holding out for something local. I have some interviews lined up in the New Year. One of them will pan out."

"That's nice," I reply, "But I know Mom's worried about money."

"We took care of that. Your Mom has a temporary job at the mall. Did she tell you that?"

"She mentioned it."

"More importantly, we closed a generous refinance on the house. That'll tide us over until I find something. Anyway, this is all grown up stuff, sweetie. I don't want you to worry about it."

"OK." But I do worry. Dad's protests to the contrary, if money weren't tight, I don't think Mom would be working at the mall. If I can get through school without taking any more money from them, that will be my contribution to the family finances.

"Oh, look, here we are." He pulls into the driveway.

I smile when I see that our house is, yet again, decorated with the only purple, green, and gold Christmas lights in the city of Easton. He must have bought them at a Mardi Gras closeout sale.

Dad insists on carrying my overstuffed bag into the house. I stand outside for a few seconds to admire the lights. I'm looking forward to relaxing and just being a daughter for a change, not super study girl or sexy party girl, which is what my life in New York feels divided into these days. I'm relieved that Dad's recovered from the funk Mom's been telling me about for months and has some good prospects, but I think I should wait until he actually has a new job before I let him give me any money.

21

CHRISTMAS DAY

Christmas morning dawns clear, cold, and cheery. Despite his upbeat holiday mood, Dad's still unemployed. Mom's temporary job at the mall will be over come the New Year, so we're economizing. We decided to forego stockings, and instead of the usual seven foot Scotch fir, a plastic mini-tree sits in the living room. Nonetheless, a small stack of gift-wrapped boxes surrounds it.

We wait to open presents until my sister Janine arrives with her husband and their two sons, my nephews. She went away to college about the time I learned to talk, so we've never been the closest of sisters, but I love being an aunt.

Around 11:00 a.m. Janine and Mike pull into the driveway. Almost before the SUV has stopped, Brian and Alex are out of the back seat and racing up the front steps to see what Grandma and Grandpa and Aunt Jenni bought them. Brian is seven and Alex is five, old enough to know what Christmas is and young enough not to be self-conscious about wanton greed.

Usually I'm crap at picking presents for the boys—last year I bought them stuffed hippopotamuses they didn't even bother to bring home—but this year Dan helped me choose. I bought them each a plastic ray gun that lights up with real electric sparks. It seemed a little violent, but Dan promised me they'd love them.

Brian unwraps his toy and screams, "Yes! A gun!"

"What do you say to Aunt Jenni, Brian?" chides Janine.

"Thanks, Aunt Jenni," says Brian with genuine enthusiasm for once. He aims the gun at his brother and pulls the trigger, then almost drops it in surprise when it buzzes and shoots sparks in his hand.

"Wow," he says, staring at the lethal (to our eardrums) weapon. "This is the coolest."

He fires at his brother again. "You're dead, Alex!"

"Am not!"

"Are too."

Rather than continue the argument, Alex drops the present he was unwrapping (clothes) and finds his equally sized box from Aunt Jenni. He rips the paper off, and before you can say Han Solo the two of them are racing around the house buzzing and flashing at each other.

I smile and whisper a silent thank you to Dan, my interpreter of the mysteries of the Y chromosome. He knows what little boys like.

With some effort, Janine manages to corral her offspring and confiscate their weaponry. They give the guns up grudgingly and only after she promises that they can play with them later outside.

After the boys have torn through the rest of their presents, Brian plays Santa, bringing each of us our gifts in turn, then waiting to watch us open them. I get a pretty, violet, wool sweater from Mom and Dad and a box of floppy disks from Mike and Janine. I bought Dad new handkerchiefs and Mom a silk scarf that Dan helped me pick out. She oohs when she opens it. I'm killing it this Christmas.

It's a light Christmas, but that's cool. I'm happy just to be with my family. I'm old enough not to need a big stack of toys to know my parents love me.

I'm reflecting on how nice this all is, when Brian pipes up. "Here's another present for you, Aunt Jenni."

"Who's it from dear?" says Mom.

I take the small box from Brian's eager hand. It's wrapped in gold foil paper, with a filigreed card with only my name on it. I eye it suspiciously. "I don't know. It doesn't say."

"Must be Santa Claus," says my father with a twinkle in his eye.

"Or Jenni has a secret admirer," cracks Mike.

I shoot him an evil look. I do not want anyone asking me questions about my love life today.

Carefully, I pull the flaps of the wrapping paper open and slide a little blue box out. Janine gasps.

I lift the lid off the box, and inside, nestled on cotton, is a silver necklace. I lift it out and drape it between my fingers. Suspended from the chain are three small diamonds followed by a large pear-shaped ruby nestled in smaller diamonds. Wow. I hold it out in front of me so everyone can see.

"It's beautiful. Thank you."

"Don't look at me," says my father. "It came in the mail a few days ago. No return address. The instructions said not to give it to you until Christmas. Do you know who it's from?"

"A friend," I extemporize, "at school, I think."

I smile and slip the necklace over my head, then tuck the pendant under my blouse. I can guess who sent it, but I'm not going to tell them. I'm not really a jewelry girl, but it's nice that he remembered me on Christmas. Maybe I'm not his one and only, but he does care about me, at least a little.

Before any more awkward questions can be asked, Alex grabs his ray gun off the table where Janine laid them down and starts shooting. "Zap zap. You're dead Brian."

Brian dives behind the couch and returns fire.

We all laugh and the necklace is momentarily forgotten. Still, I'm going to have to have a talk with Dan about being more discreet around my family.

———

WHILE DAD and Mike take the boys outside to play Star Trek or Star Wars or whatever it is they're pretending to be, Janine and I retire to the kitchen to help get dinner ready. Mom's on the back porch inspecting the turkey roasting on the gas grill. Janine chops celery for the stuffing while I mash the potatoes. If it were up to me we'd have instant, but Dad insists on only fresh potatoes for the holidays, lumps and all. Probably because he's not the one who has to mash them.

My hands are getting tired from whipping the potatoes so I pause and finger the necklace for a moment. I'll call Dan later to thank him. I hope he has someone to be with today. He has tons of friends, but he never talks about his family, at least not with me.

I start to whip again, a little more vigorously this time, when out of nowhere Janine says, "So how old is he?"

My face goes as white as the potatoes and my hands freeze on the beater, several seconds too long to be believed when I finally say, "What are you talking about?"

"Don't kid me, little sis. College boys don't give their girlfriends necklaces from Tiffany's, not even the rich ones."

"It's not that expensive," I reply. I start frantically whipping the potatoes.

"I know diamonds when I see them," says Janine. "That chain had enough diamonds to make Imelda Marcos think twice before buying it. And don't try to change the subject. How old is he?"

"Thirty-five." I look intently at the potatoes.

"Not quite as old as I would have guessed. Is he married?"

I look up in horror. "No, of course not!"

Janine throws me a look that says she doesn't believe me.

"No, really. He's not. I promise."

Janine sighs. "Word of advice. Next time he wants to give you an expensive present, real estate appreciates better than jewelry."

"It's not like that. He—" I begin to object, but then I stop. Of course it is exactly like that. Dan treats me well and buys me things, but it means nothing to him. The necklace is a rounding error on his credit card statement. I'm just another thing he's bought, like the art on his walls, or his fancy car he barely ever takes out of the garage.

The necklace I was so happy to get suddenly feels tawdry and tarnished, another payment on the installment plan.

"Do you think Mom and Dad know?" I ask, biting my lip.

"I don't think Mom got a good look, and Dad, well men never know anything about jewelry. But you probably ought to keep that thing tucked away until you go back to New York."

"Got it," I say. I return to mashing the potatoes.

"So how long has this been going on?"

"Since September. We met on campus."

"So you're still new then."

"Jenni, I understand, I do. You're young. You're having fun, and it feels like it's never going to end, but you're still in the honeymoon phase. It's all champagne and roses and fancy necklaces and I love yous."

She's wrong about the last one. That is one thing we never say, but I don't think telling her that would help make my case.

Janine continues. "Enjoy it while you can. Just don't let yourself get in too deep, OK?"

"It isn't like that," I say, but my voice is lacking conviction.

Janine sighs again. She puts down her chopping knife and comes over to me. "You've always acted so mature, I forget how young you are sometimes. How many boyfriends have you had? Since puberty. Grammar school doesn't count."

"One," I say.

"And how long did it last?"

"It's still going on."

"Not Mr. 35?"

"Yes."

"Oh God, Jenni, is he, was he, your first?"

I don't say anything, but my face must answer the question because Janine puts her arms around me. "Oh Jenni, I'm so sorry."

I was feeling pretty good, but Janine is making me feel like shit. How stupid am I? "It's OK," I finally say in a monotone that betrays my true feelings. "I like him. He's nice to me. No one else was."

Janine takes my head in her hands and looks straight into my eyes. "Jenni, listen to me. I know you're technically an adult now, but you're not experienced enough to see what's going on. This man doesn't love you. He's taking advantage of you. For now you're new enough to keep him interested, but six months is about how long it takes a man to get bored with the sex. Then he's going to drop you and move on to some other girl. I've seen it a dozen times. I'm sorry to be the one to tell you this, but you need to be ready. I don't want you doing something stupid like dropping out of school when he breaks up with you."

It's like Janine is putting all my worst fears into words, the ones that come to me when I'm alone in the middle of the night. I'm trying to hold back tears. I am not going to start crying on Christmas. "If he breaks up with me, I have to drop out of school. I can't afford it otherwise."

Janine raises an eyebrow. "I thought Mom and Dad were paying?"

"They were, some, but then Dad got laid off and my financial aid got cut."

Janine puts a sisterly arm around me and hugs me to her side. "I didn't realize things had gotten that bad. Look, I don't know what to tell you. I wish Mike and I could loan you the money, but with the boys—"

"It's OK," I interrupt. "I'll be fine. I'm taking care of it. I've taken care of it."

Janine sighs. "If things go bad, you know you can always come to me, right? We don't have to tell Mom and Dad."

Before she can say anything else or I can think of what to say to her, Mom comes back inside. So Janine knows. Someone had to find out eventually. I couldn't expect to keep it hidden forever. At least it wasn't Mom. Talking about your problems is supposed to make you feel better, but I just feel worse. While Mom chats with Janine about the stuffing, I take out my frustration on the potatoes. Handmade or not, there are going to be no lumps this year.

22

THE DRESS

I spend the remainder of Christmas break obsessing over what Janine said. It's not her fault. It wouldn't have hit me so hard if I didn't already believe it myself on some level. I'm Dan's toy of the moment, not the love of his life.

But in the end there's nothing else I can do. I'm trapped. So New Year's Eve, I'm on the 11:00 a.m. bus back to New York. Some friends of Dan's are throwing a big party, and he wants me on his arm.

He promised me it's going to be nothing like Halloween, thank God. Even so, I'm still nervous. A lot of people older than me who know how to act and behave while I stand by the wall and try not to look too awkward.

Who knows? Maybe it will be fun. Before now my New Years experience consists of staying up late to watch the ball drop on TV. At least I'll have someone other than my dad to kiss at midnight.

The dorms don't open for another three weeks, but I tell my parents that I'm going to visit Melissa in Westchester. I don't think they'll check up on me but, just in case, I call Melissa and make sure she's prepped.

"You're spending New Years with him, Jenni? And the next two weeks? That's almost living with this guy. Are you sure you're ready for that?"

Oh Melissa, if you only knew. "It's not that serious." I'm not sure how big a lie that is, or for who. "If my mother calls you, say I'm in the shower or went out to the store, and I'll call her back. Can you do that?"

"Of course, Jenni. If you need a break, I could hop the train down into the city one day. We could go window shopping."

"Thanks, I'll let you know, OK?"

Hanging with Melissa in the city does sound like fun. Dan's going to have to work a lot of the time, and it would be nice to have company besides my organic chemistry textbook. Only, then she'd want to see where I'm staying, and one look at the apartment and she'd know immediately what was going on. Maybe I can come up with a plausible story why she can't meet Dan before the semester starts.

Or maybe I should just tell her. All this sneaking around is starting to wear on me. I think she'd be cool with my arrangement if anyone would. I can't imagine telling Laura. I can hear her now: "Jenni, he's too old for you. When he gets tired of you he's going to dump you like yesterday's garbage. Why would anyone buy the cow when they can get the milk for free?"

OK, Laura probably wouldn't say the cow thing, but she'd think it. And, of course, Dan's not getting the milk for free, is he? He's paying rather a lot for it, even if I wish he wasn't. So should I tell Melissa the whole truth?

No, at least not yet. I've been keeping her in the dark for months now. It's gone on too long. So for now I guess I'm going to keep it on the down low, and pray Melissa doesn't pry too much.

———

DAN WANTED to send a driver to pick me up at the Port Authority, but I begged off. If he'd offered to come himself, I would have taken him up on it; I suppose that was too much to hope. However much time

I've spent with Dan I'm still not comfortable with servants. The pudgy doorman in his building makes me feel like the little match girl asking for an audience with the queen. Thank God, Dan doesn't have live-in help.

I can get across town by myself, overfull duffle bag and all. I've been in the city for more than a year now, if you count living on a dorm on campus as "in the city." And it's the middle of the day. I should be able to take the subway without being kidnapped.

And what do you know? I make it to Dan's apartment without breaking an ankle or even being hit on by a homeless guy. Seriously, when I'm not with Dan I can't walk two blocks in this city without at least one smelly dude who hasn't shaved since 1983 trying to pick me up. Do I give out an odor of little lost lamb or what?

When I arrive, Dan is lying on the couch in casual slacks and sock feet, reading a book. He looks like one of those models in the Land's End catalog, and I look like a bag lady. The combination of icy slush on the streets and burning heat in the subway does that to me. Maybe next time I will let him send a driver.

"Why don't you take a hot shower?" he suggests. "You'll feel better."

"So you want me out of these clothes, do you?" I try to imitate the smirk he gives when he's feeling randy. "Why, whatever for, Mr. Cortland?"

Dan surprises me with his answer. "I had a new dress sent over for you to wear tonight. You should try it on while there's still time to get it altered."

"You can get a dress altered on New Year's Eve?"

"For another—" he glances at his Rolex "—three hours. Barneys will stay open for me if they have to, but I'd rather not ask them. So chop, chop."

"OK, OK, I'm going." I unlace my boots and head to the shower.

Have I told you about Dan's master bathroom yet? It's bigger than my dorm room, and about a thousand times fancier. The tiling is immaculate. The mirrors sparkle with the world's most flattering gold-tinged light, not too dim to see anything, not so bright I can see every pore. All the fixtures are brass and work perfectly. The toilet is discretely hidden away in a separate room.

And the shower. Oh my God, the shower. Utter bliss. Thick, pulsing, hot water to massage your body, and big enough for two as I've had occasion to find out more than once. Probably big enough for three, but let's not go there. It is the complete opposite of the communal bathrooms in Hughes Hall, with their grody tiling, low pressure shower heads that drip tepid water, and drains that clog so quickly you're standing in a puddle of dirty water no matter how fast you finish.

As the warm, soothing water washes over me, my body relaxes. God, it feels good. Forget the tuition. Some days I think I'd date Dan for his shower alone. I close my eyes and tilt my head up into the spray. I don't want to go to heaven if it means I have to leave Dan's shower behind.

It's scary how comfortable I feel here. I thought home would be a nice break, but I was walking on eggshells the whole week. I'm not a good liar. Every time my mother asked me if I had met anyone at school I had to change the subject. I only survived because she was so busy with her mall job. At least Janine kept her promise not to tell our parents.

I take as long in the shower as I can get away with. I half expect Dan to slip in behind me, but he stays annoyingly, frustratingly in the front of the apartment. I think about taking care of myself with the shower massager, but I know he'd prefer me to wait for him. I guess he was serious about wanting me to try on the new dress before we get too distracted.

With a bit of regret, I turn off the water and step out. I towel myself off. Did I mention the towels? Dan has the most amazing towels, as long as I am tall and really, really thick. Before Dan, I didn't know such towels existed. I wrap it around myself and step into the bedroom.

The dress is laid out on the bed. It's a dark blue, almost black gown that should reach my ankles. I don't recognize the name on the label, though Melissa might and would probably turn three shades of green if she did. Dan doesn't skimp on clothes. I'll keep it in my closet here. I can't take it back to school. It's not like there are a lot of formal events at Fordham. The Screw Your Roommate Dance doesn't count, even if half the girls do wear prom dresses to it.

I slip the dress on and adjust it in front of the mirror. It's ankle length and surprisingly sedate for Dan's tastes. Barely any cleavage at all, and only a little skin in the back. Quite elegant in fact. I add the black pumps he bought for me last October, then turn around, admiring myself in the mirror from different angles. Needs some underwear but, otherwise, it fits perfectly. I'm glad Dan won't be asking some poor tailor to stay late on New Year's Eve on my account. I like the way it makes me look adult and sophisticated but still cute. Such a change from the jeans and sweats I'd wear if I were left to my own choices and budget. I still need to do my hair and makeup, but looking at myself like this for a moment I can almost see what Dan sees in me.

"Come on out. Show me how it fits," Dan yells from the living room, so I scurry out to show him.

"So what do you think?" I turn around and arch my back so he gets the best view of my butt. "Does it meet with your approval?"

Dan considers for a minute. "Add the necklace. It goes with the dress, and most of the other women will be wearing diamonds too."

"Oh, the necklace."

"You did get my present?"

"Yes, thank you. Only..."

"Only what?"

"I wish you hadn't."

"If you don't like it, we can take it back, get you something else. Though you should probably still wear it tonight."

"No, it's pretty." Really pretty, actually. "But getting expensive gifts from you makes me feel cheap." My economics professor would disagree, but somehow getting paid in jewelry instead of tuition makes it worse.

"Trust me. That necklace was anything but cheap."

"My sister Janine was there when I unwrapped it, and she figured out what was going on."

Dan cocks an eyebrow. "Really? Just from the necklace? I'm impressed. Your sister sounds like a pretty sharp woman."

"I may have confirmed a little more than I should have. I'm not a very good liar."

"Don't be ashamed of that, Jenni. You're very open. It's not hard to tell what you're feeling. That's one of the things I like about you."

Unlike you I could reply, but instead I say, "She doesn't think this is a good idea."

"Why not?"

"She thinks you're going to get tired of me and dump me."

Dan laughs and jumps up to grab me in his arms. I let myself fall onto the couch with him, but I keep my head turned away. He pulls me into him, and I can feel him pressing into me. "Does it feel like I'm getting tired of you?"

I don't tell him that Janine put a time limit on his attention. Six months, she said, and we're a few days past the three month mark. Three months left. Three months to enjoy the financial support and nice clothes and dining out in fancy places I could never imagine on my own. And the sex. Oh God, the sex.

If I can make it to the end of the semester, I can find the money for next year, somehow. But can I ever find another man to replace him? I look into his blue eyes. I take in his half-shaven stubbled chin, the curly hair drifting over his face, the deep scent of him, the way his arms wrap around me like a strong, warm harness. So completely unlike any of the boys I've known. He can't be the only one, but he may be the only one for me. If he lets me go, will I recover?

There's nothing I can do about it, so I don't try. "No more expensive jewelry, please?"

"OK," Dan says, though I can tell he doesn't really understand.

His fingers begin to wander. "Now that we know the dress fits, I suppose we ought to get you out of it. You don't want to mess it up before the party."

He pulls the zipper down in back as his other hand meanders up my thigh. I smile. This I can handle.

23

NEW YEAR'S EVE

We arrive at Dan's friend's building a little after ten and wow. I mean, WOW. I thought Dan's apartment was spectacular, but this place makes his apartment look like a medium-sized dorm room in St. Johns. I didn't know anybody had this much space in Manhattan. Hell, I don't know anyone who has this much space in Pennsylvania.

A butler, an honest to God butler with a British accent and everything, takes our coats. I wonder if he's full time or if they hired him for the party? A place this size probably needs a small army of servants just to clean the curtains. Dan has a maid service that comes in and cleans during the week when I'm not around, and he doesn't even let them in half the apartment. He prefers to maintain his privacy.

There must be more than a hundred people here already. The men are mostly wearing black tie like Dan, though a few rebels wear business suits instead. The women are dressed in evening gowns that cling to their stick-thin, blonde bodies like they were born in them. Their heels reach halfway to my knee. All are older than me, though perhaps averaging a few years younger than the men. Nonetheless, I am by far the youngest guest. A Fordham kegger this isn't.

I scan the room, looking for a punch bowl I can hide behind. Old habits die hard. Of course there isn't one, though there are bars on either side of the room where black-clad waiters pour drinks. Other waiters circulate through the room with trays of food.

"Who are these people?" I whisper to Dan, not that anyone would hear me if I shouted. The auditorium sized room is awash with noisy chatter, and a tango trio is playing on the far side.

"Friends, colleagues," he replies. "Don't worry. They'll like you."

I hope so. If Dan buys and sells companies, these people must buy and sell countries.

"Daniel!" a woman cries from across the room. Moments later a middle-aged, but very well preserved lady in a glittering cream ball gown sweeps across the floor toward us. I'm not sure how old she is, somewhere between Dan and social security, I estimate. Thick layers of expertly-applied makeup conceal her true age.

She plants a dry kiss on each of Dan's cheeks. "I'm so glad you could come, and who's this lovely young lady?" she asks, looking at me for the first time. "I don't believe we've had the pleasure."

"Georgia, allow me to introduce Jennifer McGrath. Jennifer, this is Georgia Duplessis, our hostess."

I'm not sure what the protocol is for meeting Manhattan royalty. I almost feel like I should curtsy, but instead I hold out my hand. Georgia clasps it with both of hers.

"Well now, let me get a look at you. Tell me, Jennifer, are you the one who's finally going to make a respectable man out of our Daniel here, or are you just for the evening?"

I don't think she intends to be mean, but my heart almost stops anyway. Dan wouldn't have told her, would he?

"Georgia, be nice," he says. "Jennifer's a very good friend. Let's not interrogate her."

"No matter," she says. "Tonight, we dance. Come you two. There are some people I want you to meet."

———

DAN IS ACTUALLY the life of the party, the complete opposite of my "hide behind the punchbowl" self. Chatting here with a Frenchman from the UN about wine, there with a city councilwoman about school policy and college scholarships. He works the room like a maestro, making everyone feel like he's their best friend.

I don't know why I'm surprised by this. Clearly, he didn't get where he is in life by hiding out in his apartment and yelling at people on the phone. Nonetheless, this is a side of him I don't usually get to see since we're rarely with other people during our time together. Until now he's mostly kept me to himself. I'm not sure what it means that he's decided to show me off tonight.

Sometime before midnight we find ourselves listening to a sweaty little pig man named Blauer declaim about the significance of "verbal art," whatever that is. He name drops a bunch of artists I'm not sophisticated enough to have heard of, my one semester of art history notwithstanding. He's particularly *enthused* (his word, he uses it about once every third sentence) about an artist named Josephus (no last name, just Josephus) who paints words on people's walls in neon blue.

"Josephus would be perfect for your pied-à-terre," he says to Dan. "When Georgia mentioned how unadorned your walls were, I simply couldn't sleep for thinking of the space."

"Is that so?" Dan replies, lifting an eyebrow.

"A unique opportunity such as this to commission a world class artist like Josephus at the nascent phase of his arc comes along rarely. It may already be too late. All Soho is positively *enthused* about his efforts." He puts a weird accent on *enthused* so the word oozes out of his mouth like toothpaste.

"I prefer a more minimalist design," Dan replies.

Blauer takes no notice of the polite brush-off and barrels onward with his sales pitch. "Exactly, and that's why my young protegé would be so perfect for your apartment." He pronounces the last word with four syllables, a-part-eh-man.

"Josephus applies his vision directly to your walls. He's already done Mia's and Yoko's residences and Mary's summer place. They're very *enthused* about him. For Mia, he did 'Sing' and for Yoko 'Act' though really it should be the other way around, shouldn't it?" He titters a little, as if he's made a joke, though frankly I have no idea who or what he's talking about. "Mary is going to have him do a second wall for her, first thing in the New Year. She's so *enthused* about his work."

"Ah, that's unfortunate. I'm afraid the first week is the only time my apartment will be free in the near future."

Blauer is not so easily deterred. "No problem at all. Josephus will only need to visit the space once so he can conceive the proper word to illuminate your lifestyle. It's short notice, but I'm sure he can squeeze you in. His team can prepare the surface and apply his vision at your convenience."

The way he describes it, it sounds charming. I'm confused about something, though, and the champagne has disengaged the filter that normally separates my thoughts from my mouth. "If it's only one word, why does he need a team?"

"Why they do the manual labor, of course. Priming the wall, taping the stencil, spraying the paint and what not. I don't concern myself with those details. One sign painter is much the same as the next." Blauer puts his hand to the side of his mouth and stage whispers like he's about to say something shameful. "They're from the Bronx."

I'm trying to wrap my head around this. "But this Josephus person, are you saying he doesn't actually paint the picture?"

My teachers are fond of saying there are no stupid questions. Judging by the look Blauer gives me he doesn't agree. He tugs at his pink bow tie and turns his piggy little eyes on me for the first time. "And you are?"

"Jenni McGrath."

"Are you an artist, my dear?"

Dan steps in before I can answer. "Ms. McGrath is a very talented young chemist."

OK, that's a slight exaggeration. Getting one A in Organic Chem doesn't make me a chemist, but if Dan says it for me, I suppose it doesn't count as a lie.

"I see. I wouldn't expect a scientist to understand the subtleties of the artistic spirit, my dear. Art is a feeling, a sensation, a small fragment of the imagination committed to physical medium. True art is a representation of the artist's soul. Who touches brush to canvas is an insignificant detail. Is a writer less of a writer if he dictates his work to a secretary? Is a composer not a composer because he hires a copyist?"

I should probably shut up now, but I can't help myself. "But why couldn't Dan hire a sign painter himself if he wants a word on his wall?"

Blauer glares at me.

"I think Miss McGrath has a point," says Dan. He's smiling now. "Why should I pay $10,000 so Josephus can hire a subcontractor to write on my wall? Why not hire the sign painter myself and save $9900?"

"If that's how you feel, you might as well take a photograph and hang it on your wall," retorts Blauer. His face, somewhat pink to start with, has shifted to full-on scarlet.

"Why, what an excellent idea!" says Dan, sticking the needle in a little deeper. "I think that's exactly what I'll do." He turns to Blauer, and does the little bow he does when he's being so overly polite it's almost rude. "Thank you so much for your expert advice. Now I'm afraid we must be leaving so we can get started on this project right away. Come, Jenni," And with that he takes my hand and sweeps me away, leaving Blauer sputtering.

In the next room, I finally lose it and start laughing. "I'm sorry. I shouldn't have said anything. I hope I didn't embarrass you."

"Don't be. The arrogant prig deserved it. There's always one in any crowd. I have to pretend to be nice to these blowhards." Suddenly his voice shifts to a more serious tone, as he takes both my hands in his. "Don't change, Jenni. Don't ever change."

"OK." I wait for him to explain more, but he doesn't. Normally I'd worry about what brought that on. For now I'm buzzed from the champagne, so I roll with it.

———

AFTER MY SET-TO WITH BLAUER, I hang back and let Dan do the talking. I really should not have gotten into that argument. It's not like anyone here is discussing the finer points of school cafeteria food, integral calculus, or anything else I might actually have an informed opinion about. Fortunately, Dan does enough talking for the both of us. I concentrate on my champagne glass, which miraculously refills like the wineskins at Cana.

At one point we join a group discussing the Knicks or the Rangers or some team. I've never followed baseball. Three couples and a priest, and oh my God, I know the priest! It is Father Dewitt, S.J., the president of Fordham. I've met him a couple of times at honors college events, but never like this. What if he recognizes me?

"Daniel!" he says with jolly enthusiasm. "How good to see you in more pleasant circumstances." He's clearly had more New Year's cheer than is wise. Lucky for him the Ram isn't covering the party.

Dan nods politely. "Father."

Dewitt's eyes light on me. "And who is this lovely young lady?" He holds out his hand, and I take it out of politeness. He shows no signs of recognizing me. In fairness, I look nothing like I look on campus. I am the complete opposite of a college student: ball gown, heels, and makeup instead of jeans, sneakers, and an inside out sweatshirt.

"This is my date for the evening, Jennifer McGrath."

"Pleased to meet you, Jennifer."

I mumble some pleasantry that is lost in the general clatter of the room. He's met me at least twice before, but I don't correct him.

"And how do you two know each other?"

My mouth clamps shut and I freeze. He's not being impolite, but this is the worst question he can ask. Dan answers before I have a chance to say something incriminating. "Jennifer and I met a few months back."

It's a reply that answers while actually saying nothing. Dan's good at that. It's a skill I should learn.

Father Dewitt laughs. Yes, he's definitely had too much champagne, not that he's alone in that. "You know the University Church is always available to you if you need it, Daniel."

"I only hope the church will still be there by the time I need it," Dan replies.

The "I" instead of "we" hits me like a punch to the stomach, one I wasn't expecting. I'm surprised how much it hurts. It's not like I was planning on marrying Dan. I didn't think Dan was planning on marrying anyone, but if he is... It hurts to be reminded of just where I stand with him. I gulp down the remainder of my champagne and try to force a smile. Neither Dan nor Father Dewitt is paying any attention to me. Father Dewitt is well lubricated, and Dan is strangely focused on the priest.

Father Dewitt continues, "I'm sure we'll manage. We've been in tough spots before. The economy will turn around soon. I hope you know how much we appreciate your help."

"It's only a bridge," Dan replies. "It won't last forever."

"Ah, but that's to worry about tomorrow. Tonight let us welcome another year." Dewitt raises his glass. "A toast, to better tidings in the New Year."

Dan raises his glass politely, but does not return the toast. He's looking at Father Dewitt, almost disapproving. There's something going on there I don't quite get.

———

YOU CAN'T BUY CHAMPAGNE. You can only rent it. I'm waiting for Dan to return from the washroom in what is either the third or fourth room (I've lost count) bigger than my parents' house. A pianist is playing show tunes on a baby grand in the far corner, or maybe it's a full size piano, and the room makes it look small.

"Shall we dance?" says Dan when he returns. He extends his hand to me. From my seated position, the light shines behind his head like a halo. An angel in a tuxedo, with a glint of the devil in his eye.

I let him take my hand in his. It is, as ever, warm and strong and so much larger than mine. He wraps my hand in his, much as I'm getting wrapped up in him. I want this to go on forever. I'm afraid it won't.

The piano player has moved onto an old song I don't know, but the music doesn't really matter. Couples swirl around the floor in each other's arms. Some of them look like they've been doing this for decades. Some of them look like they're liable to break a hip.

I try to follow as Dan leads. His left hand is on my shoulder, his right in the small of my back so that he can direct me where he wants me to go. The song is slow, and he doesn't try anything fancy as he moves me around the room, our shoes clicking across the hardwood floor, our bodies slowly rotating.

His blue eyes look down at me as I gaze up. The warmth of his hand on my back, the smell of him so close, the gaze. The feeling is too powerful. I look down and break the connection.

"Something wrong?"

"What did you mean by that? You hope the church is there when you need it?" We continue to dance across the floor. Well, he dances. I mostly follow and try to avoid stepping on his toes.

"Nothing for you to worry about. I don't expect I'll need it anyway."

The band hits a sharp note and Dan swings me around, then pulls me in close to him again. I tuck my head down and try not to start crying. Damn it, why am I so upset about this?

"Are you OK? You seem distracted."

I clench my teeth. Should I tell him what's bothering me, or bottle it up and wear a happy mask like he's paying for? If I tell him, will I seem too clingy? In the end, I decide to hide it. "It's nothing. I've just had a little too much to drink."

———

As MIDNIGHT APPROACHES, everyone starts counting down loudly. I'm giddy for no reason in particular. Some of that is probably the champagne. The energy of the room is infectious, even if it is past my bedtime.

Ten. Nine. Eight. Seven. Six. The whole room is joining in now. Even the waiters stop to look at the huge gilded clock hung from the ceiling for the evening. Five. Four. Three. Two. One.

A cry of "Happy New Year!" goes out across the room. The band strikes up one of those sappy old standards you only hear this time of year, and Dan pulls me into him and starts kissing me fervently, right there in front of everyone. I relax and go with it. If he doesn't care who sees us, I don't either. I'm with him and that's all that matters

Someone coughs pointedly in the background, but we ignore them, swept up in our own little world. After a time I can't count, we come up for breath. I'm beaming up at Dan, and he's smiling down at me. I don't care what Janine says. Six months, six years, or six lifetimes, for now I'm happy.

———

THE CLOCK IS TICKING toward 3:00 a.m. The caterers started packing up half an hour ago. Dancing and singing was fun, but I'm ready to go. Dan is probably off somewhere smoking cigars with his fellow masters of the universe in the billiard room. I haven't actually seen a billiard room, but then I haven't seen half of this castle Mrs. Duplessis calls an "apartment." I'm sure there's one somewhere.

I find a plush couch in a room off the main parlor. It's probably a $20,000 designer antique the Medicis had custom made in the Italian Renaissance, but the quality I'm interested in at the moment is that it's soft and comfy looking. I plop myself down and wait for Dan to find me.

I must be sleepier than I thought because the next thing I know, a redheaded woman in pearls and a form fitting green strapless gown is sitting next to me, looking at me. She's stunning, like she stepped out of an airbrushed magazine photo stunning.

"I see you're still together," she says, like we already know each other. "Victoria, is it?"

"Jenni," I reply. I shake my head to clear it of the champagne infused fog. She must have me confused with someone else.

"What is it? Two months now? Three?"

"Huh?"

"Dan. Mr. Cortland. You've been together two months now?"

"Um, three I think," I mumble, too woozy to give a fully coherent answer. She looks familiar. I try to place her face, but there's something missing. She's older than me, but so is everyone here. Most of the women at this party are very well-preserved, but if you look closely you can see the lines and artificially stretched skin beneath the makeup. This woman, however, is, so far as I can tell, doing without artificial assistance. Dark red hair cascades down her shoulders to frame the most stunning green eyes I have ever seen.

"How much?" she asks.

"How much?" I reply, confused.

"How much has he given you?"

"Given me?" I'm still half asleep, and the champagne is playing hackysack with my perceptions.

"I know how he plays the game, dear. What is it this time? Vet bills? Parents' mortgage? Credit card debt?"

There's something scary about this woman. I brace my arms on the shoulders of the couch and with some effort push myself up straight. I shake my head to clear it.

"Excuse me, how do you know Dan? Are you his sister or something?"

"Ha, sister. That's a good one. No, we're much closer than that. Say that I'm an old friend who has his best interests at heart. I've been there since before you, and I'll be there after you're gone. Listen Vicki—"

"Jenni," I correct her, though I don't know why. She's clearly not my friend. She stares at me with those piercing green eyes, as if trying to make up her mind, for the longest minute of my life. I shake my head again to try to fan away the champagne cloud.

She must reach a decision because her face shifts. "OK, have your fun for now. He can afford it. But when it's over, it's over. I'm going to have to pick up the pieces when you leave, and I'm not going to let him get hurt again. Remember that when it ends."

Before I can say anything, she's up and gone. I let out a sigh of relief. I didn't realize I was holding my breath. Questions swirl around my brain, adding to the confusion. Who is she? What's her connection to Dan? How does she know me, or what Dan's and my relationship really is? And what did she mean by she'll be there for him? Does she want him for herself? If she does, I don't see how I can compete.

Too many questions, too much champagne, and too little sleep to have any hope of answering them tonight.

———

"SO DID YOU LIKE THE PARTY?" Dan asks as we're undressing for bed. Surprisingly, no sex for once. We both drank far too much and are way too tired. Is this what it feels like to be married? Dan matched me drink for drink, only he was drinking bourbon instead of champagne.

"It was OK, I guess. A little weird," I reply.

"Weird how?"

"No one talked to me. I didn't know anyone. It felt like a lot of the women there didn't like me."

"A few of the men were checking you out. A couple wanted to know where I found you."

"Really?"

"Really. They left you alone because you were with me. Trust me, if I hadn't been there, the wolves would have been sniffing around you."

I kick off my heels and turn around so Dan can unzip me. "The women could have been nicer though."

"They're threatened by you. You're younger and, in most cases, prettier than they are. They're worried their husbands are going to see you and get ideas, trade them in for a younger model."

OK, that's one way to interpret it. The woman in the green dress didn't seem very threatened though, more like threatening.

"Is that what you're going to do? Trade me in?"

Dan laughs, and hugs me from the side. "Don't be silly," he says as I snuggle up next to him. "Where would I find someone younger than you?"

I know he means it as a joke, but I can't help thinking about what he said to Father Dewitt earlier. "I hope the chapel will still be there when I need it," not "when we need it." And what Janine said. Six months. And three of those are already gone.

24

WINTER BREAK

New Year's morning I wake up before Dan, miraculously without a hangover. I guess it's true what they say. If you don't want to get sick, drink better quality alcohol. New Year's Eve has faded away into a fuzzy memory of bloviating art dealers, drunk priests, and mystery women in green dresses.

Dan must be exhausted from last night. As usual he's sleeping on his back, bare chested. I watch him breathe, the night's shadow on his face before he can shave, his chest moving up and down with his breath.

There's something about him. He's so...big. He's not the tallest guy I know, and he certainly isn't the heaviest, but he's filled out to a point most boys my age are still growing into.

And although you might not know it to look at him, he's hard. (No, not like that! At least not all the time.) His arms are wider around than my legs, and it's not fat either. When I squeeze him, I barely make an impression on his skin. It's like squeezing rock.

When he holds me in his arms, I can tell he's holding back, applying the smallest fraction of his strength, and it still feels like the deepest hug ever. I'm safe in his arms, like armor. Nothing and no one can touch me there.

I prop myself up on my elbow and study him. The soft morning sunlight is streaming through the windows, reflecting off the white sheets and bathing him in a soft glow. He looks so peaceful sleeping there, almost happy. No, that's not the right word. Not happy, but content. He looks content. So different than the determined and driven Dan I'm used to when he's awake.

I'm tempted to reach out a finger and run it through his thick, curly chest hair, but I don't want to wake him. I feel like I could lie here forever watching him, watching my man, this man who wants me.

All too soon he stirs. He reaches an arm out and rubs his eye, then makes a nonverbal noise.

"Good morning," I say.

"Good morning. How long have you been up?"

"A little while. I was enjoying watching you."

"See anything you like?"

I smile. "I did. I like sleeping with you, you know."

He grins. "I've noticed. You're not exactly quiet."

"No, not that. Well, that too, but I do like sleeping with you. Just sleeping. You're warm, and it's nice. When I go back to my dorm it's lonely, not having anyone by my side."

Dan thinks about what I've said for a minute. "You could come over more often, if you're lonely. It doesn't have to be just the weekends."

The idea is tempting, living here in this little bubble, just the two of us. But in the end, it's still a bubble. It's not real. "No, I have classes. And studying to do. It wouldn't work."

I glance out the window and realize it's snowing, the first time this year. Six inches of fresh snow is magic, able to turn the dirtiest, grimiest, pervert infested, mosquito plagued city on the planet into a winter wonderland, at least for a few hours until the plows come and the salt trucks spread their poison across the pure white snow.

"Come on," I say, tugging at his arm. "Let's go play in the snow."

———

I HAVE two more weeks of vacation before the new semester kicks off. Dan doesn't. Wall Street masters of the universe don't get a winter break. I guess that's one thing broke college students have going for them. Night time with Dan is still fun, but it's weird being in his apartment without him.

The apartment doesn't seem quite as large as it did last year now that I've seen what the truly rich can afford, but it's still cavernous compared to Hughes Hall. And empty. Dan keeps it so meticulous, there's barely any evidence anyone lives here when he's not around. It doesn't even smell like him. One afternoon when the silence becomes too challenging, I find myself opening the dirty clothes hamper in the washroom, just so I can smell him and prove to myself he's real.

Everyone I know has gone home for winter break. I think about calling somebody, but Laura, Deirdre, and my parents all think I'm in Pennsylvania. Twice I pick up the phone to call Melissa and invite her down, but both times I put the receiver back without dialing. I don't know why. There was something off the last time we talked. And Janine, I don't think I want her judging me right now, even if—or precisely because—she may be seeing things more clearly than I am.

So I read ahead in my organic chemistry text to prep for next semester. When that gets too mind numbing, I visit the Central Park Zoo or the Museum of Natural History. Both are cluttered and noisy with any number of families and nannies trying to entertain bored children off from school, most of whom would rather be anywhere else.

By the time the dorms open, I surprise myself by being glad to return to my crowded four-bed quad in Hughes Hall where there's never any privacy and always something going on, even if it's an argument about whether we should eat dinner at the cafeteria or the Ramskeller. I like Dan, but two straight weeks of him with no break is a lot for a girl to take. I'll still see him on weekends, and he's promised me something special for Spring Break, but it's time to remember why I'm in school in the first place and get back to the study grind. Time and vet school wait for no woman.

25

PICTURES

The new semester is so crowded with classes, I barely have time to think. Discrete Math. Philosophical Ethics. Physics II + Lab. Organic Chemistry II + Lab. Genetics + Lab. Fruit flies. Yuck. I want to be a vet for the cute, furry animals like capybaras and opossums, not the gross ones. My last lab doesn't finish until 4:30 on Friday, which makes me later than usual to meet Dan, which means he keeps me up past midnight to make up for lost time.

Saturday morning I sleep in. It's the first good night's sleep I've had in a week. For once, Dan doesn't wake me up for a morning quickie. It's 10:30 by the time I finally rise and find him in the kitchen, paging through a coffee table book of artsy black-and-white-photographs.

I kiss him good morning on the cheek, and he grunts a response without taking his nose out of the book, so I leave him alone while I mix myself some yogurt and granola and pour a cup of coffee. Dan brews it dark to the point where I have to add almost as much milk as coffee to make it drinkable. But once I've done that and added a couple of teaspoons of sugar, it's actually pretty good. Better than the liquid asphalt in the Fordham cafeteria, at least.

I sit down at the table with my coffee and cereal, and Dan finally puts down the book and looks at me. "I've been thinking about what Blauer said on New Year's Eve."

"The art guy? If you want someone to paint on your walls, I know a couple of guys at Fordham who go out tagging on weekends. They work cheap."

"I was thinking more along the lines of photographs. I feel like there's something missing."

OK, that makes more sense. Somehow I can't imagine Dan letting anyone paint anything but white semigloss on his pristine walls. "What kind of photographs?"

"Black-and-white, I think. Something that integrates well with my existing pieces. When you're finished eating, dress up. We'll go out."

"Casual or formal?"

"Cute," he replies. "How about the leather skirt and the white lace top? And those black leather heels that show off your toes."

"OK." It sounds a little dressy for Saturday morning, but I roll with it.

It takes me about thirty minutes to get ready. When I emerge, Dan looks me over. "Perfect," he says, and I beam with pride.

Dan is dressed ultra-casual, jeans and a black T-shirt. Not that he doesn't look great in them—in fact, he looks about ten years younger than he does in a suit—but I still feel overdressed.

"Where are we going?"

"Brooklyn," he says, "and that's all I'm saying until we get there. I want it to be a surprise."

———

I DON'T REALLY KNOW the city beyond campus, Little Italy, and the Village; the latter only in the daytime. I'm completely lost almost as soon as the cab pulls away from the curb. I'm pretty sure we're heading downtown. Brooklyn's south of Manhattan? Or is that Staten Island?

After a couple of miles of traffic, the cabbie surprises me by turning straight off a city street onto a big bridge. There's no onramp or anything. Before I know it we're crossing a river, the Hudson maybe?

On the other side of the bridge, the cab winds through a series of industrial streets. I'd be nervous about the neighborhood except there are people everywhere. Not as many as in Manhattan, but way more than there are back home in Easton anywhere except the mall on Christmas Eve.

Finally, the cab pulls up in front of an old building that might be a warehouse or a factory, or at least used to be. The elevator inside is old and ratchety but big, more suited to freight than people. Dan grunts as he pushes the heavy iron grill door shut with a clang, and it clunks its way up, wheezing and moaning all the way.

We get out on the sixth floor, then wander through a series of hallways that might as well be a maze. I hold onto Dan's hand like my life depends on it, which it might. If I got lost in here, I'm not sure I could find my way out again. I imagine the headline in the Post: "Coed Lost in Brooklyn; Ate Rats to Survive."

We arrive at a heavy metal door that only has a number, 673. Dan knocks twice, hard.

Thirty seconds later, I hear a loud thunk. The door rolls open to reveal a skinny man somewhere between my age and Dan's. He has a goatee (ick!) and small, wire-framed glasses. He's dressed casually in jeans and a brown leather vest over a white T-shirt.

"Mr. Cortland, so nice to see you again. Please come in." He steps aside and motions us in with his arm.

"Terence, I have a new model for you," says Dan.

"I'm not a model," I object. As usual, Dan ignores me and talks directly to Terence.

"This is Jennifer. I'd like you to take some photos of her, black-and-white I think."

Terence looks me up and down like I'm a chair Dan's asked him to reupholster. "Yes, I think we can make some very nice pictures. Are these for professional or personal use?"

"Personal," says Dan.

"What's the difference?" I ask.

"Ah, so you're an amateur," says Terence. "Don't worry. All will be explained. It's mostly legal details. Commercial work for advertising and whatnot requires a model release. In commercial work I focus on making the clothes look good, because that's what the client wants to sell. You can't make the girl look too pretty because then the viewer focuses on her and not the outfit."

Is that why the women in fashion magazines always look coked up and half-conscious? I had wondered about that.

Terence continues. "In personal and artistic work, I try to bring out the beauty of the model herself. The clothes are secondary. It's what you see in a good portrait, or Playboy."

"Artistic. It's not the clothes I'm interested in," says Dan with the smile I'm learning to be wary of.

"Wait, do you mean, nude?" I ask, more in shock than anything.

"Don't worry. Terence is a real artist. You'll have fun." Dan says.

"What if someone sees them?"

"I want to see them. That's why I'm paying Terence to take them."

I bite my lip. "Can't you, I don't know, buy a Playboy or something?"

Dan takes my face in his hands and kisses me softly while Terence politely looks the other way. He looks into my eyes, still holding my head. "I don't want to look at those girls. I want to look at you."

I should probably be happy he prefers me to those women, even if I can't understand why. "What if I'm, like, applying for a job or something, and someone knows me from the photos?"

Dan turns to the photographer. "Terence, I own the photos, right?"

"You're paying for them," he replies.

"And you'll supply me with the prints and the negatives."

He nods. "Standard arrangement."

Dan looks back at me. "There, you see? Nothing to worry about. They're for me, nobody else, since you can't be with me all the time."

"I guess so," I say hesitantly. I have this vision in my head of being naked on the cover of some magazine displayed at every newsstand in New York. Ridiculous, I know, like one of those magazines would even want a picture of me, but the fear is there.

"Don't worry," says Terence. "We'll take it slow. You don't have to do anything you're not comfortable doing."

Dan cocks an eyebrow.

Doing things I'm not comfortable doing could be the whole theme of my relationship with Dan. Just as I'm getting comfortable with one game, we're on to the next. Sometimes I think he's deliberately trying to keep me off balance. It's like a fetish with him.

"It's OK. Let's do this. Where do you want me?"

———

TERENCE IS GOOD AT THIS. I suppose I shouldn't be surprised. Dan always pays for the best. Well, except for me of course. I still don't get that.

Terence poses me on some plastic grass in front of a roll of different backdrops. He pulls down a picture of a forested brook in the springtime. It's totally fake, but he assures me that in the pictures it will look real. He presses a button on a boombox, and light music by some indy band I'm not familiar with begins playing in the background.

I've never had any photos like these taken before, just school pictures and family snapshots. In between adjusting lights, Terence shows me how to assume different positions, mostly lying down or kneeling in the "grass."

"Flirt with the camera," he says. "You need to be about 50% past normal for it to show up on film."

It feels silly, but I purse my lips and make kissy faces. He smiles and clicks the shutter.

"Great," Terence says. "Beautiful. Now arch your back. Throw your chest out." And I do.

"OK, kick your shoes off and point your toes."

I comply.

"Roll over and pretend you're a cat."

I swipe my hand at him like it's a claw and growl. Dan laughs, but I can be a tiger if I want to. Somehow Terence makes it feel natural. He has such a guileless smile, nothing at all like Dan's.

It helps that Terence keeps telling me how beautiful and sexy I look. I'm not used to being called beautiful. Even Dan usually restricts himself to "cute" or "pretty," so when Terence finally gets around to asking me to take my top off, it seems like part of the game. I cross my hands behind my head and push my still bra-covered chest out while making a pouty face. Terence smiles and says "beautiful" again while he snaps.

I strip my skirt off without being asked so I'm down to only my underwear. It's some of the sexy underwear Dan bought me, not the Walmart cotton granny panties from back home. It looks more like a bathing suit than lingerie so it's not too salacious. And it is sort of hot in here, whatever the weather's like outside.

I roll over and kick my heels up.

"Great," says Terence, "Gorgeous. Now the bra."

I hesitate for a second, but what the hell. I've done way worse for Dan already, and I'm having a good time. I reach behind me, unhook the bra, and let it drop. For good measure, I slip my thumbs into my panties and pull them down too. I am now completely nude.

Dan is watching me intently and smiling while Terence shoots. He's seen it all before, but usually from about six inches away. This is a new angle for him.

After a few minutes, Dan excuses himself to visit the restroom. Terence hands me a robe, and begins to rearrange the lights.

"So how did you meet Mr. Cortland?" Terence asks, as he extends a long black pole from a tripod, then screws a light on top.

"We met in a bar."

"Really?" Terence looks surprised. "He never struck me as the bar type."

"What type is he?" I ask, curious. How well does Terence know him?

"Oh, I don't know. Dashing, handsome, mysterious. I imagine he picks up Russian spies on the Riviera or seduces Chinese assassins in Hong Kong, something like that."

I can't help myself. I laugh. Dan does give off sort of a James Bond vibe, even if his secret spy toys are more Pink Pussycat than Q division. (Yes, I know about the Pink Pussycat. First week freshman year, Deirdre and I went on a scavenger hunt where one of the targets was "something from the Pink Pussycat that isn't obscene." I came back with a shopping bag and some memories I still can't wash out of my head.)

Terence pulls out a big plastic cube and positions it on the fake plastic grass, then drapes a green sheet over it. As he leads me over to it, I grill him for information about Dan.

"So how long have you known Dan?"

"Six, seven years, maybe? His company hired me to do some corporate shots for an investor's report. Mr. Cortland liked my work so he started bringing me his private business." Terence puts his hands on my shoulders and turns me a little askew to the camera.

"Private business?"

"Family portraits, glamour shots, that sort of thing. Like you."

"Like me? He's brought other girls here?" I don't know why I'm so surprised. I know I'm not Dan's first.

"Every six months or so." Terence opens his camera to put in a new roll of film. "I think the last one was maybe in May?"

There's that number six again. Does everyone know about the six month rule except me?

"What are they like?" I ask nervously. "These girls Dan brings here?"

"Usually they're about your size, maybe a bit smaller, mostly brunettes, though there was that one redhead. She was fun. Smile for the camera."

I smile unconvincingly as Terence hides behind his camera. The lights flash a couple of times.

"Try sitting on your heels, and leaning back. That's the way. Now throw your head back, and open your mouth a tad. I want to get your face. There. That's it." The lights flash again.

"Do you know what happened to them?" I ask.

"Not really," says Terence. "He never brings the same girl twice. Now stretch your arms over your head, give me a big yawn, and smile."

I do as instructed, and the lights flash again, though my smile is more like a forced grin. I flip over on my side, prop my head on my elbow, and smile at the camera as the lights flash. Terence gives me more instructions, and my body makes the pose while my mind is racing elsewhere. Six months. Is that how long I have? And what happens when it's over?

———

WHEN DAN PULLS out a large manila envelope the next weekend and shows me the proofs, I don't know what to say.

"Do you like them?" he asks.

"They're beautiful," I answer truthfully.

"You're beautiful."

"I never thought so.. But these photos, they make me look like a supermodel or something."

Dan brushes one hand against my cheek, as he flips the photos over with the other. "I'll let you in on a secret. Supermodels don't look like supermodels either, not in real life. It's all in the lighting and the makeup."

"You've known a lot of supermodels?"

"A few."

I'm tempted to ask how well he's known them, but I let it pass. Some questions I don't want answered.

"Which one's your favorite?"

I turn them over one by one and consider. It's almost like I'm looking at another girl. Somehow Terence has made me look like a different person completely, a downtown woman who knows she's beautiful and isn't afraid to show it. I don't know where he found her, because that sure wasn't scared little me last weekend.

I stop at one of the last shots we took. In the picture, I'm nude and kneeling back on my heels. My body is half-turned away from the camera, but I'm looking back across my shoulder so you can see my face. I'd started to get hot under the lights. My hair was halfway to a squirrel's nest, and sweat was dripping down my face. I was half-exhausted by that point, and not completely sure what I was doing.

But that is not the woman I see in the photograph. The woman in the picture looks confident. There's fire in her eyes. This is a woman who's in the moment, ready for anything. More than ready; she's welcoming it.

"This one," I say.

"Good choice," says Dan. "I'll get it framed."

Wait, what?

———

"I'M NOT sure how I feel about this," I say the following weekend when I see where Dan has hung me. "I thought you'd put this in your bedroom, not out here in the hallway where anyone can see it."

"If it bothers you, I can move it," Dan replies, "but it works better here."

I think about asking him to move it. I figure no one's going to know it's me. I can hardly see it myself. And it's just the eighth in a line of equally tasteful black-and-white nudes. So I shake my head no. "It's fine, leave it there."

I do not ask the obvious question: who are the girls in the other seven photos?

26

THE ACADEMY AWARDS

Dan has to travel to L.A. at the end of February on some of his master of the universe business, so for the first time since finals I find myself with a free weekend on campus. My first philosophy paper of the semester is coming up and I spend Saturday in Duane library doing research. Sunday I work on my outline. My topic is Kant's categorical imperative as it applies to sexual relations, a subject that until this year was purely theoretical for me. I debate how much personal experience I can risk including. On the one hand, exploring my relationship with Dan, even with the names changed and not using the first person, would definitely give the paper some more oomph. On the other hand, if anyone did figure out who "Don" and "Leci" are, it might get me expelled. In the end I decide to play it safe and keep the paper strictly third person and formal.

By the time dinner rolls around, I have an outline in place and my sources all lined up. I'm pretty pleased with myself. It's going to be a really good paper, should be an A.

I grab dinner in the cafeteria with my roomies, a boy who thinks he's going out with Deirdre but isn't, Laura's boyfriend Joshua, and Melissa's entourage, mostly boys trying to get with her, or boys who want to get with her but are too nervous to try anything. I'm not sure any of them understand how little chance they have of getting any further than typing a paper for her. She's a strictly off-campus dater. A year ago I would have done anything to get one of them to pay attention to me instead. Now the best of them looks like a mildly cute high school kid wearing an inside out sweatshirt. How far I have come.

After dinner, the four of us hang out in our room, gossiping and chatting. Nothing serious. Laura is trying to talk Joshua into changing his major to Economics from Philosophy. Deirdre lets slip that she might be sort of half-seeing this sophomore from her calculus class, she isn't sure yet. We all scream. Melissa commences the interrogation: Where's he from? Does he have a car? What do his parents do? Is he planning on graduate school or a real job?

Around seven in the evening a knock on our door announces Tom, our resident future priest from the second floor. "Hey ladies, you want to come watch the Academy Awards down in the lounge? You know my middle name is Oscar. I was the figure model for the statue." He puts his arms by his sides and stands up straight. Imagine him painted gold, and he really does look a little like the statue. Deidre throws a pillow at him. We laugh, pick ourselves up off the floor, and head down to the lounge.

People are gathered around the TV set when we get there, about twice as many girls as boys. It's before the ceremony officially begins, but a comedian I've sort of heard of and a news anchor I haven't are interviewing celebrities on the red carpet as they arrive. Tom grabs the remote and mutes the TV, then fills in the missing dialog with his own wickedly funny impressions:

"Why it's an honor to be nominated, and if Meryl Streep hasn't already blown half the Academy, I might even win this year.

"Why yes, you're absolutely correct. I'm not wearing any underwear under this gown. How nice of you to notice.

"Actresses only win if they play a prostitute or a handicapped person, so as a deaf hooker, I think I'm a lock."

A new couple walks into camera view and stops to be interviewed.

Tom starts imitating them but I don't hear a word he's saying, because oh my God it is Dan and the redheaded woman who warned me away from him on New Year's Eve. She's wearing a different dress tonight, midnight blue instead of green, but every bit as form fitting.

"Shut up! Turn the sound on!" I shout.

Tom throws me a hurt look. "I wasn't that bad, was I?"

"No, not you, just please, turn the sound on." Someone flips a button on the remote, and Dan's voice comes booming out of the TV mid-sentence.

"...rooting for Nathan tonight."

Whatever he said must have been funny because the woman holding the microphone to his face looks like she's trying to avoid cracking up, but it's not her I'm paying attention to. My eyes are glued to the redheaded siren hanging off Dan's left arm. She's almost as tall as he is, at least in heels (which she has no trouble walking in) and the dress she's wearing, what there is of it, looks like it's painted on. And does she have a body to paint on!

The woman with the microphone has recovered enough to turn to Dan's date. "And with you tonight, I think we all recognize Kate Harrison who's nominated for Best Supporting Actress for her role in Dangerous Arrangements. Kate, what do you think your chances are?"

Shit, she's an actress; and a good one. Why have I never heard of her? The camera zooms in on her as she laughs and raises her left hand to her face to sweep away a loose strand of hair. The camera lights flash back from the diamond ring on her finger. A diamond ring roughly the size of Connecticut, and yes, it's on *that* finger.

She starts talking, but I hear none of it through the pounding in my skull. There's a sharp pain in my chest, and the room goes dark.

27

PANIC

There's a funny show on the TV. All my friends are running around the Hughes Hall lounge, like the red ants when Jimmy Dechowitz poked a stick into their nest back in first grade and I was sent home with about a thousand ant bites. I'm there too, lying on the floor, like I'm asleep.

The sound is muted so it's hard to tell what's going on, but they seem worried. Laura's on the phone. Her face is red and she looks like she's yelling at somebody. That's wrong. Laura never yells.

Melissa has grabbed me by the shoulders. She's shaking me, then she slaps me on the face. She says something, but the sound's still off so I can't hear her. Deirdre stands there biting her fingernails and looking anxious.

One of the boys says something to Melissa and she snaps at him. He reels back in surprise and almost trips over a chair.

I should tell them I'm OK, I'm just taking a nap, but that's silly. It's a show on TV. Only crazy people talk back to the TV. I'm not crazy. I'm just really, really tired.

The next thing I know I'm coughing into a brown paper bag.

"Everyone back up. Give her some room," says a male voice I don't know. Two older guys in blue jumpsuits with FEMS stenciled over the pocket are kneeling next to me. One of them has a beard.

"What happened?" I say, only through the paper bag it comes out more like "Whrgg pnnnd?"

"Lean back, keep breathing, don't try to talk," says the EMT on my left. I think I've seen him at some of the premed events. Steve or something? A lot of premeds volunteer for the campus emergency response team to pad their applications for med school.

"You passed out," says Tom. "We were watching the awards and next thing I knew you were breathing crazy. Then your eyes sort of rolled up in your head and you hit the floor. I thought we might have to take you to the hospital."

"You had a panic attack," says the other EMT, the one with a beard I don't know. "Nothing serious. You'll be fine."

"It can't be a panic attack," says Laura, who is standing over Steve. "The semester's barely started. There haven't even been any exams yet."

"No, it was a panic attack all right," says Melissa. "A girl I was in drama with had one opening night for 42nd Street. The understudy had to go on for her."

"But why, Jenni?" says Deirdre. "We were just watching the Oscars. Not even the awards. The red carpet."

"Yeah, the dresses weren't that bad," quips Tom. "Tasteless yes, especially that green frilled sack Olivia d'Abo was wearing, but not worth passing out for."

That's when I remember. The green dress. No, the blue dress. Tonight it was blue. I push the paper bag away from my face and sit up.

"Tom, who was on the TV? Who were they interviewing when I passed out?"

"You really shouldn't talk," says Steve. I ignore him. This is too important.

"I don't know," says Tom. "I think Stallone was there. And maybe Julia Roberts?"

"Michelle Pfeiffer," adds Deirdre. "She was there."

"No, the woman in the blue dress, the redhead with—" I stop. I was about to say "with Dan" but none of them know him. "She was with this good looking man in a tuxedo."

"Honey," says Tom, "That doesn't narrow it down much. Kate Harrison, maybe? She was wearing blue, Versace I think."

"Yes, that's her! Who is she?" I need to know everything there is to know about this woman.

"She's mostly a Broadway actress, but she's up for Best Supporting Actress this year. Some indy film no one saw."

"I think you're OK. We're going to pack up now," says the other EMT, but I ignore him.

"The man, who was she with?"

"Oh yeah, he was hot," says Deirdre. "I don't remember his name."

"I don't know. Some rich guy from New York," says Tom. "Randy something?"

"Dan Cortland," says Melissa. Her voice is strangely cold, almost stern.

"Is he her husband?" I ask.

Tom shrugs his shoulders. "I don't know. Maybe?"

Damn it, I need to know. Is she his wife? His girlfriend? His fiancé? Who the hell is she? But no one knows anything useful.

"You should go back to your room," says Steve. "Stay in bed for the night. Go to campus health or the counseling center in the morning."

"I'll take her," says Laura.

"I'm OK. I want to see the show." I need to know who that woman is, what she and Dan are to each other, though of course I can't explain that to them.

Laura is not moved by my pleas. "No, you need to rest. I'll take you back to the room now."

"I agree. She doesn't need to see this," says Melissa.

"I'll be all right. I don't want to screw up everyone's evening." My wobbliness when I try to stand belies my words. I'm outnumbered, and too disconcerted to resist, when Laura and Melissa each take an arm to walk me back to our room. Deirdre follows behind, asking one nervous question after another. "How do you feel, Jenni? Are you OK? Can I get you anything?" But my mind is too occupied with the redhead on TV to pay attention.

When we get back to the room, I tell them it's fine, I'm fine. They don't need to stay, but only Melissa returns to the lounge. Laura and Deirdre stay behind. It's like they're afraid of what I'll do if they leave me alone.

My thoughts swirl around this Harrison woman. Who is she? What is Dan doing with her in Los Angeles? How does her dress stay up without any visible support in defiance of the law of gravity?

This shouldn't have come as such a shock. It makes sense that Dan sees other women. I'm not his girlfriend. He never promised me he'd be exclusive. Only I wasn't ready for it to be shoved in my face unexpectedly on the TV in my dorm, you know?

But even that didn't do it. It wasn't even the Jupiter-sized ring. No, what sent me crashing to the floor was the way she looked at him, and the way he looked back at her. Like it was the most natural thing in the world. She's his age, and probably as rich as he is, and they looked like they were meant to be together.

28

BACK IN TOWN

The week drags by, one long slog of anxiety and depression. It feels like a 500 gram calibration weight is hooked to the inside of my stomach. I barely eat. By Thursday, Laura has noticed, which I know because she casually leaves counseling center pamphlets around the room with titles like, "Anorexia, the Silent Killer." She tried the same thing last year with Melissa.

I go to class, but I can't concentrate. In chemistry lab, I set a new record for most test tubes broken in one week. I think about calling Dan, but he didn't leave me a number in California and I don't want to explain to his secretary in New York why I need to speak with him.

Besides, what would I say? "Hi, I've been stalking you on TV from the other side of the country, and I want to know what you're up to." I don't have any claim on him. He's not my boyfriend, but is he somebody else's?

Instead, I fall back on the first resort of academic nerds everywhere, the library. Even though the woman in blue didn't win, it's not hard to find her name in the list of nominees in Sunday's Times. A back search through the index turns up a few mentions here and there, mostly in reviews of Broadway and off-Broadway plays. The critics think she's talented, though she's not exactly A-List. Actual biographical data is frustratingly sparse until I happen on an old Playbill that mentions she's "a graduate of Fordham, Lincoln Center."

That's too weird. Is it a coincidence? I don't know what to make of it, and there's nothing else to be found in the stacks. Then I get the idea to do what I should have done five months ago. I look up Daniel Cortland.

The papers have even less information about him. His name is mentioned once in the society pages in an article about some fancy charity event on Long Island, but briefly. It's not even clear if it's him or someone else with the same name. At least he didn't show up in the Vows column.

His company occasionally appears in the real estate section, and once I see an ad in the business section mentioning that Cortland Investments is issuing $315,000,000 of commercial paper, whatever that is. The number is so big it makes my eyes water. I read it twice to make sure I read it right. Not quite a mole of dollars, but still. No wonder my financial problems seem so trivial to him, if those are the sorts of numbers he plays with during the week.

In the end, though, I don't know much more than when I started. If I want answers to my questions, I'm going to have to ask Dan. If I can bring myself to do it.

———

DAN ISN'T due back until Sunday, so when Kathy knocks on our door on Friday to tell me I have a phone call, I tell her to say I'm not there and take a message.

A few minutes later she returns. "Some man told me to remind you to do your exercises."

"Must be a wrong—" Suddenly I realize what exercises I'm supposed to be doing. Dan must be back early, or he called from L.A. I jump up and race to the hall phone.

Dan picks up on the first ring. He doesn't even say hello. "I thought you weren't in."

I can almost hear the smirk in his voice. "I wasn't. I just got in," I lie. Then I stop. What should I say next? I've wanted to ask him all week, but now that he's on the line, I'm mute.

"I took an early plane," he says. "I want you to come over."

———

THE TRAIN into midtown is the longest 4 ride of my life. Now that I have the chance to get some answers, I'm not sure I want them. Will he be angry with me for asking? What am I going to do if she is his fiancé? Or his wife? Should I leave? Should I break it off? Can I afford to? More to the point, even if I know it's the right thing to do, can I make myself do it?

By the time I step off the elevator into his apartment, I still don't know what I'm going to say.

Dan doesn't give me time to make up my mind. Almost before I can drop my bag, he's swept me up in his arms and is kissing me, hard and urgent. "I missed you," he says.

My mind is still occupied with questions, but my body responds to him anyway. Not even willing to wait till the bedroom, he pulls me down on the couch.

He doesn't take off his pants, or mine, just drops them far enough to do what he wants. Before I can catch my breath, he's inside me, pushing and grunting with a raw intensity so hard it almost scares me.

Two minutes later he's done and I'm breathless. He's never been quite that primal, that out of control before. We lean back on opposite ends of the couch, and I try to force my heartbeat return to normal.

"That was...intense," I say.

"It was a long week."

What I say next is dangerously close to clingy, but I'm too spent and flustered from his urgency to think before I speak. "Did you..." and then I stop, my mind catching up with my mouth.

"Did I what?"

"You might have seen someone while you were away. Since I wasn't with you."

"I didn't have time for that."

I bite my lip. Should I ask? Tell him I know that's not true? It's not like I was stalking him. I didn't turn on the TV expecting to see him stride down the red carpet with a gorgeous redhead on his arm. If he wanted to tell me, he'd tell me, right? Instead of coming out with it, I dance around the elephant in the room, wondering if it's an elephant only I can see.

"It would have been OK if you did. I know we're not exclusive. You can see other girls."

"Jenni, is something bothering you?"

Oh, the hell with it. "I saw you."

"Saw me?"

"On TV. A bunch of us were watching the Oscars in my dorm, and suddenly there you were, with this actress, Kate Harrison."

Dan laughs, one loud, short ha. That is not the reaction I was expecting.

"Oh, is that what this is about?"

I pull my knees to my chest, and peek over them at him. "Well, yes."

"She needed a date. I owed her a favor. That's all."

What sort of favor, I wonder.

"She had a ring, diamond."

"Did she? I didn't notice. She probably borrowed it for the evening."

"It was on her ring finger, her left ring finger."

He cocks an eyebrow. "Really? Now that is interesting. I wonder who put it there."

"But you didn't?"

"No, Jenni. As far as I know Kate is not engaged to anyone, least of all me. Though I will have to ask her about the ring when I see her."

"You're seeing her again?"

"Jenni, she's a friend. One of my oldest friends, in fact. I'm not cutting her out of my life just because you feel a little threatened. Especially since, as you remind me, we're not exclusive."

I bite my lip again. I do that when I'm nervous. I want to believe him, but, damn it. It doesn't sound right. Men can be oblivious, but there's no way he didn't notice a rock that big. You could see it from space. And I saw the way she looked at him, and he at her. They're not just friends.

Then Dan says the last thing I expect to hear:

"Maybe I should introduce you two."

29

KATE

an's "friend" stayed behind in L.A. after the Oscars. That gives me a full week to obsess and panic about the dinner he has invited her to on Saturday night. It's irrational, I know. He wouldn't invite her if he was trying to keep a secret, but by Friday I'm wound tighter than the vibrating string experiment in physics lab. Of the final twenty-four hours I have no recollection except that it's like a ticking clock, counting down to the arrival of the woman in blue. When she finally steps off the elevator Saturday evening, it's almost an anticlimax.

Compared to Oscar night, Ms. Harrison is dressed down, a little black dress, heels almost short enough for me to walk in. However, even in the casual outfit, she's still gorgeous. Not even normal person gorgeous, movie star gorgeous. Because, duh, that's what she is.

I steal a glance at her left hand. No ring. Is that because she's not really engaged, or because she knew she'd be meeting me?

Kate kisses Dan hello—on the cheek, thank God—and turns to me.

"Hello. Good to see you again, Jenni."

"Hello." I'm cautious, unsure how to proceed.

"It's nice to officially meet the girl who's stolen my—"

"Kate," Dan interrupts.

"Oh, don't worry. No secrets spilled. I promised." She turns back to me and curls the tip of her bottom lip, like a half smile that only I can see. "But you can't expect girls not to talk."

"I'll get you two some drinks," says Dan. "Kate, bourbon for you?"

"How well you know me," Kate replies. "On the rocks please."

While Dan goes to the bar to fix the drinks, Kate sits down on the couch like she's been there before. She pats the seat next to her. "Jenni, why don't you sit and tell me about yourself."

I sit, as far to the other side as I can manage, cautiously crossing my legs in front of me. "There's not much to tell. I go to school at Fordham."

"That much I guessed. Not a lot of locals hang out in the Ramskeller."

"The Ramskeller?" Then it hits me. "That night, when I met Dan. You were with him."

"I'm shocked you forget me so easily, but I guess you had other things on your mind."

My face must redden a little, because she adds, "Don't be embarrassed. College can be tough."

"School's not that hard."

"The school part, no. The rest of it? Yes. Correct me if I'm wrong, but you weren't doing too well right then, were you?"

I nod.

"And I hope now you're doing better?"

I nod again, still not sure what game she's playing.

"I thought so. I'm pretty good at reading body language. Yours was practically screaming girl in trouble. I figured I'd better send Dan over to you before someone even more dangerous picked you off. I must admit, I didn't expect him to take it quite this far. He must have seen something in you he liked."

She sent Dan to me that night? But then—no, I have no idea what this means. Before I can puzzle it out, Dan returns with a glass of wine for me, and something stronger for her.

"So how are you two girls getting along?" he says as he hands us each our drink.

"Famously," says Kat. "I'm sure Jenni's reassured."

·No I'm not.

Dan smiles. "Glad to hear it. Why don't you tell us about the new Sondheim show?" And with that, the conversation devolves into a series of backstage, showbiz gossip that Tom would probably love, but means nothing to me. As he and Kate chatter like two old friends, no like a married couple who actually like each other, I wonder what I'm in the middle of.

If Kate really did set me and Dan up that first night, she's not his wife, or his girlfriend. There's clearly a spark between them. The way they play back and forth off each other, one slipping effortlessly into the other's sentence. It's the complete opposite of my awkwardness, never knowing when to interrupt or wait.

I'm afraid I'm something of a silent dummy at dinner. I can barely manage, "Please pass the wine," as the two of them carry the conversation without me. Kate practically bubbles with energy. Is this what all Hollywood actresses are like? It's not like I've known any others to compare.

And of course, Dan is Dan, all rugged and oozing sex and authority and power; but tonight he's more relaxed than normal, almost friendly. I've never seen him this at ease with anyone before, almost like Kate is his missing half. She needles him in a way that would earn me a harsh "Jenni," and a raised eyebrow that warns me I'm about to cross an invisible line. Coming from her, he rolls with it.

Is she his sister? He never talks about his family. Actresses change their names all the time, but usually it's from something ethnic like Leibowitz or Berlotello, not a WASPy name like Cortland. I study the two of them, but for all that Kate gives off the same easy confidence Dan does, their physical features don't match at all. Maybe a cousin?

After dessert, a raspberry sorbet that's probably delicious but I barely notice, Dan begins to clear away the dishes. "Why don't you and Kate get to know each other in the living room while I wash up?"

"That sounds like an excellent idea," says Kate. "I'm dying to hear Jenni's side of the story without you hanging over us and harrumphing every time she gets to the juicy bits."

I'm not sure I want to be alone with her. I consider feigning illness and hiding in the bedroom until she leaves; but Dan wants us to be friends for some reason. I fortify my courage with the last of the wine, and follow her into the living room.

Kate has already draped herself across Dan's black leather couch like some twenties movie star. All she needs is a cigarette holder to complete the picture, and she's ready for her close-up.

"Come join me," she says, and pats the small space beside her.

I squeeze into the corner of the couch as best I can, though she's not leaving me a lot of room.

"So now," Kate begins, "Same question as New Year's. What are your intentions with my Daniel?"

"New Year's?" Suddenly a lot of pieces click into place. "You were the woman who cornered me at Dan's friend's. You were at the Halloween party too." My voice cuts off as I remember what Dan and I were doing at the Halloween party, and what she may have seen. At least New Year's we didn't get naked in public.

"Dan and I have a lot of the same friends, though I'm surprised you forget me so easily. I suppose it was dark on Halloween, but New Year's I wasn't even wearing a mask."

"It was late. I'd had a lot of champagne."

"Hmm, you might want to think about that sometime." She glances at my hand, and I realize my wine glass is empty. I don't even remember drinking it. "But it's actually not you I'm concerned about. Daniel. How serious is this?"

One trait she doesn't share with Dan is his reserve. It's a dangerous question, one my father should be asking Dan, not his friend asking me. I don't know how to answer.

"I just want to make him happy," I finally reply. It's a weak answer, but I don't feel very strong.

"Do you love him?" she asks.

"I'm not supposed to." I'm not sure from where or why but a tear crosses my cheek, then another.

"Jenni, what's wrong?"

I choke out. "I know you could have him. You're so beautiful, and probably rich too. Please don't take him. I need him."

She flips her hair. It's a movie star flip, like Rita Hayworth, only with red hair. "Oh honey, it's not like that between us. He's an old friend."

"That's all?"

"Well, no, not all, I suppose. But I'm not going to steal him from you, if that's what you're worried about. Truth be told, I'm more worried about him than you."

"At the Oscars, on the red carpet, you were holding hands."

Kate laughs. "Jenni, if you'd spent any time in Hollywood, but I guess you haven't, have you?"

I shake my head no.

"Public dates are arranged for the cameras. Half the actors are in the closet. If someone's not with their spouse, you can bet their PR agents set them up. I needed a date who knew how to wear a tuxedo and wasn't famous enough to get the gossip columnists excited. Dan fit the bill. I'm surprised he didn't tell you this himself."

"Dan never tells me anything."

"Yes, I'm afraid that does sound like him."

"On Oscars night, you had a ring, a big one."

"A Beverly Hills jeweler paid me to wear it for the evening so my picture on the red carpet would showcase his ring. I got a bonus for making sure it was in the frame when the cameras zoomed in on me. Actresses do things like that sometimes. Despite what the tabloids print, not all of us are rich. Or at least not as rich as Dan."

"So Dan didn't give it to you?"

"No, sweetie, he didn't. That ring is safely returned to the vault, and I'll probably never see it again. It was pretty though, wasn't it?"

"I guess so." I don't really remember the ring so much as what it implied and the effect it had on me. Now that that's taken care of, I can breathe again. For the first time since the Oscars, I think.

Kate folds her legs under herself and rests her chin on her hand so she can look at me, but now it feels friendly, not like I'm frozen fish being inspected for quality. "So tell me, what do you do when you're not seducing my old college friends?"

"Study mostly. Between school and Dan I don't have time for a lot of extracurriculars."

"I hope Dan doesn't take up all your time."

"Oh no. He's good about letting me study when I need to. Sometimes it's easier to study here than back on campus. It's quieter."

"If the dorms are anything like they were when I was in school, I can believe that. Sometimes I'm amazed any of us graduated at all."

"You partied a lot?"

"You could say that. I spent my share of nights at the Lantern."

"Did Dan?"

"Dan was...driven. He had a lot to prove back then, and he wasn't going to let anyone or anything get in the way. We used to tease him about it. Said he was more adult at eighteen than the rest of us would be at forty-five."

"Sounds a little like Laura."

"Laura?"

"One of my roommates. She acts older than she is, too, but in a good way."

Kate leans in. "Tell me more."

As I launch into a discussion of campus life, I realize I've missed gossiping with someone I can talk freely with. I don't have to edit my thoughts first to keep my life safely compartmentalized.

Before long, I find myself telling Kate things I thought I couldn't tell anybody like exactly what Dan and I do in the bedroom. She grins and asks for more details. It's not that she doesn't judge me. It's that she actually approves! She's genuinely glad that Dan and I are having fun. I didn't realize how much I was itching to talk about Dan, hell to brag about Dan. With Janine, with my parents, with my roommates, I'm too worried about what they'll think, what they'll say, about our age difference, about Dan paying me, or even about how much sex I'm having. (Fordham: Catholic school. Still a lot of slut shaming and Catholic guilt to go around.)

I'm not quite sure how it happens, but I find myself laying on my back with my head in her lap, looking into her green eyes as she strokes my hair. It feels nice. "So you and Dan really didn't sleep together while he was in L.A.?"

"No, sweetie, we didn't. Not this time. Sorry to disappoint you." Kate gives me a naughty wink.

I smile back. "I'd be OK with it if you did. He didn't promise me he'd be monogamous. I sort of assumed he wasn't." Now that I'm not scared Dan is going to leave me to marry her, I really am OK with the two of them. More than OK. Kate's hot. I can't imagine Dan doesn't want to sleep with her too.

"What about you? Did you promise him you'd be exclusive?"

Weird question. "Hmm, I sort of assumed it, but I don't think he actually told me I couldn't see other people."

"Good for him. Have you taken advantage of your freedom then? Are you using your newly discovered flirting skills to drive all the other undergraduates to distraction?"

I laugh. "No. I suppose I could, but I only wear these sorts of clothes when I'm with him." I sweep my hand across my body to indicate the medium blue dress Dan bought me at Barneys. "I suppose I've noticed a couple of boys who look at me more than they used to, but they're not Dan. I'm not that interested unless he's there, you know?"

Kate twirls a strand of my hair around her finger. "Just the boys?"

"What do you mean?"

"We didn't talk about it much, but when I was in the dorms, things had a way of happening. Not all the time, but even the girls looking for a Mrs. degree tended to graduate with their horizons expanded. I went on a real gender bender spring semester of junior year. I was almost ready to join FLAG."

"What happened?"

"Oh, the usual. She graduated and I realized I was way too interested in a forward on the men's rugby team to make a permanent commitment to the lifestyle. But it was fun while it lasted." Her eyes lose focus for a minute, giving her a dreamy look, then she looks back down at me. I look back into her green eyes. There's something going on here. I'm not sure if I should say it.

Before the silence gets so supersaturated that the tension precipitates like silver nitrate in a beaker of chloride, a noise breaks me out of the spell. It's Dan, of course. He's standing in the doorway, a drink in his hand. I hop up from Kate's lap and scramble over to the far side of the couch, like a teenager caught by her father while making out with her boyfriend.

"So what have you two found to talk about in my absence?" Dan asks.

Kate throws me a knowing glance. "This and that. Woman stuff."

Dan sits down on the couch and wraps his arm around me, though he's looking at Kate. I wonder?

"So you've been sharing secrets?" Dan says.

"Nothing serious," Kate replies. "Jenni tells me she's not interested in playing with anyone else unless you're there too."

"Kate!" I exclaim in shock, by which I mean, that is not what I meant, at all!

Dan, however, reads my admittedly ambiguous exclamation as confirmation. "Oh, really? Who were you thinking about playing with then?"

At least he's smiling when he says that. There's only one possibility here, and from his smile it's clear he already knows.

Kate laughs, an almost musical sound. "You were right about this one, Daniel. She really is a delicate little flower."

Dan brushes his hand across my cheek, and I risk a glance at him. He's not angry, more like bemused. "She's a flower, all right, but I don't think she's that delicate. Not some hothouse orchid that only grows in a greenhouse. More like a wild sunflower, that grows everywhere from gardens to deserts and takes over in the end. She just needs a little water and nurturing."

He leans in and kisses me, one of his long slow kisses that makes me forget I'm alive. Then Dan breaks it off, turns, and kisses Kate the same way without taking his hand off my leg. I should be upset—here I was worried about what he and Kate were doing in L.A. and now here they are doing it in front of me—but I'm not. They're both so beautiful. As he pulls away, Kate sighs.

He kisses me again, then stands up. "Let's go to the bedroom."

"I thought you'd never ask," says Kate.

30

KATE AND DAN AND JENNI

For once, I'm glad I got a little tipsy. I don't think I could do this sober. Kate and I sit on the bed while Dan stands in the corner, surveying the room, a glass of wine in his hand. My body is as stiff as a board. Kate puts her arm around me and kisses me. I respond with all the enthusiasm of a cardboard box.

She moves her head to whisper in my ear, "Just go with it. You're going to have fun. Trust me." Then she kisses me again.

I put my hands on her back like I'm petting a dog I'm afraid might bite me at any minute.

Kate slides her hands down my back, so they're resting on my buttocks. "Open your mouth," she whispers into my ear.

Hesitantly, I do as instructed. She moves her mouth over mine, and slides her tongue inside. Our tongue tips touch, and I feel a momentary shiver. Startled, I pull back and stare at her.

Kate is smiling. She reaches out a hand to touch my breast, and runs a finger across it, then back up. Even through my shirt, my nipple hardens under her touch. Kate continues to massage my nipple with her finger, then leans in to kiss me again. As her tongue finds mine for the second time, I recognize the beginnings of sensations that until now only Dan has evinced in me.

Before those can grow any further she releases me and stands up. I watch her walk over to Dan's sound system to inspect the CDs. The way she moves is mesmerizing. It's like watching a ballet dancer perform. She finds a disc she likes, takes it out of the jewel case, and inserts it into the player. Soft instrumental music starts playing.

Kate returns to the bed and holds out her hand. I take, it and she pulls me up. She interlocks her hands behind her head so she's facing away from me and Dan, and whispers, "Unzip me."

I pull the zipper down the back of her dress. Then Kate makes a shimmying motion with her hips, and the dress magically puddles around her feet. Underneath she's wearing black lingerie and sheer black stockings. Her body is as perfect out of her dress as inside it.

She gives an over-the-shoulder glance to Dan who is watching us with his enigmatic smile, then turns back to look at me again. She lays a hand on the back of my neck and pulls me in for a kiss. I open my mouth and let her tongue find mine, twirl around it with the heady aroma of the wine we've drunk flavoring every touch.

It's different than kissing Dan. She's less forceful, more playful with the motion of her tongue in my mouth, but still arousing. Without taking her mouth away, she begins expertly unzipping my dress. Then she breaks off the kiss long enough to effortlessly slip my dress off my shoulders.

A little more awkwardly, I finish the job and let it drop to the floor. I can feel Dan's gaze on us, hear his breathing going deeper, though I don't think he realizes it. My heart is pounding in my chest heavier than any time since that first night with Dan. Kate and I face each other, front to front. She puts one hand on my rear to bring me closer to her and uses the other to move my hand to her breast. I'm not sure what to do, but I circle it gently over the silk fabric of her bra. I must do something right because she tilts her head back and moans.

Kate reaches behind herself and unclasps her bra. She tosses it aside and places my hand on her exposed breast. "Harder," she whispers through clenched teeth, and pushes my hand into her with her own.

Dan yanks his tie off and begins stripping off his shirt. "Fuck watching, I want you two now."

He tosses the shirt over a chair and heads for the bed. Kate throws out an arm to block him. "Hold it, lover boy. We'll get to you. Let the girls play first."

To my surprise Dan accepts the rebuke without objecting and seats himself in a chair by the wall. Wow, I didn't know I was allowed to do that.

Kate returns her attention to me. She puts one hand behind my neck to hold me in front of her as she looks into my eyes. "Are you ready for this?"

I don't think I can speak, but I nod. Only Dan has ever gazed at me from this distance before, but his face is rougher, more demanding. I feel her reach down and softly slide a finger between my legs. She goes slower than Dan, and more steadily, but she begins to move in time with my breathing. At first I try to hold the pose and stay balanced, but soon I'm gasping and leaning on her for support. Then we reach a point where the only thing holding me upright is her. It's certainly not my legs. The feeling washes over me, and I clench my arms around her involuntarily.

When I'm ready to come up for air, my face is drenched in sweat. Kate smiles at me. "So you enjoyed that?"

Still not ready to talk, I nod.

"Good. I'll show you some tricks later. Meanwhile, let's add a player to this game. Daniel, get over here."

"Finally," he growls. In less time than it takes to read this, he's sprawled out on the bed.

"Sit up, lover boy," Kate commands. Again, to my surprise, Dan obeys. Kate unbuckles his belt and in on swift motion yanks his pants down to his ankles. He moves to kick them off, but Kate stops him with a hand on his knee. "Leave them there. I don't trust you without a little control."

Dan looks at me and raises an eyebrow, but I shrug. I'm not the one in charge here and, I'm starting to understand, neither is he. Kate is a force of nature. Instead, I huddle up next to him and drape my left arm around his shoulders. He kisses me once, lightly, then we both turn our attention to Kate who kneels down in front of us, between Dan's legs.

Kate grasps his penis with her hand, then leans forward and licks it from bottom to top in one long slow motion. Dan groans, and I can already see the first drop of moisture seeping out from the tip.

I lean into Dan, grab the bottom of his T-shirt, and pull it up over his head, all without looking away from what Kate is doing below. She's put her mouth around it and moves down halfway, then back up again. The steady motion back and forth is hypnotic. From his glazed look, Dan is hypnotized all right.

Kate flicks her eyes to catch my attention, then tilts her head to the side. I catch her meaning, and slide out of the bed to kneel next to her.

She hands Dan to me and I try to imitate her slow, steady motions. To my surprise, she doesn't move aside but pushes her head lower and begins to lick Dan's balls.

I look up at Dan as I lick. His head is tilted back, his eyes half-closed, and he doesn't seem fully conscious. I glance back at Kate. Her eyes are bright and she's smiling. I smile back. I've never been able to take this much control of him before.

Kate sticks out her tongue to touch the tip of his erection and I do the same. She starts flicking her tongue across the engorged head, and I imitate.

Suddenly Dan moans, his eyes roll back in his head, and he releases a near fountain that somehow manages hit my face, Kate's face, a spot in the hair behind my ear, and probably a few places I don't notice. A few drops dribble down my throat. He usually has more control than that. I can't help it. I giggle. Kate smiles and laughs too.

Kate rises from her knees and sits next to him on the bed. He's still panting, out of breath. She brushes a hand across his cheek. "Some things never change, do they, lover?"

He looks at her with open mouth but can't think of anything to say to that.

After Kate and I make a quick trip to the bathroom for some washcloths and hot water, Dan is still hors de combat. Normally that means at least a few minutes of cuddle time while he recovers, but tonight there's a third person in the mix. Kate grabs my hand. "Come on, Jenni. Why don't we have some girl time?"

Nervously, I join her on the bed, while Dan scoots to the side. She puts a hand behind my head to hold me while she looks into my eyes. She smiles like this is a game between two friends.

When she tilts her head and leans in, I meet her halfway and the tips of our tongues touch. Her breath is sweet, like raspberries. She slides one hand down my back while the other cups my breast, massaging my nipple. The hair on my body is starting to stand up, tingling like there's static electricity in the sheets.

Gently, Kate lays me down on my back and kisses me again. Then she starts moving down my body, kissing my chin, my neck, my collarbone. She stops at my breasts, and I almost cry in frustration, but then she touches her tongue lightly to first one nipple, then the other. Her circles each one, applying more pressure now. The feeling is exquisite and I almost climax from that alone.

I don't know how long she stays there. It feels like a moment. It feels like forever. But finally she lifts herself up from my chest and runs a finger down my torso from between my breasts, down my belly to just above, and takes it away at the last second. I squeak in frustration.

Kate smiles enigmatically, then places her hands inside my thighs and pushes lightly. Compliant, I spread my legs apart. Kate leans down, placing her head between them. Her green eyes look up at me, as if silently asking if I'm ready for this.

I should probably think a little more about what's going on here, but I'm too far beyond rational to worry about things like the gender of the person touching me. All I can manage is a tortured, "please." I'm not even sure if I say that out loud or just think it.

Kate must see whatever she wants to see in my face, because she buries her head further in and reaches her hands out to grasp my sides. I feel the wet strength of her tongue slip across my spot and I scream incoherently. My head throws back, my hands clutch Kate's flame-colored hair, and I'm convulsing, shaking, shivering.

When Kate rises, I notice that Dan has been watching us this whole time. He doesn't look upset.

Kate scoots up to lie next to me. "So, how was that?"

"Great." Not the most eloquent description I admit, but it gets the sentiment across.

"Good. Take a minute to catch your breath. Then, it's my turn."

My face freezes. Kate catches my hesitation. "Don't worry. It's easy. I'll show you." She pushes herself up so she's sitting against the wall. Then she opens her legs wide in a position that leaves no doubt she's a natural redhead. I don't think I've ever had this clear a view of a woman's parts before, mine included. Not that it's unattractive. Quite the opposite, but I'd be embarrassed to pose like that, even for Dan.

She puts a finger near the top. "This is the clitoris. You know where your clit is, right?"

I blush but nod. I am a biology major, and I figured out where mine was when I was nine. Still, the way she uses the word, it's a lot more direct than I'm comfortable being.

"We'll start simple. Put your tongue here and lick softly. Every woman likes it a little different, so I'll tell you if you need to speed up or slow down, or go harder or softer. Got it?"

I nod and get ready to bend down.

"Good girl. We'll leave the fisting for next time."

Dan sputters loud enough to make me jump.

"Oh dear," Kate says, with a mischievous gleam in her eye. "I think I've shocked your boyfriend. We better go slow so we don't scare him."

I smile and bend down, while making a mental note to research fisting later. It's fun watching Kate play with Dan, the unteasable.

Kate's saltier than Dan, and hairier too, at least along the good bits. But she responds quickly, and she's more vocal, letting me know that she likes what I'm doing. "Harder. OK, faster. Up a little. OK, there. Oh God, that's good."

"Fuck it," says Dan in his gruff voice. "I'm not waiting for you two to be done." He grabs my hips from behind and positions his cock along my backside. I'm so relaxed there's not even the usual jolt as he enters me.

"Keep going, girl," Kate says. I remember I'm a more active participant than I usually am in this position. I can't rest my head in the pillows and let Dan control the pace. I get back to work on Kate, trying to time my own motion to coincide with Dan's enthusiastic thrusting behind me.

Kate's body begins to contract. Her hips squeeze in against my head, her hands clutch the sheets. "Oh, fuck," she says as her pelvis bucks upward. At this point, Dan would be done, but with her I'm not sure so I keep going.

"Oh fuck," she says again. "Fuck, fuck, fuck." She's shaking all over.

Finally, she grabs my hair. "Enough, please. Enough."

"Was that good?" I ask in all innocence.

"God, yes."

"Hey, I'm still here," says Dan from behind me.

I look at Kate from about three inches away and she gives me a sly smile which I interpret as, "Men, what are you going to do about them?"

I suppress a giggle and rest my head on Kate's thigh, basking in the afterglow while Dan finishes inside me, after which we all collapse on the bed in a happy, sweaty, pile of exhausted limbs and random body parts.

As usual Dan is up and out for his morning run around the reservoir before I wake, only this morning that doesn't mean I wake up alone.

"Hi," I say to Kate.

"Hi yourself," she says with a wicked look in her eye.

She runs a finger down my leg, and I squeal. "Stop, that tickles."

"Oh well, maybe later. You want some breakfast?"

Kate eats yogurt and granola. It's a welcome change from the meat and eggs Dan likes to cook. I figure I'll never have a better opportunity to grill Kate about our definitely mutual friend out of his earshot. "How long have you known Dan?"

"Since college. I don't remember how we met. I was at Lincoln Center and he was at Rose Hill so we weren't in the same classes, but we hung out with a lot of the same people." Kate gets a faraway look and smiles.

"So were you and he ever, you know?"

Kate laughs. "A few times. OK, more than a few. He did know his way around a woman's body, as I'm sure you know."

She throws me a knowing glance, and I blush a little. Yes, he does.

"His level of skill and enthusiasm was unusual in college boys back then. Probably still is, though I suppose you know more about that than me."

Actually I don't, but I stay quiet and let her continue.

"As you can imagine, he was rather in demand. He wasn't rich yet, but we were young and no one much cared about money. I can't say either of us was exactly monogamous. Sometimes it felt like Fordham was one big puddle of hormones. All us kids from Catholic school who were finally out of our parents' houses and away from the nuns."

I can imagine. I know a thing or two about that dynamic myself. "What happened then?"

Kate swirls some more granola into her yogurt and takes a bite. "Oh, the usual. We graduated and mostly went our separate ways. A few teachers, a few social workers. Some of us went straight into law school or an MBA. One or two joined the Jesuits and went off to do missionary work. Dan took a job he hated on Wall Street. I went on active duty and flew helicopters."

"You were in the Air Force?" Somehow Kate is not my picture of a military pilot.

"The Army. I attended Fordham on an ROTC scholarship so I owed them a few years. Not the smartest thing I ever did, I'll admit. Nothing's so boring as being a soldier in peacetime, but they did teach me to fly."

"Wow." I'm beginning to think Kate is the coolest person I have ever met in my life. "So how did you get into acting?"

"I always planned on being an actress. I was a theater major as an undergraduate. After I got out of the Army, I took a job in New York flying a traffic copter and started going to auditions again. Only then—"

The ding that announces an arriving elevator interrupts her.

"Oh, Dan must be back," I say.

Thirty seconds later he strides into the kitchen, sweaty from his morning run, and heads straight to the refrigerator for a carton of orange juice. "Good morning, ladies. Are you two getting along?"

"Famously," says Kate. "But I have a 10:00 a.m. phone call with my agent, so I'm going to head home. It's been fun, but I'll leave you two love birds to whatever you can imagine."

Dan comes over to the counter with his juice. "Sounds good. We still on for tennis next week?"

"Of course," Kate replies, and gives him a chaste peck on the cheek. Then, to my surprise, she puts her arms around me and gives me a considerably less chaste kiss. "Don't be a stranger, OK?" Then with a wink, she's out the door.

When we hear the elevator begin its descent, Dan puts down his juice and turns to me. "So what do you think of Kate?"

"She's really nice."

Dan chuckles. "You seemed to think she was a little more than 'nice' last night."

"OK, I admit it. She's amazing. Did you know she can fly a helicopter?"

"Yes, I believe she's mentioned that before. But are you feeling good? No more concerns about strange women in blue dresses?"

"Yes, I'm good," and I realize I'm telling the truth. Kate is Dan's friend, and maybe a little more; but she's my friend too and that makes me happy.

"Good," says Dan, taking a big swig of orange juice, "Because after I get showered off, I want to spend some time with just the two of us."

I smile. I'm ready for that too.

31

CHAPEL

March in New York City is still winter, but Dan keeps me more than warm enough. Meeting Kate has actually helped me relax around Dan. I feel more secure with him now, safer. I've stopped worrying that he's going to dump me and run off with some model. (That's a logical AND by the way. He might run off with some model, but he's not going to do that AND dump me. Discrete math this semester.) I don't have to be better than all the other women, just good enough that he wants me too. I know that's not how I'm supposed to feel, but it's a huge step up from worrying that doom is waiting in high heels around every corner.

Plus, Kate is the first real *friend* of his I've met. Sure, Dan is always sociable with the various doormen and drivers and salesladies who populate our weekends—almost frustratingly so sometimes—but he doesn't invite any of them back to his place for drinks and poker. Kate's actually on his level, his equal if such a thing can be imagined. Of course, she's also really, really hot. Dan is no longer the only one I'm picturing in my head on the rare occasions when I'm alone in my dorm room.

Who knows? Maybe I'll even get to meet his parents. I wonder if he has any siblings, maybe a younger brother? Would he be as attractive as Dan is? I wonder if Dan shares things with his brother (brothers?). Oh my God, that would be hot. OK, breathe Jenni, breathe. Some fantasies need to be kept to myself.

Not that life is all cream and chocolate. There must be a law of conservation of worry since the time I don't spend obsessing over Dan is freed up to obsess over school. The first organic chem midterm is coming up before spring break. There's so much to memorize, and half of it begins with the letter A: alcohols, alkanes, alkenes, allylic carbon, alkynyl anions, aromaticity, acyl substitution, and at least eighteen different kinds of acids. How is this possible less than two months into the semester? It's like Professor Bolotowksy used my A in the first semester as evidence that he wasn't moving fast enough. It took every chemist in the world two hundred years to figure this stuff out, and I'm supposed to learn it all in five weeks? Forget Lavoisier. Chemistry was invented by the Marquis de Sade.

Sunday evening I'm so absorbed in my organic chemistry textbook that when Dan comes up from behind and touches me on the shoulder, I almost fall off the couch.

"Jumpy, tonight, are we? Maybe I can do something about that." As he sits down next to me and starts massaging my shoulders, I close the book and lay it next to me. Normally I'd be tingling with the thought of where his fingers were going next, but right now I'm too anxious about losing study time to enjoy it.

I consider asking him if we can skip sex tonight, but that's not the deal I made. I wonder if I can satisfy him quickly with my fingers? If we don't have full sex, I'll be good for another couple of hours of studying before bed.

I flip around so I'm facing him and begin fumbling at his zipper. To my surprise, Dan pushes me away.

"Jenni, what's wrong?"

"Nothing's wrong. Let's just do it."

He takes my face in his hands, one on each cheek, so I have to look directly at him. "Jenni, tell me the truth."

I exhale deeply. "Really, it's nothing. I have this damned chemistry exam tomorrow. I can't get it out of my head. I'm afraid I'm going to flunk, or get a B."

Dan laughs. "You say it like those two outcomes are the same."

"A B would bring my GPA down. Do you know how hard it is to get into vet school?"

Dan lets go of me and comes over to the front of the couch. "You're not feeling it, are you?"

"No," I say, looking down. I should be, but I'm not. "It's OK. We can still have sex. Give me a minute to take off my clothes."

Dan pulls me into him. I rest my head against his shoulder but look away.

"Jenni, it's OK. I don't want to make you do something you don't want to do."

"I don't have to? It's OK if we skip a night?"

"Sure, though I wouldn't want to make a habit of it, but I don't think you should study."

"I have to study. I have a test. If I don't pass then this is all for nothing."

"Not for nothing, I hope, but I've been watching you study all weekend. You know this material. You're going to ace the exam. You're just nervous. At this point you need a good night's sleep more than you need to stay up late and cram a few more formulas in."

I snuggle in a little closer to him. "I don't know. What if there's a question about nitrile hydrolysis? I haven't memorized the reaction from ethanenitrile to ammonium ethanoate via ethanamide yet."

"I have no idea what you just said, but if they ask about nitrous whatsis, leave the question blank. You'll fail the exam, get an F in the class, flunk out of school, move back to Pennsylvania, never get a job, and die alone in a hole."

I hit him with a throw pillow. He laughs. When he puts it that way, maybe I am obsessing over this a little too much. It is only an exam.

"Do you want to go back early? Spend the night in your dorm so you don't have to take the subway in the morning?"

"Can I?" I didn't think I was allowed to ask for that. "That would be great."

"Get your things. I'll drive you up. Just promise me one thing."

"What?"

"When you get back, it's straight to bed. No more studying tonight."

———

DAN DOESN'T LIKE to talk while driving so we speed up the FDR in silence. Not that I blame him. New York drivers are insane. I got my license at sixteen, but no way would I even think about driving in the city. Instead, Dan looks at the road and I look at him. How did I get so lucky? Stumbling across him must have used up nineteen years of good karma, and then put me in the hole for the next nineteen.

There's not much traffic at this hour on a Sunday night, so we make good time and arrive on campus a little after nine. The security guard waves us by without asking to see ID. He probably thinks Dan is my father, dropping me off after a weekend at home, but I'm not sure I care about that any more. He's with me, and that's enough. Who cares what the rest of the world thinks?

Dan parks the Lexus in front of Hughes Hall. I turn to give him a quick kiss goodnight, but he stops me by putting a finger on my nose. "Now remember, no studying. You're going straight to bed."

"Yes, Dad." I'm smiling when I say it.

Dan makes a harrumphing noise like he disapproves, but I can tell he's playing. That's when I get the idea. I haven't been on campus on Sunday night often since I started seeing Dan, and never with him. Would he?

"You know, it's not very late. There's something we could do."

"You want to get a drink in the Ramskeller?"

"Actually, I was wondering if you wanted to go to late Mass."

Dan leans back into the driver's seat. "Wow, I'm not sure what I was expecting you to say, but it certainly wasn't that. I haven't been to

Mass in, well, I'm not sure how long. I think if I walked into church, the saints might step off their pedestals and toss me out."

I scoot over and take his right hand in mine. "It's fun. Everyone on campus goes. It helps you relax, get ready for the week. I think it would be good for me." I think about adding, "It might be good for you too," but decide against it.

"Are you sure you want to do this? Your friends might be there. I know you try to keep your life on campus separate. You'd have to explain who I am."

He's right, but I surprise myself by realizing I don't care all that much. Keeping the secret is becoming more of a burden every week. I'm tired of having to be quiet when Deirdre and Melissa gossip about boys they like, or what they've done.

"If anyone asks, I'll tell them you're my friend from the city." Let them imagine the rest. I don't have to tell them everything.

"OK then, let's go to Mass."

I squeeze him tight and give him a quick peck on the cheek. I don't know why, but this makes me really happy.

As usual, the 10:00 p.m. service is packed. Dan and I are scrunched up together in a pew near the back. I'm feeling so warm and peaceful I genuinely don't care who sees us. That's what I love about this service. It feels like everyone there loves you, and everything's going to be OK.

And everything really is right with the world with Dan next to me. I don't think about tomorrow's test, or tuition money, or what happens over the summer. I don't really believe in God any more, especially not during finals, but sitting here, praying and singing along with everyone, God doesn't seem as impossible as he usually does.

Dan has never shown the slightest interest in religion, so I'm surprised when he knows all the responses and hymns. He slips right into it like he goes every week. I'd guessed he was Catholic since he went to Fordham too, but I thought he'd have forgotten by now. Unless when he goes jogging in the morning he's actually sneaking out to mass? No, that would be too weird.

Dan skips Communion. I figure I have plenty to confess so I skip it too. Maybe I'll visit the campus ministry tomorrow after the exam for a quick absolution. Honestly though,, I can't really believe that what I'm doing with Dan is wrong. Everything feels so perfect and right.

After Mass is over, Dan walks me back to Hughes Hall, holding my hand the whole way. He doesn't say anything, but he doesn't have to. In front of the dorm, he kisses me, then kisses me some more.

"So this is good night," he says when he finally lets go.

I'm not sure what I'm thinking. OK, I'm not thinking, but I don't want the night to end. I look up at him coquettishly. "It doesn't have to be. You could come up."

"To your dorm room?"

"Um hum."

"Won't your roommates be there?"

"Deirdre has the top bunk, but she went on some sort of retreat for the weekend. Laura usually sleeps in Joshua's room. Melissa is probably asleep."

"You don't think we'll wake her up?"

"We can be quiet. Even if she wakes up, she won't know who you are. I've had to pretend to be asleep for all of them over the last two years, more than once. For one night, they can do it for me."

"Alrighty then," Dan says with a smile.

———

I DON'T WANT to turn the light on for fear of waking Melissa, so I take Dan's hand and guide him into the room by what light comes through the window. I think the jig may be up when Dan stubs his toe and lets out a curse word. I freeze, waiting to see if Melissa wakes up but she doesn't move.

We undress as quietly as we can and slip under the covers.

It's actually kind of hot having to do this in the dark in the single bed with Melissa asleep on the other side of the room. Dan usually takes charge and tells me what he wants, but we need to be quiet so we feel each other out by touch and experience without words passing between us. We lay on our sides in the bed facing each other. Dan has his arms around me and kisses me deeply. I feel him growing against my leg as my own body prepares to receive him.

When I think I'm ready, I reach down between us and rub my palm along him. I roll onto my back, and Dan repositions himself between my knees. I take him in my hand and guide him in.

Dan begins to thrust, in and out, in and out. He's normally so vigorous; tonight he is controlled, slow, steady, rhythmic.

As the feeling builds in me, I realize I'm the weak link in this plan. Dan usually grunts a bit. When I'm not too swept away to notice, his face gets this really funny scrunched up look when he comes. Otherwise he's pretty quiet about it. I'm Little Miss Can't Keep My Mouth Shut. It's never been a problem in Dan's apartment, but with Melissa asleep on the other side of the room I'm suddenly very conscious of how loud my breathing gets as he's moving up and down inside me.

Too late I try to control myself, clenching my teeth, curling my toes hard, grabbing the bed tight in my hands, trying against all my natural inclinations not to make a sound as Dan ever so slowly strokes in and out. The tension is agony. Somehow having to hold it in makes everything more that much more intense. As Dan lifts himself up and slides that extra inch higher against me, I bite my lip hard to keep from yelling. In the end, only a soft "eep" escapes from my mouth as my entire body convulses and the bed shakes.

Dan pulls out and kisses me. He hasn't finished yet, so he takes my hand in his and places my palm where he wants it. Holding me softly, he guides my hand to show me the rhythm he needs. I rub up and down, first gently, then not so gently. I put my other arm around his back. I try to time my speed to coincide with his breathing. Finally, he explodes into my hand and relaxes back onto the bed with a sigh.

Usually we get to sprawl out in Dan's king bed afterwards and recuperate, but my tiny dorm bunk doesn't have the room. We stay pressed together while I fall to sleep in his arms, so relaxed I don't even think about the test tomorrow or how I'm going to explain this man in my bed to my roommates in the morning.

———

WHEN I WAKE UP, Dan is gone. He must have snuck out and driven back to Manhattan after I fell asleep. I'm a little disappointed, but at least this means my secret's still safe. I do a quick check to see if he left any evidence behind, though I'm not sure what I could do if he did, since Melissa has already risen and vacated the room. I'm relieved not to find one of his socks or, worse yet, underwear, incriminatingly positioned on my desk. Having reassured myself that my reputation is still intact, I grab my backpack and head to the cafeteria for a quick bite before Maxwell's demon torments me with another chemistry exam.

Or not. I zip through the test in 45 minutes, spend 15 minutes checking my answers, and spend the next hour contemplating the finer points of institutional ceiling tiles in fluorescent light. I may have over-studied, and I certainly over-worried.

At lunch, I spot Melissa in the cafeteria and wave her over. She sits down with a green salad of Fordham's least wilted lettuce and a paper basket of fries. This should be my first warning since she rarely eats lunch and never carbs. She lays the fries in the middle of the table to share. Then she tears open a plastic packet of reduced fat French for the salad. "So you got lucky last night." It's a statement, not a question.

"Oh, you heard us?" "Spill. Was it the mysterious boy you're running off to visit every weekend?"

I chew a fry while considering how much I can safely say. I settle for, "Yes, that was him. But please don't tell anyone, OK?"

Melissa puts her palm up in a gesture of feigned shock. "Of course not. I've been quiet until now, haven't I? But if he's spending the night on campus, people are going to find out. Laura probably already knows. She's just too polite to call you on it. Nobody goes home to visit their *parents* that often. So who is he? Why all the secrecy?"

"It's complicated."

"That much I guessed. Why? Is he a Jesuit?"

"No, of course not!" It's not as shocking a question as it sounds, though. I know at least two girls in the senior class helping novices rethink their vows. Then I remember, Melissa has seen him, at least once. "Do you remember Oscar night, when I passed out?"

"It's one of the EMTs?"

"No. Do you remember who was on the TV, being interviewed, right before I collapsed?"

"Is he famous? Is that why you're being so secretive?"

"No, he isn't. But he has friends who are, and he doesn't want to see his name in the papers. That's all."

Melissa takes a french fry out of the basket, holds it in front of her face to study it for a moment, then puts it back. "I don't know. It still sounds sort of weird that he doesn't want to meet your friends. If he's just having a little fun, OK. But if this man is really serious about you..." Her voice trails off leaving the implied question hanging in the air.

Instead of answering I pick up a handful of fries, and I don't put them back. How does Melissa always manage to go straight to the one thing I'm trying the hardest not to think about?

Melissa continues, "How'd you two meet anyway?"

"We met in the Ramskeller last semester. You remember when everyone started freaking out because their financial aid was cut?"

Melissa nods.

"It happened to me too, and I thought I was going to have to drop out. Only he helped me...figure out what to do about it. We got to talking and one thing led to another, and well, you know. If it wasn't for him I wouldn't still be here." Not the whole story, but as much as I'm willing to reveal for now.

"Why? Is he giving you money or something?"

I spew half chewed fries across my plate. Apparently Melissa didn't need the whole story. She always was smarter than me. When I finally finish coughing, it's too late to lie. "Please don't tell anyone," I whisper.

Melissa puts a hand across her heart. "Of course not, Jenni. I thought it might be something like that. He didn't seem like your type."

"Oh, and who is my type?" Not my favorite topic of discussion but anything to move the conversation away from my arrangement with Dan.

"I don't know, some nice sophomore boy. Maybe Tom."

I make a face. "Tom's just a friend, and anyway he's with Sharon now."

"I hear that isn't going so well, and didn't he sleep over with you last year?"

God, I was trying to forget that. "Yes, he did, and that's all we did too, sleep I mean. He was a perfect gentleman." Much to my disappointment, I might add. Not that I was interested in him like that, but I thought it was time to just get it over with, with somebody, you know?

Melissa takes another forkful of salad and considers it before spooning it into her mouth. I don't think I've seen her eat a fry yet although they're almost gone. "Jenni, how do you know this man's not taking advantage of you? Men like that, they promise you the moon. Then the bill comes due, and suddenly you're yesterday's newspaper."

"Dan's not like that."

"Jenni, you're sweet, but it makes you a little naïve at times. You forget not everyone is as nice as you, and men can take advantage of that. You ought to think hard about breaking this off."

"Not that hard. I can't afford to leave. Without him, I can't stay in school."

"Can I meet him? I'd feel better if I knew him a little, knew where you were going, that you were safe."

Not an unreasonable request. "I'm not sure. He's a very private person."

"You two didn't sound very private the other night."

Touché. "OK, I'll ask so long me this is between us. I'm not ready for the world to know yet."

Melissa reaches across the table to take my hand in hers. "I promise, Jenni. You and me. I won't tell a soul."

32

ASKING A FAVOR

L uxurious as Dan's bedroom is, we don't always make it there. More than once we've made a mess in a place that makes me pray he tips the cleaning service really well.

This afternoon Dan has selected the living room couch for our bacchanal. His hand cradles the back of my head, holding me in place while he kisses me. I'm down to my panties so there's nothing stopping him when he brushes the other hand across my left nipple, which instantly hardens. Then he moves it to the other side and rubs it lightly across my right breast. I shiver involuntarily.

Dan licks his finger, slips it down under my panties, and rubs it right across the spot. He rubs it back and forth, slippery with his spit. Just as I feel a climax beginning to build inside me, he stops. I gasp in disappointment.

Dan hooks his thumbs into my panties and pulls them down so I'm completely naked. I'm starting to breathe heavily. I know what's coming next.

He puts a hand across my chest and pushes me back so I'm lying on the couch. I'm barely down before he's stripped off what's left of his own clothes and positioned himself on top of me. He takes the back of my neck in his right hand and holds my head so I can't look anywhere but him while his other hand parts my legs. He slides his body in between them so that he's positioned right. He moves slowly up and down without penetrating so that each stroke slides along my clitoris while we're staring into each other's eyes from about six centimeters apart. I almost release but I hold it, waiting for what I know is coming.

Finally, when I think I can't take it anymore, he repositions and enters me. As he thrusts I begin to convulse. Thirty seconds later we're both done.

After the necessary cleanup, we both return to the couch to relax in the afterglow and do nothing in particular. Five minutes post-coital is usually when Dan's at his most relaxed and agreeable which makes it the best time to ask him for something. Who says I don't have any feminine wiles? Maybe I'm not in Melissa's class yet, but I'm learning.

As he lays on his back and I not so absent-mindedly run a finger through his chest hair, I bring up the subject that's been on my mind since Melissa raised it last week.

"So I've been thinking..."

"Yes?"

"Last weekend, when you brought me back to school and we went to Sunday night service—"

"And other things, don't forget. I don't want to spoil my reputation as the devil incarnate." He gives me a grin that belongs on a devil, that's for sure. A very sexy devil. I hope five minutes wasn't too long to wait for this conversation. I glance down. Nope, still recuperating. I return to twirling my finger along his chest.

"You were taking a big risk, being together on campus like that. Someone might have seen us."

"Are there still rules against boys staying over in the girls' rooms? I wouldn't worry too much about that. I can handle a snoopy RA if it comes to that."

"I know, and that's not what I was thinking. But at the beginning you were really specific that I wasn't supposed to tell anybody about us. I had to sign that paper and everything."

"The NDA? That still applies."

"I know, and I haven't broken it. I haven't told anyone about us. Only it turns out Melissa wasn't as asleep last Sunday night as I thought."

Dan raises an eyebrow. "Really?"

"It's OK. She won't tell anyone, but she already knew something was going on. She's had to cover for me with my parents a few times, like at Thanksgiving and New Year's, and I swore her to secrecy. But that's it. I haven't even told Laura or Deirdre."

"That sounds all right then."

"I know, but Melissa's a really good friend. She's worried that she hasn't met you. I feel guilty hiding you from her."

"Do you trust her? Can she keep a secret?"

"For sure. She's not like Deirdre. She hasn't told anyone else about us yet."

"Jenni, what are you asking?"

This is the big one. I prop up on my knees so I'm looking right at him. "I wondered if we could invite her out with us sometime. Maybe pizza in Little Italy or something. So she can get to know you, see that you're not the 'devil incarnate'."

Dan sits up and gives me a serious look. "Jenni, is this important to you?"

I nod. "It is. I know it's not part of our agreement, but it would make me feel so much better if at least one of my friends could get to know you." And Melissa is the one to meet, for sure. There's no way Laura would ever approve of this, and Deirdre can't keep her mouth shut. No, it has to be Melissa.

He puts his head down and thinks silently while I hold my breath. Then he says one of the most unexpected things I've ever heard him say. "You're right."

"I am?"

"It's not fair to ask you to keep part of your life walled off like that. There are people who wouldn't approve of this and might try to use it against me; but if your friend can be discrete, it's OK if she knows about me. Not pizza though. Why don't you invite her over for dinner next Saturday?"

I peck him on the lips in gratitude. "Thank you!" I blurt, and I really mean it. There's a genuine smile on my face. If he's willing to meet my friends, then maybe this relationship has fuel for more than the six months Janine forecast. Before he has time to rethink, I lean down to kiss him again, slower this time. I move my fingers lower, and although I don't really plan it, pretty soon we're off for round two.

33

DINNER PARTY

Dan is making some fancy beef dish that takes about three hours to prepare. Thank God he doesn't expect me to cook for him. I could never live up to his standards. I was pretty impressed with myself the first time I made hot dogs without using a microwave.

The entire kitchen smells like meat. That's another reason I couldn't ask Deirdre. She's in the middle of one of her six-week vegetarian phases that usually lasts until she goes home and smells her father's cheese steaks. Dan has no patience with "salad heads." His words, not mine. Although Melissa sometimes seems to subsist on a diet of lettuce leaves and air, she has no pity on small, defenseless farm creatures and will happily tear into a cheeseburger when politeness demands it.

The doorman calls up to announce Melissa at the stroke of seven. Dan is busy putting the final touches on the dinner, so I go to the elevator to wait for Melissa. A minute later I hear the beep that signals its arrival. I open the door to the foyer, and my jaw drops to the floor.

Melissa always takes a lot of care with her appearance, but tonight she has turned it up to eleven. She's wearing five inch gold fuck me pumps that push her legs up beyond all decency. Her skirt is short enough to get her thrown out of more than one priest's classroom, and her blouse is so sheer it's hardly there at all. A tiny gold evening bag is slung across her shoulder, barely big enough for a subway token. I assume she's not planning on spending the night since there's nowhere to hide a change of clothes. I'm wearing the little black dress from Barneys and flat sandals that probably cost Dan more than my parents' mortgage payment, but suddenly I feel underdressed.

Melissa winks at me conspiratorially. "So where's this mysterious boyfriend of yours?"

I shake my head to clear out the haze. "He's in the kitchen getting dinner ready."

"Rich and he cooks. You should marry this one fast."

I ignore the implied dig. "Come on in. I'll introduce you."

We meet Dan coming out of the kitchen. Since we have company, he's dressed for dinner, black slacks, white shirt, and tie.

"Hello," says Dan with way too much twinkle in his eye. "You must be Melissa. Jenni's told me so much about you." He offers her his hand.

Melissa takes his hand politely and leans in to kiss him none-too-chastely on the cheek. She has a few inches on me to start with, and in the heels she barely needs to lean up to reach him.

"Funny, she's told me almost nothing about you." Her voice is interested, too interested if you ask me. I want Dan to like her, and vice versa, but maybe not so much, so fast.

"Why don't we go into the living room and have a drink?" Dan asks.

In the living room, Dan mixes the drinks, bourbon on the rocks for him, vodka and tonics for me and Melissa. Melissa watches him like a cat watching her owner get the cream out of the refrigerator. When he bends down for a second to look for a bottle of tonic water in the mini-fridge, Melissa makes an exaggerated wow face at me. I smile politely. I can't deny it. He is hot.

Dan brings us our glasses and takes one end of the couch. Melissa plops herself down on her knees right next to him, sprawled out so that I don't really have room to join them. I take the red chair.

"So Mr. Cortland...." says Melissa.

"Please, call me Dan."

"Oh, I don't know if I can do that. Maybe Daniel?"

Dan raises an eyebrow. "I suppose so."

"All right, Daniel." She draws out his name in a purr.

Dan glances my way, and I shrug my shoulders. I'm not sure what he was expecting, but it wasn't this. When Melissa sets her mind on something, she is a force of nature. I can't control her. He's on his own for this one, and his eyes may be bigger than his...lower parts. I did warn him. I just wish she were a little less forward.

Melissa continues. "Jenni told me you went to Fordham too. You must have graduated right before we started."

"A few years earlier than that, I expect."

"You didn't stay in the Bronx, though. How'd you end up here? Were you born in Manhattan?"

"No, I wasn't."

Hah. I could have told Melissa she wasn't going to get anywhere asking him about his past. Dan is the master of the non-answer.

"Really? So this isn't your family home? It's so...big for one person."

"Maybe a little. I picked it up the last time Manhattan real estate dipped. It was a good investment."

"That's smart."

"Smart, lucky. Hard to tell the difference sometimes."

Melissa laughs. "Oh, I'm sure you're not just lucky." She bats him on the arm playfully.

Something buzzes in the kitchen. "Time to turn the roast again." Dan lifts himself off the couch. "Jenni, why don't you give Melissa a tour of the apartment while I get the salads ready?"

"Sure," I reply, eager for the opportunity to show off. The apartment is the second most exciting thing about dating Dan, and until now I've had to keep it to myself.

"So how big is this place?" Melissa asks as we walk down the hall.

"I don't know. Dan owns the whole floor. Maybe 5,000 square feet? I never asked him. Do you need to freshen up? I can show you the guest bathroom. It's a lot cleaner than the one in Hughes Hall."

"Jenni, is this you?"

I glance back to see what she's referring to and freeze. Melissa is staring wide-eyed at one of the last photographs Terence took, the one where I'm kneeling with my face turned back toward the camera. Half my face is obscured by my hair but not enough so you can't tell it's me, and nothing else is obscured by anything. Dan promised me no one would see it but him. Then he went and hung it on his wall. I briefly consider denying it, but the photographic evidence is too blatant.

"Oh, um, yeah. It is. I forgot that was there. Dan had that taken a couple of months ago."

"Wow, girl. I don't know what to say. I'm going to have to reevaluate. I had you pegged as this little waif from the burbs, and here you are with a secret rich boyfriend who's taking nude pictures of you. I'm impressed."

"Um...thanks?"

"Oh, don't look so embarrassed. You look good. Whoever did this is a real artist. Did Dan take it? I should ask him to take my picture."

"He has a photographer friend, with a studio. Somewhere in Brooklyn I think."

"Does he do this a lot? Are these other pictures all his girlfriends too?"

"I don't know. Maybe. Some of them." For the first time I realize there's no picture of Kate on the wall. That may be significant, but Melissa doesn't give me time to stop and think about it.

"So you're not exclusive?"

The question makes the hairs on the back of my neck rise. "They aren't around any more." Even as I say it, I wonder if it's true.

Melissa nods knowingly.

We walk the rest of the way to the bathroom in silence. Melissa washes up while I stew. I lied to her. I don't know who these women are, or whether Dan stills sees any of them or not. For a while I thought it didn't matter, but from the way my gut churned when Melissa asked if we were exclusive, maybe it does.

———

I'M sure the dinner is as delicious as always, though I hardly notice. I could be eating the plastic trays from the cafeteria for all I notice. I'm too absorbed watching Melissa interact with Dan.

As I watch them banter, I realize they're actually quite alike, aside from gender and age. They're both wicked smart, way too pretty for their own good, and surprisingly circumspect about their pasts.

Dan asks Melissa where she's from, and all she says is "Westchester."

Melissa asks him where he grew up and his answer is the even less specific "New York."

I'm afraid the dinner is going to be nothing but one long awkward silence, but fortunately they discover a shared interest in the history of New York City. Melissa is taking a social science elective on the subject this semester. I can't really follow the conversation—I thought LaGuardia was an airport?—but at least they find some common ground.

By the time we've finished a couple of bottles of wine and dessert —cream puffs from a French pastry shop a few blocks away that are so full of sugar it's like mainlining Count Chocula—Dan and Melissa are laughing like old friends.

Before long, Dan is sweeping the plates away. While he's in the kitchen, Melissa turns to me. "Jenni, I had no idea. I thought I knew a few tricks, but now I feel like I ought to be asking you for lessons. When I got out of the cab and saw the building where he lived, I figured your boyfriend would be ugly, or collecting social security or something. But he's gorgeous. How'd you land him?"

"I don't know. We met in the Ramskeller."

"No, not where. How? No offense, but you're really punching above your weight here. It's not easy getting a real man to pay attention to a teenager. I know you can get them into bed." She puts up a hand. "Don't ask me how I know, but you've been with him for almost a year now."

"Closer to half a year."

"Whatever. What's the secret? Does he have a mad wife locked in the attic? Or is he really kinky, and there's something only you'll do for him?"

I'm a little fuzzy on exactly where the line between normal and kink is drawn. It's not like I have a lot of experience to compare to. "I don't know. Is a blow job kinky?"

Melissa shakes her head. "Not even."

"He thinks my feet are cute."

Melissa scoots her chair over closer to me. "Oh come on, there has to be something worse than that. You can tell me. What's the wildest thing you've done with him?"

Involuntarily my mind flashes back to the night with Kate. I don't say anything, but my face goes red enough for Melissa to squeal. "I knew it. There is something. Come on, truth or dare. I'll start. You want to know the wildest thing I ever did?"

"Sure," if it will move the conversation away from what Dan and I do in the bedroom.

Melissa stares up at the ceiling and a dreamy looks comes across her face. "This was a couple of years ago, between junior and senior years in high school. I'd gone away for a long weekend at CYO camp. A priest and a nun ran the camp, but most of the counselors were seminarians from St. Joseph's. Two of them were the most beautiful boys I'd ever seen, but it was the last night, and I couldn't choose, so I went with them both."

"You had sex with two boys the same night?"

"I had sex with two boys at the same time."

"Wait, you mean..."

"One of them had the key to the pool, so we snuck out for a late-night 'swim.' Only we didn't bring our bathing suits, and we never got in the water. We unrolled a pool mat on the concrete. One was behind me and one was in front. It was dark, but they could see each other. They were from the seminary so I figured they'd already done that much."

I try to visualize the geometry. Only in my head it's not two random seminarians. It's Dan and Tom, and—OK, let's leave that one for next week when I'm alone.

Melissa bounces forward. "OK, I told you mine. Now you tell me yours. What's the wildest thing you ever did? Don't leave out any details."

I take a sip of the port Dan brought out with dessert. "I don't think I can top that. I never had a three-way with two guys."

"You slut! You did it with another girl didn't you?"

Crap, I wasn't going to tell her that. "Well, yes." I say with eyes downcast, but a playful smile on my lips. I can play the bad girl too. I'm no longer the innocent little naïf from Easton Melissa met first day of freshman year.

"So spill. Dan must have been the guy. Who was the other girl? Was it Deirdre? I bet it was Deirdre."

"No, of course it wasn't Deirdre. It was no one you know. A friend of Dan's. It was a one time thing."

"So are you into that, then? Women? Or is this just something you do for Dan?"

I think about that. It's a really good question. "I don't know. We only did it once."

Melissa peers over her wine glass at me. The reflection off the crystal makes her eyes sparkle. "So is Dan in the habit of inviting extra women over for the evening?"

"It was just the one time."

"But you enjoyed it, right?"

I can't believe I'm about to admit this but, "Yeah, I did."

"And now you invited me over."

I sit up straight as I suddenly realize what she's thinking. "Melissa, no. That's not what I meant. I didn't plan. I just wanted you two to meet, and really, that's all."

"Shh, it's OK. I don't mind. It's kind of flattering."

Something clatters in the kitchen, and I grab at the excuse to hop up and make a quick exit. "I should see if Dan needs something."

"You do that. I'll wait here." She smiles at me enigmatically.

I need Dan to myself for just five minutes. I catch him in the kitchen loading the dishwasher. "So, um, look, about Melissa..."

"She seems very friendly."

"Yeah, that's sort of what I wanted to talk to you about."

Dan cocks an eyebrow. "Oh?"

"I think might have let something slip I shouldn't have. I mean I know I'm not supposed to talk about us, but now that you've seen how she can be..."

Dan closes the dishwasher and gets serious. "Jenni, did you tell her about our arrangement?"

"No! Absolutely not." I don't like to think about that myself. As long as the checks go straight from Dan to the bursar's office, and I never have to touch one, I can live with myself.

"OK. What then?"

"I sort of mentioned Kate, and how she spent the night. I mean, she doesn't know the details, but now I think she thinks, maybe that's why I invited her here?" I look up at him to see how he reacts.

Dan wipes his hands and hangs the dishtowel on the rack. "I take it you two haven't actually talked about this."

I shake my head. "No."

"Do you want her to spend the night?"

It's a little weird. Kate was fun, but Melissa is my roommate and we share a very small room. I imagine Melissa in bed with us. In bed with me. Brushing my hand down her side. Running my fingers through the blond hair that puddles around her shoulders as we look into each other's eyes while Dan watches us. Her smiling at Dan the way she smiles at a boy sideways when she wants him to do some-thing for her. The soft tone in her voice when she's asking a professor for an extension on a paper. My breath catches. Shit, I'm actually getting turned on. "Maybe. What do you think?"

"I think Melissa is a very attractive young lady. Also, I suspect Melissa may be a little more proactive than you're giving her credit for." He closes the dishwasher and hits the cycle button. "Tell you what. I'll take the lead. You don't have to say anything. If she seems game, I'll close the deal. If not, she can go back to the Bronx, none the wiser. No harm, no foul."

What the hell? Melissa's a big girl. She can take care of herself if anyone can. Unlike Deirdre, she's not the least bit hesitant telling men no. "OK."

"Good girl," says Dan, and before I have time to think about what I just agreed to, we're off to find Melissa.

In the living room, the three of us cuddle up on the couch and Dan regales us with some stories I've heard before, but they're new to Melissa and she reacts with obvious interest, laughing at the jokes, batting him on the arm and saying "No!" when he gets to the climax.

It's making me a little nervous to see her flirting so brazenly with him. She can turn on the charm when she wants something—like a boy to run to Pugsley's at 11:00 p.m. and bring us back a pizza—but she's never gone this far. She's acting like a sorority girl three drinks past any judgment whatsoever, and I know she didn't drink that much. I watch her. I wonder what she wants from Dan; though with him, she may have met her match.

"So Melissa, has Jenni been telling you stories about me?" Dan says.

"She has. I don't know whether to believe them."

"Don't, the truth is much, much worse." He flashes his teeth in that wicked grin he has.

"So Daniel," Melissa says in a more girlish voice than normal, "what do you do when you're not seducing innocent young coeds?"

Dan puts a finger on Melissa's cheek and half looks into her eyes with his head cocked back. "You're claiming to be innocent, are you? Somehow I doubt that."

"Say I'm not that innocent. What would you do to me if you could?"

"Who says I can't?" replies Dan, still smiling like a cheetah looking at a baby gazelle. He puts his hand on the back of her head to hold her and kisses her lightly, on the lips.

Melissa's breath catches audibly, whether from the kiss or because I'm sitting right here on the other side of them, I don't know. Dan breaks the kiss, and turns to me. He repeats the kiss, his hand in my hair now but without taking his right arm off Melissa's shoulders. When he breaks away, I look at Melissa for her reaction.

For just a second, a hint of nervousness flickers across Melissa's face. Then it's gone. She looks at me, questioning. I smile back and shrug my shoulders. She's used to being the one in charge, the one calling the shots. I don't think she realizes yet what she's stepped into here.

Dan stands. "Ladies, perhaps we should take this party to another room?"

34

FRIENDS AND LOVERS

Before things get started, I tell Dan that Melissa and I need to get ready and half-drag her off of him and into the en suite. I close the door behind us and take a deep breath. Crap, how can I say this? Something's off here, but I'm not sure what.

"What's up, Jenni?"

"I want to make sure you're OK with this. I know Dan can be a little intimidating, but he's not going to make you do anything you don't want to do. You can tell him no if you don't want to."

Melissa doesn't take the hint. "I'm fine, Jenni. Your boyfriend's really hot. Super hot."

"If you're worried about taking the train back this late, he'd be happy to pay for a cab. You don't have to stay over if you don't want to."

"You don't have to worry about me. I'm cool."

I can't tell her I'm getting cold feet, and I really don't want her to fuck Dan. Not after inviting her over her and everything I already told her. Plus, that's not the agreement I made with Dan. "It's a little weird, you know? Last time I didn't really know the woman, but you're my roommate and we live together."

Melissa puts a reassuring hand on my shoulder and looks at me.

"What's college for anyway if not a little experimentation? But maybe we ought to agree that what happens in Manhattan stays in Manhattan."

"Yes." No problem there.

"And we won't do any lesbian stuff. That'll make it less weird. Dan looks big enough for both of us."

I nod. Not totally what I'm worried about, but I'll take it.

Melissa takes me by the hand and reaches for the doorknob. "Now come on. I'm dying to see if Dan looks as good with his clothes off as he does with them on."

———

SHE'LL HAVE to wait a little longer to find out. In the bedroom, Dan has doffed his jacket and tie, but is otherwise still fully clothed. He's leaning nonchalantly on a chair and looking at us as we come out. His gaze still gives me the shivers.

He holds out his arm and Melissa walks straight up to him, wraps her right arm around his neck, and stretches up to kiss him, this time on the mouth. I mentally kick myself for not adding a no kissing rule to the no lesbian stuff rule when I had the chance. As she breaks the embrace, she sighs softly and whispers something to him. I strain to catch the words but can't make them out.

Then Melissa turns and walks to the bed giving Dan, and incidentally me, a clear view of her ass. Frankly, it's on the skinny side, but I have to admit the five-inch heels help her make the most of it.

When she reaches the bed, she turns around and smiles at Dan, only at Dan. Her attention is laser focused on him. I might as well be a lamp or a dresser, for all the notice she takes of me. She reaches around behind herself, and suddenly her blouse and skirt are falling around her feet. It's like a magic trick. I usually have to ask Dan to help me out of an outfit like that.

Two more snaps and Melissa's underwear joins the rest of her clothes on the floor. She's still smiling at Dan, hiding nothing. We're roommates so I've seen most of this before, but never so brazenly posed for inspection. There isn't an ounce of fat on her, and in my opinion she could use a little. Dan, though, doesn't seem to mind. He reaches over and takes her in his arms. He pulls her in, puts his strong left hand on her forehead, and runs his fingertips down her side in a move I know well. It's sort of funny watching it instead of feeling it, but I know from experience exactly how it makes a girl tingle. Melissa lets out a little "eep" as the shiver rushes through her. I know she's had sex before, but I can't imagine she's ever had it with someone who's as good at it as Dan is.

Then it's Dan's hand in Melissa's crotch as he kisses her. I can see his tongue slip into her mouth. Dan's hand pulsates between her thighs, and suddenly Melissa grabs him, closes her eyes, and clenches her fingers behind his back as her body shakes.

Dan smiles at her and keeps right on going as Melissa gasps and moans. She's putting on quite a show, if it is a show. Her golden hair is flying. She looks like she's trying to say something, but all she finally manages is an irreverent, "Holy fuck."

Embarrassed, I look away. I don't think the plan was for me to be a voyeur tonight so I slip off my shoes and do the best I can at wriggling out of my dress, while trying not to listen to the noises Melissa is making. They don't form complete sentences, or even complete words, but this isn't English class and I get the drift.

By the time I'm plausibly naked, Melissa and Dan are horizontal on the bed. Dan's unbuttoned his shirt and kicked off his shoes, but is otherwise still clothed.

I join them in the bed, and Dan briefly smiles and reaches for me. Before he can say anything, Melissa is unbuckling his belt. She slips her hand in and out it pops. Dan is, of course, ridiculously erect, not that this is an unusual state for him. Melissa doesn't miss a beat. She wraps her hand around it and begins stroking. Dan unbuttons his shirt and hands it to me. I lay it over a chair, and turn back to them. Melissa and Dan have moved to a kneeling position, their bodies pressed together and mouths locked. It's mildly interesting in a Discovery Channel sort of way, but I thought I'd be a more active participant.

When they finally come up for air. Dan turns to me. I get ready to snuggle in, but instead he mouths, "Wait." Then he strips his pants off and passes them to me. I fold them as best I can and lay them with his shirt on the chair. It only takes me a second, but it's long enough for Dan to have pushed Melissa onto her back and entered her. Her legs are wrapped around him like a pair of skinny anacondas. The view from outside is not attractive. Is this what Dan looks like when he's inside me?

I try to figure out where to insert myself in this tableaux vivante—I learned that word in art history class last semester—but I'm not sure there's room for a piece of paper between the two of them, much less a second girl.

The best access seems to be from behind Dan. I scoot over, but one of Melissa's legs gets in the way. I have to climb off the bed and come around from the other side.

Hesitantly, I reach out my hand to try stroke Dan as he's sliding in and out of her, but the angle is awkward and instead my hand slips down Melissa's thigh. She squeals, not a fun squeal, and I snatch it back.

OK, moving from the front was stupid with the two of them squashed together like that so I reach around behind Dan and start to tickle him, very lightly, softly like he showed me how. Only then, Melissa slips her head out from under him long enough to give me a glare that makes me curl up.

Dan slows for a moment and looks at me. "Jenni, why don't—"

Then Melissa lets out a half moan/half scream and bucks underneath him. "Oh, like that Daniel. Don't stop."

I'm not sure how to make this work. Kate was different. She seemed as interested in me as in Dan and vice versa. It was more like the two of them paying attention to me. This is more like it's Dan and Melissa having sex and I'm the servant hiding in the closet who can't slip out without admitting she shouldn't have been there in the first place.

In the end, I give up and lie on my back and wait for the two of them to finish. Melissa is moaning and crying. "Oh God, Oh Daniel,

Oh God, Oh Daniel, please don't stop, Oh God, Oh Daniel." It's like a mantra. I'm not sure who she's trying to hypnotize, him or her or me.

I want Dan to stop and call me over, let me be part of this, but he just keeps moving. I know how long he can last when he wants to draw things out. Listening to the two of them, it feels longer than ever.

When I can't take it any longer, I make an excuse. "I have to pee," I announce loudly.

Dan mutters something in response about coming back, but he's talking into Melissa's breast and Melissa moans so I give up and get out of the bed. Dan and Melissa are wrapped up in each other. It's sort of ugly and gross, all asses and legs and backs. Neither notices when I grab some underwear and a robe and go out into the hallway instead of the bathroom.

Lying on the couch in the living room, I'm numb. What did I think would happen? I'm yesterday's newspaper compared to Melissa. Of course, Dan would rather be with her than me. He should be with someone like her. She knows how to wear the right dress for a party and talk to people without making a fool of herself. She already fits better in his world than I ever will. Maybe they'll even get married. Guys like him aren't for girls like me. It's over. Why was I so stupid? I don't even have anyone to blame but myself. If I hadn't wanted him to meet my friends, if I hadn't invited Melissa over, if I hadn't let him sleep over after chapel. If, if, if.

I'm still lying there cataloging my mistakes when Dan comes into the room. He's naked but I stare at the ceiling.

"Jenni, are you OK?"

"I'm fine," I reply in a monotone that betrays my lie. "You can go be with Melissa."

"She's washing up," He sits down beside me on the couch, so I have to sit up too, but I keep looking at the ceiling. If I look at him right now, I'll break down.

"What happened to you? I looked around and you were gone."

I cross my arms and pull my knees to my chest. I'm not going to cry. I'm not going to cry.

Dan wraps an arm around me, then moves my head so I have to look at him. "Jenni, you have to talk to me. I can tell you're upset, but I can't read your mind."

I glare at him. Like he wasn't right there in the room. Like he doesn't know exactly what was going on. But he only stares back at me blankly. Before I can think of anything to say, Melissa comes in. She's wearing one of Dan's three-zillion thread count cotton bathrobes.

"Hey, you two. I had fun. We should do that again." She hops down onto the couch next to us and kisses Dan on the cheek. "Did you have fun?"

"Yes," Dan says.

"Yes," I lie.

Dan smiles and pulls me to him but he's looking at her. "That was intense. Are you OK?"

"More than OK," says Melissa with a big smile.

He should be asking me if I'm OK. I'm not OK I shout inside my head, but what I say is, "Me too."

35

REGRETS

When I wake up Sunday morning, Melissa is already gone. She's not usually one to let herself be packed off to the Bronx with a friendly goodbye, a kiss on the cheek, and cab fare. Maybe she's as interested in avoiding awkward silences over breakfast as I am. We're still sharing a shoebox-sized room for the last few weeks of the semester. Even if the night hadn't headed straight into the crapper, we'd still have to look at each other, knowing what we did. Awkward doesn't begin to describe it.

Even if Melissa had said no and laughed it out, which is sort of what I expected her to do, even if we hadn't shared Dan, she'd still know about us. Why did I tell her so much? The one silver lining is that she's not going to want what we did to get around campus any more than I am, so my secret stops with her. Still if I had a do over, I wouldn't let her into the borough of Manhattan, much less Dan's apartment. To say I didn't think this through doesn't begin to cover it.

Monday morning, I'm so nervous about how Melissa's going to react that I let two 4 trains go by without getting on. When I finally do get back to Hughes Hall, it turns out that, as usual, my imagination has outrun reality.

"Oh, hi Jenni," says Melissa, who is putting the final touches on her eyebrows in front of the mirror on her desk. "Welcome back."

"Um, hi." She's acting surprisingly perky, almost Deirdre like. I'm cautious. I toss my bag onto my bed, and sit down in my chair. Laura and Deirdre are out already. I guess it's as good a time as any to wake the elephant in the room.

"So, um, are you OK? Everything good?"

"Yeah, why wouldn't it be? I had a great time. Thanks for inviting me. Dan really knows what he's doing. Maybe we can do it again some time."

"I don't know. I was thinking it was sort of a one time thing, like for his birthday, you know?"

"Oh, OK. Let me know if you change your mind. Anyway, did you hear about Tom and Sharon? They broke up this weekend. I haven't gotten the whole story yet, but they had a big fight in front of Edwards Parade about how much time Tom was spending with Brett. Then Tom accused of her being paranoid. She said, 'I know what I saw'," and with that Melissa is off and running with the latest dorm gossip, and it's like the whole weekend didn't happen. I don't know how she does it, but I guess she isn't as obsessed with Dan as I am, which, when I think about it, is a very lucky thing.

———

THE WEEK SLIPS by with the usual lethal mixture of organic chemistry lab and philosophy. Seriously, like science majors don't have enough work already. Why does the university make us suffer through liberal arts courses they don't even care enough about to hire a real professor to teach instead of a grad student? But I digress.

Friday afternoon can't come too soon for me, but come it eventually does, and I am once again packing my books for a weekend with Dan. A weekend when I have him all to myself, I might add.

Then Laura pops through the door. "Oh Jenni, I'm glad I caught you. Someone called for you on the hall phone earlier. Ms. Parent something?"

Ms. Parenton is Dan's secretary. I've never met her, but he's mentioned her once or twice. The couple of times I've talked to her she sounded very efficient.

"What did she want?"

"Let me find the paper. The message was sort of strange, so I asked her to repeat it so I could write it down." She roots around through some notebooks on her desk. "Ah, here it is."

Laura begins to read. "Mr. Cortland had to go out of town on business so he won't be able to meet you in Manhattan at his apartment as usual. Please stay on campus this weekend."

"Oh." My face falls. I guess I should be grateful that Dan can spend as much time with me as he does. But still, I was really looking forward to getting away with him this weekend, just the two of us, unlike last weekend's disaster. Now I'm stuck in the boring-ass Bronx with nothing to do but eat bad cafeteria food and study. I start taking my textbooks out of my bag and putting them back on my desk. I'm so wrapped up in my own disappointment that I'm surprised when Laura asks the obvious question.

"Jenni, who's Mr. Cortland?"

I freeze, my hand gripped tight around my super thick Organic Chemistry text.

Laura repeats the question. "Jenni?"

My mind races as I try to think of a plausible lie. Wrong number? No, she asked for me. Shit, why did she ask for me? Until now Dan's always been good about being discrete. Maybe his secretary didn't know she wasn't supposed to leave a message? Shit.

"Jenni, is this what you've been doing every weekend? Not going home to your parents?"

"Laura, I don't know. I'm just...please don't tell anyone, OK?"

"Jenni, of course I won't tell anyone if you don't want me to, but why do you think you have to hide it? If you have a boyfriend, that's cool. None of us are nuns."

"It's...complicated."

"So you're dating somebody off campus. It's no big deal. I guess he's little older if he has a secretary calling for him. It's not like you're turning tricks on Fordham Road."

Oh Laura, if you only knew. Half of me wants to come clean and tell her everything. Half of me wants to hide in the mythical steam pipes under Keating Hall and not come out until graduation.

"I know. I'm just not ready to tell anyone yet. Please, can we keep it our secret? For now?"

Laura doesn't understand, but in the end she agrees not to say anything. I know I can trust her to keep quiet. Thank God Laura took the call instead of Deirdre. Deirdre couldn't keep a secret if her financial aid depended on it (sort of like mine does).

———

THIS ISN'T the first weekend Dan has skipped, but before now he always gave me enough advance notice that I could plan something to do, either term papers or test prep, or a trip into the city with the roomies. When we do that I am very careful to stay away from anywhere Dan and I have been. Not that this is too hard since Dan prefers places that are a thousand times past our student budgets.

This weekend, however, I'm left at loose ends. I finished all my homework for next week by Thursday night. Deirdre's off on another campus retreat. Joshua's family in Connecticut invited Laura up for the weekend, and Melissa is nowhere to be found. Maybe she went home to visit her mother. That's lucky. I'm not sure I'm ready to spend a weekend alone with her. Melissa may believe that what happens off campus stays off campus, but I'm still a little weirded out by last weekend.

I try to study for the upcoming finals, but my head isn't in it. It's too nice a Spring day to spend cooped up in the library. Instead, I treat myself to a trip to the Bronx Zoo, practically around the corner from campus though most students manage to finish four years here without ever entering its gates. However, it's depressing walking around alone, watching all the couples and families. Maybe I can get Dan to take me next weekend. He'd enjoy the colobus monkeys. I can imagine his big, booming voice making up over-the-top soap opera plots about their familial relations. "Look, Jenni, that one is cheating on her husband with the younger monkey, but she doesn't know that Big John over there is secretly in love with her and he's planning to murder the husband so he can share her bananas."

I leave after only an hour. At least I got out in the sunshine for a little while.

No reason to rush on the way home so I take the long way around, up Southern Blvd and through the parking lot. As I round the corner of Edwards Parade, I spot a big black Lexus parked in front of Hughes Hall, a car I know. Dan's car.

My heart leaps. He must have come home early. He didn't have to drive up here himself. If he'd called, I would have hopped the first 4 train into town. I pick up my pace, almost skipping I'm so happy to see him. And then I freeze.

Because Dan isn't in the car. He's standing next to it, and Melissa is standing next to him, facing him. Neither of them sees me. They're looking at each other. Then the next thing I know she leans up, puts her arms around his neck, and kisses him. It's not a long kiss, but it's long enough not to leave any doubt what's going on.

Before I can break down completely, I turn and run.

Somehow I make it to the women's room on the first floor of Keating Hall before the tears come. It's the same one where I collapsed after the dean told me my financial aid letter wasn't a mistake. The irony burns like hydrochloric acid. Seven months and I'm right back where it all started.

36

DEAR DAN

Keating Hall is empty on weekends so I manage a good long cry without being interrupted. After a while, I'm not sure how long, I wear myself out. Then the recriminations start.

How, how could I be so stupid? Why did I introduce Dan to Melissa? Of course he'd pick her over me. She's smarter, prettier, and more sophisticated. I was starting to let myself think that this might be something real. That I meant more to him than another photo on his wall. Stupid, stupid, stupid!

OK, breathe. What now? Do I have to drop out? No, spring semester's almost over. I'm pretty sure Dan has already paid the bill. I can finish out the year. Maybe get a loan for next year. As if it matters. As if anything matters any more. Funny, I kept telling myself I was only doing this to pay for school, but now that school is the only thing I have left I don't think I care about it at all. All I can think about is Dan and Melissa.

I can't go back to our room, not after this. If I see her, I'm going to break down. And of course I can't go to Dan's place. Maybe I can sleep on Tom's floor, or Laura might ask Joshua to let me crash in his room.

Or there's Theresa. She lives off campus so she has more space. I can shuttle back and forth between friends' rooms until finals are over.

OK, it's not going to be easy, but I can do this. One day at a time. One night at a time. I feel like throwing up every time my thoughts circle back to that kiss, but I need to be level headed. I cannot let this derail me.

Tom's roommate is away for the weekend so Tom lets me borrow his bed. Most importantly, Tom doesn't ask me too many questions when I tell him I can't go back to my room.

"I won't be any trouble," I promise.

Tom smiles. "No problem. If you want to talk about it, I'm here. But you don't have to. No pressure."

"Thanks, Tom." Spontaneously I hug him. He freezes for a second, then hugs me back. "You really are a good friend."

Saturday night I sleep fitfully, if at all.

Sunday I barely get out of bed. You can only cry for so long. Eventually nothingness takes over. I'm numb, just numb. Biology forces me out of bed long enough to use the toilet. By Sunday evening I'm functional enough to consume some empty calories at the cafeteria. I'm worried I might run into Melissa there, but she's probably eating with Dan tonight. I wonder if he cooks for her too? Probably. He likes to cook.

Dan never promised me he would be exclusive. He didn't ask me to be either, though any chance otherwise was mostly theoretical. I didn't even think about anyone else, not seriously at least. Not that it was too hard. Even the boys here who are as pretty as he is, they're not him. Intellectually, I can see that he's not the only attractive man on the planet, but somehow given the choice between him and anyone else, the answer is always him. Is it too much to expect that he'd feel the same way about me?

I guess it is.

I sort of assumed Dan saw other women when he wasn't with me. Mostly I tried not to think about it, didn't ask him what he did during the week, at least not until he walked across the TV screen with Kate on his arm. But it never occurred to me that he might hook up with one of my friends.

And I brought her to him! That's the stupidest thing. It's all my fault. Scariest thought: has Dan actually broken up with me? If that's what he wanted, he'd tell me, right? Oh shit, what if he wants us both? Me and Melissa switching off every other weekend? It is exactly the sort of thing he would do and expect me to go along with. But if that's what he's planning, why did he lie and tell me he was going away this weekend?

Dinner is spaghetti with meat sauce. It tastes like nothing. Not bad, that would be normal, but nothing. I twirl a piece of spaghetti around my fork while I think. No, I can't do it. I don't care what Dan wants or what he expects. There's a stone in my stomach when I think about it. I promised him no commitments, no drama, but I can't. Absolutely not. I cannot go through that again, not even if that's the price I have to pay to stay in school. As much as I want to graduate, as much as I want to be with him, there comes a point where the cost is too high.

OK. That's it. Decision made. I push my chair back from the half-finished plate and stand up. If Dan wants Melissa, he can have her; but he's not getting me too. I'm not going to be his backup plan any more. And if school is what it costs, so be it.

I'm not happy about it but enough moping around. What was it Janine said? Six months? I made it seven, and got an extra year of school in the bargain. That's something right?

I drop my tray at the dish counter and, in a burst of energy, decide to get some ice cream for dessert on the way out. The ice cream isn't as good as the Haagen Dazs Dan buys, but right now some cheap chocolate therapy is just what I need. And damn it, I deserve it after the weekend I've had.

Marching across campus in the orange twilight with my ice cream cone held high, I decide I'm going to sleep in my own bed tonight. Melissa won't be there anyway. Dan only let me come home Sunday night that once. God, what was I thinking, letting him sleep over? If anyone had seen us, but I guess that was the least of my worries.

"Oh hey, you're back early," says Deirdre, when I march into our room.

It takes me a few seconds to realize she doesn't know I stayed on campus this weekend. She's the only one of us who's still completely in the dark. I should probably tell her, but I don't have the strength, so I lie.

"Yeah, I don't think I'm going to go home again until after exams so you're stuck with me on the weekends now. Put a sock on the door if you need the room to yourself."

"Cool. About that…" and we're off into a long and involved discussion of her love life. Deirdre recounts what happened at the Martyr's Court party last weekend and how, somehow, that explains why she's now seeing Will 2 instead of Will 1, except that she's not really into either of them but she thinks that Alex might like her if he could just forget about his girlfriend back in New Jersey.

As I sit on the bed and listen to Deirdre chatter on, I realize I've missed this. I've been so wrapped up in Dan this year that I've barely had any time for my friends. I may only have a few weeks left, less than a month, but I resolve to make those weeks count. Just because I don't have Dan any more doesn't mean I don't have friends.

————

WHEN I WAKE up Monday morning, Melissa's bunk has not been slept in. Half of me is still upset that mine has. The other half is relieved that I don't have to see her. That is a conversation I am not looking forward to. Maybe if I'm lucky she'll stay with Dan for the rest of the semester. Then I can go back to Pennsylvania and never have to see either of them again.

Meanwhile finals are approaching fast and I still have class. I surprise myself by actually looking forward to organic chem. Right now it's the least anxiety producing part of my life, which should give you some idea of how fucked up I am. I may not be the complete basket case I was two days ago, but I still feel like someone ripped my heart out of my chest and pureed it for the Monday night mystery meat in the cafeteria.

Professor Bolotowksy is explaining enols and enolates and carbonyl reactions and I don't know what else because I'm slowly coming to the uncomfortable realization that I'm not finished with Dan yet. I've made my decision—and even if it was a painful one, that's big pile of carbonyl reactions lifted from my shoulders—but I haven't actually told him. Until I do I'm not going to be free.

After class I go back to my room. Thankfully it's empty. I sit down at my desk and take out some paper and a blue pen. I could use the word processor in the lab, but this feels like a letter that should be handwritten.

"Dear Dan," I begin and that's where I stop. How exactly do I do this? I have even less experience breaking up with somebody than being with somebody. Has he already broken up with me or am I breaking up with him? What exactly is the protocol here?

A knock at the door interrupts my deliberation. It's Kathy from down the hall.

"Hey, Jenni. Glad I caught you. My roommate took a message for you earlier. Some man called. Allison told me to tell you he said it was important that you call him back before five. She wrote it down."

Briefly my heart jumps with the irrational joy that it might be Dan with an explanation for all this, but the yellow sticky note Kathy hands me has an unfamiliar number and name, Lawrence Fredkin.

"Allison made me promise to give it you when you got in. Something about a deadline?"

"Yeah, OK, thanks. Tell her I got it. I'll call him back when I get a minute."

Kathy leaves and I slap the note down on my desk and return to the letter. Where was I? I guess there's nothing for it but to write and let the ink flow where it may. I begin:

Dear Dan,

I'm sorry I can't face you in person, but I can't. It's too painful.

I know I wasn't supposed to get involved. You were always clear this wasn't a "relationship." I wasn't your girlfriend and you weren't my boyfriend. We were two consenting adults (you a little more adult than me, I suppose) having some fun, no strings attached.

And I thought I was OK with that. I honestly did. Sometimes I was. Only along the way things got complicated. When I was with you, everything was fine. Better than fine, in fact. I'd be lying if I said I didn't enjoy some of it.

But then I'd go back to campus where thoughts of you—where you were, what you were doing, who you were with—started to eat at me. First Kate, and now, well, you know. I don't think I can go through that again.

So I think it's best if we don't see each other any more.

Oh God, I can feel the tears starting to come. I try to squint them back. I have to get this over with. There's no use drawing it out. I scribble as fast as I can:

I appreciate everything you've done for me. I'm sorry it didn't work out. I hope you'll respect my decision. Please don't call.

I almost sign it "Love, Jenni," then catch myself. Love is the one thing this relationship never was. "Respectfully yours"? "Sincerely yours"? Too formal. "Your friend"? Is that even true?

In the end I sign it with my name:

Jenni

There. Done. Now put it in an envelope and bring it to the post office and it's over. I think I have a blank envelope in my drawer somewhere. I pull it open and push aside the old blue books, paper clips, and birthday cards. A white corner sticks out from underneath the October issue of Discover. As I reach for it to seal this relationship once and forever, the door opens and Melissa comes in.

37

THE RAM

Melissa comes up short when she sees me sitting at my desk. I don't think she was expecting to find me here.

"Oh, hi," she says.

"Hello," I reply. My tone is flat.

"Jenni, are you OK? You sound off."

"I saw you."

She pretends ignorance. "Saw me what?"

"I saw Dan picking you up in front of the dorm on Saturday. I saw you kissing him."

"Oh. Look, Jenni, I can explain."

I put a hand up to stop her. "Don't. Don't lie to me. You can do anything you want, but not that."

"So, um, look, I don't know...Um." She's at a loss for words. This is a first.

I continue. "I don't blame you. I know what he's like. I know what he does. I'm sure you started out thinking it was only a talk, then maybe a drink, then a kiss. It's not your fault. It's the way he is, but I don't want to hear about it, OK? Anyway, I made my decision. It's over."

"Um, OK?"

"I don't blame you if you want to be with Dan. Maybe you'll last longer than I did. Or not. I don't know. But can you do me one favor?"

Melissa pulls her desk chair over and sits next to me. Her face is a mask of concern. "Sure, Jenni. Anything. You know that."

I take a deep breath. I made my decision, but this is still hard. "Ask him not to come back to campus, OK? Here. Give him this." I stuff the letter into the envelope and hand it to her. "It explains everything."

"You're breaking up with him?" Melissa sounds shocked.

"We were never really together, but I guess you knew that, right?"

Melissa leans back. Her expression is pained, almost mournful. "Wow. I wish I'd known before...I just wish you'd told me sooner." She leans in and puts a hand on my shoulder, "Look, Jenni, maybe you should leave campus. Visit your parents for real for a few days. Give yourself some time to process this. I don't think you're going to want to be here for the next few days."

"You know I can't leave, not with exams. I have to finish out the semester. It may be my last one." I smile ruefully.

———

I USUALLY SLEEP in and skip breakfast on Tuesday because I don't have class until 10:30. I'm still half-asleep when Laura and Deirdre burst into the room.

Deirdre shoves a copy of the school paper, The Ram, under my nose. "Jenni, is this you?"

I push the paper away and sit up in the bed. "What?" My eyes aren't focusing yet, so I rub them with my hands.

Deirdre plops down on the bed next to me. She's panting and her hair is flying every which way, like she ran here. Has she been crying? "In the school paper. There's an article on the front page. It sounds like you."

"It's not her," Laura says firmly. "That is not Jenni. No way."

"Let me see." I pick up the paper, and my face goes white. Dan's photo is right there on the front page, but it's the headline that smashes me across the cheek:

FORDHAM BOARD MEMBER IN IMPROPER RELATION-SHIP WITH STUDENT

Quickly I scan the article:

Daniel Cortland, FCO 1979 and member of the university Board of Trustees for the last two years, has been using the campus as his own private singles bar, The Ram has learned.

Cortland, who recently voted in favor of both tuition increases and financial aid cuts, has been offering "scholarships" to financially compromised undergraduates who spend time with him at his Manhattan apartment on Fifth Avenue.

Cortland's position on the Board of Trustees provides him access to student data. "At first, I thought it was strange that a board member would want to see individual student financial records," said junior administrator Lisa Tortello. "He said he was heading a committee to determine whether money problems were causing students to drop out." The Ram was unable to confirm the existence of any such committee.

One Fordham sophomore interviewed by the Ram, whose name is being withheld at her request, found herself unable to cover her tuition following financial aid cuts earlier in the year. Cortland offered to arrange a "private scholarship" in exchange for her spending weekends with him at his Manhattan apartment. In addition Cortland supplied her with numerous gifts of clothes, expensive jewelry, and cash.

"My father had been laid off. My financial aid was cut. I was going to have to drop out of school. I didn't know where to turn so when Daniel offered to help me, it didn't feel like I had a choice," said the sophomore. "I was already sharing a dorm with three other girls, and I got all my textbooks used or from the library. Work study didn't come close to covering the bill. There was no other way I could afford to keep going. When he offered to help, I thought he meant he'd help me get my financial aid back.

"I know I shouldn't have agreed to meet him at his apartment, alone, but he was busy. It made sense that he couldn't come up to campus. Only when I got there, he made it obvious that this was a private arrangement, something the school didn't need to know about. If I did this for him, he'd take care of my problems. I didn't want to, but I didn't think I could say no."

As of press time, calls to Mr. Cortland's office have not been returned.

I drop the newspaper on the sheets. It feels like someone kicked me in the stomach. If I weren't already in bed, I'd collapse. I clutch the blanket in my fists and try to hold on.

Dan's on the Board of Trustees? He never told me that, though it would explain what he was doing on campus that night. And he's responsible for me losing my financial aid? Did he do all this to coerce me into his bed? Dan's controlling, but he's not that manipulative, is he?

Then again, how well do I really know him? I've never met his family, and very few of his friends. I told myself he was a very private person, but maybe that's not it at all. Oh crap, was he hiding me because he didn't want anyone to know what he'd done? Is that why he made me sign the NDA way back at the beginning? Because he was doing something illegal? And if that's true, what is he going to do now that the story is out? He's going to see this. There's no way he's not, and he's going to think I said those things about him, that I think that about him. If he thinks I betrayed him like this... A small piece of me is suddenly very cold and very afraid.

"Jenni, is it you?" Deirdre asks again.

"I didn't talk to the Ram," is all I can mumble. The gist of the article is correct, and there are a lot of details that point to me. The reporter claims to have talked to someone, and I know I didn't talk to any reporter about this. Could the reporter have made up the quotes? Do reporters do that? It's only a campus paper, not the New York Times. But then how did they find everything out?

"Jenni, do you know this man?" Laura says.

"Jenni, please tell me it isn't you," Deirdre says. She looks desperate, like she's just finding out there's no Santa Claus.

I'm too devastated to lie. "Yes," I say softly. I muster enough strength to look at her but that's it. There's nothing else I can say.

Deirdre grabs me and hugs me. "Why didn't you tell us? We could have done something." She starts sobbing.

Laura looks shocked. "Jenni, it's true?"

I pat Deirdre on the back and look at Laura. It's too much. None of it makes any sense, but I can't deny it any longer. Defeated, I slump into Deirdre's arms. "It's true."

Deirdre holds me tight in her arms and I let her. "Oh Jenni, I'm so sorry. It's not too bad. The article doesn't name you. I don't think anybody but us could figure out you're the girl they're talking about."

Poor Deirdre, concerned about my nonexistent reputation. I suppose I should be too, but all I can think about is what a fool I've been. My heart is torn apart into a thousand little pieces. And it's my own fault too. I knew what this was. I knew what I was signing up for. I knew Dan wasn't my boyfriend. But I ignored all the evidence and believed it anyway. Why? How could I be so stupid? Only now that my heart has been torn out of my chest, stomped on, and smeared all over the floor for everyone to see, can I admit it. I loved him. I wanted to believe he loved me too.

Laura is pacing back and forth across the room, like a tiger in a cage that's way too small for her. It takes her three and half steps to get from one side to the other, then turn around again. She's almost monologuing. "Should we sue the Ram for libel? No, that doesn't work if the article's really about this Cortland man. You could sue him, or maybe the university. It's probably a breach of privacy. The university shouldn't have let him see your records."

"We can't do that," Deirdre pleads. "If we do, everyone will know it's her."

"Only if it goes to court," Laura replies. "The university will want to settle this fast and quiet."

"Everyone, be quiet," I say. "I'm not suing anyone."

"You don't have to make up your mind now, Jenni," says Laura, "but you should talk to somebody. I know a professor at the Law School who's all about women's rights. She has tenure so I bet she would help us."

"No, I just want this to go away. We're not going to tell anybody, OK? Not even if you swear them to secrecy." I look straight at Deirdre as I say this. Please, please don't tell anybody.

"Of course, Jenni," Deirdre replies. "Nobody." Laura scowls but doesn't say anything.

———

FOR THE NEXT forty-eight hours I do not leave our room except to go to the bathroom. I live on cereal Laura and Deirdre smuggle out of the cafeteria. I think about calling Dan, but really what is there to say to him? Why are you such a controlling asshole? Why did you rescue me when I was trapped with no way out? Why aren't you the man I want you to be? Why couldn't you just love me? Did you have to pay for it? Why did you have to make it all so cheap?

In the end there's nothing I can say.

The article is the talk of the campus. Usually the Ram sits in bins collecting pigeon poop, but all copies of this week's issue were gone within an hour. Laura takes economics with one of the reporters, and he told her that the administration is threatening to shut the Ram down and expel everyone involved if they reprint. They are livid about the article and have been pressuring the paper divulge their source so they can expel her.

This is the first time in anyone's memory the Ram has printed a story hot enough to censor. The editor-in-chief, a communications major, has hooked up with some professors from the law school. They're having a grand old time defending the First Amendment and academic freedom. Meanwhile, I hide in my room, praying no one connects the dots and outs me.

Surprisingly few students have actually read the article. Anyone who wasn't up and out by 10:00 a.m. missed it. Not that this stops them from speculating on the identity of the unnamed sophomore.

The favorite seems to be a hard-looking punk rock girl named Dora. Dora is extremely attractive, only she dresses aggressively in army surplus and dyes her hair purple on a campus otherwise split between preppy and grunge. She stands out enough for everyone to know who she is; but no one really knows her, so she makes the perfect suspect. As far as my roommates have heard, no one has mentioned me.

The pain gradually shifts to simple numbness. Friday morning, Laura informs me that she has had enough of my moping. I have to get out of bed, take a shower, and leave the room. I'm growing tired of smuggled Cheerios so I grudgingly agree.

The shower helps some. I still feel awful, but at least I'm not gross. As I leave the bathroom, two freshman girls from down the hall spot me and and gape open-mouthed like I'm Mary Magdalene back from the dead, but don't say anything. Weird.

Deirdre thinks I should dress up a bit, but I can't bring myself to do more than throw on some jeans and sweats. We hurry out of the dorm to hit breakfast before it closes. There's a funny feeling in the air, but honestly I'm too numb to care. Whatever.

As we make the short trek to the cafeteria, several groups of students stop talking about whatever they're talking about and look at us. One pair of girls coming the other direction openly stares at the two of us. Do I know them? I glare back, but they don't say anything, just watch us pass.

As we're about to enter McGinley Center, Tom bursts out of the big glass doors. He's panting. "Jenni, thank God I found you. Have you seen this?" He thrusts a newspaper into my hands, not the skinny campus paper but one of the thick city tabloids, the New York Post.

It's rolled up when he hands it to me, but as I unroll it my stomach drops. The headline isn't quite as classic as Headless Body Found in Topless Bar, but it's close:

CATHOLIC SCHOOLGIRL BY DAY
PROSTITUTE BY NIGHT

And right below it are two photos, both unmistakably me. One in my old high school uniform and one completely, totally naked.

38

THE POST

The front page of the tabloid is split vertically down the middle. On the left I'm holding my books and looking off to the side, like I'm talking to someone who's been cropped out. I guess the Post copied it from my high school yearbook or the St. Agnes school newspaper.

But on the right: oh my God. It is the naked profile of me kneeling that hangs in Dan's hallway. They've covered my nipples with a black bar, but I'm looking straight at the camera and smiling.

"Has, has everyone seen this?" I stammer to Tom.

"The bookstore stopped selling it when they realized what was inside, but yeah, pretty much. Some seniors went off campus, bought a stack in Little Italy, and have been hawking them for ten bucks each."

Panicked I flip to page four. There's a photo of me (clothed, thank God) kissing Dan somewhere in Manhattan. Below it, the headline reads:

THEOLOGY, CHEMISTRY, AND SEX ED

Sexy Fordham sophomore, Jennifer McGrath, arranged a very special scholarship with Board of Trustees member Dan Cortland after her financial aid was cut last fall, sources tell the New York Post. Tuition at the Jesuit university in the Bronx has been rising faster than the rate of inflation for several years. However, it was financial aid cuts that forced at least one student into an uncomfortable position.

McGrath has been seen around town for months with venture capitalist and Fordham alumnus Cortland, causing not a few tongues to wag at the difference in their ages, but only recently has the true nature of their relationship come to light.

"We thought she was going home on the weekends," said roommate Deirdre Llewellyn. "We had no idea this was going on."

Shit, shit, shit! I knew Deirdre couldn't keep her mouth shut.

According to another close friend whose name we have agreed to withhold, Cortland "likes Jenni to dress up in her Catholic high school uniform. Sometimes he wears a priest's collar and tells her to confess her sins to him, then has her do penance on her knees."

According to classmates interviewed by the Post, Jenni (as her friends call her) is known on campus as a hard working pre-med who studies a lot and doesn't participate in extracurricular activities or go to parties. "She was so quiet. We didn't even think she had a boyfriend," said one classmate interviewed by the Post.

"I gave her an A. She was a bright, if shy, student," said Jane Samuels, Associate Professor of Anthropology.

Students and faculty were divided on the apparent arrangement.

"It's not fair," said Roslyn Wells, a junior business major. "I had to borrow a lot of money to stay in school while she ran off to play in Manhattan with her rich boyfriend. You shouldn't have to sleep with a billionaire to pay for school."

Senior Pablo Regas was more understanding. "Times are tough. She's an adult. It's nobody's business but hers who she dates."

"I think the administration ought to take a hard look at what they're driving students to," said Pierre Blum, S.J., a novice studying for the priesthood. "Fordham should be accessible to everyone, without requiring them to go into sex work."

Professor Linda Rothwell of the theology department added, "I think we need to focus on the impropriety of a member of the Board of Trustees abusing his position to take advantage of young women. This is only the latest incident in a long history of the Catholic hierarchy treating women as lesser human beings."

When asked to comment, Fordham Dean Dennis Maresca issued the following statement. "Fordham endeavors to make a world-class education available to all through a combination of scholarships, need-based financial aid, and work study. We have strict policies prohibiting personal relationships between faculty and students." Mr. Maresca declined to answer whether board members were considered members of the faculty under these policies.

When contacted, Mr. Cortland's office said he was not available for comment. However, his attorney called back an hour later with the following statement: "Any relationship that may or may not exist between Mr. Cortland and Ms. McGrath is a private matter between two consenting adults. We fail to see how this is newsworthy. We categorically deny any allegations of impropriety."

As of press time, Miss McGrath, who shares a dorm room without a telephone with three other students, could not be reached for comment.

I stare at the words on the page, willing them not to be there, willing them to change into some other girl's name or vanish like invisible ink. They remain stubbornly in focus. That's when my world goes dark for the second time.

———

"Jenni. Jenni, are you OK? Do I need to call FERS?" Tom is shaking me and tapping me on the face. For some reason I'm on the sidewalk.

"No, no ambulance," I force out with what little breath I have left.

Laura is standing, pressed up on the other side of me, waving some curious students away. "It's OK. She got a little light headed. Nothing to see here."

One of them stops anyway, and tries to get around her. "Is that—"

"Leave!" she snarls. "None of your business," and she physically blocks him with her body.

"Help me get her up," Deirdre says to Tom.

Tom kneels beside me. "Jenni, are you OK? Do you want to go home?"

Home. Oh God, yes. Anywhere but here. Anywhere away from Fordham and Dan Cortland and tabloids and just away. "Yes, home," I stammer.

"OK, we'll take you back to the dorm," Tom says.

"No," I state, more sharply than I intended. "Not to the dorm. I can't stay here. I'm going back to Easton."

———

DEIRDRE SITS ON HER BED, biting her hair and looking embarrassed. Good. Maybe if she hadn't talked to the Post, they wouldn't have figured out who I was. She probably didn't even know she was talking to a reporter, but I don't care. Given how chatty she is, they probably didn't even have to ask her any questions, just stand next to her and take notes while she blabbed my secrets. A little voice in the back of my head reminds me that Deirdre didn't know all the secrets the Post printed, even the ones that were true, but right now I need someone to blame who isn't me.

Laura watches me pack. "Jenni, be reasonable. You can't leave now. At least finish the semester, in case you change your mind and want to come back later."

"And what good would that do me?" I snap back. "Who's going to care whether I dropped out after my sophomore year or halfway through? Either way, it's a failure. I want to be out of here as fast as possible."

Laura doesn't know what to say to that, so she says nothing. She doesn't deserve me being this cold. It's not her fault. She's trying to help, but anger is the only emotion I can summon and if I let that go I'm going to collapse. I need to hold it together at least until I get to the Port Authority where no one knows me and everyone looks away from a dirty person crying in the corner. I rip open my dresser drawer and begin shoveling underwear into my duffel bag.

I leave my textbooks and notebooks. I won't need them any more. All my nice clothes are at Dan's, and he can keep them. I never want to see them, or him, again.

The phone in the hall keeps ringing while I pack. Kathy knocks on our half-open door, then walks in without waiting to be invited. Probably wants a quick look at the freak before she's gone forever.

"Jenni, there's a man on the phone asking for you. He used your full name."

"Tell whoever it is I left school." Why not? It's the truth. Or it will be in ten minutes.

Deirdre looks at me. "Are you sure? Maybe it's your boyfriend."

Ever the romantic, she's got the puppy dog eyes like she really wants it to be him. But he would have had his secretary call, and she always calls me Miss McGrath. Probably a reporter from some other paper that got scooped by the Post.

"Deirdre, I don't want to talk to anybody, OK? Why don't you do something useful for a change and take the phone off the hook."

Deirdre looks hurt. For a moment I think she may start to cry, but she leaves to take care of the phone without arguing. Good. One less thing to worry about.

Only my desk drawer left. I yank it open. It's overstuffed with letters and cards from my family and friends back home, even a few photographs. There's one on top of the four of us roommates freshman year. We're all giggling and laughing. I think it was taken the first couple of weeks of school, while we were all still drunk on the freedom of living away from our parents for the first time, before we knew how rough it was going to get. There's nothing in the drawer from Dan. He never went in for letters or pictures, at least not pictures of him.

I throw the papers into my duffel bag on top of the clothes. No need to be neat. Then I buckle the bag shut, and bend down to hoist it over my shoulder for my last hike to the D train. Before I can heft it, Deirdre comes back through the door with Melissa in tow.

Laura pops up from her chair. "Melissa, thank God. Tell Jenni she's being stupid. She can't give up now."

"You're leaving?" Melissa asks.

"Yep."

"So I guess you saw the Post?"

"No, I decided to throw my education in the garbage because everything is peachy." The bile practically drips off my lips. God, why can't I help being nasty to my friends? It's not even her fault, not really.

Melissa shrugs her shoulders. "I don't know. Maybe she should go. I think I'd leave if something like this happened to me."

Laura slumps back into her chair, defeated. Guess she was counting on Melissa to back her up, but then there are some things Laura still doesn't know. "You're sure? This is what you want?"

"Of course it's not what I want. It's what I've got."

"I guess this is goodbye then," says Laura.

"Goodbye."

"Be well," says Deirdre.

"Whatever." I hoist the duffel over my shoulder and stomp out of the room. I don't look back to see if they're watching me.

39

EASTON

To my surprise, I don't start crying in the elevator, or even on the long hike to the D train. For once the creeps on Fordham Road leave me alone. Something in my attitude must tell them I'm not a girl to be messed with today. I'm itching for a target for all this anger.

On the subway, I see three different people reading the Post. At first I'm afraid someone will recognize me, but no one does. No one in New York looks at anybody anyway. With my clothes on and my hair up, I'm another grungy student, one of ten thousand, not worth a second glance. Thank God for the anonymity of the big city. Maybe if Rose Hill were more like this and less like high school I could have toughed it out.

While I wait for the next bus to Easton, I sit on a hard plastic bench and stew in the general unfairness of life. I was almost starting to feel like I belonged in Dan's world of designer clothes and doorman condos. What a crock. Maybe I should have paid more attention when the Trotskyists came door-to-door in the dorms recruiting for the revolution.

On the ride home, I stare out the window at the trees whipping by on I-78. I've come this far on adrenaline, anger, and shame; but as the bus rolls across New Jersey, I realize there's one more thing to worry about. What am I going to tell my parents? I'm not sure which is worse, the anger I imagine on my father's face or the disappointment I imagine in my mother's. What was it Frost said? "Home is the place where, when you have to go there, they have to take you," but does that still apply when you've been naked on the front page for eight million people to see? My parents don't read the Post—no one in Easton does—but they're still going to want to know why I'm home before exams. Even if they don't know already, someone's going to tell them eventually.

I was always the good girl, the one who studied hard and didn't cause trouble. Janine was the hellion who drank, got knocked up at seventeen, and married way too young. Only in the end, her life turned out OK and I screwed up way worse than she ever did. It just took me a couple of years longer to get there. Way to go Jenni.

When the bus drops me off in Easton, I use a pay phone to call Mom to pick me up. My fingers are shaking so much I mis-key the number twice and have to start over. The third time, I slam the receiver back on the hook before I finish.

I can't do it. I can't tell my parents I dropped out, not yet. They were so proud of me for getting into Fordham, and they've had such a tough year. I can't do this to them. There's only one person left I can call.

I pick up the phone again. This time I finish dialing.

Janine answers on the third ring. "Hello."

"Hi, it's Jenni. I'm at the bus station. Can you pick me up?"

———

JANINE IS as good as her word. When I tell her what happened, she doesn't nag or say I told you so, not even when I get to the part about being naked on the front page. She hadn't seen, or even heard about, the story in the Post. Maybe there's hope that our parents haven't seen it yet either.

"Wow," she says when I finish telling the story. "That is seriously fucked up."

I nod. "So, can I stay?"

Janine hugs me. "Oh Jenni. You can stay as long as you need to. I wish you'd come to me sooner. Maybe we could have, I don't know, done something."

There's nothing she could have done, but I appreciate the thought.

"Have you told Mom and Dad yet?"

"I was planning to. I really was, but then, I couldn't. You know?"

Janine nods. "There's one thing I don't understand, though. How did the Post get the picture they printed?"

"I'm not sure, but I think Dan gave it to them. He's the only one who had it."

"Why would he do that?"

"He must have been furious with me. I guess he saw the first story in the Ram. It made it sound like I told them about him, even though I didn't. He must have thought I betrayed him. He was always very clear that he didn't want to show up in the papers. He made me sign something about that when we first met. I'm probably not even supposed to be telling you this now, only, cat's sort of out of the bag."

Janine mulls it over. "I don't know. Even if this man was that angry with you, I don't see why he'd want more publicity. If I were in his place, I'd wait for it to blow over."

"Maybe he figured his name was already out there, and he'd moved on to Melissa. Might as well drag me through the mud too."

"Pardon my French, Jenni, but this Dan person sounds like a Grade A controlling asshole. I'm glad you got away from him. Nothing's worth that sort of abuse."

Almost reflexively I open my mouth to defend him, but I stop. As much as it hurts, she's right. This relationship was wrong from the start, and no river in Egypt can change that.

———

A COUPLE OF HOURS LATER, Janine is on the phone with Mom. I'm listening to half the conversation and trying not to vomit.

"Yes, she's here with us. She's OK, or as OK as can be expected given everything."

There's a gut-churning silence while Janine listens to the other end.

"I'm not sure that's a good idea."

More silence.

"Um hmm, I see."

She cradles the phone on her shoulder while she reaches for a pen. "OK, if you think so. Talk to you later. Bye Mom."

"So what did she say?" I burst out as soon as she hangs up the phone.

"They saw the paper. A friend of Dad's read it and told him."

My face drops. So much for my last hope that I could hide this from them.

Janine continues. "They've been worried sick about you. Mom's been calling the school every two hours, only no one there will talk to her. Dad's locked himself in his study and only comes out to use the bathroom. Mom was almost ready to drive to the Bronx to look for you. Anyway, she's driving over to see you."

———

THE CONVERSATION with my mother in Janine's kitchen is possibly the most uncomfortable we have ever had, though not for the reasons I was expecting.

"I'm so sorry we couldn't afford to help you out, Jenni."

No matter how many times I tell her none of this is her fault, I don't blame her for anything, this is all on me, she won't stop apologizing. I had no idea she felt so guilty about our money problems.

"Mom, how about Dad? Where's he?"

Her face gets that forced rictus of a smile again. "He's fine, honey. He just needs a little time."

I suddenly get a sinking feeling in my stomach. "Mom, are you two getting a divorce?"

She recoils in shock. "What? No, of course not."

"Then what is it?"

"He's having a little trouble processing the news. His friend Aaron called him to ask if he'd seen the paper. We hadn't yet, and when Aaron told us what was in it, he thought it was a bad joke. Your Dad got angry with him and hung up, told him not to call back. Only then he went out and bought a copy, and there you were."

"I'm sorry, Mom."

"Don't be, Jenni. It's not your fault. That man took advantage of you. If we'd been better parents. If we had saved a little more—"

"Mom! I told you not to blame yourself."

"Sorry honey. I can't help it. If only we—"

"Mom!"

"Sorry, sorry. We'll figure something out. I promise. I don't know what yet, but maybe I can get another job. Your father will find something this summer. We got a good deal refinancing the house, more than we thought the old place was worth. That's helped out a bunch. It'll all work out. You'll see."

I already told her that I was done with school, but she isn't really listening to anything I say, and I don't have the strength to repeat myself until she gets it. I let her continue talking until she says, "Why don't you come back with me? You can stay in your old room."

"I don't know. What would Dad think?"

"I know he wants to see you, sweetheart. Whatever else happens, he loves you."

"I know. I do. It's that...He must be disappointed in me."

"Oh, honey, no. Nothing you could ever do would make us disappointed in you. He's upset because you were hurt, and that hurts him too. It would be good for you both if you came home now."

"I don't know. Maybe, if you're sure it's not going to make things worse."

"Oh honey, of course I'm sure."

In the end I let myself be talked into going home. At least my old bed will be more comfortable than Janine's couch.

————

SEEING MY MOM WAS BAD. Seeing my father for the first time since the news hit is ten times worse.

"Hey slugger," he says.

"Hi, Dad," I reply. Then we stand in the living room in awkward silence for a minute that feels like an hour, both of us looking at the carpet.

"So, um, I guess I should go to my room now."

"OK. See you at dinner." He hits me lightly on my shoulder and goes back to his study. I guess it's going to take both of us some time to get used to what happened. At least he didn't scream at me. That's something, right?

I spend the next day in bed in my pajamas, watching Family Ties reruns. Around three o'clock I gather enough strength to venture out to the kitchen and fix myself a bowl of generic Cheerios. As I'm pouring the milk, my mother asks me to get the mail. It's probably an excuse to make me put on clothes, but I agree anyway.

The mailbox is at the end of our driveway. As I walk back, I page absentmindedly through the junk mail and catalogs, when suddenly a thick envelope with the familiar logo of Cortland Investments jumps out at me. Only it's not addressed to me. It's addressed to Robert and Julia McGrath.

Is Dan writing to my parents? Why? I stand outside for several minutes trying to decide whether to open it. In the end, I can't. Instead, I go back to the kitchen and sit down with my cereal.

"Mom, what's this thick envelope here?" I try to be as nonchalant as I can as I hand it to her. Fortunately my mother is not the suspicious type.

"Here, let me see." She puts on her reading glasses. "Oh, that's from the new mortgage company, honey. I told you we refinanced. After IBM laid your Dad off last year, we needed the extra money. We were living off credit cards and when they ran out, I don't know what we would have done. But then this company from New York bought the mortgage and offered to let us take out more equity."

I try to hold my voice steady. "When exactly did this happen?"

"I don't know. After your father was laid off, so it couldn't have been earlier than September. It took a little while to get the paperwork done. Maybe late October? Yes, it was. I remember we were thinking about not giving out candy this Halloween to save a little money, but then we got the big check, so we figured we could afford it."

No way this is a coincidence. A few weeks after I start seeing Dan, he buys my parents' house? Why? I was already deeper in debt to him than I could ever pay back. Did he think he needed a backup to hold over me in case I dropped out? Which, of course, I have just done.

Nervously, I twirl my spoon through the milk without actually taking a bite. My appetite has vanished as suddenly as the blue in an iodine clock. So what happens now? Is he going to foreclose? Is this how he forces me to go back to him? Or does he even want me back? Is it too much to hope he forgets he owns my parents' house?

Truth is, I don't know what he's thinking, and the not knowing is like a bot fly larva crawling around under my skin. I stare at the phone on the wall. If I called him, would he take the call? And what would I say to him if he did?

"Please don't foreclose on my parents' house even though I broke my promise and ran away without telling you. And trust me, I didn't talk to the papers, even though they say I did."

Yeah, right. I wouldn't believe that story myself, and Dan is less gullible than me. The mere thought of talking to him is making my heart pound, and not in a good way. More in the "a lion is coming to eat me and I'm tied to a tree" way. I can hear the thump thump thump of my heart pounding. I swear I can almost see my hands shaking.

"Jenni, what's that noise?" says my mom.

Startled, I look up. Shit, it's not me. The room really is shaking. The cheerios are bouncing around in the bowl, the windows are rattling, and it sounds like a hurricane is coming down the street. Only there aren't any hurricanes in Pennsylvania.

The noise is loud enough to rouse my father from his study. He comes into the kitchen more animated than I've seen him for months. "Julia, call 911. Some idiot's landing a helicopter in the middle of the street."

No, no way. He wouldn't. He couldn't. Not here. Not now, not at my parents' house.

Oh, who am I kidding. Of course he would. It is exactly like him. Land a helicopter of all the ridiculous things in the middle of a suburban street with no thought for the neighbors or me or anything except how he's going to get to me twenty minutes faster to yell at me.

The thumping is starting to die down and the windows are shaking a little less.

No, I am not having it. Not here. What incredible arrogance. Showing up like this after everything he put me through. Like I haven't already been humiliated enough.

"Jenni, do you know what's going on?" my mother asks.

"It's for me, Mom. Let me deal with this."

"Jenni, are you sure? You look a mess. Why don't you go freshen up? I'll call the police."

"It's OK, Mom. Don't call the police. Please, give me a little privacy, OK?"

She looks like she's about to say something, but then thinks better of it and sits down.

I grab my barely touched cereal and stamp into the living room. Fine, if that's how he wants it to be. It's time to let him know he can't have anything he wants. I told him not to come after me. I wrote him a letter even. Despite all his promises, he's not willing to let me make a clean break. Well, to hell with him.

I stand in front of the door working myself into a righteous fury. Let him see what I really look like without all his fancy makeup artists and expensive clothes. Let him see the real Jenni McGrath in her natural habitat, frizzy hair, Walmart pajamas, and store-brand cereal.

By the time the doorbell rings, I know exactly what to do. I tear the door open and throw my bowl right in his smug face. "What the hell are you—" and then I freeze in horror.

"I know we're not besties, but I was hoping I might rate a better reception than that," says Kate.

40

HELICOPTERS

"I am so sorry," I say to Kate for about the hundredth time as we sit across my parents' kitchen table. "There's a dry cleaners only a few blocks away. They can have it done in an hour."

"Forget about it. I'll get my suit cleaned in town." Although Kate has changed into some of Janine's old clothes I found stuffed in the back of a closet, she still looks like a movie star. Somehow she manages to make Janine's pre-baby weight overalls look like the latest grunge style from Seattle and not at all like mom jeans.

"Are you sure? It's no trouble." I've learned enough in eight months of running in Dan Cortland's world to realize that the suit I doused in milk and cheerios cost somewhere in the vicinity of my parents' mortgage payment.

"Jenni, please stop worrying about it. My suit is the least of your worries. We have more important things to talk about."

"Can I get you some coffee?"

Kate taps her chin. "Coffee, yes, that would be nice, thank you."

I hop up from the table, grab the can, and start scooping the coffee into the brewer. My parents have quietly absented themselves, though I'm sure I'm going to be interrogated later about this woman who parks helicopters in the middle of our street. I have no idea how

I'm going to explain her. Dan, at least, they understood, if not exactly approved of. Kate, I think the truth would shock even Janine and give my father a heart attack.

When the coffee starts dripping into the pot, I return to the table. I can't begin to guess why she brought the helicopter, but there's a more important question first. "So, why are you here?"

Kate leans back in her chair. "Huh, I thought that was obvious. I love Dan."

I stare at her in open-mouthed shock.

"Sorry, let me rephrase. Dan is one of my oldest friends, and I care about him like a brother. I can't lie to you of all people and tell you it's purely platonic, but it's not possessive either. I'd like to think you're my friend too, and when I see two of my friends making each other miserable though their own thick-headedness, I feel like I ought to do something about it. Does that explain things?"

I shake my head. "Honestly, no."

Kate sighs. "You may be a little too young to understand this, but please believe me when I say that I would never do anything to come between you and Dan."

The coffee maker dings and saves me from having to come up with a response to that. I excuse myself for a second to pour. Honestly, she's even more confusing than Dan is.

"How do you take your coffee?"

"Black, I think. I'm not in the mood for more milk just yet."

I pour Kate's coffee into the bluebird mug I made at summer camp when I was eight, and sit back down at the table. "I'm not sure how I feel about all this. Why isn't Dan here?"

Kate takes a sip of coffee and makes a face, but chokes it down. I never was any good at coffee.

"Male pride, I suppose. I thought about kidnapping him and tossing him in the helicopter, but I'm not sure his ego could take it."

I think she's joking about that. 90% sure.

"Mostly, I wasn't sure how you felt. You did run away. You might not want to be found. Dan's in bad enough shape already. I didn't want to fly him out here if you were only going to throw milk in his face."

"Again, I'm really sorry about that."

"You've had your own problems to deal with, or the same problems from a different angle. Otherwise you wouldn't need me to tell you this, but Dan's been storming around New York like a gorilla pawing through ant hills, making life a living hell for everyone around him. First the mess in the newspapers, and then you disappeared on him without a word. He sent someone to look for you at your parents' house, but your father threatened to call the police on him."

What? Mom didn't tell me that. Way to go, Dad.

"What does he want?" I ask with some trepidation. Dan's scary enough when he's calm. Dan angry I really don't want to encounter.

"Do you really not know? He wants you."

"Why? I thought after the stories in the papers, he never wanted to see me again."

Kate nods. "Seeing you naked on the front page of the Post certainly didn't help."

My face goes redder than phenolsulfonphthalein in a 10.0 base. That's still the most embarrassing part of this fiasco. If I had thought anyone other than Dan would ever see those pictures, I never would have posed for them. It's too late to do anything about it now, but I still want to run and hide when I think about it.

Kate continues. "I managed to talk him down from doing anything too rash, convinced him he ought to at least hear your side of the story before he said or did anything he couldn't take back. So, what is it?"

"Huh?"

"Jenni, I'm not at the top of the A-list but I've been in the spotlight enough to know I shouldn't trust everything I read in the papers, especially not the Post. What's the real story?"

"I don't know. I woke up one morning and there was an article in the Ram about me. It didn't mention my name, but it was obviously me. Unless I'm not the only Fordham sophomore Dan's paying."

"So that much was true? Dan's been paying for you to attend school?"

I nod. I thought she knew that.

Kate looks thoughtful. "Can't say I'm too surprised. He always was an easy touch when a pretty face swam into view. It's gotten him into trouble more than once, though I must say you've taken it to a new level."

"I didn't want to," I object. "I really do like him. It's not the money. I would have been with him, even if he was a penniless grad student. He was the one who insisted on paying. I didn't ask him to." I don't know why, but I need to hang onto that. This was his idea from the first. I never asked him for any of it.

Kate leans forward. "I don't doubt you. I've seen my share of women who were after Dan's money, and you most definitely do not fit the profile. For one thing, if you were, you wouldn't have run away when you had him on the hook like that."

That makes zero sense. Dan was never the one on the hook in this relationship. It's like she's been watching a whole different movie than me.

Kate takes my hands in hers. "Jenni, I've known Dan for half my life now. You're not the first woman Dan has—" she pauses to look for the right word "—adopted."

"There've been others?"

"A few, though none who lasted. They hang around for a couple of months, then disappear. I think the record before you was eight months. I assume Dan pays them off."

Oh God, it really isn't me. It's him. It makes sense, I guess. I'm not sure if I should feel better or worse now that I know I'm the latest in a series.

"So why? Why does he have to pay?"

"He didn't, not always." Kate stops and looks at her coffee. "I'm not sure how much I should tell you. Some of this he should probably tell you himself. You know how private he is. I don't want to betray his trust, but Dan has had some...problems with the women in his life. Not his fault really, but he got hurt, badly, more than once.

Some men might give up or hide out after what he went through. Move to another country. Join the priesthood. Hell, even switch to men. He took a different path."

"He decided to pay for it?" I don't try to hide my incredulity.

Kate stirs her spoon in her coffee. "I'm not going to say I agree with his choices, but I do understand them. It gives him a sense of control, of being in charge. And he needed that."

I try to imagine Dan not being in control and fail. He is the most in control person I know.

"Jenni, I'm the last one to tell you Dan doesn't have issues, but you can't believe everything you read in the papers." She smiles ruefully. "Trust me on that one. Though speaking of the papers, that's the one thing I don't understand. Why did you talk to the reporters?"

"I didn't," I object. "I wouldn't betray him like that. No matter what. He has to know that."

"Maybe you did and didn't realize it? Journalists can be very sneaky, especially with people who don't know how the game is played. You think you're talking to a friendly stranger in a bar, or amongst friends, and you don't know they have a tape recorder in their purse."

"No, nobody, I swear. I was very careful not to tell anyone." I was too ashamed to tell anyone, I could add.

"That is a mystery then because it sure sounds like they talked to somebody. And if it wasn't you and it wasn't Dan, I don't know where they got this story in the first place. But I really do think you owe it to him to at least listen to him, hear his side of the story."

"I don't owe him anything," I say with a vehemence that surprises me. "He got what he paid for."

"Then if not for him, for yourself. Whatever happens, you need closure. Whatever he did, whatever he thought, I know you weren't just in it for the money."

"I don't want to see Dan again, ever." As the words come out of my mouth, I realize I mean them. It's not a happy feeling, but it is a complete feeling. I've made my decision. It's over.

"OK, not Dan then, not yet. Is there anybody else who matters to you? I know breaking up is rough, but the end of a relationship is not the end of your life. You still have friends who want to see you again."

It's like Kate knows right where to cut me to make it hurt the most. With Dan, I can let anger be my guide; but Laura, Deirdre, even Melissa, there's nothing there but shame and it's all on me.

"I'm sorry," I say. "If I could put this all behind me and pretend it never happened, I would, but I can't. Now that everyone knows, and is talking about me, whispering behind my back...I'm sorry. I just can't."

"Jenni, I went to Fordham too. I know how small townish Rose Hill can seem. But trust me, it will blow over. Sure, people are going to talk, but most of them are only jealous it was you instead of them. Your real friends will still be there for you, no matter what."

I think about that for a minute. Laura's a rock, and Deirdre doesn't have a mean bone in her body, even if she doesn't know when to keep her mouth shut. Even Melissa didn't do anything I didn't ask her to do. She's probably six months away from living in the same hole in the ground as me. Would they really still be my friends, even when everyone on campus is gossiping about me? Yes, they would, and I can't put them through that, not after everything they've done for me. "No, I'm sorry but no."

Kate sips her coffee. "OK, so you won't go back for Dan and you won't go back for your friends. Final question then, and if you're still intent on living the rest of your life as an old maid in your parents' basement, I won't stop you. What about your education? That's why you did this, right? Are you ready to throw that away?"

I bite my lower lip. That is the one thing she could say that really sinks its hooks into me. I've been so wrapped up in my personal disasters that I haven't given any thought to class or exams.

I actually thought I had gotten through anxious and reached numb, but being reminded that I'm about to miss a test starts my stomach flipping up and down in my abdomen, anatomically impossible as that is. I have never missed a test in my life. I've lost track of the calendar, but I think it's Monday. And if it is...

I glance at the clock on the wall. "It doesn't matter. The chemistry final starts in thirty minutes. Professor Bolotowksy doesn't give make-ups. I've already flunked it."

Kate smiles at me, like she knows something I don't.

"What?" I ask.

"Jenni, I have a helicopter."

41

FINALS

Before confirmation, my eighth grade class went on a retreat that was supposed to teach us how to be good, adult Catholics. Although at the time it felt like one of the most meaningful and intense experiences of my life, only three things have stuck with me from that weekend: the location of Easton's local makeout spot, a telephone game in which the one piece of the message that survived being passed through twenty hormone-addled tweens was "hot pink pants," and Sister Roberta intoning in her Irish accent that, "Times of trouble show you who you really are."

She may have been right about that. These are certainly my times of troubles; and what I have found out about myself is that when everything is stripped away, at the core I am an annoying teacher's pet who actually likes tests. I can give up Dan. I can give up the money, but I can't bring myself to give up the chance to nail down one last straight A report card.

Kate lands the helicopter on Edwards Parade and gives me a quick hug as the rotors rev down. "Good luck, and don't give up. Whatever you think, it's not over yet."

"Thanks," I say as I grab my backpack. "For everything."

I crack open the door, and jump out onto the lawn. A group of boys have stopped playing hacky sack long enough to gape. I'm getting used to being gaped at, but if they recognize me I'm going to have even more explaining to do. Landing a helicopter in the middle of campus probably isn't explicitly prohibited in the student handbook, but I'm sure the dean can think of some rule we broke by landing here.

Time enough to worry about that later. If the dean wants me gone, he's going to have to throw me out. I'm not going to make it easy for him by flunking. I sprint the rest of the way to Mulcahy and slide into an empty seat in the back row of the lecture hall just as Teresa is handing out the last of the blue books. Professor Bolotowsky shoots me a dirty look from down in front, but he doesn't say anything. Most of the class is already too absorbed in the exam to notice me. Thank God for the tunnel vision of premeds during finals.

Two hours later I flip the blue book closed and hand it to the TA. I grab my bag and bolt for the door while most of the class is still trying to squeeze in an extra answer or two.

Despite my lack of studying, I think I did pretty well; and it was, surprisingly, relaxing. For the first time since my world fell apart, I was too preoccupied with balancing reactions and molecular formulas to worry about Dan, the New York Post, my roommates, or the mess I've made of my life.

Of course, the exam was only a temporary reprieve. I still have to deal with all that.

I pull the hood of my sweatshirt over my head and somehow manage to walk back to Hughes Hall without anyone stopping and pointing. I suppose it helps that I look nothing like the sexy photos in the Post. For the moment I'm just another mousy sophomore with a backpack slung over one shoulder. Move along folks. Nothing to see here.

My blessed anonymity lasts until I walk through the front door of Hughes and run smack into Laura.

"Um, hi," I mutter.

Laura stares at me for a moment like I've turned into Bigfoot, then grabs me in a big hug. I freeze, more in amazement than anything else. Laura is the least huggy person I know.

"Oh my God, Jenni are you OK? Where have you been? We were so worried about you. We tried calling your parents, but they didn't know where you were and we thought you'd lied to us again and gone off to be with your boyfriend, only then he showed up here looking for you, and he didn't know where you were either, and—"

"Wait a minute," I say, breaking into Laura's frantic monologue. "Dan came here?"

"Yeah, he showed up a couple of hours ago, looking really serious. Melissa started acting really weird with him, all touchy feely. Only when we told him we didn't know where you were, he said he wanted to talk to Melissa alone, so Deirdre and I left the room."

Shit, shit, shit. What was he thinking?

Laura is still talking. "We probably should have insisted on staying, though, because right after we left there was a lot of shouting and yelling. You could hear it all the way down the hall. Deirdre and I didn't know what to do. We were about to call campus security, but then Melissa came running out of the room and ran down the stairs, and I'm not sure where she went. Only now you're here, and like, can you get him out of our room?"

"He's still here?" I exclaim.

"Well, yeah. I thought I said that."

Shit. I thought I had time to prepare for this. OK, Jenni. Take a deep breath. You can do this.

———

Deirdre is waiting outside the door to our room. Her face lights up when she sees us. "Jenni," she squeals, and hugs me. "Where have you been?"

"Shh, it's OK," I say, patting her on the back. "I'll tell you later. Is Dan still in there?"

Deirdre nods enthusiastically. "Yes, and Jenni? He's really hot." Deirdre doesn't seem nearly as weirded out by this fiasco as Laura.

"Wait here," I say.

Laura frowns. "Are you sure? You're OK being alone with him? He seemed sort of scary. Maybe I should call campus security, just in case?"

"No, no police. You two wait outside. I'll be OK." I think I'm telling them the truth. Despite all he's done, Dan has never been violent with me. Then again that was before his name got splashed across page four of the Post.

"No," Laura says. "I'm not letting you be alone with him. If you're going in, I'm coming with you."

"Me too," adds Deirdre. "I'm not missing this."

"Fine," I say and add a sigh of exasperation. I need to do this before I lose my nerve, and I don't have time to babysit them. The door is unlocked. I open it and step inside.

Dan is looking out the window with his back to the door, but I'd know his backside anywhere. He turns around when the door opens, and a look of relief washes across his face. "Oh, thank God," he says, and in three big strides he's across the room and grabbing me up in his arms. "Where have you been? I thought something happened to you."

"I'm fine. I went back to Easton. Kate found me."

"Kate?" He looks puzzled. "Fuck it, that can wait." He starts to glow with that fire he gets as he leans in to kiss me. Only this time, I stand firm and turn my head away.

"Jenni, what's wrong?"

I put my hands on his chest and push. Reluctantly he lets go.

"Is it true? What they wrote about you in the Ram?"

"The Ram?" He looks puzzled.

"That you raised the tuition, then looked for girls who couldn't pay?" Looked for me, I should add.

"No, Jenni. How could you think I'd do something like that?"

"It was in the paper, in the Ram, and the Post. Did they lie?"

Dan turns away and looks toward the window. "It's complicated."

"How complicated can it be? Are you on the Board of Trustees or not? Did you vote to raise the tuition or not?"

"Yes, I am on the Board, and yes, I did vote for a tuition increase; but Jenni, you don't understand the situation." Dan pauses, then turns to Deirdre and Laura, "Would you two ladies mind leaving us alone for a few minutes?"

"No way," says Deirdre. Her eyes are wide with excitement.

Laura scowls and crosses her arms across her chest. "I'm not leaving her alone with you."

"Fine," says Dan, a hint of exasperation in his voice. "The news was going to come out sooner or later anyway. The university's bankrupt. They took a real bath in the market crash last year. The endowment went from about a hundred million dollars to close to a billion dollars in the red, almost overnight."

"A billion dollars?" says Deirdre, like she's never heard a number that high.

"Wait, that doesn't add up," objects Laura. "Even if the market went to zero, and it didn't, the university still wouldn't end up owing money."

Dan looks at her, sizing her up. "The treasurer had leveraged the endowment by buying complex derivatives that were supposed to outperform a rising market. If the market went up, the university stood to make a lot of money."

"Only it went down instead, and multiplied the losses," finishes Laura. "Still, to lose that much, they must have been leveraged twenty to one."

"More like twenty-five to one. In the circumstances, it was exactly the wrong thing to do. Excuse me, who are you?"

"Laura Cartmeyer. I'm pre-law with a major in economics. Hindsight's 20/20 and all, but isn't that a very risky position for a university to take?"

"It is, which is why your former treasurer is currently having some uncomfortable discussions with the New York State attorney general's office. Meanwhile, the only reason the gates are still open is that I loaned the school a lot of money, money I would like to get back some day. And yes, I voted to raise tuition, by twelve percent. I had to fight damned hard on the Board to keep the increase that low.

The administration wanted to raise it thirty-five percent, and another thirty percent next year."

Laura's face scrunches up as she does the math in her head. I can do it too, but thirty percent or 300, it's all money I don't have. Plus, I have other things on my mind. "I'm sure this is interesting to you finance geeks, but that's not the only thing. What about the student records? The Ram said you went through them looking for girls who couldn't pay."

"That's a lie," Dan says firmly.

"So you didn't look at our financial aid forms?"

"I skimmed a few forms, eight or nine, to get an idea of what was going on. I have no idea whose forms they were. They were paper and numbers, not people. I made copies of all the records so the accountants at my company could figure out just how deep a hole the university was in, and how much it was going to cost me to bail it out. I didn't trust that the administration was giving me the real numbers. That was the first time I knew how bad things had gotten. Jenni, if I read yours, I don't remember it. I had no idea who you were until I met you that night in the Ramskeller."

I'm not sure if I should believe him or not. I don't understand a word he said about the endowment, though it seems to have calmed Laura down for the moment. Leverage is for physics class and derivatives are calculus.

"So you were trying to protect us?" asks Deirdre, getting to the heart of the matter.

"Yes, I was. I'm sorry I didn't do a better job. My accountants estimated that with the loan, and a smaller tuition increase, we could keep the school open another year or two until the market turned around and the endowment recouped some of its losses. There wouldn't be more than two percent or so of students who'd have to drop out. It sounded better than the twenty percent who would have had to leave under the administration's plan. Only then I met Jenni, and suddenly that two percent didn't seem like a good tradeoff anymore."

Laura looks at me. "Jenni?"

Is it true? Could he really have been trying to help us? Help everyone? I know nothing about finance or stocks or market crashes, except that it messed up my life. I want it to be true. I really do. I look up into his eyes. He's waiting for me to believe him, to trust him. When he looks at me like this, wanting, pleading he looks like a little boy asking his mother for a puppy. I do believe him. I can't not believe him. But that only makes the next part harder.

I take a deep breath. I've been imagining this scene for days, but getting the words out still feels like pushing cement blocks uphill, and not the frictionless kind we use in physics problems either. I open my mouth and close it, twice. Finally, I force the words out.

"OK, I believe you."

His face lights up. "Jenni, I'm so glad."

I put my hand up again. "Wait. I'm not through. I believe you. You weren't taking advantage of me. You were trying to help in your own weird, infuriating, fucked up way, but that's not enough. I still can't be with you."

Dan looks like I've kicked him straight in the heart, which is fair enough since that's about how I feel. He puts his hands on my shoulders and I let him, but I look away.

"Jenni, is it the newspapers? I don't know how they got those photographs, but I'm going to find out. And it's going to blow over. By this time next year, no one will remember it."

"No, it's not the newspapers. It probably should be, but it isn't."

"Then what?"

"Yes, Jenni, what is it?" says Deirdre, eagerly, like she's watching one of her soaps, and it broke for commercial at the crucial moment.

"Maybe you should read the letter I gave Melissa for you. It explains everything."

"You gave Melissa a letter for me? Why would you do that?"

"I know you've been seeing her too, Dan. Melissa admitted it."

"Jenni, listen to me. I have not been seeing Melissa."

"Wait, are you talking about our Melissa?" says Deirdre.

"Yes," I say to Deirdre. To Dan I say, "Don't lie to me, not now. I saw you two together."

"You saw us together? When?"

"The weekend you told me you were out of town, only I saw you picking her up in front of the dorm. So don't lie to me now."

Dan sighs. "Jenni, I was hoping I wouldn't have to tell you this but —" he turns to Laura and Deirdre. "Excuse me, do you two think we could have a moment alone? This really is private."

"Nope, no way," says Deirdre, who is sitting on her hands and almost bouncing on her bed. "This is too good."

Laura assumes an almost military posture. "Sorry, I'm still not sure I should trust you."

"Fine, I was hoping to spare everyone the embarrassment, but if you all have to know—" He takes a deep breath, like he's steeling himself to say something really hard. Before he can force it out, I hear the thunking sound of our door unlocking.

We all turn our heads to see who it is, but of course only one other girl has the key, Melissa.

42

MELISSA

Melissa comes up short, almost like she's about to trip on her overly high heels. She clearly wasn't expecting to see us here, at least not together. She looks at the floor, takes a deep breath, and looks up again as if nothing has happened.

"Daniel, I wasn't expecting you to still be here." She nods in the direction of Laura and Deirdre. She's pointedly ignoring me.

"I could say the same to you," Dan replies. "Your friends have been telling me some very interesting stories. I wonder if you have an explanation?"

"Why Daniel, whatever do you mean?" She steps over to us and sidesteps me so she's facing Dan. She reaches up to brush her hand on his cheek, but he bats it away.

"Melissa, I want to know exactly what you've been telling people about us."

"Don't worry, I haven't given away any of your secrets. I could have, but I didn't. I was very careful about that, lover." She taps her hand on her purse.

"Melissa, I told you an hour ago and I'm telling you again, we are not lovers."

"OK, if you say so," she says with a smile and a bat of her eyes that says she's just playing along.

Dan takes her by the shoulders and looks straight down into her face. "Melissa, this has to stop, now."

Melissa's face quivers, and for a second I think she may be about to cry, but she recovers her composure. "Daniel, why are you being like this? Is it because they're here?" She stands up on her toes so she can whisper in his ear, but I'm standing right next to them and I hear every breathy word. "We can go back to your apartment, or your car if you don't want to wait. You know I'm always ready for you."

I knew Melissa could be forward, but this is extreme, even for her. Dan, however, doesn't seem to be responding, at least not in the way I'm used to. Instead, his face tightens. He pushes Melissa back down by her shoulders and says, "Melissa, listen to me." His voice is firmer, sterner than I have ever heard it. "I've tried to be polite and respect your feelings, but polite isn't working. I came here today for Jenni, not for you. That's all."

Melissa touches Dan on the arm. "That's OK. I don't mind. You can see her on the side if you need to. I know a man like you—"

"Melissa," Dan practically barks. "You are not hearing me. There is nothing between us."

"That's not true. You know it isn't." Then she looks directly at me and her voice drops an octave. "You know it too. You were there as I recall."

Deirdre gasps. "Jenni, does she mean you three all..." Laura shushes her, but not before my face goes beet red. I thought I had no secrets left to be embarrassed about, but I was wrong.

"That was a mistake," says Dan. "I invited you to join us because I thought you were Jenni's friend. I was wrong. It's not going to happen again."

"I am Jenni's friend. But I can't stand by and let her do this to you, betray you like this. Friend or not, I have to tell you the truth. Daniel, I know you care about her but she doesn't feel the same."

"That's a lie," I finally manage to blurt out.

Melissa looks at me. "I'm sorry, Jenni, but it's true. I can't keep your secrets any longer. Not when they're hurting everyone. You don't fit into his world. You can barely stand to be with him. I could tell that the night we were together. You're hanging on for the money. You told me so yourself."

"Jenni, is this true?" says Dan. He sounds almost hurt.

"That's, that's...I didn't say that."

Melissa smirks. "'I can't afford to leave. Without him, I can't stay in school.' Your exact words, Jenni. I remember them well. Is there some other way to take them?"

She's twisting my words. That's not what I meant. Can't he see that? I should say something, but I'm frozen in panic.

Melissa sounds so calm, so rational while my stomach is winched so far up into my throat, I can barely breathe. Melissa turns back to Dan and continues. "I'm sorry to be the one to tell you this, but it's for the best. I don't want to be with you for your money. I like you for you. I'm the girl you need. I know it. You know it. Even Jenni knows it when she's honest with herself. Isn't that right, Jenni?"

"No," I splutter, but she ignores me.

"Daniel, I can live in your world. She can't. I can keep a secret. She doesn't know what a secret is."

"What do you mean?" asks Dan.

Melissa continues. "I'm sure you figured it out already. You just didn't want to believe it, that she could betray you like that. There's only one person who could have taken those pictures from your apartment, who knew all those things to tell the newspaper, who needed money badly enough to sell herself out for a few dollars." Then she turns her head to look straight at me.

I stumble backwards and almost trip onto the bed. No, no, I didn't. I couldn't. Why would I? He can't believe that about me. He can't.

Dan turns and looks out the window. He waits for what feels like an eternity before speaking. "I suppose you're right. When those stories came out in the papers, I didn't think about anything for days except who might have done it and why. A man like me makes enemies. It's the cost of doing business, but you're right. Most of my enemies don't know those particular facts, and I don't think any of them could have taken the photos from my apartment. That does narrow it down."

Melissa's lips are curling upwards ever so slightly. "It isn't true!" I shout in my head, though the words don't escape my mouth.

Dan continues speaking while looking out the window. "I suppose you do know me better than I would have guessed, given how little time we've spent together, better than Jenni in some ways, I think. You're right that when I realized who gave that story to the newspapers, I didn't want to believe it. I don't like thinking badly of anyone, especially someone who was, how did you put it? 'A lover'? And I'm afraid today has confirmed my suspicions."

Melissa's smile is growing. She's practically beaming now, while I'm falling deeper into a black pit. It's over. He doesn't love me. He doesn't trust me. He's going to replace me with her.

Dan continues. "There's only one little thing that doesn't fit."

Deirdre pops forward excitedly. "What's that?"

"There wasn't only one person who knew enough to give those stories to the papers, who'd been in my apartment, and who could have taken that picture. There were three."

"Three?" Melissa says, confused.

"Three?" I ask.

"Three," Dan says, looking at Melissa, "and you were the second."

I'm not sure what he means, but Melissa must figure it out before me—she always was faster than me. "No, you're wrong. Jenni did it. Jenni talked to the newspapers. You read the article, same as we all did. It was her. We all know it. They talked to her." She points her finger at me, but for the first time she doesn't sound certain.

"But did they?" says Dan. "The article in the Ram never used her name. They talked to somebody, but they only identified her as 'a sophomore sharing a quad in Hughes Hall.' Now assuming the reporter checked all her facts, and that's a big assumption for a college newspaper, that still only narrows it down to the four of you." Dan looks around the room. He glances at me, then Laura, then Deirdre, then back to Melissa.

"Not me, I didn't do it," says Deirdre.

"I have no idea what you're talking about," says Laura.

"But the Post. The Post named her," objects Melissa. "They published her picture."

"Yes, they did, and I do have to wonder about the ethics of a journalist, or a friend, who would do that to a nineteen-year-old girl. But unlike the Ram, they never claimed to have talked to Jenni herself. They had any number of named and unnamed sources on campus, but not Jenni. Or am I wrong about that?"

This last question he addresses to me. I shake my head no. "I think someone might have left a message, but I didn't call him back."

"You probably should have. If you had, maybe the Post would have realized they were being played, and we could have shut this whole fiasco down sooner. But it's too late for that."

"I thought I was doing the right thing," I mumble under my breath, but Dan ignores me and turns back to Melissa.

"Besides myself, three people knew enough to give that story to the Ram, and had been in my apartment since I hung that photograph. One you don't know, but I'd trust her with my life. Then there's Jenni, who seems to be the one this whole debacle was designed to hurt. So Melissa, that leaves you."

Wait, what? I try to process what he's saying. Dan thinks Melissa outed me? That doesn't make any sense. Why would she...how could she?

"I did it for you," Melissa says to Dan softly, though not so softly I can't hear. "You wouldn't see the truth so I had to show you. She's not right for you. She's not smart enough or good enough for you. I am. You know that."

"I'll be the judge of who's right for me and who isn't," Dan replies. "Melissa, this is over."

"No, Daniel, it's not."

"I don't see that you have much say in the matter. I've told the guards at my office and the doormen at my building not to let you in. If you come back again, my lawyers will file a restraining order against you. Is that clear enough?"

"I didn't give the Post all the photos. I could have but I didn't. I held some back, the bad ones."

I bite my lip. What photos is she talking about? The pictures of me that Terence took? Too late for that. That ship has sailed, crossed the ocean, and docked in Timbuktu. What could be worse than the one the Post already printed? It's physically impossible to be more naked than that.

"Melissa..." Dan says in a rising tone with a hint of a threat.

"Do it, I don't care," and to my surprise I actually mean it. I've had enough of being ashamed, and I'm not going to do it any more, even if it means the whole world gets to see me. It's not like the black bar in the Post left all that much to the imagination.

"Not you, you slut, him." Melissa points at Dan. "You're going to be with me, or I'm going to show her and everyone what you really are."

"Dan, what's she talking about?" I can't imagine she can force Dan into anything he doesn't want to do, but she sounds so sure of herself. What could possibly be so bad that it would make Dan agree to be with her?

Dan looks down at her. "Melissa, were you in my study? Did you take something from my desk?"

Melissa's voice gets even again. "It's OK with me. I don't care if you want to do that. I won't tell anyone. But you have to be with me, not her. With me."

"Melissa," he says, "I don't care who you show those pictures to."

"I will. I'm not bluffing. I mean it."

"I know you will. Do you have them with you?"

A momentary glimpse of fear crosses her face. Dan is much bigger than her. If he decides to take whatever she has by force, she can't stop him. She throws a quick glimpse at Laura and Deirdre, who look confused. I don't think they have any clue what's going on. Melissa takes a deep breath and straightens her back. "I do, but you can only have them if you agree. It's for the best. You'll see."

"Melissa," Dan says, his voice getting firm like a strict father addressing a child, a voice that brooks no resistance. "Give them to me." He holds out his hand.

Melissa wobbles on her heels, as if she's uncertain what to do.

"Melissa," says Dan, deeper now.

Melissa looks nervous. She reaches her right hand into her purse and takes out a fat white envelope. She hands it to Dan.

"It's going to be OK now, right? We'll be together, right?"

Dan glowers at her briefly, then looks down at the envelope in his hand. Half of me is desperate to see what's inside it. Half of me is terrified to find out.

Dan flips back the unsealed flap and riffles through the contents. I expect him to slip the envelope into his coat pocket, but instead he hands it to me. "Here, these are for you."

Shocked I take the envelope from his outstretched hand. Melissa makes a mewling noise like a strangled kitten. Whatever she was expecting him to do with the envelope, it wasn't this.

I finger the envelope nervously. I'm not sure I want to look. I glance at Dan, and he nods. I take a deep breath and reach in.

I'm not sure what I expect to find—a will, money, a signed confession to the Kennedy assassination—but instead my hand pulls out a dozen black and white prints of two very well muscled men maybe a couple of years older than me wearing not a sock between them. One of them is a blonde Adonis I've never seen before, but the other—well, let's just say I know him by more than his face.

"Are these you?" I ask, though I already know the answer.

"They are. I did some modeling after I graduated. At the time, I needed the money."

"They're...beautiful."

"Thank you."

"Let me see," squeals Deirdre, but Laura grabs her and pulls her back before she can get a look. I push the photos back into the envelope and stuff the envelope in my pants pocket. I am not letting Deirdre or Laura see these. Nope, not going to happen.

"It's OK. You can show your friends if you like. I'm not ashamed of them—" he looks at Melissa "—even if some people think I should be."

Melissa opens her mouth to say something, but she must think the better of it, because instead she reaches for the door. Then, as I think she's about to walk out of my life forever, she stops and turns back around. "Just so you know, Daniel, I really was trying to protect you. You two are wrong for each other, even if neither of you sees it. Call me if you need a shoulder to cry on when she dumps you."

And before I can begin to parse what she means by that, she's out the door.

"That bitch," says Deirdre.

"Maybe I should I go after her?" Laura asks, though her heart clearly isn't in it. The drama's still here.

"So, do you have any other questions?" says Dan.

"Where did she get these?" I ask, studying the photos more closely. The way Dan and the other man in these pictures are looking at each other—and more than looking—with such naked intensity, it's maybe not the question I should ask; but it's the only question I feel safe asking in front of Deirdre and Laura.

"I assume she took them from my apartment, either the first weekend or one of the times she came over after that.

"So you did see her without me?"

"She seems to have a way of convincing doormen to let her in when I'm not home, one of them in particular. He isn't working for us any more."

"Not Carl?" I gasp. Carl is one of my few friends in Dan's world.

"No, David."

"Why didn't you tell me?"

"I didn't want to embarrass her. She was clearly more than a little interested in me. She seems to have trouble taking no for an answer. And she's not bad at playing the frightened little girl when she thinks that will get her what she wants, though I'm beginning to realize that's an act. The last time she said it wasn't safe to take the subway back to the Bronx and wanted to sleep over. I didn't want her in my apartment for one minute longer than necessary, so I drove her back here."

"That's when I saw you together. She was kissing you."

"Her idea, not mine. I tried to discourage her. I should have been more forceful."

"That weekend though. You told me you were going out of town. That's why I was so surprised when I saw your car, even before I saw you with Melissa."

Dan looks puzzled. "I don't remember that. You told me you needed to stay on campus to study."

"No, I didn't."

Laura interrupts, "Um guys, that's not quite what happened."

Surprised, we both look at her. For a minute we forgot there was anyone else in the room.

"Jenni, Mr. Cortland didn't talk to you. I did. And I didn't actually talk to him either. His secretary called for him. I wrote it down and gave you the message."

That's right. She did.

Laura continues. "And Mr. Cortland, did Jenni tell you she was staying on campus or...?"

"I was in a meeting when she called. Ms. Parenton gave me the message."

"So if neither of you actually talked to the other one, if maybe there was someone who knew you both well enough to leave messages pretending to be someone the other would trust, and it all got relayed through a third party..." Laura's giving us the look our freshman philosophy professor would use when she was waiting for us to figure out the answer to a paradox.

Dan and I speak in unison. "Melissa."

"I guess telephone isn't just a game for eighth grade confirmation classes," I say.

Dan shakes his head. "I feel like a grade A idiot. I knew she was trying to manipulate me, but I had no idea."

"You two got played," says Deirdre.

Dan turns back to me. "Jenni, I'm sorry this happened like it did. I should have told you what was happening sooner. I thought there wasn't any reason to get you involved or make you worry about it. That was a mistake, but I'm not ready to give you up, not yet. So, are we good?"

"You two look so cute," Deirdre says. "I'm so happy for you."

"Jenni?" says Laura.

"No," I reply. "We're not."

43

JENNI

"Noooo." The high-pitched cry of desperation isn't me. It's Deirdre. It's the same cry she used when General Hospital killed her favorite doctor in an ill-timed piano accident. "Jenni, you can't give him up. You can't. He's your prince. You have to be with him."

I glance to Laura for support, but she shrugs. "I can't believe I'm saying this, but for once I agree with Deirdre. I think you ought to give him another chance. You can break up with him next semester if it doesn't work out."

I sigh. OK, I'm going to have to do this myself. I look at Dan. Oh God, this is hard. He looks like a puppy at the pound realizing I'm not going to take him home after all. I've never seen him look this vulnerable. And now I'm about to kick him again.

I take a deep breath and begin. "I'm sorry. Melissa or no Melissa, I can't do this any more. I thought I could, but I can't. It's tearing me up inside. We have to end it. I'll find some other way to pay for school next year."

"Jenni, why? Have I done something? Have I hurt you?"

"No, you've been good, better than I deserved, better than I even thought I was allowed to hope for. And I enjoyed our year together. I really did. I hope you know that."

"But then why..."

"Shh, let me finish, please. I don't think I'll have the strength to say this twice. After I left, when Kate found me, I was numb. I didn't want to get out of bed. I barely had enough energy to eat. But then she told me you wanted me back, and it was like she filled a needle full of adrenalin and jammed it straight into my heart. Only then I crashed just as fast because I knew I couldn't have you."

"I don't understand. You can have me. That's what I'm here for."

"I couldn't have you like I wanted you, like I needed you. I'm not cut out for this kind of relationship. I can't party with you on the weekends and then go back to campus like it doesn't affect me, because it does. I'm in love with you, and I know it's not fair, and it's not the agreement, and you can be with whoever you want to be with. But when I think of you with Melissa, or probably twenty other women I don't know, I can't take it. It hurts too much. I want you all to myself, to be mine like I'm yours; and I can't have that so I can't have any of it."

I look at Dan, begging him to please understand, to not make this harder than it already is, to leave and let me break down in private. Only he doesn't go. He looks, not shocked, exactly. Maybe querulous?

"Jenni, I haven't been with any other women. Not since I started seeing you."

"But what about the deal? No strings attached. I didn't have a claim on you. I remember. You were very clear about that."

"I know," Dan says. "I remember too. And I tried. In the first couple of months, I dated a few times while you were back on campus. Only when it came to it, I didn't want to."

"You didn't want to?"

"I didn't want to be with anyone else. The women I went out with were nice enough, I suppose, but they weren't you. I only wanted to be with you. There was Kate and Melissa, because I thought you'd enjoy it, and you were still with me. But when you weren't with me? Never."

He can't be serious, can he?

Dan continues. "I didn't let myself admit what I was feeling at first. I simply enjoyed the time we had together. It was...magical. When I was with you, I felt free, like the weight of the world was lifted from my shoulders. Then you'd go back to the Bronx, and I'd spend the rest of the week counting the hours until you came back to me. I didn't want anybody but you. I don't want anybody but you. What I'm trying to say is, I love you Jenni McGrath."

And before my brain can fully process what he's said, my body has jumped three meters ahead. We're in each other's arms, and we're kissing again, deep and wet and hot and passionate.

I don't know how long we stand like that, pressed up against each other, trying to merge into each other, but all too soon Laura clears her throat.

"Ahem, now that that's settled, it is still finals week, and I have an econometrics exam to study for, so if you two don't mind..."

I break the liplock reluctantly, though I don't let go of Dan or stop looking into his eyes. "Sure, we'll get out of your way. You can have the room."

Dan is smiling more openly and looks happier than I've ever seen him, like a little boy. A little boy who's 6'2" and oozing sex, but still innocent and happy. I'm sure I'm smiling like a Cheshire cat too. He has his arms around me and his hands locked firmly to my backside.

"I don't want you to leave yet," I say.

"I hear a but coming."

"I want to go back to Manhattan with you, this minute. I really, really do. Only..."

"Let me guess. You have exams?"

"And I haven't studied for them at all. I'm going to fail genetics if I don't at least open the book. It would be a shame to flunk out now after everything you and Kate did to keep me here."

Dan laughs, but it's a happy laugh. "OK, you go study. But you're going to owe me extra time after the semester's over, with interest, you understand?

"Count on it," I say.

EPILOGUE

Twenty years later:

I got a machine printed letter from Fordham in the mail today:

Dear Jennifer:

I don't have to tell you that Fordham is a special place.

Is that special like the kids on the short bus are special? Or special as in special high intensity training?

An elite institution that is not elitist.

Translation: we'll take anybody, if their parents' bank balance is high enough.

Students are admitted based not on their ability to pay, but on their qualifications and character.

Wow. There's a howler, though I can't actually claim it's false. Fordham did indeed admit me without concern for my ability to pay, and it was only by my qualifications (nineteen-year-old virgin) and character (willing to do anything for money) that I made it through.

I can't say I planned any of it. Lord knows Fordham didn't. At the time, they would have rather I quietly disappeared and never darkened their doorstep again. There was some muttering about expelling me and another slut shaming article or two in the Ram, but

Dan has really good lawyers and he's not afraid to use them, so nothing much ever came of that.

Then Amy Fisher hit the headlines and I was yesterday's fish wrap, no more noticeable on the street than Rachel Hotchkiss or Denise Smith. You don't remember them? Exactly. In the end I was one more forgettable New York Post headline. Andy Warhol was right. We really are all famous for fifteen minutes; and even if it's fourteen minutes longer than I needed, my fame did fade out pretty quickly.

Some people would even call this a happy ending. I got my prince. He loved me. And we all lived happily ever after. Well, no, actually. Because then came junior year.

ABOUT THE AUTHOR

Lecy Elliotte graduated from Fordham shortly before the events of this novel with a degree in Classical Languages. Her financial aid was not cut off, and she did not have nearly as interesting a love life as Jenni does. She currently lives in Brooklyn. This is her first novel.

For more books and updates:
www.lecyelliotte.com

 twitter.com/LecyElliotte

www.ingramcontent.com/pod-product-compliance
Lightning Source LLC
Chambersburg PA
CBHW061551100726
47898CB00002B/329